The Illegitimate Heirs: Luke, Zach and Jake

KATHIE DeNOSKY

MILLS &
BOON

Published in Great Britain 2013
by Mills & Boon, an imprint of Harlequin (UK) Limited,
Eton House, 18-24 Paradise Road, Richmond, Surrey TW9 1SR

THE ILLEGITIMATE HEIRS: LUKE, ZACH AND JAKE
© by Harlequin Enterprises II B.V./S.à.r.l 2013

Bossman Billionaire, *One Night, Two Babies*, and *The Billionaire's Unexpected Heir* were first published in Great Britain by Harlequin (UK) Limited.

Bossman Billionaire © Kathie DeNosky 2009
One Night, Two Babies © Kathie DeNosky 2009
The Billionaire's Unexpected Heir © Kathie DeNosky 2009

ISBN: 978 0 263 90572 4
ebook ISBN: 978 1 472 00145 0

05-1113

Harlequin (UK) policy is to use papers that are natural, renewable and recyclable products and made from wood grown in sustainable forests. The logging and manufacturing processes conform to the legal environmental regulations of the country of origin.

Printed and bound in Spain
by Blackprint CPI, Barcelona

BOSSMAN
BILLIONAIRE

BY
KATHIE DeNOSKY

Kathie DeNosky lives in her native southern Illinois with her big, lovable Bernese mountain dog, Nemo. Highly sensual stories with a generous amount of humor, Kathie's books have appeared on the Waldenbooks bestseller list and received a Write Touch Readers' Award and a National Readers' Choice Award. She enjoys going to rodeos, traveling to research settings for her books and listening to country music. Readers may contact Kathie at PO Box 2064, Herrin, Illinois 62948-5264, USA or e-mail her at kathie@ kathiedenosky.com. They can also visit her website at www.kathiedenosky.com.

This series is dedicated to Charlie, the love of my life.

A special thank you to Kristi Gold and Roxann Delaney for laughing with me, crying with me and being there for me through the ups and downs. I couldn't ask for better friends. You're the best.

And to Tina Colombo for believing in me through thick and thin. I can't thank you enough.

Prologue

"We're not for sale, Mrs. Larson," Lucien Garnier refused flatly. "And I'm sure you'll agree that trying to build a relationship of any kind at this stage is out of the question."

Completely unaffected by his blunt statement, Emerald Larson stared across her highly polished Louis XIV desk at one of her recently discovered grown grandchildren. She could understand his and his two siblings' anger. It had to have been quite disconcerting to discover that instead of the struggling artist he'd portrayed himself to be, their father Neil Owens was really Owen Larson, the philandering, footloose offspring of one of the richest, most powerful women in the corporate world. But then, she hadn't been overly happy to learn that in his youth, her late son had left a bevy of women pregnant and on their own.

Since learning of her grandchildren, Emerald had arranged for all of Owen's children to claim their birthright and take their rightful place within the Emerald, Inc. corporate empire. She had successfully built a relationship with her three other grandsons and set them up with companies of their own, but the trouble was, she didn't know exactly how many children Owen had fathered or even if she'd found all of them. It was only in the past few months she'd learned that her son had impregnated yet another woman—not once, but twice. His affair with a young Frenchwoman visiting the San Francisco area on a student visa had resulted in a set of twin sons, Lucien and Jacques. Then, ten years later, Owen had returned to the woman and rekindled the affair, only to leave the poor dear girl pregnant again, this time with a daughter, Arielle.

The fact that Francesca Garnier had been the only woman Owen had returned to was bittersweet for Emerald. It was heartening to learn that her hedonistic son had loved the woman as much as he was capable of loving anyone, but disappointing to realize that in the end, his self-absorption had won out and he'd left Francesca behind—just as he'd done with the others.

But the past was just that—the past. There was little Emerald could do about what had taken place all those years ago. The only thing to be done now was to forge ahead and focus her efforts on righting things between herself and the three Garnier siblings.

"I can well understand your irritation, Lucien, but think about what I'm offering you and your brother and sister. Each of you will receive a multimillion-dollar trust fund, as well as complete control of one of my companies."

"We don't need your money or your company," Jacques reiterated.

"I understand that you and Lucien are wealthy enough in your own right now to never want for anything," Emerald acknowledged, nodding. Turning her attention to her only granddaughter, she smiled. "But what about you, darling? I'm sure your teaching salary is adequate enough to provide you with the basics, but what I'm offering is financial security for the rest of your life. You'll never have to worry about taking care of yourself or your—"

"Arielle is fine," Lucien interrupted, his glare formidable. "Jake and I have always taken care of our sister and we always will. We'll see that she has everything she needs."

"And you should both be commended for the sacrifices you've made to raise her." Emerald was completely impervious to his dark expression. "After your mother's untimely death, you not only did an excellent job of taking care of your sister, you both held jobs, as well as finished your education. That's a huge undertaking for two boys barely twenty years old."

"We wouldn't have thought to do it any other way," Lucien countered, shrugging off her compliment.

Emerald watched the girl eye one brother and then the other before Arielle sat forward in her chair.

"I could never express how much I appreciate everything the two of you have done for me throughout the years," Arielle spoke up, finally breaking her silence.

"But I'm a grown woman now, Luke, and I'm perfectly capable of taking care of myself and making my own decisions." She turned her full attention on Emerald. "Luke and Jake might not be interested in what you're offering, Mrs. Larson, but I certainly am."

"No, you're not." The twin brothers glared daggers at their younger sister.

"Oh, yes, I am."

Arielle's determination was almost palpable and it did Emerald's heart good to see that her granddaughter didn't seem the least bit affected by her older brothers' intimidating scowls. The child reminded Emerald of herself some fifty years ago.

"You two can do what you please, but I'm going to accept the trust fund and whatever company Mrs. Larson deems suitable for me to take over."

Their lack of agreement on the issue was the very opening Emerald had been looking for to seal the deal. "If you'll excuse me for a few moments, I have something that requires my immediate attention," she interjected, rising from her desk chair. "While I'm gone, I think it would be wise for the three of you to discuss my proposal." Walking to the door, she turned back. "But keep in mind, this is all or nothing. You all agree to accept everything or forfeit the opportunity completely."

Stepping into the outer office, she pulled the door shut behind her and walked over to her assistant's desk. "Get the acceptance papers ready for my grandchildren to sign, Luther."

"Have they accepted your gift, madam?" Luther Freemont asked in his usually stiff manner as he reached for a file on his desk.

Emerald glanced at her closed office door, smiling contentedly. "Not yet. But rest assured, they will."

She hadn't intended to put stipulations on her gift to the Garnier siblings, but her twin grandsons' determination to decline her generosity left her little choice. Being one of a few women over the past fifty years to carve out her place in the "good old boy" network of the corporate world, she'd learned when and how to manipulate a situation to her benefit. And she certainly wasn't above pulling out all the stops to get what she wanted—even if that meant playing hardball with her own grandchildren.

Confident that everything was going her way, Emerald glanced at the clock on Luther's desk. The Garnier siblings should have had ample time to reach an agreement.

"I'll page you when we're ready to sign the documents, Luther," she instructed, walking back to the door.

When she re-entered her private office, she smiled at her grandchildren still seated in front of her desk. It was time to incorporate the Garnier siblings into the Emerald, Inc. empire.

One

"Haley, I want my calendar cleared for the day and you to be in my office in five minutes. There's something I need you to do."

Haley Rollins stared open mouthed as Lucien, or as he preferred to be called, Luke Garnier passed her desk on the way into his private office. For the past five years, every weekday morning at promptly eight-thirty, he'd arrived at the corporate offices of Garnier Construction, ordered her to get him coffee and expected her to be in his office to review his day's itinerary. But today he was more than half an hour early and failed even to mention the requisite cup of coffee.

What on earth could have happened that would cause a man so set in his ways to deviate from his routine?

Something was definitely in the works and if the

look on his handsome face was any indication, he considered it to be of the utmost importance. Her usual Monday morning slump vanished.

Reaching for her phone, Haley made quick work of rescheduling his appointments, then after a quick trip to the break room for the coffee she knew he wanted, entered Luke's office a few minutes later. But as she walked across the room, her eyes widened and she had to remind herself to breathe. She never got tired of looking at the sexiest man she'd ever seen.

He had removed his suit coat and stood at the plate glass window behind his desk, staring pensively at the downtown Nashville traffic on the busy street below. With his hands stuffed into the front pockets of his trousers, the gray fabric had pulled taut over his tightly muscled derriere, drawing her attention to the narrowness of his hips, while at the same time his crisply pressed, tailored white shirt emphasized the width of his broad shoulders. The contrast was amazing and a testament to his excellent physical condition. And it was becoming increasingly difficult to hide her reaction to him.

"You're three minutes late," he said without turning around.

Bringing her wayward thoughts in check, she calmly set his coffee mug on the desk. "I had several calls to make in order to free up your day."

She wasn't surprised that he knew the moment she walked into the room, even though the plush carpet made the sound of her late entrance inaudible. Luke Garnier missed very little. And he never hesitated to comment on his observations. Ever.

"Sit down, Haley. There's something I want to talk over with you." His tone of voice denoted the serious nature of their discussion and for the briefest of moments, a tiny shiver of trepidation coursed through her.

She'd been extremely careful, but had he finally realized that his efficient, reliable, emotionless executive assistant had done the unthinkable? Had he discovered that she'd developed a huge crush on him practically from the moment he interviewed her for the job five years ago? That she might even be in love with him?

Seating herself in the leather armchair in front of his desk, she gave herself a mental shake. Her feelings for him had been the only thing that he'd failed to detect and she had no reason to believe that had changed. She'd never given him the slightest indication that she viewed him as anything more than her workaholic boss. A boss who made no secret of the fact that he had no interest in anything that took his attention away from Garnier Construction. His business was a very demanding mistress and that was just the way he preferred it.

"How was your trip to Wichita this weekend?" she asked when he continued to stare out the window. He hadn't shared the reason for his last-minute trip or whom he'd been meeting with, but Haley had no doubt it was the cause of his early arrival at the office this morning. "Did everything go well?"

His shoulders slowly rose and fell, indicating he took a deep breath before he finally turned to face her. "It actually depends on how you look at the outcome."

His noncommittal answer confused her. She'd never known Luke Garnier to be indecisive about anything.

He was the type of man who viewed things as either black or white, up or down, right or wrong. Gray areas in his business or his personal life were quite simply nonexistent.

Frowning, Haley shook her head. "I'm not sure I understand."

"I wouldn't expect you to." His intense blue gaze pinned her to the chair for several long moments as he decided exactly how much he wanted her to know about the meeting, then raking his hand through his thick black hair, he took another deep breath. "I've just become the new owner of Laurel Enterprises."

She couldn't have stopped her surprised gasp if she'd tried. "This is huge, Luke. Laurel Enterprises is the largest, most successful builder of vacation rentals and log homes in eastern Tennessee. Maybe in the entire state."

He nodded. "Laurel and all of its holdings are mine now."

"Congratulations! How on earth did you get Emerald, Inc. to relinquish it?" she asked, somewhat in awe of the achievement. She had seen him accomplish several seemingly impossible goals in the past, but obtaining Laurel Enterprises from the infamous Emerald Larson had to be an all-time best, both professionally and personally.

"Let's just say I had the inside track on gaining control of Laurel and leave it at that for now," he replied, giving her a one-shouldered shrug.

His answer only served to confuse her even further. As his executive assistant, Haley knew almost as much about Luke's vision and goals for Garnier Construction as he did. And she couldn't, for the life of her, figure out why he wasn't more triumphant about the acquisition. For someone whose already quite lucrative construction company had just doubled in size, he was being extremely reserved about it.

But she knew better than to ask why he wasn't more enthused. If he wanted her to know how he'd pulled off the deal, he would tell her.

"Well, whatever magic you used to convince them to sell to you worked beautifully. You've been wanting to expand into that area of the business for some time." She smiled. "Shall I set up an appointment with your attorney to examine the purchase agreement?"

"No, all paperwork was taken care of over the weekend."

"Should I contact your banker to have the funds transferred?"

"No need. Laurel has already been signed over to me. *Free* and clear."

Surely she'd misunderstood. "Excuse me? Did you say *free?*"

When his vivid blue eyes met hers, he gave her a half smile. "Yes."

Unable to believe what she was hearing, Haley sat forward. "Emerald Larson, the most successful woman in the corporate world, the first woman to crack the top five of the Fortune 500 list, just *gave* you the company?"

"Yes, but that's not what I want to discuss with you," he said, his tone indicating that the subject was closed. He lowered himself into the high-backed executive chair behind his desk. "I've come to the realization that now that I own the largest construction company in the

South, I need someone to ensure the continuance of Garnier Construction long after I'm gone. I need an heir."

She wasn't sure what shocked her more, his admission that Emerald Larson had handed him Laurel Enterprises on a silver platter or that he suddenly thought he needed someone to inherit his assets. "What brought this on?" she blurted before she could stop herself.

To her surprise, he didn't seem at all upset that she was questioning his decision. "My brother and sister aren't the least bit interested in the construction business," he explained. "Jake is perfectly content being the most expensive divorce lawyer in Tinseltown and Arielle adores teaching preschool kids whatever children that age need to learn. That's why I've decided to hire a surrogate and produce an heir of my own."

Haley knew her expression conveyed her disbelief, but she was beyond caring. "Don't you think that's a little drastic? Having a child is a huge step."

Luke shook his head. "It makes perfect sense. To make sure that the Garnier name will be a force to reckon with in the construction business for decades to come."

"And you think that having a child will make that happen?"

"I believe it tips the odds in my favor, yes."

"But it will take years before a child would be ready to learn all that you have to teach."

"That's why the sooner I get started, the better."

Luke could tell from the look in her turquoise eyes that Haley thought he'd lost his mind. And truth to tell, he wasn't entirely sure he hadn't done that very thing.

But after seeing Emerald Larson's desperation to

find family members to take over her vast holdings, he'd realized that building a corporate empire meant nothing without someone to carry on the legacy. That's why he had thought about who would take over his company and what they would do with it when the time came for him to retire.

It had taken a couple of sleepless nights, but to be certain Garnier Construction continued to grow and prosper long after he was gone, he concluded he would have to spend years grooming his own replacement. And who would have more of a vested interest in learning all that he knew than his own son?

That's when he'd decided to have a child. Luke could start by taking him to the job sites as a toddler, then by the time the boy understood how to avoid the pitfalls of the business and how to encourage Garnier's growth, he'd already be familiar with the way the operation worked.

"Are you really serious about hiring someone to have your baby?" she asked, finally finding her voice.

"Yes."

He wasn't at all surprised by Haley's astonishment. He'd had much the same disbelieving reaction himself when the idea first took shape. But the more he'd thought about it, the more it made sense to hire a surrogate from a reputable agency in order to produce his heir. The last thing he wanted or needed was the hassle of finding someone, then the trouble of convincing the woman to have his child without the slightest possibility of a future together. It would be much easier to choose a woman who had already decided to serve as a surrogate.

"If you think about it, it's actually the smart thing to do."

She raised one light brown eyebrow. "Maybe it makes sense to you. But I seem to be missing your rationale on this."

Why he felt compelled to explain himself to her was something of a mystery. He never explained his reasoning or actions to anyone, for anything. But he suddenly felt it was very important that Haley understand.

"I need an heir. I don't have a wife, nor do I want one. That's why surrogacy is the obvious answer. I get what I want without any further obligation to the boy's mother. Once the heir is born, she goes her way and I take the child and go mine."

"And you're definitely going through with this?" she asked, looking more doubtful with each passing second.

"Yes." He leaned back in his desk chair. "I want you to research the state laws and compile a list of reputable agencies specializing in surrogacy. I'll expect it on my desk by noon."

"Is there anything else you need?" she inquired, rising to leave.

"No. That will be all for now."

As he watched her close the door to his office, Luke could tell that she strongly disapproved of his decision. But he knew her well enough that she wouldn't voice her objections. And that was one of the many reasons Haley Rollins made the perfect executive assistant. She was amazingly efficient, had business instincts that rivaled his own and knew when to voice her opinions and when to keep them to herself.

An hour later, Haley breathed a tiny sigh of relief as she closed the Internet browser on her computer. It appeared that Luke would have to forego his plan of producing an heir through a surrogate. From everything she found on the subject, the state of Tennessee had taken a clear stand and only allowed married couples to enter into surrogacy agreements.

Nibbling on her lower lip, she glanced at his closed office door. It wasn't that she didn't think Luke should have a child of his own. She did. But only for the right reasons. And she certainly didn't consider having a baby simply because he needed someone to run Garnier Construction eventually to be one of them.

Unfortunately, her boss wasn't the type to give up that easily. He'd made up his mind, set his course of action and that was that. There wasn't a doubt in her mind that he would somehow find a way to get what he wanted. He always did.

Her chest tightened at the thought. She'd been giving babies a lot of thought herself after receiving a birth announcement from a friend and would give almost anything to have a baby. Considering her feelings for Luke, she'd like nothing more than for him to be her baby's daddy. But aside from the fact that he'd never looked at her as anything more than his extremely competent executive assistant, she wanted all the things he wanted to avoid. She wanted love, marriage and the close family life she'd never had.

She slowly pushed away from her desk and walked over to tap on his office door. There was no sense in thinking about any of that now. His plan had run into a huge obstacle and was effectively stalled, at least for the time being.

"Luke?" He was on the phone and motioned for her

to enter, so she seated herself in front of his desk as she waited for him to end the conversation.

"I'll be there on Saturday. Set up a special meeting for me with the office staff, then I want to visit the job sites to meet the construction crews. In the meantime, reassure them that I have no plans to make any major changes. Their jobs are just as secure now as they were when Emerald, Inc. owned Laurel Enterprises."

Hanging up the phone, he turned his attention her way. "I take it that you've already compiled the list of surrogacy agencies?"

"I didn't get that far," she stated, shaking her head. "It appears that your plan has run into a bit of a snag."

"And that would be?" he prompted.

"State law allows only married couples to hire surrogates."

She could tell when he rubbed the back of his neck with his hand that he wasn't at all happy with the news. "Are there any exceptions?"

"If there are, I couldn't find them." Shrugging, she added, "There are a few states where the law is more liberal on surrogacy, but this isn't one of them. However, it doesn't appear to be illegal to enter into a verbal agreement with a woman as long as there's no compensation other than medical expenses and she willingly signs over her rights to the child."

"Did you consult with my attorney?" he asked, a deep frown creasing his forehead.

She shook her head. "Mr. Clayton is out of town for the next week and I hesitated calling anyone else due to the discretion needed for a matter this sensitive. Besides, from everything I could find on the issue, the state law is quite consistent—married couples only."

Luke nodded slowly but remained silent, mentally reviewing what new course of action to take. "In other words, I need to find a woman with the traits I want and one who would also sign over her custodial rights immediately after giving birth." He looked thoughtful for several long moments. "That would be taking a huge risk without the protection of a binding contract."

Haley should have known he'd immediately start thinking of other options to obtain his goal. That was the way Luke worked. When he ran into a roadblock, he found the best way around it.

But the thought of another woman bearing his child caused a tight knot to form in the pit of her stomach and she suddenly felt the need to escape his presence. "I've decided to take the rest of the day off," she announced, quickly rising to her feet. "And if I were you, I wouldn't count on me being here tomorrow."

"Why? What's wrong?"

She wasn't surprised by his puzzled expression. In the five years she'd worked for him, she had never taken time off other than her annual two-week vacation. But she wasn't about to explain what she didn't fully understand herself. He wouldn't want to hear her explanation anyway.

And really what could she say to him? Oh, by the way, I love you and it breaks my heart to think of you having a child with another woman.

No, she needed space to regain her perspective and come to grips with the fact that no matter what it took, Luke would find a way for his outrageous plan to work. She wasn't part of it.

Walking to the door, she turned. "To borrow one of your favorite phrases when you don't wish to share details…let's just say I feel like taking the time off and leave it at that."

"All right, that's it." As he hung up the phone, Luke sent his desk chair sailing backward and quickly rose to his feet. "I'm going to put an end to this ridiculousness once and for all."

Grabbing his suit jacket from the coat tree, he stuffed his arms into the sleeves and headed for the door. Nothing had gone right since Haley walked out of his office yesterday and she had just called in "sick" for tomorrow. Facing another day with Ruth Ann, the temporary secretary, was completely intolerable and he wanted to know what the hell was going on. He didn't for one damned minute buy Haley's weak excuse that she just didn't feel well.

"I'll be out of the office for the rest of the afternoon, Ruth Ann," Luke growled as he passed the woman seated at Haley's desk. "If you can figure out how, forward all my calls to my cell phone, otherwise just take messages."

"A-all right, Mr. Garnier," she answered in a whiny tone that further irritated him. "W-will there be anything else?"

"No."

Ruth Ann's voice not only resembled the sound of fingernails scraping the surface of a blackboard, she looked and acted as if she was scared to death of him. And that was only scratching the surface of the many problems he had with Haley's temporary replacement.

To say the woman was absolutely incompetent would be the understatement of the year. Ruth Ann couldn't make a decent cup of coffee, couldn't find anything in a simple alphabetic filing system and found the phone to be an utter and complete mystery to her. She somehow reached the public relations coordinator for the Tennessee Titans football team while attempting a conference call with his satellite office in Atlanta.

He needed Haley back on the job immediately. She kept his office running like a well-oiled machine. Not to mention the fact that she made a damned fine cup of coffee.

As Luke navigated the late-afternoon crosstown traffic, he dismissed his current woes with Ruth Ann. He was on his way to find out what the problem was with Haley and believed she would be back on the job the first thing tomorrow morning.

But as he turned the SUV onto the street leading to Haley's apartment complex, his thoughts strayed to his other dilemma. He still needed to find a surrogate. A woman he could trust, as well as have all the qualities he wanted for his heir. And that wasn't going to be easy.

Oh, he knew several women who would be willing to volunteer for the job, and some of them even possessed a few of the traits he wanted for his son. But there wasn't one he could trust to bear him an heir without the benefit of a signed legal agreement. He needed a trustworthy and loyal woman like Haley—one with intelligence and business instincts to match his own. A woman as trustworthy and loyal as Haley. And one who kept herself in good physical condition, was easy on the eyes and enjoyed good health like…Haley.

Parking the Escalade in front of Haley's apartment, Luke took a deep breath before he switched off the engine, exited the SUV and briskly walked to her door. As he pressed the doorbell, he stepped back and waited impatiently for her to answer. When the door swung open, he didn't bother waiting for her to invite him in and brushed right past her into the small living room.

"Luke, what are you doing here?" she asked, looking as surprised as he'd ever seen her.

Smiling, he reached around her and closed the still wide-open door. "I wanted to let you know that I've chosen the perfect surrogate."

"No offense, Luke, but I really don't want to hear anything about this. I don't care who you choose, I just don't want to hear about it," she declared, folding her arms beneath her breasts in a defensive manner.

The action called attention to the size and shape of the pert mounds and the fact that she obviously wasn't wearing a bra. Without a second thought, Luke let his gaze drift lower to her trim waist, shapely hips, then down the length of her long, slender legs.

Damn! If there was ever a woman built for making love, it was Haley Rollins. Odd that he had never noticed how enticing her figure was. Of course, he'd never seen her in a pair of Daisy Duke cutoffs and a hot pink tank top before, either.

As he raised his eyes to her face, he marveled at how feminine she looked. At the office, she always wore her long blond hair straight and most times tied back at the nape of her neck. But today she wore it loose and the soft curls caressed her heart-shaped face and drew attention to her delicate features.

"Luke."

There was a warning in the tone of her soft voice. A warning that he'd never heard before and found completely intriguing. And one that he had every intention of ignoring.

When she impatiently tapped one bare foot, he grinned. "Who are you and what have you done with my business minded executive assistant?"

She glared at him. "I'm not working today, remember? I can wear whatever I like at home. And besides, I wear these when I'm cleaning. Now, would you please tell me why you're here, Luke?"

He grinned. "I've already told you. I've chosen the woman to be my surrogate."

"And you felt compelled to share the news with *me?*"

"Yes."

"Couldn't all this have waited until I returned to the office?"

"I don't see any reason that it should." Walking farther into the room, he shook his head. "I only made my choice a few minutes ago. On the way over here."

"Good for you," she said, sounding less than enthusiastic.

He pointed to her couch. "Have a seat and I'll explain."

"Fine." Clearly running out of patience, she sat and looked up at him expectantly. "Let's get this over with."

"I had several requirements in mind when I made the decision to hire a surrogate. There is only one woman I know who meets all my expectations and who I can trust with something this important," he summarized.

"I know I'm going to be sorry that I asked, but what are you looking for?"

"I want an intelligent woman with excellent business instincts." When it looked as if Haley intended to speak again, he held up his hand to stop her. "I also want her to be reasonably nice looking and in excellent physical condition."

"It sounds to me like you want a superhero," she offered, rolling her eyes.

"I didn't think of it quite that way, but in a sense you might be right," he mused, chuckling at her evaluation. She had no idea that as far as he was concerned she was assessing herself.

He'd always admired Haley's quick wit and he was more confident now than ever that he'd made the right choice. She was definitely the woman he was looking for.

"And you think you've found this paragon?" she prodded.

"Yes." Before she could react, he walked over, took her hands in his and asked, "Haley Rollins, will you have my baby?"

Two

Time stood still and Haley wasn't entirely certain that her heart hadn't come to a complete halt as well. Luke was asking *her* to be his surrogate? He actually wanted her to have his child?

She opened her mouth, closed it, then opened it again as she desperately tried to find her nonexistent voice. The fact that he saw her as the perfect means to produce his heir rendered her utterly speechless.

"I can tell by your reaction that you weren't expecting this," he laughed.

Never in a million years.

"And I don't need your answer right now," he added.

Good. Because that would require words and right now I couldn't put two words together to save my own soul.

He gave her hands a gentle squeeze, then reached for his suit jacket. "I want you to sleep on it tonight and, since you're taking tomorrow off, spend the day thinking about it. I'll pick you up around seven tomorrow evening for dinner. You can give me your answer then."

In a total state of shock, all Haley could do was stare at him. When he pulled her to her feet and led her to the door, she couldn't have protested no matter how hard she tried.

Opening the door, he turned and, reaching out, lightly touched her unruly curls. "By the way, you should wear your hair like this more often. It looks very nice." Then, without another word, he stepped out onto the sidewalk and pulled the door shut.

Haley felt as if she'd fallen down the rabbit hole and landed squarely in the middle of Wonderland. When she'd gotten up yesterday morning, she'd had no idea that in a little over twenty-four hours, her life would take such an unexpected turn. Nor would she have ever thought the man she'd dreamed about for the past five years would get some wild notion that he needed an heir and that she was the only woman to make that happen.

Slowly returning to the couch, she plopped down and let her gaze wander aimlessly around the room. How could everything look the same when the whole world had been turned completely upside down?

As the gravity of Luke's request began to sink in, she shook her head. There was no way on God's green earth that she could help him with his cockamamy plan. She couldn't—wouldn't—do that to a child. To her child.

Her child.

She was pretty sure that, as her father's housekeeper used to say whenever someone expressed a desire to procreate, she had "baby fever." Not because she didn't have plenty of time to have a child. She did.

At twenty-eight years old, she certainly hadn't heard the ominous ticking of her biological clock. Nor did she anticipate that happening for quite some time.

She had, however, watched several of her friends find love, get married and have babies. In fact, just last week Haley had received an announcement from her college roommate about the birth of her second child. And that seemed to intensify the void, her desire that she wanted more than anything else in life—a family of her own.

Just the idea of holding her own baby, of watching him or her take the first steps, of hearing the first words and seeing a sweet toothless grin brought tears to her eyes. She wanted a baby to love and be loved by in return.

But that wasn't what Luke had in mind. He wanted an heir to carry on at Garnier Construction, not a close family who loved, laughed and together weathered whatever storms life sent their way. And she was old-fashioned enough to believe that the choice to conceive should be based on the desire to love and nurture, not a good business decision. If she went along with his ludicrous plan, he'd raise their child alone and she'd be completely out of the picture. She'd lived that type of existence and she couldn't do that to a child, couldn't bring an innocent baby into a childhood like hers. Although the circumstances weren't exactly the same, she knew all too well how it felt to have a workaholic father who always put business first, who relied on nannies and his housekeeper to raise his motherless daughter.

Nor could she do that to herself. Unlike her own mother who abandoned her shortly after birth, nothing would ever keep Haley from being part of her child's life. She had every intention of being there each day to love and guide him or her as they made the journey to a happy, productive adulthood.

Unfortunately, Luke Garnier was a formidable negotiator. She knew as sure as she knew her own name that he would not stop until she agreed to his crazy scheme.

Luckily for her, she knew him well enough to know exactly how to deter him from his mission. But in doing so, it meant effectively ending any romantic fantasies of being more than his glorified secretary. Her chest tightened with intense emotion. It saddened her deeply, but she couldn't see any other option.

Taking a fortifying breath, she rose to her feet and walked into the spare bedroom she'd turned into her home office. As she seated herself at the desk, she took a tablet and pen from the drawer and began compiling her list of conditions. Demands that she was certain Luke would find to be deal-breakers and send him running away from her as fast and far as he could possibly get.

The feel of Luke's hand at the small of her back as the hostess led them to their table sent an interesting little shiver straight up Haley's spine and she focused all her attention on walking it to the table in her three-inch high heels without breaking her neck. Instead of dressing for style, she should have worn a more sensible—and a lot more comfortable—pair of shoes.

But her decision to wear the ridiculous shoes had

been a psychological crutch of sorts. Luke was well over six feet tall and she'd wanted to feel as if she were more on his level. The only problem was, he still towered over her by at least eight inches. So much for trying to psych herself up for their dinner meeting, she thought as they reached the table. All she'd succeeded in doing was to increase the chance of a broken ankle.

When Luke held her chair for her, she noticed that the table was strategically located in a dimly lit corner of the upscale restaurant and gave them a maximum amount of privacy. Knowing Luke, he'd specifically requested it when he made the reservation so they could talk freely without anyone eavesdropping.

"Hello, my name is Martin and I'll be your server for the evening," a young man said as Luke took his seat across from her. "Would you like to see our wine list, Mr. Garnier?"

"That won't be necessary, Martin," Luke answered. He gave her a smile that curled her toes inside her ridiculous shoes as he requested an extremely expensive label and vintage of wine, then added, "We'll both be having the house salad with house dressing. And for the main course we'll have prime rib, baby carrots and asparagus."

Martin nodded. "Good choice, sir. I'll be back in a few moments with your wine."

Haley wasn't at all surprised that Luke had ordered their dinner without consulting her or the menu. That was the type of man he was—a take charge kind of guy, who expected everyone to go along with whatever choices he saw fit to make.

"Did you enjoy your day off?" he asked conversationally, once the young waiter had placed their wine glasses in front of them, then silently moved away. "Were you able to give a significant amount of thought to my request?"

Leave it to him to bypass her need to respond to the small talk and get right to the sole reason they were having dinner together.

"I haven't been able to think of anything else since you left my apartment yesterday afternoon," she said truthfully. "You really gave me a lot to think about."

"Have you reached a decision?"

She stared at his handsome face as she mentally readied herself to recite the list of demands she'd spent the day memorizing and knew would have him rescinding his proposition in less than a heartbeat. But being prepared for what she had to say didn't make saying it any easier.

"Yesterday, when you asked me to consider doing this for you, I don't recall you mentioning anything that would give me an incentive to help you," she clarified, choosing her words carefully. "What would I get out of this besides gaining a significant amount of weight and a few stretch marks?"

"After I left your place, I gave that some thought," he agreed, nodding. "And there's no question that I would take care of all medical expenses, as well as give you as much time off from work as you'd like. With pay, of course."

He made it sound so simple. Had he even considered the permanent changes her body would undergo or the possible risks if the pregnancy was problematic? And what about the emotional devastation she would endure when it came time to give him custody of her child?

"That isn't nearly enough," she declared, flatly. "I want more." She shook her head. "No. That's not correct. I want *a lot* more."

His eyes narrowed and she could tell that he hadn't anticipated her rejection. "What exactly is it you want, Haley?" he finally asked.

"I'm sure it's a lot more than you're willing to give," she stated, taking a sip of wine.

"Name your price and we'll see." There was a challenge in his voice, indicating that he was about to go into serious negotiation mode.

"I never said I wanted money," she offered, staring at him over the rim of her glass.

He cocked one dark eyebrow. "Then what do you want?"

Haley slowly placed her wine goblet on the table and took a deep breath. She was about to reveal the hopes and dreams she'd had since childhood to the man she quite possibly loved, then listen to him reject each and every one of them.

"I don't expect you to understand how I feel about this, but I'm a traditionalist. When I have a baby, I have every intention of being a mother to my child. I'm going to be there to get her up each morning and tuck her into bed each night. I'll be there to see her first steps and hear her first words." She had to pause a moment to keep the emotion out of her voice as she finished. "And every minute of every single day, my child will have the comfort and security of knowing that she's loved and cherished by her mother."

A frown creased his forehead. "Is that it?"

"No."

"There's more?" The lines on his brow deepened and the tone of his voice indicated that he thought she was being extremely unreasonable.

Nodding, she stated the final demand, certain he'd find it completely unacceptable, giving up on her as his surrogate once and for all. "When I have a child, Luke, I intend for her to have a mother and father who are equally responsible for raising her, as well as living under the same roof and sharing the same last name."

His intense stare was intended to intimidate, but as far as she was concerned, this was one issue that was nonnegotiable. He might as well get used to that fact.

"In other words, you want to get married," he said after several uncomfortable moments of silence.

Their waiter chose that moment to bring their salads and she waited for him to leave before she answered. "When I have a baby, yes, I have every intention of being married and making a stable, loving home for my child to grow up in."

"Anything else?"

Shaking her head, she reached for her fork with a trembling hand. "No, I think that just about covers the subject."

Silence reigned over the table as they ate and she knew Luke was contemplating ways to change her mind. But that wasn't going to happen and the sooner he realized it, the better off they'd both be. Then they could forget that he'd even brought up the subject and resume being an executive assistant and her workaholic boss.

"Did you find everything to your satisfaction?" the waiter asked while he removed their plates.

"As always, the meal was excellent," Luke answered. Turning to her, he inquired, "Would you like something for dessert, Haley?"

"No, thank you. I'm positively stuffed." Smiling, she looked up at the server and crossed her fingers beneath the table for the lie she was about to tell. "Everything was delicious."

In truth, she couldn't have said whether they'd had prime rib or a piece of shoe leather. She'd been far too preoccupied wondering when Luke would tell her that he found her requirements completely unacceptable and that he was officially deleting her from his short list of surrogacy candidates.

Nodding, Luke handed the waiter a credit card. "I think that will be it for this evening. Have the valet bring my car around to the front."

Once Luke had taken care of the check and they walked out of the restaurant, they had very little to say to each other. The drive home was little better and Haley was more than relieved when he parked the car, walked her to her door and bid her a very quick, very platonic good-night.

Confident that he'd given up on the idea of her becoming the surrogate for his child, Haley felt her mood dip into sadness. When she'd told Luke what she wanted, she'd been revealing the dreams she'd carried for the past five years. And knowing there wasn't a snowball's chance on a hot July day that any of them would come true now, was almost enough to send her running to the freezer for the carton of triple fudge nut ice cream she kept on hand for just such depressing occasions. Instead, she opted to change into her nightshirt, pour herself a small glass of white wine and watch the nightly news on television before turning in for the evening.

But half an hour later, as she crawled beneath the sheets on her bed and reached to turn off her bedside lamp, the phone rang. The caller ID revealed Luke's cell number and her heart skittered to a stop.

This is it, she thought, taking a deep fortifying breath. He was calling to tell her that he found her requirements totally unacceptable and he would be searching elsewhere for his surrogate.

"Hello, Luke."

"Have you already gone to bed?" His deep baritone sounded so darned smooth and sexy it sent tiny little shivers straight up her spine.

"Uh…yes, but I hadn't gone to sleep."

"Good. Get out of bed and get to the front door."

Her scalp tingled and a wave of goose bumps shimmered over her arms. "Why?"

"Because I'll be there in about thirty seconds and I want to get this thing settled tonight."

"Can't we discuss this over the phone?" she asked, throwing back the covers and scrambling out of bed. Holding the phone between her shoulder and ear, she frantically searched for her robe. Where on earth had she put the thing? She rarely wore it because she never had overnight visitors.

"No, I'd rather talk in person," he said as the doorbell rang. "Now, open the door and let me in, Haley."

At the sound of him ending the call, she tossed the phone on her bed and, giving up on finding her robe, pulled her raincoat out of the closet. "All right, I'm coming," she muttered when the bell rang again. Shrugging into the coat, she hurried down the hall to the entryway. "Somebody needs to remind Mr. Luke Garnier that patience is a virtue."

When she opened the door, Luke walked right in as he'd done the day before. "Are you going out?" he inquired, turning to eye her coat.

Pushing the door closed, she pulled the coat's belt tight around her waist. "I couldn't find my bathrobe and you wouldn't stop ringing the doorbell."

"You don't keep your robe handy?" he asked as he walked into the living room.

"I live alone and if I want to walk around without a robe, there's no one here to care," she replied, wondering why she bothered to explain herself. It was her business, not his. "Now, what do we need to discuss that can't wait until tomorrow morning, Luke? I thought I made my position quite clear at dinner."

"You did," he said, nodding. "And I've given it a fair amount of thought."

She couldn't tell what he was thinking from his expression, but knowing him, he was there to get her to come around to his way of thinking. "I'm not changing my mind, Luke."

"I didn't think you would." Staring at her, he took a deep breath.

Here it comes, she thought, anticipating his rejection of her requirements.

"I've decided that the terms you laid down tonight are within reason and I'm willing to accept them," he stated as if closing a business deal.

Her heart felt as if it lodged in her throat at the same time her knees gave way. Sinking down on the couch, she could have sworn that the walls started to move in on her.

"W-what did you say?"

"We'll get married this weekend right after you sign a prenuptial agreement covering the protection of my assets, shared custody of my heir and a fair settlement for you if and when the marriage ends."

"But…we…I mean, you—"

"I assume that since you haven't indicated otherwise, you'll be in the office tomorrow morning?" he interrupted.

Unable to find her voice for the second time in as many days, all she could manage was a short nod.

"We can discuss the details and refine our agreement then," he continued. "Now, get some sleep. We have a big day ahead of us."

Haley watched him walk to the door, then close it with a click that seemed to echo throughout the room. She couldn't move, couldn't speak and rational thought was completely out of the question.

What on earth just happened? Had her commitment-phobic boss really just informed her that they would be getting married for the sole purpose of having a baby? And this weekend, no less?

Knowing that sleep would be out of the question, she took off her raincoat and tossed it on the back of the couch. As she prowled the room like a caged tiger, she tried to arrange her tangled thoughts into some semblance of order.

The man of her dreams, the very man who clearly stated he had no time for love and marriage, was willing to become her husband. And his only purpose for making her his wife wasn't because he loved her and wanted to raise a family with her. He was willing to marry her in order to have her bear him an heir.

She stopped in the middle of the room and barely suppressed a scream. Every one of her dreams was well on the way to becoming reality and for all the wrong reasons.

She wanted love and all the bonding that went with it. She wanted a lifetime emotional commitment, not a prenuptial agreement. But to Luke, their union would be just another business arrangement.

As she stood there, she couldn't help but wonder where her plan had gone wrong. And what had possessed him to agree to her demands?

But most important of all, how in the name of all that was holy was she going to talk him out of following through with it?

Three

The next morning, Luke slid a folder across his desk for Haley's perusal. "I've taken the liberty of having an attorney who specializes in family law draw up a pre-nuptial contract for you to sign."

"How did you manage to get this done so quickly?" she asked, looking a lot like the proverbial deer caught in the headlights of a car.

"You can get just about anything done in a short amount of time for the right price." He nodded toward the document she hadn't yet touched. "I think you'll find the agreement spells out what is expected from both of us when it comes to joint custody and parenting the boy. It also covers what we'll both keep and what compensation you'll receive when the marriage is dissolved."

She looked a little distressed. "And when will that be?"

"Whenever we both agree that we'd like to move on with our lives." He shrugged. "I'm sure we'll know when the time comes." Leaning back in his chair, he motioned toward the folder. "Take your time to read over the contract, then sign it and have it back on my desk by the end of the day."

"It's so generous of you to give me an ample amount of time to think over what I'll be signing," she said, her tone sarcastic.

He stated what he saw as obvious. "I don't intend to drag my feet on getting this finalized. You laid down the terms, I've made the decision to comply with them and we'll get married on Saturday morning. But between now and then we have a lot to do."

"What's the rush?" she asked, hiding a yawn behind her delicate hand. She looked thoroughly exhausted and he'd bet his next multimillion-dollar deal that she hadn't slept a wink the night before. The thought that she'd soon be in his bed caused his heart to stall and a slow smile to tug at the corners of his mouth.

"Why wait?" he responded, answering her question with one of his own. "I want to get started making you pregnant as soon as possible." That instantly brought her fully awake and added quite a bit of color to her unusually pale cheeks.

"You can't be serious. We'll be sleeping together?" She shook her head and the curls brushing her flawless cheeks fascinated the hell out of him. "I don't remember you mentioning anything about that last night."

He smiled. The idea of waking up with her in his arms each morning was becoming more appealing with each passing second. "I didn't think I'd have to. The last I heard, that's what married people do."

Her turquoise eyes grew wide. "But the only reason for the marriage is to have a child. I thought we'd be sleeping in separate rooms and visit a doctor for some kind of medical procedure. That's what we would be doing if we weren't getting married."

"You assumed wrong." He couldn't stop himself from giving her a wicked grin. "I have all of the required equipment, sweetheart. And let me assure you, everything works just fine. I see no reason for us to resort to a turkey baster when I'm perfectly capable of taking care of the job myself."

He almost laughed out loud at the shocked expression crossing her pretty face. "But we barely even know each other outside of this office. And you've made it quite clear that you have no expectations of the marriage lasting for any length of time after the birth."

Had he heard a hint of panic in her voice?

Interesting.

"That's not exactly true. I said we'd know when it was time to move on. That could be a month, a year or even ten years after the birth before that happens. But that's not the point," he said, shaking his head. "I can't think of a better way to get acquainted than making love. Besides, if I have to get married to get the heir I want, you can damned well bet I'm going to enjoy all of the benefits of the marital institution. And that includes sleeping with you." Heat began to gather in his lower belly and anticipation filled his chest. There were definite advantages to meeting her demands.

He didn't think it was possible, but the blush on her

cheeks changed from pink to a deep rose. Was it possible that Haley found the idea of making love with him less than appealing? Or could it be that she was a bit more innocent than he'd anticipated?

Deciding to find out, he stood up and rounding the desk, took her by the hand to help her to her feet. "While you read and sign the prenup, I'll make the arrangements for our trip to Pigeon Forge," he said, taking her into his arms.

"W-what are you doing?"

"Giving the woman I'm going to marry a hug," he responded, drawing her a bit closer. Holding her to him increased the heat in his lower body and sent a shaft of excitement straight through him.

At first, she stood stiffly in his arms. "We aren't going…to be married…here in Nashville?" she asked, sounding delightfully breathless.

"No."

When he drew her even closer, Luke felt a tiny tremor course through Haley and instantly knew his suspicions about her innocence were right on the mark. He normally liked his women to be a little more experienced. But for reasons he couldn't put his finger on, he found Haley's inexperience oddly touching.

"I have an important meeting with the management employees of Laurel Enterprises and I want to tour my new properties and meet the construction crews," he explained, enjoying the feel of her silky hair against his cheek. "And since there are several wedding chapels in the Pigeon Forge area where we'll be staying, it just makes sense for us to get married while we're there."

"This is a…" She paused. "…huge step. I'm not

entirely certain we're doing the right thing. Are you sure you want to go through with this?"

"I am."

"Really?" She didn't sound as if she believed him for a minute.

He nodded. "You told me that it would take us getting married before you'd have my son and I'm complying. In some courts, a verbal agreement is as binding as any contract. And unless you've changed your mind about us being married, I'd say we have a solid deal, sweetheart."

"No, I haven't changed my mind."

He smiled. "I didn't think so." Releasing her, before she realized just how much he looked forward to making her pregnant the old-fashioned way, he picked up the folder containing the prenuptial agreement. "This is fairly basic and straightforward. After you sign it, I want you to take the rest of the day off, as well as tomorrow."

"Why?" she asked, looking confused. "I thought you said we had a lot to accomplish."

He nodded again. "I need to review the agenda for my meeting with the Laurel employees, call the charter service to arrange our flight and reserve a wedding chapel for the ceremony."

"But you normally have me make those arrangements for you."

"You'll be too busy."

She frowned. "Doing what?"

"You'll need to pack, inform management that you're giving up your apartment and decide whether to store your furniture or donate it to an agency for the homeless." He walked back around the desk and reaching for his suit jacket hanging on the back of his chair, removed his wallet. "I almost forgot. I have to attend a charity thing at one of the museums tomorrow evening and I need a date. I want you to go shopping for something new to wear," he said, handing her one of his credit cards. "And while you're at it, you might as well get whatever you're going to wear for the marriage ceremony on Saturday."

To his amazement, she looked as if he'd offered her a poisonous snake instead of the small harmless piece of plastic. "If I want something new to wear, I'll get it myself." She sounded more than a little offended as she scooped up the folder containing the prenup. "For your information, Mr. Garnier, I'm not destitute. You pay me more than enough to be able to afford whatever clothes I wish to purchase."

As he watched her leave his office in an obvious huff, he wondered what he'd said to upset her. Didn't men buy things for their spouses anymore?

Of course, he and Haley weren't married yet. Maybe she took exception to him paying for things like that before they'd made their union official.

But the way he saw it, it was already a done deal. They had a verbal agreement, would soon have a signed prenup and within a few days a marriage certificate. End of story.

Staring at his computer screen, Luke still couldn't quite believe that in two days, he'd be a married man. Hell, he'd spent the better part of his adult life avoiding anything more than a casual relationship with any woman. And he'd never so much as entertained the idea of getting married. So why was he jumping into the deep end of the marital pool with both feet now?

Haley had every trait he wanted for his heir—intelligence, a good head for business and excellent health. And for another, he couldn't get her to have his son without the benefit of marriage. Yet, when he'd first heard her requirements to agree to his plan, he'd rejected the idea outright and given serious consideration to looking for a different woman. But the more he'd thought about it over the course of their dinner together, then later on the drive to his place after dropping her off at her apartment, the more sense it made and the more appeal it held.

She was extremely passionate about mothering a child and that would definitely work to his benefit. He had several satellite offices throughout the south, requiring a certain amount of travel, and juggling a small child with all the paraphernalia required for his care would be counterproductive. Besides, he would have had to hire a nanny to care for his son until the boy was out of infancy and old enough to go with him to the actual job sites anyway. But with Haley sharing custody of the child, Luke wouldn't have to worry about finding someone suitable to give his son the quality of care he expected.

And then there was the more pleasurable aspect of marriage. Until he'd stopped by to ask her to be his surrogate, Luke had never seen Haley outside of the office and certainly not wearing anything other than the conservative suits she seemed to prefer for her job.

But when she'd opened her door and he caught sight of her long, slender legs in those extremely short little cutoffs and the size and shape of her pert breasts in that snug tank top, it had damn-near knocked his socks off. It had been like he was seeing her for the very first time and every one of his male instincts had come to full attention—reminding him in the most basic of ways that he hadn't had the pleasure of a woman's company in his bed for a very long time.

His lower body tightened even more. In two short days, Haley would be his and he would be making love to her quite frequently. Just the thought of having those shapely legs wrapped around him and her soft body cradling his caused the heat deep in the pit of his belly to flicker into a flame.

"Here's your signed prenup," Haley said, choosing that moment to walk into his office. When she tossed the folder onto his desk, then turned to leave, she added, "And unless you wish to issue another edict about what I need to do before we make the trip to Pigeon Forge, I'll be leaving the office now."

So that was why she'd become so upset. She obviously viewed his suggestions about her apartment and buying something new to wear as high-handedness. He'd have to remember that calling all the shots at the office was one thing, but he'd have to exercise a little more diplomacy when they were discussing what he thought she should do in her personal life.

"Before you leave there's just one more thing. Are you using anything for birth control?" He knew she wasn't presently seeing anyone, but that didn't mean she wasn't prepared.

Her cheeks colored the pretty shade of rose they always did when he mentioned anything to do with sex. "No. That's not an issue."

"Good."

"Is there anything else?" she asked, her gaze not quite meeting his.

"I'm pretty sure what I told you earlier covers everything," he said, unable to stand up without her seeing the evidence of his arousal. "I'll give you a call this evening to let you know what time I'll pick you up for the charity event tomorrow evening."

She shrugged one slender shoulder as she continued toward the door. "Whatever."

"Haley?" When she stopped and turned to face him, he grinned. "There is one more thing I really think you should consider doing."

"What?"

Her withering glare might have stopped a lesser man, but it didn't phase Luke one damned bit. Nor did it stop him from a little teasing.

"Be sure to get plenty of rest between now and Saturday." He gave her a suggestive wink. "I plan on getting our little project started this weekend."

When her cheeks turned bright pink and she fled his office like something chased her, he laughed out loud. Getting married just might prove to be more fun than he'd first thought. At least temporarily.

As Luke held her hand to help her out of his limousine, Haley glanced at the other couples arriving for the museum's annual charity event. She recognized several prominent businessmen, a couple of them Luke's rivals, and she knew they were attending for the same reason Luke was—meeting potential clients. Making a contact at a social function could mean the difference between signing a lucrative contract to build the next high-rise to grace the Nashville skyline or watching the competition walk away with the job.

"It's good to see you again, Luke," a distinguished-looking elderly gentleman greeted them as they walked through the museum's entrance. He pumped Luke's hand, then turned to give her a friendly smile. "And who is this lovely young lady?"

"My executive assistant, Haley Rollins," Luke answered, already scanning the crowd in the atrium. "Haley, I'd like for you to meet Max Parmelli, the curator of the museum and the head of this year's charity drive for the city's homeless shelters."

Holding her hand, the older man leaned forward to kiss the back of it. "It's a real pleasure to meet you, Ms. Rollins."

She smiled at the pleasant older man, but Luke prevented any other greeting when he placed his hand to her back and guided her through the crowd toward a group of men standing by the fountain in the middle of the room. One of them she recognized as a former client of Garnier Construction who she knew in the very near future was going to be expanding his current building, if not contracting for a new one.

"Why don't you look at some of the exhibits or get something for yourself at the buffet tables?" Luke advised, his attention clearly focused on the men by the fountain. "I'll find you in a few minutes."

Effectively dismissed, she watched him join the group before heading toward a display of artifacts believed to belong to the ill-fated Romanov family of Russia. She really wasn't all that interested in any of the exhibits, but she couldn't—wouldn't—just stand there like a little lost puppy, waiting for Luke to once again grace her with his attention.

Sighing, she wandered around the museum, wondering what on earth she'd gotten herself into. It hadn't been lost on her that Luke had introduced her to the curator as his executive assistant, instead of his fiancée or future wife. Nor did he have any compunction about dumping her in favor of soliciting a possible repeat client.

But she really didn't have any reason to complain. He'd made it quite clear that he was only marrying her because he couldn't get her to have his heir any other way. And she was going through with their arrangement because she wanted a baby more than she'd ever wanted anything in her entire life.

Haley smiled as she absently gazed at a delicate, elaborately decorated egg. She was finally going to have her own baby—a child she would love and nurture and who would love her unconditionally in return. And the fact that Luke was going to be the baby's daddy made her decision to go through with their agreement much easier. The only fly in the ointment was the fact that Luke didn't love her, nor did he make any pretense that he expected their marriage to last.

"It looks pretty fragile, doesn't it?"

At the sound of the male voice at her shoulder, Haley turned to find a nice-looking man with dark blond hair and sparkling green eyes standing next to her. "Yes, it does," she said, really taking a look at the Faberge egg in the glass case in front of her for the first time.

"Back where I come from, we fry up the eggs for breakfast and throw the shells away," he remarked, laughing.

"And home is Oklahoma or Texas?" she asked, recognizing his southwestern drawl.

"Beaver, Oklahoma, to be exact," he announced proudly.

"And you?"

"I was born and raised in Atlanta." She walked to the next display case containing pictures of the Romanov family shortly before their deaths. "But I've lived in Nashville since I was in college."

"Never went to college myself," the man disclosed, shaking his head as he followed her. "I left home right after graduating high school with a fifty dollar bill in my pocket and an old guitar slung over my shoulder." He grinned. "That was fifteen years ago and I've been here ever since."

"So you're in the music business?" she asked politely.

The man looked shocked for a moment before giving her a wide grin. "You're about the sweetest thing I've come across in a long time. What's your name, darlin'?"

She caught sight of Luke coming toward them like a charging bull. "Haley, I need you to come with me." The censure she detected in his voice startled her.

"Haley is it?" the man beside her repeated, smiling. "Pretty name for a pretty lady."

She ignored the man's compliment as Luke came to stand on the other side of her. "Is something wrong?"

"No. I just want to get your opinion on one of the paintings offered here that I thought would make a nice addition to the office." Before she could respond, he glared at the friendly man standing beside her. "You'll have to excuse us."

When Luke took her by the elbow and strongly urged her in the opposite direction, she gave the man an apologetic smile. "It was nice talking with you."

He nodded. "You, too, Haley. That's just my luck, though. All the pretty ones are already spoke for."

She frowned as Luke hurried her toward a gallery on the opposite side of the atrium. "Are you sure there's nothing wrong?"

"We'll talk about it later," he said, leading her to an abstract painting. "Right now, I want your opinion on this. Do you think this would be appropriate for the reception area?"

She stared at him before she finally shook her head and turned her attention to the painting. "I'm not the person you should be asking about this."

He looked surprised. "Why not?"

"Because I prefer a more realistic rendering," she elaborated, pointing to a beautiful landscape down the long wall. "I especially love scenes like this."

"Really?" Shaking his head, he glanced from one painting to the other. "I wouldn't have guessed that about you."

"I'm sure there's a lot about me you'd never guess," she murmured, moving on to view another canvas. If he was surprised by her taste in artwork, he'd be shocked right down to his Italian loafers to learn how she truly felt about him.

While Luke arranged the purchase and delivery of the landscape she had chosen for the Garnier office on Monday, Haley continued looking at the array of artwork.

"You know, that picture looks like something my

nephew did when he was in kindergarten," a familiar voice remarked from behind her.

Turning, Haley smiled at the man she'd talked to earlier in the room displaying the Romanov treasures. "You wouldn't happen to be following me, would you?"

He grinned. "Would it bother you if I said yes?"

"It wouldn't set well with me."

Haley glanced up to see Luke walking toward them, his expression anything but pleased. "Come on, Haley. It's time I took you home."

"There you go again, trying to steal her away from me," the man said good-naturedly.

Luke placed his hand to her back. "Pal, she's not yours for me to steal away. She's already mine and you might as well give up the chase. It's not going to happen tonight or any other night."

Surprised by his possessive words, Haley didn't even think to protest as Luke guided her to the exit. But when they stepped onto the sidewalk in front of the museum and she finally found her voice, she asked "What was that all about?"

He gave the valet instructions to call for his limo before turning to face her. "Do you even know who you were talking to?"

"No. Why?"

Luke's frown eased a bit. "That was country music's bad boy, Chet Parker. Surely you've heard about his womanizing. He has quite a reputation."

She glanced over her shoulder at the museum's entrance. "You can't be serious," she said, amazed that she hadn't recognized the country music superstar.

"He's divorced again," Luke advised disgustedly.

"And I'd say he was sizing you up as his next candidate."

Haley shook her head. "I doubt that. We were just chatting about the displays."

"Guys like Parker don't strike up a casual conversation with a woman. Not without an ulterior motive." When his limousine pulled up to the curb, Luke helped her into the back, then slid in beside her. "Just keep in mind that you and I have a deal. And it doesn't include the likes of Chet Parker."

A mixture of anger and disappointment settled in the pit of Haley's stomach. Luke wasn't acting possessive because he cared for her, he was just concerned that she might find a reason to renege on their agreement.

Thankful the ride to her place was short, when the driver parked the car in front of her apartment, she gathered her evening bag and readied herself to escape Luke's presence. If she didn't, she wasn't entirely certain she wouldn't bop him on top of his thick head with her sequined clutch.

Unfortunately, he had other ideas. When the chauffer opened the door and Luke got out to help her to her feet, he wrapped his arm around her waist and started up the walk to her door.

"There's no need to see me inside. I'm perfectly capable of finding my own way."

"I'm sure you can," he said as he continued to escort her to the front step. Taking her key from her, he fit it into the lock and opened her door. "But I always make sure my date gets inside safely."

"Your date? I wasn't aware that's what I was tonight," she retorted, unable to stop herself.

"Of course you were."

She shook her head. "Let me see. You didn't ask me to go to the event with you, you told me that we were going. Then this evening, I was introduced as your executive assistant and immediately dismissed in favor of a potential client. And at no time during the evening do I remember you referring to me as your date or being treated like one, unless you want to count that little display of macho possessiveness with Chet Parker."

He looked at her like he didn't have a clue what she was talking about. "You are my assistant and I'm sure you recognized the client I was talking with. I don't need to tell you how profitable his business could be for Garnier Construction. And as far as Parker was concerned, he needed to get the message that you're unavailable."

Suddenly too tired to explain what he was obviously missing, she reached for her key. "On second thought, just forget it. You probably wouldn't understand if I drew you a picture."

"Oh, I get it." He held her key just out of reach. "You feel that I neglected you this evening."

"No," she lied. That was exactly the way she'd felt, but for one thing, he had no idea that she had romantic feelings for him. And for another, he didn't see her as anything more than his executive assistant, who had obviously lost her mind and agreed to help him with his cockamamy scheme to have a baby.

"Please, give me my key. I'll see you tomorrow morning when you pick me up to go to Pigeon Forge," she responded, holding out her hand.

To her surprise, he shook his head and wrapped his arms around her waist to draw her to him. "I can't let you think that I was ignoring you." He smiled as he ran his index finger over the scooped neckline of her dress. "Or that I didn't notice how sexy you look in this little black number."

Haley felt as if her heart bounced down to the pit of her stomach, then rebounded to lodge in her throat. His strong arms holding her securely to his tall, solid frame and the intention in his dark blue gaze sent a shiver of sheer delight through her. How many times in the past several years had she imagined him looking at her that way? Or what it would feel like to be in his arms and have him kiss her?

But when he lowered his head to cover her mouth with his, reality far exceeded any of her fantasies. Light and tender, his firm lips moved over hers with such care it robbed her of breath and sent a delicious warmth flowing in her body.

Tingles of excitement rushed through her when he used his tongue to coax her mouth to open for him. Haley couldn't have denied him access to her inner recesses if her life depended on it. She wanted to experience every nuance of Luke's kiss, wanted to taste him and have him taste her in return.

As his tongue mated with hers, her knees gave way and she raised her arms to his shoulders to keep from falling. Never had a kiss left her feeling as if every bone in her body had been turned to soft, malleable putty.

But all too soon Luke eased the pressure of his mouth on hers and nibbled tiny kisses from her lips to her ear, then down to the hollow below. "I'll be by around seven in the morning to get you," he whispered, sending a wave of heat coursing through her.

"Th-that's awfully early," she noted, distracted by his warm breath feathering over her suddenly sensitive skin.

"I want to get the wedding out of the way before I meet with the Laurel employees," he stated, releasing her to step back.

Being doused with a bucket of ice water couldn't have been more effective in ending the sensual feelings he'd created within her. Of course he'd think of their wedding as an inconvenience to be dispensed with as quickly as possible in order to get back to business as usual.

"Don't bother," she said, plucking her key from his fingers. "I'll meet you at the airfield."

Walking into her apartment and closing the door before he could argue the point further, Haley barely suppressed the urge to scream. She hadn't expected him to feel the same about their wedding as she did. After all, she might love him, but he barely knew she existed beyond the office. Yet, it certainly would have been nice for him to view the ceremony as more than just fulfilling one of the details of their agreement.

She shook her head as she entered her bedroom to change into her nightgown. Her father's housekeeper used to warn her to be careful what she wished for because she just might get it.

Haley had never understood what the woman meant more than she did at that very moment. Tomorrow she would have everything she'd wished for. She would become Luke Garnier's wife—albeit temporarily—and quite possibly within the next year, the mother of his child.

So why wasn't she happier about it? And why did she feel like she was embarking on a journey that could very well end up destroying her?

Four

The following morning, barely an hour after they were picked up by a limousine at the Knoxville airport, Haley walked down the aisle of a little log wedding chapel in Pigeon Forge toward Luke and the rotund minister waiting to unite them in holy matrimony. Dressed in a black pin-striped suit, pearl gray shirt and burgundy tie, Luke looked as handsome and confident as she had ever remembered seeing him. And within a few short minutes, they would be husband and wife.

Unbelievable.

After all these years, the man of her dreams had finally seen her as more than his glorified secretary. The only problem was, when he finally did take a second glance in her direction, all he'd been able to see was a fertile egg and an incubator.

When she reached the end of the aisle and stopped beside Luke, the grandfatherly minister smiled. "Please turn to face one another and join hands."

Haley was sure she stopped breathing when Luke captured her hands in his and smiled down at her. His encouraging expression and the feel of his solid palms against hers sent tingles rippling up her spine and reminded her that later on that evening, she'd feel those same strong hands elsewhere on her body, exploring, caressing, teasing.

"Are you ready to put the final touch on this deal?" he asked, completely unaware of the direction her thoughts had taken her.

"I...um, suppose I am," she murmured, not at all surprised that he refused to acknowledge their marriage as anything more than one of his business agreements.

"Good. The meeting with the Laurel people is due to start in..." he glanced at his watch "...a little less than forty-five minutes."

"Of course." She glared at him and before she could stop herself, added, "I couldn't possibly expect you to keep them waiting for something as trivial as your own wedding."

Frowning, Luke looked at her like she'd sprouted another head. "You knew that I'd scheduled the meeting for today."

Didn't he realize that no matter the reason for a marriage, a woman's wedding day was special to her? That having the groom rush off to a business meeting immediately following the ceremony wasn't exactly the stuff a woman's dreams were made of?

"It doesn't matter," she said, resigned that he would never understand.

His smile faded and clearing his throat, the minister interrupted their verbal sparring to ask "Are y'all real sure you folks want to go through with this wedding?"

"Yes," Luke declared, his tone leaving no doubt he meant it.

When the man turned his attention her way, she glanced up at Luke. Even though she was keenly disappointed over his insensitivity, the time for backing out of this fiasco had come and gone. She'd given her word and that was something she tried never to go back on. Besides, she wanted a baby—his baby—more than she'd ever wanted anything and she wasn't going to pass up the opportunity for the child she wanted to be that of the man of her dreams.

"Yes, I want to marry him," she admitted, surprised by the surety in her own voice.

"All right, I guess if you're both agreeable, we'll get started then," the minister indicated, sounding more than a little doubtful as he opened his book of wedding vows. "We are gathered here today to join this man and this woman in the bonds of—"

Staring at Luke, she heard very little of the blessedly brief ceremony and was surprised when the minister asked, "Do you have a wedding ring for your bride, son?"

Luke frowned. "No."

"It's really not that important anyway," she said, hoping her voice didn't reflect her disillusionment.

She didn't know if Luke had forgotten about a ring for her or if he purposely hadn't bought one. But either way, it was one more detail about her wedding day that she'd just as soon forget.

The man raised one bushy gray eyebrow, then shaking his head turned to the groom. "Luke, do you take Haley to be your lawful wedded wife, to have and to hold, for richer or poorer, in sickness and in health, as long as you both shall live?"

There wasn't even the slightest hesitation in his rich baritone when Luke gazed into her eyes and answered, "I do."

The minister nodded, then turned to her. "And Haley, do you take Luke to be your lawful wedded husband, to have and to hold, for richer or poorer, in sickness and in health, as long as you both shall live?"

"I…uh…yes. Yes, I do." Knowing their marriage was only a temporary arrangement, she hated making a vow she knew for certain wouldn't be kept.

As if he couldn't quite believe what he was about to say, the minister shook his head as he announced, "Then by the power vested in me by Sevier County and the great state of Tennessee, I now pronounce you husband and wife." He gave Luke a questioning look. "Son, if you want to kiss your bride, now would be the time to give it a try."

For the briefest of moments, as she watched Luke lower his head, she thought he was going to brush her lips with his and that would be the end of it. But the light of challenge she detected in his intense gaze a split second before he wrapped his arms around her and pulled her to him, warned her that the kiss was going to be anything but casual or brief.

Haley caught her breath and when his mouth settled

over hers, every cell in her body seemed to zing to life. At first, his firm, warm lips moved over hers with such tender care, such thoughtfulness, she felt as if she might just melt into a puddle right there on the chapel floor. But when he tightened his arms and pressed her even closer, her heart began an erratic cadence and a current of electrified heat coursed from the top of her head all the way to the tips of her toes.

The feel of his solid body against her much softer one as he coaxed her mouth to open for him caused an interesting little swirl in the most feminine part of her and Haley didn't have the presence of mind to put up so much as a token protest. Allowing him access, she leaned into him as he stroked and teased. But when he engaged her tongue in a game of advance and retreat, she felt as if her knees had turned to rubber and she wrapped her arms around his trim waist to keep from falling in an undignified heap at his feet.

She'd been kissed many times before, but never like this, never with such tenderness and purpose. Not even their first kiss had affected her as profoundly, and by the time Luke eased away from the caress, Haley felt completely and irrevocably claimed.

She silently stood by Luke's side as the chapel's photographer snapped several pictures, then handed him the disk of still shots and a DVD of the ceremony, along with their newly signed marriage certificate.

"Thank you," Haley murmured as Luke took her hand in his and led her up the aisle and out of the chapel door to their waiting limo.

"I've got to hurry to make the meeting with the Laurel employees on time," he said, helping her into the backseat of the long black car. When he slid in beside her on the plush leather seat, he checked his watch, then tapped on the window separating them from the driver. "Take me directly to the Laurel Enterprises office in Gatlinburg, then drive Ms. Rollins up to the Mountain Crest Lodge."

"You don't want me to attend the meeting with you?" Since she was his executive assistant, she'd been included in several employee meetings in the past and she'd assumed that would be the case this time.

He shook his head. "Besides meeting with the office staff, I'll be touring a couple of job sites and talking to the work crews. But I plan to be back in time for dinner this evening."

"Will I need to go shopping for food?" At least buying a few groceries and preparing a meal would give her something to fill the empty hours of the long day ahead.

"No. I've arranged for a caterer to make dinner for us. And the housekeeper will oversee the clean-up in the kitchen before she leaves for the evening."

After college, Haley had done her own cooking and cleaning and she liked it that way. Having someone perform those duties for her again was going to take some getting used to.

It took a moment for her to realize that the car had stopped in the parking lot of Laurel Enterprises on the outskirts of Gatlinburg. As with most of the other build-ings in the area, it was a log structure that complimented the surrounding environment, instead of detracting from it.

"What am I supposed to do for the rest of the day?"

Being abandoned by her new husband right after they exchanged vows, then sequestered in a mountaintop lodge with nothing to do wasn't exactly the way she'd dreamed her wedding day would unfold.

"It's a nice spring day. You could sit on one of the decks and enjoy the view of Mount LeConte," he said, waiting for their driver to open his door. "Or you could spend the afternoon relaxing in the hot tub." He started to get out of the car, then turned back. "But whatever else you decide to do, make sure that you get plenty of rest." Giving her a quick kiss and a smile that spoke volumes, he winked. "If you'll remember, we're going to start making a baby tonight."

All the way up the mountain to the lodge where they would be staying, Haley tried to remind herself that her marriage to Luke was one of convenience. He viewed their union as the means to an end—a way to get the heir he wanted.

But no matter how hard she tried, she couldn't help but resent the fact that he wasn't even willing to take their wedding day off from work. Nor could she stop a keen sense of sadness from filling her. She'd always envisioned having a baby with a man who loved her and was as devoted to her and their child as she intended to be.

And although she'd known and accepted that theirs was a one-sided relationship, that knowledge did very little to help her stifle an almost uncontrollable urge to let the flood gates open and have herself a good cleansing cry. Nor did it keep her from wanting to tell the driver to turn around and take her back to Nashville and the safe haven of her comfortable little apartment.

* * *

Long after the limousine driver let him out in front of the Mountain Crest Lodge and drove back down the mountain, Luke stood staring at the dark windows of the huge three-story log structure. Haley hadn't bothered leaving a light on for him and he couldn't say that he blamed her. Hurrying off immediately after the wedding ceremony to meet with the Laurel people, he'd left her to fend for herself on their wedding day. That was probably more than enough to get him nominated for jerk of the year.

He checked his watch. It was well past midnight and he'd missed most of his own wedding night as well. He didn't pretend to be an expert on the subject by any means, but even he knew that kind of behavior fell short of what was expected of a newly married man. And especially one who had wed for the sole purpose of making his partner pregnant. But the truth of the matter was, he hadn't expected the intensity of his reaction to Haley when he'd watched her walk down the aisle toward him or the emotions that he'd experienced during the ceremony. Wearing a simple, sleeveless white dress and with her hair in that curly style he'd liked the day he stopped by her apartment, she had been absolutely stunning. And he still had a hard time believing that in the five years she'd worked for him, he hadn't once taken notice of how beautiful she was.

But it was when she'd looked up at him with those trusting turquoise eyes, that a need to protect and take care of her threatened to overwhelm him.

And if that wasn't enough to throw him for a loop, the kiss they'd shared at the end of the brief ceremony was. When he'd kissed her the night before, it had been quite promising and more than a little pleasant. But it couldn't compare to the kiss they'd shared to seal their vows. The feel of her soft, sweet lips beneath his and the need to possess her had been staggering. He'd never in his entire thirty-six years experienced anything even close to that with any other woman.

That was what sent him rushing off to meet the Laurel people. He'd needed the distance to regain his perspective on the matter.

Unfortunately, the meeting ran a lot longer than he anticipated, then he'd learned of a labor dispute that threatened to shut down work on several job sites. By the time he'd straightened out the problem so that the jobs could resume the next week, it was well after midnight. And if missing the wedding dinner he'd arranged for them and not being there to make love to Haley on their wedding night didn't lock up the prize jerk award for him, he didn't know what would.

He sighed heavily as he started up the steps to the front door of the lodge. As he keyed in the security code and opened the door, he wondered if she would honor their agreement of having his child. But as he walked through the great room on his way to the master suite, he shook his head. There was no doubt in his mind that Haley would hold up her end of the arrangement. If there was one thing he knew about his executive assistant, it was that her word was as good as any signed contract. And he'd known from the minute she'd outlined her conditions that if he accepted her criteria, she'd go through with it.

Still, that didn't change the fact that she probably expected a lot more from him on their wedding day.

Luke narrowed his eyes at the sight of his big empty bed. The comforter was still in place, indicating no one had been in it. He looked around the room and noted that her overnight case was nowhere in sight.

Where the hell was she?

His strides purposeful, he crossed the great room and taking the stairs two at a time, went in search of his wayward assistant. There were seven other bedrooms in the place and Haley had damned well better be in one of them.

By the time he got to the door at the end of the hall, Luke was already planning to call the housekeeper and put the woman through the third degree about when Haley had left and if she'd indicated where she was going. But when he glanced in the last bedroom, his irritation instantly disappeared at the sight before him.

The moonlight streaming through the floor-to-ceiling windows bathed the room in an ethereal light. Haley looked like a golden-haired angel curled up in the middle of the king-size bed. Walking over to wake her and ask her why the hell she wasn't in his bed in the master suite, Luke stopped short at the iridescent trace of tears on her flawless cheeks.

She'd been crying?

Without warning the protectiveness he'd experienced at the wedding chapel began to spread throughout his chest and he didn't think twice as he quietly shrugged out of his suit coat and began to loosen his tie and unbutton his shirt. Tossing them on the chair across the room, he removed his shoes and socks, then unzipped his trousers and added them to the growing pile of clothes. Careful not to wake her, Luke pulled back the covers and stretching out on the bed beside her, reached out to take Haley into his arms.

As he pulled her against him, he thought he heard her murmur his name in her sleep, but he didn't have time to dwell on what that might mean when she moved to snuggle against him and placed a delicate hand on his bare chest. The feel of her slender body aligned with his and her soft palm against his hair-roughened flesh sent heat streaking at the speed of light down the length of him and he concentrated on drawing in his next breath.

Suddenly, and completely without warning, the memory of their wedding kiss came rushing back and his body hardened so fast it left him feeling light-headed. The memory of the feel of her perfect lips against his had him wondering what the hell he'd been thinking. Why had he put work ahead of what he knew for certain would have been one of the most exciting nights of his life?

Luke glanced down at Haley's head cradled on his shoulder. He'd like nothing more than to wake her and make love until they both collapsed from exhaustion. But all things considered, he doubted she'd be overly receptive to the idea of sharing her body with the man who had abandoned her in favor of work.

Tightening his arms around her, he forced himself to relax and concentrate on getting some much needed sleep. The first thing in the morning, he'd let her know he regretted the way things had gone the evening before. And once she was in a more congenial mood, they could spend the rest of their stay in the mountains on the pleasurable task of making her pregnant.

* * *

Trying her best to prolong her tantalizing dream, Haley moved closer to the warm, hard masculine body lying next to her. But one by one, as her senses woke up, she became aware of several things at once. The feel of crisp hair beneath her palm, the light woodsy scent of a man's cologne and the sound of soft snores chased away the last traces of sleep and opening her eyes, she found herself face-to-face with Luke.

Her sharp intake of breath must have wakened him because the corners of his mouth slowly curved up in a sleepy smile a moment before he opened his eyes. "Good morning, sweetheart."

"What are you doing here, Luke?"

His low chuckle caused a wonderful fluttering sensation deep in the pit of her stomach and made every one of her feminine instincts come to full alert.

"If you'll remember, we got married yesterday. This is where I'm supposed to be."

"Oh, *I* remember." She shook her head and started moving away from him. She wasn't letting him off the hook that easily. "But I was under the impression that you had forgotten all about that."

The smile on his handsome face faded and before she knew what was happening, he reached out and pulled her back to him. "I really regret that I missed having dinner with you last night." He used his index finger to brush a strand of hair from her cheek. "But during my meeting with the Laurel office staff, I learned about a labor dispute with the work crews which had to be resolved immediately or there would have been a walkout on Monday."

Her skin tingled everywhere he touched her, but Haley tried her best not to notice. As far as she was concerned, no matter what the reason for their marriage, there was no excuse for a man to completely ignore a woman on what was supposed to be one of the most important days of her life.

"There's always going to be something that needs your attention." She tried to wiggle out of his grasp, but his arms were like two steel bands holding her firmly against him.

"That's true," he said, confirming her suspicion that she would always come in a distant second to Garnier Construction. He pressed a kiss to her forehead. "Would you like to know what's going to claim my attention today and tomorrow?"

"Not particularly." She wasn't interested in hearing about labor problems or another meeting with office managers. All she wanted to do was take a shower, get dressed and pack for their return trip.

"That's too bad because I'm going to tell you anyway," he continued as he ran his hand down the outside of her thigh, then back up, bringing the tail of her nightgown to her waist. "Today and tomorrow, you will have my complete and undivided attention."

Haley wasn't sure if her heart skittered to a stop because of what he'd said or from the feel of his hand slipping beneath her gown to caress her lower back. "B-but I thought…I mean, you said we would be going back to Nashville early this morning."

"I've decided that we need time to rectify the situation you brought to my attention the other day at the office. We need to get to know each other on a more…personal level," he said, giving her a smile that warmed her all over and left no doubt about what he had in mind. "We'll head back home in a couple of days."

"Home? Meaning your mansion?"

He nodded as his finger traced the lace edge of her panties. "Didn't you inform the complex that you would be moving? Surely you didn't think you'd be returning to your apartment, did you?"

She shook her head. "I…still have to…move my clothes." How was she supposed to think with his fingers dipping beneath the scalloped trim?

"Don't worry. I had some of my staff move your personal effects after we left yesterday," he stated, his voice low and intimate.

Haley froze. "You did what?"

He kissed her shoulder. "Everything will already be unpacked and put away by the time we get back on Tuesday."

She couldn't believe what she was hearing. "Your arrogance has no bounds, does it?"

"What do you mean?" He had the audacity to look truly puzzled.

"Did it ever occur to you that I might not like someone else handling my underwear?"

He smiled as he continued to touch her and every stroke of his warm palm on her suddenly sensitive skin increased the heat building deep inside of her. "I don't…know what surprises me more…your arrogance or…you taking a day off from work," she explained, struggling to catch her next breath and trying desperately to remember she was irritated with him.

"Why would my taking time off surprise you?" he asked, his warm breath close to her ear.

"The only time I've ever known you to take a day off from the office was when your sister graduated from college," she retorted, trying to concentrate on something besides his hands moving steadily over her body. She was definitely losing the battle.

"I'm not all work," he insisted, slowly easing her to her back. When he leaned over her, his smile and the gleam in his vivid blue eyes told her in no uncertain terms exactly what he meant when he added, "Believe me, I do know how to play, sweetheart."

"I'm, uh, sure you do," she hedged, staring up at him. "But I don't think—"

"That's all right. I'll do the thinking for both of us," he interrupted as he brought his mouth down to cover hers.

His lips teased and caressed, making Haley forget anything she'd been about to say. Wrapping her arms around his broad shoulders, she gave up trying to think and lost herself to his tender exploration.

How could she even begin to form a rational thought when she was lying in bed with a half-naked man? The very man she'd fantasized about for over five years? The man who was kissing her like she was the most desirable woman he'd ever known?

When he used the tip of his tongue to trace the edge of her mouth, she couldn't deny him entry. She wanted to once again experience his taste and the feeling that Luke was claiming her for his own.

Her pulse sped up and she wasn't entirely certain it would ever return to normal when he slowly slid his hand from her back to her abdomen, then up to the underside of her breast. Never in her wildest imaginings could anything have felt more sensual as when he cupped the soft mound and began to relentlessly tease the puckered bud with the pad of his thumb.

"You're so sweet," he said, breaking the kiss to nibble his way down her throat to the top of her nightgown. When he raised his head, he gave her a smile that heated her all the way to her soul at the same time he used his finger to trace the delicate lace edging at the neckline. "Let's get you out of this."

Before she could respond, he tossed the comforter back and propping himself up on one elbow, used both hands to rip the thin cotton garment from the top all the way to the hem.

Gasping, she reached for the sheet. "Good heavens, Luke, you didn't even give me the chance to take it off."

He was not the least bit apologetic when he shoved the sheet farther from her grasp. "I didn't want to waste the time."

"That was the only gown I brought with me…I didn't expect to be staying more than one night," she explained, covering her breasts with her palms.

Taking her hands in his, he moved them to her sides. "Don't try to hide from me, Haley. We're married. There's no reason for you to be embarrassed or shy with me."

"But couldn't we learn about each other on a more personal level with our clothes on first?" she asked as a fiery flush heated her cheeks.

She knew he thought she'd lost her mind, but that couldn't be helped. To have their relationship go from strictly business with no contact outside of the office one day, to being married and naked in bed together the next was more than a little intimidating. And even though she'd dreamed that one day he'd notice her as a woman instead of just his competent assistant, in her fantasies, things between them had never progressed this far this fast.

"I told you before that there's no better way for a man and woman to get acquainted than making love," he reminded, lowering his head to kiss the tip of her breast. "Besides, the sole reason for our getting married was for me to make you pregnant." Laughing, he traced the valley between her breasts all the way down to her navel. "And that would be hard to do with clothes on, sweetheart."

When he lowered his mouth to her overly sensitive nipple, a swirl of heat gathered in the very core of her and Haley forgot about everything but the way Luke was making her feel. Shamelessly threading her fingers through his thick black hair to hold him to her, it took a moment for her to realize he'd slipped his hand below the band of her silk panties.

Inch by slow inch, he caressed his way to her most secret parts, and she thought she'd melt from the delicious heat threading though her veins. The intense longing he created was like nothing she had ever known and she didn't even try to stop her moan from escaping.

"Look at me, Haley," he said, raising his head from her breast. When she did, his smile sent another wave of tingling sensations straight through her. "In the past few minutes, I've already learned several things about you that I wasn't aware of before."

"R-really?"

Smiling, he nodded. "You like the way I make you feel when I touch you here." When he moved his fingers to dip inside and stroke her intimately, every fiber of her being hummed with pleasure.

"I…oh…y-yes."

"And you really like for me to do this," he added, nipping at the tip of her breast with his firm lips.

When he took the bud into his mouth to draw on it deeply, exquisite feelings flowed to every nerve in her body and her will to resist became nonexistent.

Unable to make a sound, she nodded as Luke continued his gentle assault on her senses. Completely lost to the feelings he was creating within her, she didn't have the slightest clue when he'd removed her panties and his boxers. But the feel of his bare body against hers and the solid strength of his arousal as he pressed himself to her thigh, brought back some of her sanity and she shivered from nervous anticipation.

"I've gotten to know you quite well already, sweetheart," Luke informed, kissing her. "But now it's time you learned something about me."

"W-what…would that…be?" she asked, finding oxygen in extremely short supply.

"I want you," he said, nudging her legs apart with his knee. "I want to be deep inside of you. Right now."

As he moved to cover her, she closed her eyes and lay back against the pillows. The electrifying excitement he'd built inside her was undeniable, but so was a fair amount of nervous apprehension.

He'd said that making love was a good way to get to know each other on a more personal level. And there was something very important that he was about to find out about her. Something that she was fairly certain he would have never guessed.

What was Luke going to think when he found out? How was he going to react when he discovered that his wife had never been acquainted with any other man the way she was about to become acquainted with him?

Five

Luke felt Haley's body tense as he guided himself to her and his protectiveness returned tenfold. "Open your eyes, sweetheart." When she did, he thought he saw a brief shadow of fear in her blue-green gaze. "You do trust me, don't you?"

She stared at him a moment before she slowly nodded. "Y-yes. But there's something I should probably tell you."

"Do you want me, Haley?"

"Y-yes."

"That's all I need to know." Giving her what he hoped was a reassuring smile, he brushed her soft lips with his, cutting off anything she was about to say. "It's going to be all right, Haley. I know you haven't been seeing anyone and it's probably been a while. But I don't want you to worry. We're going to be good together and I promise to take care of you." He moved his lower body forward a fraction of an inch. "I'll make sure that you get as much pleasure from our lovemaking as I do, sweetheart."

As he entered her, Luke gritted his back teeth and forced himself to go slow in order to allow her body to adjust to the invasion of his. He'd been right in his assumption that she didn't have a lot of experience at making love. She'd been too inhibited about him seeing her body and he could tell that she'd been genuinely surprised by the way he'd made her feel when he'd touched her. And if that hadn't been evidence enough to prove his theory, the mind-blowing tightness surrounding him now was.

But when he met a slight resistance within her, then the feeling that he'd pushed past a thin barrier, he froze and tried to come to grips with his newest discovery about her. He'd thought it had been some time since she'd been intimate with a man, but it had not even crossed his mind that Haley might still be a virgin. After all, she was twenty-eight years old and extremely attractive. He couldn't believe some man hadn't swept her off her feet at least once.

"You've never had sex." He hadn't meant for the words to come out more as an accusation than a statement of the fact.

"No," she whispered. A couple of tears slipped from the corners of her tightly closed eyes and Luke felt like the biggest fool alive.

He knew she was experiencing a bit of discomfort and careful to hold his lower body completely still, he wrapped his arms around her and cradled her to him. "It's okay, sweetheart. I know it must be uncomfortable, but try to relax. Just a little more and you'll have all of me."

He waited until he felt a slight easing of her feminine muscles surrounding him, then moving forward, joined their bodies completely. The realization that he was claiming her in a way that no other man had, caused the possessiveness within him to reach heights that he never expected and didn't even want to think about.

But concentrating on more pressing matters, he ignored the fire in his belly that urged him to complete the act of loving her. Her body needed more time to get used to the newness of accommodating his. And the very last thing he intended to do was hurt her any more than he had already done.

"It's a little better now," she said, opening her eyes. The spark of desire he detected in the turquoise depths and the easing of tension in her slender form reinforced her statement and he knew that the unfulfilled passion he'd created within her was beginning to return.

As he eased his hips back, he captured her gaze with his. "I want you to promise me that you'll let me know if I'm hurting you in any way."

"I promise," she repeated, bringing her arms up to encircle his shoulders.

The feel of her arms embracing him and her soft body accepting him almost sent him over the edge. But focusing all of his attention on making things as easy for her as was humanly possible, he slowly began to rock against her.

His body demanded satisfaction, but Luke refused to give in to his own needs without ensuring that he'd first met hers. He knew it wasn't always enjoyable for a woman the first time she made love, but even if it killed him, he was going to see that Haley found their love-making at the very least pleasant and if he had his way, quite pleasurable.

When her body began a tentative movement that joined the rhythm of his, he knew his efforts had been worth the hell he'd been going through to ensure her comfort. But all too soon he felt her gently tighten around him, signaling that she'd reached the pinnacle and was about to find the ecstasy he was determined to give her. Deepening his movements, he waited until he felt the trembling of her delicate body beneath his and heard her softly cry out his name before he let go of the slender thread he held on his control. Only then did he give way to his own desire and allow himself to find the release he so desperately needed.

Luke's pulse pounded in his ears and he thought he just might pass out from the rush as he thrust into her one final time and wave after wave of intense pleasure flowed through him. As he filled her with his essence, he felt as if he'd been completely drained of energy and eased himself down on top of her.

He wasn't certain how long he lay covering her as he tried to catch his breath, but when he finally gained enough strength, he moved to her side and gathered her to him. "Are you all right?"

"That was…" She paused as if trying to find the right word. "…absolutely amazing."

Smiling at the fact that he'd taken her virginity and still managed to bring her pleasure, he reached down to pull the sheet over their rapidly cooling bodies. "I promise next time our lovemaking will reach incredible status."

"Really?" She shook her head. "I don't see how it could be any better than what I just experienced."

"That's because you haven't had anything to compare it to." He hugged her close and tried not to dwell on the possessiveness that threatened to consume him. "My mission is to see that every time we make love the pleasure keeps getting stronger for you."

"I'll have to take your word for that," she conceded, sounding extremely sleepy.

He kissed the top of her head pillowed on his shoulder. "Get some rest, sweetheart. We'll talk after you've had a little nap."

As he held Haley while she slept, Luke couldn't quite wrap his mind around the fact that he was the only man to make love to her. Had he ever been a woman's first time before?

If he had, he knew for certain he would have remembered it. Taking a woman's virginity wasn't something a man was likely to forget.

Glancing at Haley sleeping so peacefully next to him, several questions kept running through his mind. Why had she waited so long to be with a man? If she'd been holding out for the permanence of marriage before taking that step, why had she agreed to birth his heir when she knew their arrangement would eventually end? And how had she managed to save herself from players like Chet Parker, who were out there just looking for the right opportunity to swoop in and seduce a woman as beautiful and innocent as Haley?

When Haley moved closer to him in her sleep, he tightened his arms around her and kissed her soft cheek. He didn't want to analyze his uncharacteristic protectiveness toward her or the unfamiliar need to possess her. They'd reached an agreement and she was his for now—the woman he'd chosen to be the mother of his child. As far as he was concerned, that was reason enough.

Oh, he still wanted answers to his questions regarding her lack of sexual experience and an explanation of her motives for agreeing to have his child. But he wasn't overly concerned about getting them right away. As he got to know her better, he'd learn her secrets and reach a satisfactory conclusion to the mystery of Haley Rollins.

In the meantime, he had every intention of enjoying the pleasure of making love to her every night and reaching his goal of soon having an heir to inherit the vast holdings of Garnier Construction.

Slowly opening her eyes, Haley found herself alone in the big log bed and wondered if she'd been dreaming. After all this time imagining what it would be like, had she really slept with Luke?

As she stretched to loosen the kinks of sleep from her limbs, the feel of the sheet sliding over her bare skin and the interesting little aches in her lower body quickly told her that they had indeed consummated their marriage. Her cheeks heated as the memory of what they'd shared in the early predawn light came flooding back.

Luke had seen her as no other man had and made her feel things she would have never thought possible. But once he'd learned she was a virgin, his incredible patience and the extra care he took to reduce any discomfort she might have had touched her deeply. He'd seen to it that her first experience making love was pleasurable and even though their marriage was destined to end one day, she'd never be sorry that she'd waited for her husband.

"I see you finally woke up, sleepyhead," Luke greeted her cheerfully, shouldering the door open. He carried a breakfast tray with two plates of delicious-looking food, glasses of orange juice and a single rose in a glass bud vase. "Time to rise and shine."

His thoughtfulness was unexpected and quite touching. "I haven't had breakfast in bed since I was child," she reminisced, holding the sheet to cover her breasts as she sat up. "And I was too sick to care about eating anything then."

"Well, I hope you have a hearty appetite now, because Mrs. Beck outdid herself," he noted, referring to the housekeeper. "I think she cooked every breakfast food known to man."

"Could you get my overnight case, please?" Haley requested, wanting to retrieve the new bathrobe she'd purchased for the trip.

"Uh-oh." He gave her a sheepish grin. "When I got up and went to shower and change, I moved it to my room."

"What am I going to put on?" she asked, looking around for something—anything—to wear.

"I really like what you're wearing now," he observed, setting the tray on top of the dresser.

"I'm naked under here."

"Bingo."

Her cheeks heated at his lascivious grin. "Seriously, what am I going to wear?"

"I think you wear *nothing* very well," he commented, rocking back on his heels. "It really looks good on you."

"Will you be serious?" she pleaded, feeling a little desperate. "I can't even go downstairs to get my clothes without something to cover up with. Poor Mrs. Beck would probably have a massive coronary."

He looked thoughtful. "I guess you might have a point."

"I do have a point." She shook her head. "And unless you intend for me to stay in this bed the rest of the day, I need something to put on."

"Staying in bed presents some very interesting possibilities," he responded, his grin widening. When she tugged the sheet free from the end of the mattress, he pulled the tail of his shirt from his jeans. "If you're that adamant about it, I'll have to make the sacrifice."

She stared shamelessly as Luke unbuttoned the garment and revealed his wide chest. Earlier when they'd made love, she'd been too nervous and preoccupied with the newness of it all to pay a lot of attention to his physique. But as he shrugged out of the shirt, her breath caught and her heart did a funny little thump against her rib cage.

His body was absolutely perfect. Every muscle from his shoulders all the way to the waistband of his low-slung jeans was well-defined and he was most definitely the type of man dreams were made of. At least, her dreams.

When he handed her the shirt, then stood there expectantly, she forced her thoughts back to the matter at hand and shook her head. "Turn around."

His smile sent a wave of sizzling warmth shimmering over her skin. "Sweetheart, I saw your body when we made love and believe me, you have no reason to be self-conscious. You're beautiful."

"I'll have to take your word on that," she remarked, refusing to give too much weight to his appreciation of her body. "But it's extremely difficult to throw caution to the wind after twenty-eight years of keeping myself covered up."

Apparently deciding she meant business, he finally blew out an exaggerated breath, shook his head and turned his back to her. "We've already made love once and I anticipate doing so again quite frequently. It won't take long before I know your body as well as I know mine."

"In less than a week, we've gone from nothing more than boss and employee to sleeping together," she tried to explain, pulling on his shirt. The delicious masculine scent surrounding her as she buttoned the garment caused Haley to feel warm all over. "We only went on one date—if you want to call it that—and that was the night before we got married."

When he picked up the breakfast tray from the dresser and turned to face her, his expression was thoughtful. "So what you're saying is, you don't switch gears quite that fast."

"Something like that." Maybe he was beginning to understand how she felt.

"I guess that makes sense," he said absently as he set the tray over her lap, then lowered himself to sit on the mattress beside her. He looked pensive for a moment. "Since we're discussing your inhibitions, were they the reason you were still a virgin?"

She knew he'd be curious and ask about it. "It's quite simple, really. I went to a very strict, private high school for girls. In our Freshman year, we were encouraged to take a pledge to stay pure until we married. I promised that I would." Reaching for a slice of crispy bacon, she shrugged. "Besides, I never met a man that I cared enough about to be intimate with."

"Never?"

"Oh, I was tempted a couple of times in college with one or two of the guys I dated." She shook her head. "But I always found a reason not to break my vow. Probably because it just didn't feel right with them."

"Do you always keep your word, Haley?" His question was casual enough, but she could tell he was extremely interested in her answer.

Swallowing the bacon she'd been nibbling on, she nodded. "It's not always easy, but if I tell someone that I'll do something, I try my best to do it." She smiled. "I have had to break my promises a few times, but I've never made a habit of it."

"So that's why you followed through when I called your bluff about having to be married," he proclaimed, capturing her gaze with his. "You gave me your word."

Haley nodded again. She wasn't overly surprised that he'd figured out that she was discouraging him when she laid down the terms to have his baby. He was very perceptive and it was one of the many reasons he was such a highly successful businessman.

"Knowing how you feel about relationships, I thought mentioning marriage would dissuade you," she admitted. "If I'd tried to back out when you said you were agreeable, you wouldn't have given me a minute's peace until I honored my word."

"That's true, but why didn't you just reject my request outright?" he asked, obviously trying to figure out what made her tick as he took a big bite of his scrambled eggs.

"Because I know you well enough that when you set your sights on something, you don't give up. You're like a dog with a juicy bone." Picking up her glass of orange juice, she gazed at him over the rim. "Would you have abandoned the idea of me having your child if I'd said no right away?"

Chuckling, he shook his head. "Not a chance in hell, sweetheart."

"My point exactly."

"So, if you know me so well," he argued as he placed his fork on his empty plate, "why do you keep insisting that we need to get to know each other further?"

How could she explain that it was the little everyday things that she wanted to know?

"Do you have any idea why my hair is straight when I'm at the office, but when I'm at home it's curly?" she finally asked.

His expression clearly stated he thought she'd lost her mind.

"Bear with me for a minute."

He gave her a dubious look. "Okay. I assume you're like my sister and use a curling iron when you want to make your hair curly."

"Just the opposite." She couldn't help but laugh. "I use a flat iron to take the curl *out*."

"Your hair is naturally curly?" He shook his head. "I wasn't aware of that."

"That's what I meant about knowing each other. Don't you think that's something a man would know about the woman he has a child with?"

He looked thoughtful. "I suppose it might be since it's a trait that could be passed on to my son." Grinning, he winked at her. "But it's certainly not a requirement for having sex."

Luke wasn't going to concede easily. But neither was she.

"I know how you take your coffee. Do you know how I prefer mine?"

He was silent for several seconds before he finally answered. "No."

"That's something else most couples know about each other by the time they walk down the aisle or have a baby." She smiled. "And just for the record, I don't drink coffee because I don't like the taste of it."

"I never noticed," he acknowledged as he picked up the tray. "But I think I have an excellent way of remedying this little problem you think we have while learning each others' likes and dislikes."

"Really? What would that be?"

"We're going to take a drive across the mountains over into North Carolina. And while we're traveling, we'll take turns asking questions about the little everyday things." He looked quite pleased with himself. "It won't take any time at all and we'll know each other quite well."

"But I thought you had plans to stay here for the rest of the weekend," she reminded him, fascinated by the play of muscles in his broad back as he balanced the tray and walked to the door.

Stopping, he turned. "That was before I took your virginity."

"What does that have to do with anything?" she asked, getting out of bed to find her clothes and take a shower.

Luke suddenly groaned, closed his eyes and drew in a deep breath.

Alarmed by his uncharacteristic behavior, she went to him. "Are you all right?"

When he opened his eyes, the intensity in his incredible blue gaze warmed her. "Do you have any idea how sexy you look wearing nothing but my shirt? Or what a turn-on it is for me just knowing that you don't have anything on underneath it?"

"Not really." She wondered if he knew how sexy he looked *without* a shirt.

"The reason we need to go for a drive is because if we don't, I'm going to put down this tray, carry you back to bed and make love to you until we both collapse from exhaustion." He glanced away. "And that wouldn't be a good idea right now."

Had he changed his mind about wanting her to become pregnant immediately?

"Why not? Isn't that a prerequisite for making a baby the old-fashioned way?"

"Sweetheart, nothing would make me happier than making love to you all day and all night." He gazed at her and shook his head. "But you're new to this and I'm sure you're a little sore. If we wait until this evening, it might not be as uncomfortable for you as it would be now."

Haley felt as if her cheeks were on fire. She wasn't used to discussing something so intimate and personal. "Oh, I...um, didn't realize."

"We'll make love again tonight." He gave her a quick kiss, then walked out into the hall. "Now, do me a favor. Go down to the master suite and get ready. We'll leave as soon as the rental car agency can have a car delivered."

When she started to walk past him, he shook his head.

"Let me go first."

"Why?"

Giving her a look so sensual it could have easily turned a stone to mush, he started down the hall. "Because if you walk downstairs ahead of me, I'll end up hard as hell. And when I take the tray back to the kitchen, I don't think Mrs. Beck could stand the shock of seeing me in that condition."

"That might even traumatize her more than me wearing nothing but a sheet," she said, laughing.

Luke snorted. "Knowing Mrs. Beck, I'd put money on it."

As Haley followed him toward the stairs, a tiny feminine thrill flowed through her at the knowledge that he was that attracted to her. She wasn't foolish enough to think that just because he wanted her, that he cared deeply for her. But if he desired her now, maybe one day he would develop true feelings for her.

As Luke steered the rental car into a parking area at Chimney Rock in North Carolina, Haley gazed at the lush green mountains surrounding the natural monolith. "I see why this location was chosen for several movies. It's absolutely gorgeous. Can you imagine how fantastic the hiking must be around here?"

Turning off the car's engine, he smiled. "Did I just learn another little known fact about you that I wouldn't have guessed? Are you a hiker?"

"Not anymore." She looked out at the panoramic view. "But I used to go hiking all the time when I was younger."

"Let me guess. One of the college boyfriends appreciated nature."

"Not hardly. They might have gotten their hands dirty." Just the thought of any of them going anywhere that took them outside of a climate-controlled environment was laughable. "My passion for hiking started long before college. I went on nature walks when I joined the Campfire Girls. Then later, when I was in high school, I joined the hiking club."

"Interesting."

"What about you? Do you enjoy any outdoor activities?" She grinned. "Surveying the work-in-progress at a job site doesn't count."

He laughed. "But that's outdoors and I do enjoy watching another Garnier project take shape."

She shook her head. "That's something I already know about you. Remember, we're supposed to be sharing the unknown."

"Right. Let's see, Jake and I used to go on an annual camping trip in the Sierras," he replied, referring to his twin brother. "But in the past several years, we've both been so busy that we haven't had time."

"Did you enjoy those trips to the mountains?" she asked, trying to imagine what it would be like to have a family to share things with.

Looking thoughtful for several seconds, he nodded. "We'd spend an entire week fishing and catching up on what plans we were making to advance our careers."

"You should make the time to do that again, Luke." If she had a brother or sister, nothing would stand in the way of their spending time together. "You know what they say about taking the time to smell the roses."

"I'll keep that in mind," he indicated, getting out of the car to come around and open the passenger door for her. "What about you, do you have a family tradition with one of your siblings?"

Taking the hand he offered to help her out of the car, she tried not to meet his questioning gaze. If she did, he might see how truly alone and sad she'd always felt.

"I was an only child," she revealed.

"Really?" Closing the car door, he put his arm around her waist and tucked her to his side as they walked to the edge of the scenic overlook. "I wasn't aware of that."

Before he could question her further about her family, she pointed to a black bear and two small cubs that waddled into a clearing on the slope below. "Aren't they adorable?"

He snorted. "I suppose, if you like a lot of fur and really big teeth."

"I love babies of all kinds," she confirmed as she watched the two cubs engage in an impromptu wrestling match.

"What about alligator babies?" Turning her to face him, he pulled her close. "They don't have fur, but they do have a lot of teeth. You don't think they're cute, do you?"

The feel of his arms around her sent a languid heat flowing through every part of her. "Well, they may not be as sweet as a live teddy bear, but I'm sure the momma alligator thinks they are."

He stared at her for several long moments, then slowly lowered his head to capture her lips in a kiss so tender it brought tears to her eyes. Thoughtful and sweet, Luke explored her with a thoroughness that made her feel as if he truly cherished everything about her.

But when he slipped his tongue inside her mouth to taste and tease, the kiss became so steamy that Haley felt as if the earth moved beneath her feet. Stroking her inner recesses at the same time he pressed his hips against her belly caused an empty ache to settle deep in the most feminine areas of her body. The feel of his strong arousal and the mastery of his kiss caused her knees to give way and she clung to his solid strength for support.

"I think we'd better head back. Otherwise, I'm going to abandon my good intentions and make love to you right here and now," he vowed, breaking the kiss. "Besides, there's one other place I think you'd enjoy seeing."

"Really? Where would that be?" she questioned, not really caring as long as they were together.

"You'll see," he promised, guiding her to the car.

Two and a half hours later, as they stepped onto the moving walkway that led through the acrylic tunnel at the aquarium in Gatlinburg, they were immediately surrounded by thousands of species of aquatic creatures. "This is wonderful, Luke," Haley declared, marveling at the activity surrounding them. "It's like being underwater."

"You find this interesting, do you?"

"Absolutely." She smiled at a couple of orange and white striped fish gliding effortlessly through the water. "Aren't they sweet?"

Luke snorted. "I've never associated that word with fish." He smiled suddenly. "Let me guess, you're thinking of the cartoon movie that came out several years ago about a lost clown fish."

"You know about that?" she asked, somewhat surprised. She wouldn't have thought he'd have known anything about a children's movie.

Nodding, he shrugged. "Arielle insisted that Jake and I had to take her to see it when it first came out. It was part of her birthday present and we couldn't get out of it."

"Did you enjoy it?"

"I suppose it was a good kid movie," he commented, gazing at a shark lazily gliding toward them. "But I normally prefer psychological thrillers or action/adventure movies."

"Not the best for a growing child." She paused, then glancing at him from the corner of her eye to make sure she had his attention, she went on. "You do realize that you'll be taking in a lot of cartoon films once the baby gets old enough to enjoy them."

He frowned and it was obvious that he hadn't thought past grooming his heir to take over his business holdings once the child was old enough. "Why don't I leave that part of the parenting to you?" he finally suggested.

"Why don't we do that part together?" she shot back. "Don't you think a child would like to go a few places and do a few things with both parents at the same time? It would be nice for our child to know her parents are on good terms. And you do want the baby to grow up to be happy and well-adjusted, don't you?"

"Of course, but I hadn't really given activities and the like a lot of thought." He was silent for a moment as if digesting what she'd said. "But it probably would be a good idea for us to do things together with him."

Satisfied that she had Luke contemplating the emotional needs of a growing child, she decided to give him one more thing to think about. "You know that the baby could turn out to be a girl."

He looked thoughtful. "Something else I hadn't considered. I just assumed my heir would be a son."

"Would it make a difference if we had a daughter?" she asked, needing to know how he would react if she had a girl.

"No. I've met several women with excellent business instincts. You included." As they stepped off the moving walkway, he turned to face her and the expression on his face caused heat to shimmer over every inch of her. "You're going to be a wonderful mother, Haley, and not just for the traits I want passed on to our child."

"You really think so?"

He nodded. "Now, what do you say we head back to the lodge? I think it's time we stopped talking about the baby and get started making one."

Several hours later, standing on the balcony staring out at the night sky, Luke watched a shooting star disappear behind Mount LeConte as he thought about the day's events. He'd had one of the most fascinating, and at the same time, frustrating afternoons of his life. And Haley was completely responsible.

On one hand, he'd been intrigued by the things he'd learned about her. He now knew that her favorite color was lavender, that she couldn't resist anything chocolate and that she had a weakness for babies, whether they were human, animal or fish.

He smiled at the thought of her reaction to the mother

black bear and two chubby little cubs they'd observed when they stopped at Chimney Rock. Her excitement and joy at seeing the baby animals at play had sparkled in her turquoise eyes and been reflected in her soft laughter. And he couldn't get over how happy he'd been to share the moment with her. She was going to be a wonderful mother and he was convinced now more than ever that he'd made the right choice for the mother of his heir.

But on the other hand, the day had been sheer hell. He'd noticed things about her that he'd never paid attention to before—how sweet and feminine her voice sounded, how pretty she was when she smiled and how graceful and sensual every move of her body was when they got out of the car at the scenic overlook and when they'd strolled through the aquarium.

He'd spent every minute they were together in a perpetual state of arousal. All he'd been able to think about was getting back to the lodge, taking their clothes off and making love to her the entire night.

And that was what really had him perplexed. After making love to her, he'd started thinking less about having sex for the purpose of making her pregnant and more about giving her immeasurable pleasure. In fact, she'd been the one to remind him about having the baby and how they should share the responsibility of raising the child.

"Mrs. Beck and I finished cleaning up the kitchen," Haley said, walking out onto the deck. "She said to tell you she's leaving and will be back tomorrow morning in time to prepare breakfast."

At the sound of her voice, Luke glanced over his shoulder. She looked amazingly beautiful in her yellow blouse and khaki slacks, but he liked the way she'd looked in his shirt a hell of a lot better. Or better yet, out of it.

The thought caused his body to tighten predictably and he forced himself to remember what she'd just said. "You didn't have to help Mrs. Beck. That's what I pay the woman for."

"I'm used to it," she advised, walking over to stand next to him. "Even before I moved out on my own, I sometimes helped my father's housekeeper with the cooking and cleaning."

It was her first mention of anything about her family. "I take it your folks are fairly well off?"

Earlier in the day, he wondered why she deflected the sibling talk. She had at least met his siblings the few times they'd stopped by his office and knew that after their mother's death, he and Jake had raised their younger sister. But he knew absolutely nothing about her family, beyond her telling him that she was an only child.

"My father wasn't overly wealthy, but he did all right," she finally stated, shrugging.

"And your mother?"

"Was completely out of the picture." He watched her cross her arms beneath her breasts and fix her gaze on the mountains.

Haley's defensive body language and the sadness he detected in her voice surprised him. "We don't have to talk about it, sweetheart," he ventured, reaching for her.

When he took her into his arms and held her close, Luke wondered what had happened to her mother. But remembering the look on her pretty face when she'd asked him at the aquarium if it would matter if his heir was a girl made him wonder about the relationship she shared with her father, as well. But his curiosity could wait. She clearly didn't want to discuss any of that now.

He could respect that. The anger and resentment caused by an absentee parent was certainly familiar ground for him. Besides, he had no intention of spoiling what had, up until that moment, been a damned good day.

"Why don't we get in the hot tub and relax for a while before we go to bed for the night?" he asked, nuzzling her soft curls.

"I can't." She sounded less than certain as she brought her arms up to his shoulders. "I didn't bring my swimsuit."

Nibbling on her earlobe, he smiled when he felt a tremor course through her. "We don't have to wear suits. In fact, I think it would be a lot more fun to go skinny-dipping."

"I—I don't think so."

Her breathy laughter sent a shaft of heat straight to the region south of his belt buckle.

"If I couldn't drop the sheet in front of you this morning, what makes you think I could go skinny-dipping with you in the hot tub this evening?"

"Well, for one thing it's dark and we're alone on this section of the mountain." He trailed kisses down the column of her neck. When she sagged against him, he added, "And for another, I promise I won't peek until you're settled in the water."

"Why am I having trouble believing that?" Her throaty question sent his blood pressure soaring.

He chuckled. "How did you know I used up all of my allocated honor for the day?"

"Just a lucky guess."

When she threaded her fingers in the hair at the nape of his neck the heat in his lower belly turned into a hungry flame.

"I suppose we could wear our underwear in the hot tub," she suggested.

His internal heat flared out of control and threatened to turn him to a cinder when she kissed the exposed skin at the open collar of his shirt. "I've got an even better idea, sweetheart," he revealed as he swung her up into his arms. He carried her through the French doors of the great room and straight to the master suite. "Why don't we skip the hot tub and just go to bed?"

Six

As Luke cradled her to him, Haley put her arms around his shoulders and allowed him to carry her to his bedroom. They'd spent a wonderful day together with moments that she would never forget. And if she hadn't been sure she loved him before, Haley knew for certain that she did now.

When he set her on her feet at the side of his bed, then reached over to switch on the bedside lamp, Haley's heart thumped so hard against her ribs she was truly surprised it wasn't deafening. She hadn't anticipated they would be undressing in front of each other or that the light would be on when they did. But it appeared that was exactly what Luke had in mind as he bent to remove both of their shoes and socks. Straightening, he pulled her back into his arms.

"If we'd gotten in the hot tub without our clothes on, you were going to peek, weren't you?" she asked.

Grinning, he nodded. "Shamelessly, sweetheart."

"I think I probably would have, too," she admitted.

"I assume this means that after today you feel we've reached a more personal level and you're more comfortable with me?" he commented, sliding his hands from her back down to the curve of her hips.

"I know you think I've been ridiculous about our knowing more about each other. But you only knew Haley Rollins, the executive assistant who runs your office." She raised her gaze to meet his. "I wanted you to learn about Haley Rollins, the woman."

His gaze was positively sizzling as Luke studied her before he slowly began to lower his head. "And I'm glad I got to know the real Haley. You're warm, compassionate and…" He brushed her lips with his. "…so damned sexy I can't keep my hands off you."

When his mouth covered hers, Haley's eyes drifted shut and her heart soared. Maybe there was hope. Maybe in time Luke could learn to care for her as deeply as she loved him.

But as his firm lips explored her with a tenderness that robbed her of breath, she lost herself in his kiss and abandoned all speculation of what the future might hold for them. All that mattered was she was in his arms now and it felt absolutely wonderful.

As he coaxed her to open for him, she didn't think twice about parting her lips and granting him access. She wanted to once again experience the mastery of his kiss and taste his growing need for her.

Tentatively touching her tongue to his, a tingling excitement filled every cell of her being and she felt as if her insides had been turned to soft, warm butter. Wrapping her arms around his trim waist, her heart raced and the delicious warmth spread inside her as she enjoyed the feel of his hard masculine body pressed so closely to hers.

Slowly easing the pressure of his mouth on hers, he broke the kiss and leaned back to capture her gaze with his. "Why don't we get a little more comfortable?" he suggested, reaching to release the button at the top of her blouse. His slow, promising smile sent shivers coursing throughout her body. "Do you have any idea how much I'm going to enjoy taking these clothes off you?"

"I really…hadn't given it…a lot of thought," she said breathlessly. His fingers grazing her breasts as he unfastened the next button made it seem as if the air had suddenly been sucked right out of the room.

"Have you given any thought to what it would be like taking my clothes off?"

Every night in her fantasies for the past five years, but she wasn't about to admit that to him. "I'm certainly thinking a lot about it now."

By the time he finished with the buttons on her blouse, then slid the silk fabric from her shoulders and down her arms, Haley wondered if she'd ever draw another breath. The feel of his hands skimming over her skin as he whisked the top from her body was absolute heaven. She wanted his touch, wanted to again feel the same delicious sensations he'd created within her that morning. But just when she thought he would remove her bra and touch her the way he had when they made love, he surprised her.

"Let's make this a little more equal, sweetheart," he offered, taking her hands in his to guide them to the front of his shirt.

She knew what he was doing and she loved him all the more for it. Luke wasn't only making an attempt to help her feel more comfortable by allowing her the freedom of undressing him, he was encouraging her to do a little exploring of her own.

As she worked the first button free, she kissed the warm, tanned skin just below his collarbone. "I think I'm really going to like this."

"And I think it's going to kill me," he muttered, sounding more than a little winded.

"You don't like what I'm doing?" she asked as she pushed another button free. She kissed the exposed area, then glancing up at him, kissed her way to the next button. "Would you like for me to stop?"

"Not on…your life." He paused as if trying to arrange his thoughts. "Don't get me wrong, sweetheart. What you're doing feels damned good." When she released the next two buttons and nibbled all the way down his chest to the rippling muscles of his abdomen, she was thrilled at the sound of his sharp intake of breath and the shuddering of his body. "But if you go much farther, I'm going to be finished way before we ever get started."

"Hmm, I don't think that would be good," she confessed, smiling as she pulled the tail of his shirt from the waistband of his low slung jeans.

Laughing, he shook his head. "No, it wouldn't be good at all." Looking up at him, Luke's eyes were tightly closed and a muscle along his jaw was working overtime. "Are you feeling all right?" she asked, thrilled that he seemed to be enjoying her efforts to arouse him.

"I will be real soon," he answered.

When he opened his eyes, the intense blaze of passion in the dark blue depths heated her all the way to her feminine core.

His gaze held her captive as he slowly shrugged out of his shirt, then reached behind her to make quick work of unfastening her lacy bra. When he slid the straps down her arms and tossed it at their feet, he took her hands in his and stood back to gaze at her.

"You're absolutely beautiful, Haley. I don't ever want you to doubt that."

He must have expected her to cover herself because before she had an opportunity to react, he pulled her to him. At the initial feel of soft, feminine skin meeting hard, masculine flesh, the fluttering in her stomach went completely berserk and tiny electric charges skipped over every nerve ending in her body. The delightful abrasion of his chest hair against her sensitized nipples was so sensual, so incredibly exciting, Haley never wanted it to end. And apparently the sensations were just as intense for him as they were for her.

A groan rumbled up from deep in his chest and he took a deep breath a moment before he shook his head. "This was a mistake," he said, splaying his hands over her bare back to hold her to him.

"W-why do you say that?" She was truly surprised that her vocal cords still worked, let alone that she had the capability of putting words into a coherent thought.

Sliding his hands from her back down to her hips, he cupped her bottom and pulled her more fully into the cradle of his hips. The solid ridge of his arousal pressed to her lower stomach threatened to send her into a total meltdown and she had to force herself to breathe.

"You've made me harder than a chunk of granite." Holding her to him with one arm, he reached for the waistband of her khaki slacks. "I want you so damned much I'm about to explode."

As spirals of heat twined their way throughout her body to gather in an ever-tightening coil at the apex of her thighs, Haley couldn't speak. Weakened by the urgent desire building inside of her, she grasped Luke's biceps to stay on her feet.

"You feel so good," he said as his lips moved over her collarbone, then down the slope of her breast.

As he unfastened the closure at the top of her slacks and lowered the zipper, she unbuckled his belt and released the snap of his jeans. Then, feeling bolder than ever, she toyed with the tab at his fly a moment before slowly easing it downward a fraction of an inch.

"I thought we were supposed to be…" Her heart skipped several beats when her fingers brushed the insistent bulge straining to be released from the denim fabric. "…taking each other's clothes off."

When he shuddered and caught her hands in his, their eyes met and the hunger she saw in the navy blue depths sent a shiver of anticipation skipping over her. "Haley, before this night is over, I fully intend for you to know every inch of my body, as I'm going to know every inch of yours," he said, his voice sounding deeper and sexier than she'd ever heard it.

As she watched, he finished lowering his fly, shoved his jeans and boxers down his long muscular legs, then stepped out of them and kicked them to the side. When he straightened, he stood proudly in front of her and she knew he was giving her the luxury of perusing his body without the hindrance of feeling self-conscious about her own.

With her stomach fluttering like a swarm of butterflies had been trapped inside, her gaze slowly slid from his muscular midsection down to his lean, well-toned hips, then beyond. Her breath caught in her throat and her pulse pounded in her ears at the sight of his proud, heavily aroused sex surrounded by a thick patch of crisp dark hair.

"Oh heavens," she said, her gaze flying up to meet his.

As he wrapped his arms around her and drew her to him, his smile made her feel as if she were the most desired woman alive. "I give you my word that making love this time will be easier, sweetheart," he promised as he slid his hands to her waist. "I'm going to give you nothing but pure pleasure."

Unable to find words adequate enough to express how she felt, Haley simply nodded and waited for him to lower the last barriers between them.

"Do you have any idea the hell I've gone through today just knowing what your clothes have been hiding?" he asked, when he added her slacks and panties to the pile of clothing beside them.

"I-I didn't…realize—"

"Let's get into bed while we've still got enough strength left to get there," he cautioned, his words vibrating against her lips.

"That's probably…a good idea," she agreed, trying to catch her non-existent breath.

The world suddenly tilted precariously when he

lifted her in his arms to gently place her in the middle of his bed. As he stretched out beside her, she briefly wondered if he was thinking about making love to her or if he was concentrating on making her pregnant. But as he pulled her to him and she saw the raw hunger in the vivid blue depths of his eyes, she forgot about the purpose behind their union and concentrated on the way he was making her feel.

As he kissed her with a tenderness that robbed her of patience, heat streaked from every part of her to gather in a pool in her very core and she briefly wondered if she'd ever breathe again. But when he cupped her breasts and chafed the overly sensitive tip with the pad of his thumb, a shiver rippled the length of her spine and she moaned from the pure pleasure of it.

"Does that feel good, Haley?" he asked as he nibbled tiny kisses to the rapidly fluttering pulse at the base of her throat.

"Y-yes."

He slid his hand over her ribs to her waist. Then, as he kissed his way from her collarbone down the slope of her breast, he moved his hand to her hip. "Would you like for me to do more?"

"I-If you don't, I think I'll go out of my mind," she groaned, meaning it. She needed his touch, needed his lovemaking like she needed her next heartbeat.

The overwhelming hunger in her lower belly quickly turned to an emptiness that needed to be filled when he took the hardened bud into his mouth and teased her with his tongue at the same time he touched her intimately. Tremors of desire ran through her at the speed of light, but when he slipped his finger inside it felt as if fireworks had been ignited in her soul.

Wanting to bring him the same kind of pleasure, she flattened her palms on his chest and caressed the firm pads of his pectoral muscles, then used her fingertips to trace the lines of his abs on the way to his flat lower belly. But unsure if she should touch him as intimately as he touched her, her hands stilled.

"Go ahead, sweetheart. I promise I won't break," he reassured her, taking her hand in his to guide her to his rigid flesh.

As she encircled his hard masculinity, Haley was encouraged by his deep shuddering groan and she took the liberty of measuring his strength, of teasing his velvety tip and exploring the softness below. But all too quickly Luke took her hands in his and brought them back to his wide chest.

His gaze never left hers as without another word he nudged her knees apart and moved to settle himself between her thighs. "Only pleasure this time," he repeated as he slowly moved his hips forward. "I promise."

Trusting him as she'd never trusted any other man, she didn't even think to be apprehensive. She wanted him to love her, wanted him to take her back to the heights of ecstasy that he'd taken her to that morning.

A shimmering heat began to dance behind Haley's tightly closed eyes when she felt the blunt tip of him against the most feminine part of her. "Please make love to me, Luke. I need you inside. Now."

The blood in her veins felt as if it flowed to the beat of a sultry drum as he slowly began to enter her. Wrapping her arms around his broad shoulders, she reveled in the exquisite stretching of her body as she became one with the man she loved.

When their bodies were completely joined, Haley closed her eyes and lost herself in the intimacy of it all. It felt as if there was no beginning and no end as he set a slow, leisurely pace and wave after wave of pleasure began to consume her. Tension, sensual and exhilarating, began to grip every fiber of her being. Apparently sensing that she was rapidly approaching the peak, Luke deepened his thrusts and she suddenly broke free of the ever-tightening need holding her captive.

Basking in the delicious crescendo of sensations overcoming her, she clung to him to keep from losing herself and held him close in an effort to prolong the feelings. Then suddenly, she felt his body go perfectly still a moment before he hoarsely called her name and joined her in the peace of sweet release.

Haley tightened her arms around Luke and tried not to think about their arrangement being temporary. How long after she became pregnant would he still desire her? Would he view the pregnancy as "mission accomplished" and lose interest in their lovemaking?

And what would happen if she didn't get pregnant right away? Would Luke become impatient and end their arrangement prematurely? Would he decide to find someone else to have the baby both wanted so badly but for different reasons?

She forced herself to end her disturbing speculation as he rolled to her side and drew her to him. All too soon her questions would be answered. Until then, she would store up every memory that she could for the cold, lonely nights when she would be without him.

* * *

Cursing a blue streak, Luke bolted out of bed and hurriedly searched for his jeans in the pile of clothing on the bedroom floor. Who the hell would be calling him at this hour of the night? And why couldn't he find his damned cell phone?

"Do you have any idea what the hell time it is?" he demanded when he finally found his phone and ended its incessant noise.

"I don't give a damn what time it is, we need to talk."

At the sound of his twin brother's voice, Luke growled, "This had better be important, Jake."

"There's something wrong with Arielle," Jake said, unaffected by Luke's harsh tone.

Luke's irritation at being wakened in the middle of the night instantly disappeared at the mention of his younger sister. "Is she all right? What's happened? Does she need a doctor?"

"I'm not sure." Jake paused. "She tells me she's fine, but when I called her this evening she was sobbing her heart out. Again."

"Again? You mean this has happened before? How recently? And why haven't I heard about it until now?" Luke demanded. Normally, he and Jake shared everything. Especially their concerns about their younger sister.

"She begged me not to say anything to you the first time it happened," Jake answered. "And I figured it was just one of those emotional things women do when they have a bad day."

Checking to see if his conversation had disturbed Haley, Luke found her still sleeping peacefully in his bed. Satisfied, he turned his attention to the matter at hand. Normally a very happy person, Arielle rarely cried unless something was terribly wrong.

"How many times has this happened?"

"Twice," Jake confirmed. "And you and I both know this isn't like her."

"Did she tell you why?" Luke inquired, quietly opening the door and walking into the great room.

"I asked, but she wouldn't tell me. And that's what has me concerned. She's never kept anything from us before." Jake's frustration was evident in his tone. "The only thing she would say was we couldn't fix everything for her and that she'd work it out on her own."

That wasn't like their younger sister at all. From the time she could talk, Arielle had shared everything that went on in her life with them and never hesitated to come to either one of them with whatever problem she had.

"Maybe she's having second thoughts about this deal she insisted we all make with Emerald Larson," Luke offered, thinking aloud. God only knew he'd had more than his fair share of misgivings.

"I seriously doubt it." Jake snorted disgustedly. "She told me last week that she's already put in her resignation at the preschool, given notice on her apartment and couldn't wait to move to Dallas."

Luke remained silent as he thought of what could possibly be wrong with their little sister. "Don't women sometimes cry when they go through that hormonal change each month?" he asked, wondering if Haley was prone to mood swings.

"How the hell should I know? If you'll remember, when Arielle went through puberty, we didn't have a clue what to tell her and ended up having our secretaries talk to her about what was going on with her body," Jake huffed, sounding just as clueless as Luke felt. "Since neither one of us has a wife to talk to her, should we have your assistant give her a call and find out what the deal is? They seemed to hit it off pretty well the last couple of times she and I flew into Nashville for a visit."

Luke took a deep breath. He'd intended to call Jake and tell him about his plan for an heir and his agreement with Haley once they returned to Nashville. But since he had his brother on the phone, Luke figured there was no time like the present to fill Jake in.

"Well, you're half right about that statement," he admitted, anticipating his brother's reaction. "You might not be married, but I took the plunge this weekend."

There was a shocked silence before Jake shouted. "You did *what?* And why didn't I hear about this sooner?"

"I didn't make my decision until this past week."

"What the hell were you thinking?" Jake countered, sounding thoroughly disgusted. "Haven't you been listening when I tell you about all the nasty divorce cases I handle?"

Explaining his reasons for wanting a son, Luke carefully omitted Haley's name when he told his brother about the agreement they'd reached. His brother had been teasing him for several years about having hired Haley to add beauty to the Garnier offices. Odd that Jake had noticed years ago what Luke had only recently discovered about her. But then, Jake had always taken an interest in every woman he'd ever laid eyes on.

"Are you sure you can trust this woman?" Jake sounded more than a little doubtful. "How long have you known her?"

"Five years and I have no reason not to trust her," Luke confirmed, realizing that he'd never put his faith in any other woman the way he did Haley. "She's above reproach."

"I wish I had a dollar for every time I've heard that." Always the divorce attorney, Jake demanded "What about a prenup? Please tell me you had her sign one."

"Signed, sealed and airtight," Luke answered.

"You should have had me look it over," Jake groused, clearly disappointed that he'd been excluded from Luke's plan.

"I would have if there had been time," Luke reiterated, meaning it. "But I needed to move on this before she changed her mind."

"So what if she had? I'm sure you could find another one willing to be the surrogate," Jake said reasonably. "And you might not have had to get married to get what you wanted."

Luke shook his head. "I didn't want anyone else. This woman is perfect. She has every trait I'm looking to pass on to my heir."

Several long seconds passed before Jake spoke again. "Well, now that you're out of the running, I guess it won't bother you if I make my move on that sweet little assistant of yours. You know how hot I've always thought she was."

"I have it on good authority that Haley's husband wouldn't appreciate your plan to include her as the object of one of your sexual interludes," Luke grumbled, suddenly more angry with his brother than he could ever remember and not entirely sure why.

He told himself it was because Jake was a notorious player and changed women as often as he changed his socks. But the truth of the matter was, Luke couldn't stand the thought of any other man touching Haley.

Jake was silent before he finally spoke again. "Well, I'll be damned. Haley is my new sister-in-law, isn't she, Luke?"

Still trying to come to grips with the uncharacteristic possessiveness threatening to consume him, Luke ran his hand over the tension building at the back of his neck. "Yeah."

"I wondered how long it would take for you to finally wake up." Jake sounded genuinely surprised. "I'd almost given up on you noticing what a looker she is."

"I told you the sole purpose of the marriage is to have my heir. It's only a temporary thing."

To Luke's immense displeasure, Jake laughed like a damned hyena. "You keep telling yourself that, bro, and you might just start to believe it."

If Luke could have reached through the phone, he'd have cheerfully choked his twin. "Did anyone ever tell you what a smart-ass you are, Jake?"

"You do just about every time we talk," Jake declared, his continued laughter irritating Luke beyond words.

Luke took a deep breath. "We've spent more than enough time talking about me and my current situation. Can we get back to the real reason you woke me up in the middle of the night?"

"I just wanted to give you the heads up about Arielle,"

Jake confirmed, his voice turning serious. "Maybe you can figure out what's wrong the next time the two of you talk."

"I'll give her a call when I get back to Nashville," Luke indicated. "If I find out anything, I'll let you know."

"Okay." His brother paused a moment before adding, "And in the meantime, you tell that sweet little woman of yours that her favorite brother-in-law said 'welcome to the family.'"

"It's temporary, Jake."

"So you say, bro. So you say."

"Shut up."

"Then I don't suppose you'll have a problem with me kissing the bride the next time I see her?"

Luke knew that his brother was baiting him, but it didn't seem to matter. "Try it and die."

At the sound of Jake's hearty laughter, Luke punched the end button and walking back into the bedroom, tossed the cell phone on top of the pile of clothing on the floor. He wasn't sure who he was angrier with—Jake or himself.

In all fairness to Jake, he'd just been his typical devil-may-care self. But Luke, on the other hand, had abandoned his usual reserve and displayed all the self-control of an enraged bull.

What he couldn't understand was why his brother's kidding bothered him so much. And why, when Jake mentioned making a move on Haley and then warned that he was going to "kiss the bride," Luke had been angry enough to bite nails in two.

But as he looked at Haley still sound asleep, he abandoned his speculation. He had a warm, willing woman in his bed and a lot more pleasurable things on his mind than his smart-aleck brother's sense of humor.

Seven

A week after their return to Nashville, Haley gathered a report on one of Garnier's current building projects and walked into Luke's private office. "I've run the numbers on the Robinson build as you requested and it appears that we're going to come in under budget by at least a few hundred thousand dollars, maybe a little more."

"Good to hear," Luke said without looking up from his computer. "Close the door, Haley."

Anticipating a confidential discussion on one of the current Garnier construction projects, she closed the door and sat down in the chair in front of his desk. Since their return to the office, they'd resumed their business-as-usual relationship during the day. Luke was still the no-nonsense, workaholic boss he'd always been and she was the executive assistant he relied on to keep his office running smoothly. To the outward eye, everything was just as it had always been, no single thing had changed. They even drove to the Garnier office in separate cars.

But at home it was an entirely different story. When they were alone in his mansion, Luke was warm, compassionate and an absolutely insatiable lover. And she was the object of his attention from the moment they closed the door until they walked back out the next morning for work.

Looking up from the computer screen, he motioned for her to come around to his side of the desk. "There's something here I think you'll want to see."

When she rounded the desk, she glanced at the computer monitor. It wasn't even turned on. But before she could question why he'd been intently focused on a blank screen, he turned his chair sideways, wrapped his arms around her waist and pulled her down to sit on his lap.

"Good lord, Luke, what are you doing?" She'd assumed that his hands-off attitude at the office had been to keep from feeding the ever-present rumor mill. "What if someone notices your door is shut?"

"No one will think anything is out of the ordinary," he said, nipping at the sensitive skin along the column of her neck. When he leaned back to look at her, his grin was as promising and wicked as she'd ever seen it. "I'm the boss and you're my executive assistant. It's not at all unusual for us to have a private meeting with the door closed."

"That's true, but what about—"

When his mouth covered hers, Haley abandoned

trying to reason with him. Luke still hadn't informed anyone about their marriage beyond his twin brother. But she wasn't surprised when he told her on the way back to Nashville that he'd let Jake know about their arrangement. Being mirror twins, they had always shared a special bond.

As Luke began to nibble at the corner of her mouth, coaxing her to open her lips for him, she relegated all thought of his relationship with his brother to the back of her mind and responded to his unspoken request. As his tongue slipped inside to mate with her own, liquid fire raced through her veins and an exciting little charge of electric current began to gather into a need deep in the pit of her belly.

He moved his hands to lift her arms to his shoulders, giving him free access to her breasts and emitting a tiny moan, she arched into his palms. His taste, his tender teasing and the feel of his hands gently caressing her caused a delightful tightening in her lower stomach and she wished with all of her heart they were somewhere besides the Garnier office.

"Do you know what I think?" he prompted, when he finally broke the kiss.

He expected her to form a rational thought after a kiss like that and with his hands still holding her breasts, his thumbs still gently circling her nipples through her clothing?

Laying her head on his shoulder, she kissed his neck. His whole body shuddered and a tiny feminine thrill coursed through her at the knowledge that she could affect him that way.

"I don't have a clue what you have on your mind, but

I'm sure you're going to tell me," she whispered close to his ear.

"I'm thinking that I'd like to take you home for lunch," he stated, his tone hoarse.

"Really? And just what would be on the menu?" she inquired, leaning back to give him a wide-eyed innocent look.

The hunger in his incredibly blue eyes caused her stomach to do a funny little backflip. "You."

"I would love to go home for your kind of lunch," she agreed, regretting what she was about to say next. "But we have a luncheon meeting scheduled with Ray Barnfield to go over the figures for his new office building and I doubt he'd be very happy if we called to reschedule. And since we don't have a signed contract yet, he might even decide to go with another construction company."

"Damn, I forgot about that." Luke looked as disappointed as she felt. "No, rescheduling is completely out of the question. We've worked too hard on this project to risk losing it now."

"I assume you still want me to go along?" When the meeting had been set up, he'd mentioned as much.

He nodded. "I want you to present the materials estimates to Ray, then I'll jump in with the projected deadlines and close the deal."

Over the past five years, they'd worked out a system of presenting proposals to potential clients as a team and it had proven to be very effective, winning several lucrative contracts for Garnier Construction.

"I'll get Ray's file ready," she indicated as she started to get off Luke's lap.

"Hey, where do you think you're going?" he chided, tightening his hold on her.

"The meeting is scheduled for one o'clock." Smiling, she pressed a kiss to his lean cheek. "And if you expect me to help you bring this deal to a satisfactory end, I need to have all of my ducks in a row."

He gave her a quick kiss, then set her on her feet. "While you're getting everything lined out for the meeting, there's something else I want you to do."

"What would that be?"

His expression held a wealth of promise. "Call and cancel my appointments for the rest of the day and arrange for Ruth Ann to take over for you as well."

She had a pretty good idea why they were taking the afternoon off but felt compelled to ask, "Is there a reason we won't be back in the office this afternoon?"

"Once we leave the restaurant, we'll both be going home for dessert." His wide grin promised an afternoon of sheer ecstasy. "If you'll remember, we have a baby to make, sweetheart. And I'm taking immense pleasure in this little project."

Careful not to wake him, Haley slipped from beneath Luke's arm and got out of bed to search for her robe. Her tears were not only threatening, they were imminent and walking out onto the master suite's balcony, she let them flow freely down her cheeks as she considered what had taken place earlier in the day.

The meeting with the client couldn't have gone better. Together, she and Luke had presented plans and a cost estimate that enticed Mr. Barnfield and by the end of the luncheon, the man had verbally agreed to have

Garnier Construction build his new high-rise. Then, when she and Luke had left the restaurant, he'd brought her home and they'd spent the rest of the afternoon and most of the evening making slow, passionate love.

But for her, the day had been bittersweet. When they'd arrived at the restaurant, Luke hadn't introduced her to the client as Haley Garnier. He'd seemed to stress the point that she was Miss Rollins, his executive assistant.

She knew she was being completely unreasonable about the matter. But it still hurt to think that she was married to the man she loved with all of her heart and he couldn't find it within himself to tell anyone that she was his wife. Even if it was temporary.

How could he be so caring and considerate when they made love and not acknowledge her as his spouse?

Swiping at the tears running down her cheeks, she walked over to the railing to stare out at the night sky. She'd known when she agreed to have his baby that their marriage was an appeasement—a way to get her to go along with his plan.

But he hadn't even bothered to buy her a wedding ring. Would it be such a crime for him to refer to her as his wife for however long their union lasted? Couldn't he at least give her that much?

"What are you doing out here, Haley?"

At the sound of Luke's voice, she quickly tried to wipe away the evidence of her emotions with the back of her hand. "I just needed a little fresh air. I hope I didn't wake you."

"No. What woke me was rolling over and not finding you there beside me where you're supposed to be."

When he came up behind her and wrapped his arms

around her waist to pull her back against his chest, she closed her eyes and willed away a fresh wave of tears. No matter how he introduced her to people or how brief their marriage, she was in his arms now and she would have to content herself with that fact.

"What's wrong, sweetheart?" he asked, holding her close.

"N-nothing."

"Don't give me that. You've been crying. I can hear it in your voice." Turning her to face him, he shook his head. "And I want to know why."

Unable to meet his questioning look for fear of giving herself away, she focused on his wide bare chest. "Women cry for a variety of reasons. It doesn't necessarily mean that there's something wrong."

He tilted her chin up until their gazes met. "Could one of those reasons be a hormonal thing?"

"Sometimes."

Looking thoughtful, he stared at her for several long seconds. "Do you think we've achieved our goal?"

"It's probably too early for any symptoms indicating that I'm pregnant."

He was silent for several moments before his amiable expression turned to a dark frown, as he contemplated something.

"Luke?"

Taking a deep breath, he finally explained. "When Jake called the other night, it wasn't just to catch up with each other. He told me he'd talked to Arielle and she was sobbing her heart out. But she wouldn't tell him why." He shook his head. "We figured something had to be wrong."

"I suppose that could have been the case," Haley

conceded, nodding. "But women aren't like men. We don't keep things bottled inside. There are times when we cry simply to relieve tension and stress."

Luke mulled over what she'd said, then running his hands over her back in a soothing manner, he asked "Is that why you were crying just now?"

"Yes."

It was as good an excuse as any she could come up with. And in truth, she had been stressing. But his refusal to acknowledge her as his wife was something he wouldn't want to discuss.

"I think I know what you're worried about," he said, pulling her close.

"You do?" She seriously doubted he'd understand even if she told him what the problem was.

He nodded. "I'm sure it's normal to be frightened about getting pregnant and all the changes your body will go through." Kissing her tenderly, he held her to him. "But you aren't going to be alone, Haley. Unlike a lot of men, I don't consider my job finished once my son is conceived. I'll be with you throughout this whole thing."

The sudden tension she detected in his large frame confused her. "Is there something going on that I don't know about?" Haley asked.

Pausing, he finally took her by the hand, walked over to a grouping of patio furniture, then lowering himself into one of the wrought iron chairs, pulled her down to sit on his lap. "I believe I've told you before about me and Jake raising Arielle after our mother was killed in a car accident."

Haley nodded.

"Do you know why we were left with that respon-

sibility, instead of our father taking care of our sister?"
When she shook her head, he continued. "Because the
bastard wasn't anywhere around. He took off shortly after
our mother learned she was pregnant with Arielle. The
same as when he learned she was expecting me and Jake."

"Your father left your mother—"

"Twice," he finished for her. "She loved him with all
of her heart and trusted that he cared the same way
about her. But all she got out of the bargain was three
kids to raise alone and the heartache of watching the
jerk continually walk out on her."

With sudden clarity, Haley saw the reason behind
Luke's avoidance of relationships. He obviously never
intended for anyone to have that kind of power over
him.

"Oh, Luke, I'm so sorry. That must have been so difficult for all of you."

He shrugged his shoulders. "There's no reason to be
sorry. We did just fine on our own and I'm thoroughly
convinced we were better off without him."

She didn't know what to say. Her father might have
completely ignored her after her mother had left Haley
on his doorstep, but he'd at least furnished a roof over
her head and food for her to eat. Apparently, Luke's
father hadn't even bothered to stick around long enough
to see to his children's basic needs.

"But the story doesn't end there," Luke continued,
staring out at the gardens beyond the balcony railing.
"We recently learned our mother wasn't the only
woman to fall for his line of bull."

"You have another sibling?" she guessed.

Shaking his head, he sighed heavily. "More like

three. All brothers. All from different mothers. And all from different parts of the country."

Shocked, Haley could well understand his bitterness. "Your father certainly believed in sowing his share of wild oats, didn't he?"

"Oh, yeah." Luke was silent a moment before he went on. "I suppose you could consider Jake and I the lucky ones. At least we got to meet the man once when we were ten. The others never had that opportunity. They didn't even know his name."

"Why did your father return after all those years?" she interjected.

"He just showed up at the house one day, stuck around long enough to impregnate our mother with Arielle, then took off again." A chill slithered up her spine at the sound of Luke's harsh laughter. "Of course, Jake and I may have met him, but we didn't really know who he was, either. It wasn't until we learned about our half brothers that we discovered he'd been using an alias when he was with our mother. Instead of the starving artist he'd portrayed himself to be, he was a notorious womanizer with a bottomless bank account."

"When and how did you find out about your brothers if they didn't know who their father was?" she queried.

"After he was killed in a boating accident somewhere in the Mediterranean, our paternal grandmother hired a team of private investigators to look into her son's past escapades to see what damage he'd left in his wake throughout the years. She knew all along about the other three boys he'd fathered. But she only recently discovered that Arielle, Jake and I were also illegitimate grandchildren."

"That must have been heartbreaking for her," Haley

said, feeling compassion for the poor woman. "She was cheated out of watching all of you grow up and being part of your lives."

"Believe me, that old bird is a survivor," he corrected, his tone indicating he had no pity for his grandmother. "She probably wouldn't have taken the time to pay much attention to us anyway."

They fell silent for several minutes before Luke asked "Now that you've learned all about my family secrets, what about you? Why wasn't your mother part of the family picture?"

His question caused a knot to form in the pit of Haley's stomach. Millie Sanford may have given her life, but the woman had never been a mother to Haley.

"There really isn't a lot to tell," she began, wondering if Millie ever regretted her decision to give away her baby girl. "Shortly after I was born, she showed up and told my father that I was the product of their one-night stand and she was going to put me up for adoption if he didn't want to claim me."

"I'm sorry, sweetheart." Luke's arms tightened around her. "But if she didn't intend to keep you, why did she go through with the pregnancy?"

Haley had asked herself that a thousand times over the years and never came up with any answers. "I don't really know. I've often wondered if she thought she'd make it on her own with a baby, then decided it was too difficult once I was born. Or maybe she gave me up because she wanted me to have all the opportunities she couldn't give me."

His strong hands massaged the tension in her lower back. "I'm sure it was something like that."

She sighed. "But if that had been the case, you'd think she would have stayed in touch with my father to see how I was doing throughout the years."

"Have you tried to get in touch with her?" he asked, quietly.

"I've thought about it, but I don't even know where she went after she left me with Dad. Besides, what would I say? Oh, by the way, I'm the little girl you abandoned all those years ago." She shook her head. "If she'd wanted anything to do with me, I'm sure she'd have contacted me by now. After all, it's not like she didn't know who she left me with."

They fell silent before Luke asked "So it was just you and your dad all these years?"

"More like just me." She tried not to think of how lonely she'd felt growing up. "Dad was married to his work—always at the office or on a business trip—and even when he was at home, he never seemed to know what to do with me or how to relate to me. He left my care to our housekeeper, Mrs. Arnold."

"In other words, she raised you."

"Yes." Her chest tightened. "And now that I'm older, it's too late. My father passed away while I was in college and we'll never be able to have a relationship."

"Is that why it's so important for you to be a mother to the baby we're going to have?" Luke coaxed, his tone so gentle and caring that she couldn't stop a tear from slipping down her cheek.

"Yes." Suddenly feeling as if every ounce of her energy had been drained away, she laid her head on Luke's shoulder and snuggled into his embrace. "I don't ever want my child to go through the uncertainty of not feeling loved…and wanted," she revealed haltingly as sleep began to overtake her. "I intend for my baby to feel secure in the knowledge that she's the most…important person in my life."

Long after Luke heard Haley's breathing become shallow, indicating she'd drifted off to sleep, he sat holding her securely against him. He understood now more than ever why she'd been adamant about what it would take for her to have his son and why she'd insisted on joint custody. She wanted to protect his heir from the same type of loveless existence she'd been forced to grow up in.

Cradling her to him like a small child, he rose from the chair and carried her into his bedroom. He and his siblings had been lucky compared to Haley. They might not have had a father, but they'd had each other and they'd certainly known their mother. From the moment they were born until the day she died, Francesca Garnier had devoted herself to her children and left them with no doubt about how much they meant to her.

But Haley hadn't had that kind of childhood. She'd had no one to love her the way a child needed to be loved.

As he placed her on the bed, then stretched out beside her, Luke gathered her close. Emotions he wasn't at all comfortable with and certainly wasn't about to acknowledge filled his chest almost to the point of bursting.

But he stubbornly willed them away. He'd seen firsthand the emotional pain his mother suffered when his father rejected her love and there wasn't a chance in hell that he'd ever open himself up to that level of devastation.

Haley was a warm, compassionate woman who had

a lot of love to give and deserved a man with the capacity to love and cherish her just as much in return. Unfortunately, he just wasn't the right man for the job.

"Mr. Lucien Garnier, please hold for a call from Mrs. Emerald Larson."

Luke rolled his eyes at the sound of the stiff, formal voice of Emerald's personal assistant, Luther Freemont.

"Lucien, I'm so glad I caught you before you left the office for the day," Emerald said, coming on the line. "Did the transition from our management to yours go as smoothly as anticipated?"

"There were a couple of minor issues with the labor force, but nothing I couldn't straighten out," he responded, wondering why the old girl was fishing for answers from him, when they both knew she still had her share of loyal contacts in the Laurel offices.

"Excellent. I'm happy to hear things are moving along on that front."

"But you aren't calling to find out how I've done with Laurel Enterprises, are you?" Luke asked, running out of patience.

"No, I'm not."

"Why *are* you calling, Mrs. Larson?" he demanded.

"Considering our relationship, don't you think calling me 'Mrs. Larson' is bit formal, Lucien?"

"I've only known about you for a few weeks. Surely you don't expect me to call you Grandmother," he declared. "I told you when we first met that building a relationship at this stage of the game would be next to impossible."

"And I completely understand," she agreed, sounding

as if she really meant it. "If you'd like, why don't you call me Emerald, dear."

"All right, Emerald. And for the record, most people call me Luke."

"I prefer calling you by your given name."

"You'll do whatever pleases you anyway," he retorted, using his hand to rub the tension building at the base of his neck.

She laughed. "Of course, I will."

"Now that we have that settled, to what do I owe the pleasure of this call, *Emerald?*" he asked, wishing he'd ducked out of the office ten minutes earlier. If he had, he wouldn't be having this chitchat with her.

"I'm going to be in Nashville this weekend and I would very much like for you to attend a reception being held in my honor." She paused. "Your three other brothers will be in attendance and this would be an excellent opportunity for you, Jake and Arielle to meet them."

"Half brothers," Luke corrected.

"Yes, of course." To her credit, the old gal didn't even try to pretend she was offended by his bluntness and continued as if he hadn't pointed out the obvious. "Arielle is coming with me from San Francisco to fly into Nashville and I'm certain your twin brother plans to come from Los Angeles for the occasion. Will I be able to count on you, as well?"

He should have known when they all agreed to Emerald's offer that it would come with a considerable amount of strings. "I'll have to check my calendar and get back with you," he hedged.

"Wonderful. I'll expect to see you at eight on Saturday evening in the main ballroom at the Gaylord Opryland

Hotel." Before he pointed out that he hadn't committed to anything, she added, "And of course it goes without saying you're more than welcome to bring a guest."

"Of course," he repeated, rolling his eyes once more.

"I look forward to seeing you again, Lucien. Goodbye."

As he hung up the phone, he shook his head. He had to give her credit for one thing: Emerald Larson was damned good at getting what she wanted. Unless he missed his guess, Jake had been fed the same line of bull about her being certain Luke would be attending and now they'd both been roped in.

But the more he thought about it, the more it could work to their advantage. If Arielle was going to be there, maybe he and Jake could pull her aside and get to the bottom of what was going on with her.

And Luke had no doubt she was hiding something. She'd been avoiding his calls the past couple of weeks and that was the longest they'd ever gone without talking.

Checking his watch, Luke turned off his computer and rolled down his shirt sleeves. Haley had left an hour ago to run a couple of errands and it was time he called it a day, as well. He had a soft, sweet woman waiting on him at home. And he couldn't wait to get their evening started.

Eight

"It's negative," Haley announced, peering at the results window on the little white stick in her hand.

"Are you sure these things are accurate?" Luke asked, looking over her shoulder. "Maybe another brand would be better."

"From everything I've read, this test is the most accurate," she answered, checking the back of the box for the second time.

She picked up the instruction insert from the early pregnancy test and read through it again. "It says to retest a few days later if there are doubts about the results."

"You might still be pregnant." He grinned as they walked out of the master bathroom and over to the bed. "And in the meantime, all we have to do is relax and enjoy each other."

She smiled. "I'm sure you're up for the challenge."

Wrapping her in his arms, he rested his forehead against hers. "I can't help myself. You're just so damned desirable when you wake up. And when you walk into my office with my coffee. And—"

"I think I get the idea," she said dryly as she crossed the room to remove her robe and get into bed. "You're blaming me for your insatiable needs."

"I didn't have this problem before we started making love," he countered, walking over to remove his watch and place it in a small tray on top of the dresser. His grin turned positively wicked. "Do you know why I spend so much time sitting behind my desk at the office?"

Propping her pillow against the headboard, she leaned back against it. "I assume it's because you're working."

"Nope." He walked over to his side of the bed. "It's because I've been watching you or thinking about making love to you and I'm too aroused for people not to notice."

"So you're saying we can't go out in public together anymore?" she teased.

He shook his head as she watched him lower his boxers. "No, but when we are out, I find that I'd rather be here making love to you." He paused. "And speaking of going out in public together, I almost forgot to tell you about the reception on Saturday evening at the Opryland Hotel."

"For anyone I know?" she asked, shamelessly watching him. She loved his body, loved watching the play of muscles as he moved. It was just so darned sexy.

"You don't know her, but you do know *of* her," he commented, climbing into bed. "It's Emerald Larson."

Turning on his side to face her, he pulled her close. "But I don't want to talk about her now. I have more exciting things on my mind."

"Oh, really?" Haley couldn't keep from smiling at the promise on his handsome face and completely abandoned all thought as his firm lips nibbled and coaxed with a skill that stole her breath.

But when his tongue parted her lips to deepen the kiss, it felt as if he'd ignited a pyrotechnic display within her soul. A flickering light danced behind her closed eyes and a delicious warmth flowed through her veins as he stroked the inner recesses of her mouth, then encouraged her to explore him in kind.

Tasting and teasing him as he'd done her, her pulse quickened when she felt him reach for the lace hem of her gown. The feel of his palm as he slid it up her thigh and over her stomach to the underside of her breast, sent a searing current of heat dancing over every nerve in her body. But when he cupped her fully and lightly brushed his thumb over her hardened nipple, the heated desire swirling inside her quickly turned into a hungry flame.

She wanted him with a fierceness that she never imagined and running her hands over his side, then his hip, she took him in her palm to explore his length and the power of his need for her. She felt his entire body shudder a moment before he broke the kiss, then leaned back and shook his head.

"It's been brought to my immediate attention that one of us is overdressed for what we're about to do here," he said, sounding winded.

"Since you're the one not wearing anything, I suppose that would make me the guilty party."

Toying with the neck of her gown, his smile turned into a wicked grin a moment before he used both hands to rip the light cotton fabric all the way down to the hem.

"I'm not going to have any nightgowns left," she complained, not in the least bit upset.

His promising grin stole her breath. "Not that you're going to be needing them anytime soon, but if you insist, I'll buy you new ones." Quickly dispensing with her tattered nightgown, he hooked his thumbs under her panties. "And we definitely don't need these, either."

Raising her hips to help, a wave of electrifying desire covered every inch of her as he slid the offending garment down her legs, then tossed them over the side of the bed to the floor. Her wildest fantasies could not compare to the erotic thrill Luke created every time he removed her clothes.

"I don't know why you bother with them anyway. You know I'm just going to take them off of you," he said, pulling her against him.

"But you told me you enjoyed doing just that."

"Getting you out of your clothes is part of the fun." He frowned suddenly. "But I don't want to dwell on that now. Where were we before getting you out of your clothes became the big issue?"

"I believe you were going to explain why I don't need nightgowns and panties," she reminded, suddenly feeling quite breathless.

"No, I believe I told you that I intended to show you." He lightly brushed her lips with his as he pressed himself even closer.

Her eyelids drifted shut as she relished the feel of their bodies pressed close. His hard contours against her much softer curves excited her as little else could and sent a tremor of sheer delight straight through her to gather into a pool of need deep inside.

"Open your eyes, Haley."

When she did, the intense look in his eyes caused her heart to pound erratically. Hunger, urgent and undeniable, sparkled in the vivid blue depths and just knowing that she'd created such deep need in him as well sent threads of heated passion twining throughout her entire being.

He continued to hold her gaze with his as without a word he slowly slid his hand down to her knee, then back up along the inside of her thigh. Ripples of desire skipped over every nerve in her body and an extreme restlessness began to overtake her. She needed to be one with him, to have him buried so deeply inside her that she lost sight of where she ended and he began.

"Please...Luke," she said, amazed at the sultriness in her own voice.

"Only if you promise me something," he warned, lifting her leg over his.

"What?" At that moment, she would promise him almost anything if he would quench the fire threatening to send her into total meltdown.

"I don't want you to close your eyes." Taking her hand in his, he helped her guide him to her. "I want you to look at me while I'm inside you, Haley." Easing his hips forward, his jaw tightened and his eyes began to blaze with a feral light as he slowly began to enter her. "I want to see the moment when you realize there's no turning back, that I'm going to take you over the edge and put my baby inside of you to love and nurture."

"I promise I'll try," she whispered, placing her hand

on his chest. The steady rhythm of his heart matched the beating of her own and in that moment she'd never felt closer to him.

Her soul filled to overflowing with love as he completely joined their bodies, then slowly began to move within her. His gaze continued to hold hers as he built the bond between them to a fevered pitch and sensations, exquisite and sweet, flowed through her.

But all too soon the connection grew, changing, evolving into something that Haley never wanted to end. A sudden delicious tightness gripped her body, then quickly shattered to send her spinning out of control. Shivering from the force of her release, she heard herself whimper his name as every cell in her being melted with pleasure and she clung to him to keep from being lost.

Feeling the sweet languor of fulfillment wash over her, she watched Luke's eyes darken a moment before his body stiffened and he crushed her to him. He thrust himself into her one final time and as she felt the honeyed warmth of his life force flow into her, she knew that she could never love any other man the way she loved Luke. He owned her heart, her body and her soul.

On Saturday evening as he waited for the doorman to announce his and Haley's arrival to the guests at Emerald's reception, Luke glanced at her and wondered for at least the hundredth time in the past three weeks why it had taken him so long to see how beautiful she was. Her long blond curls cascaded over her bare shoulders like a golden waterfall and the strapless black evening gown she wore accentuated her slender feminine form to perfection.

"Mr. Luke Garnier and Miss Haley Rollins," the doorman finally announced to the crowded ballroom.

He thought he felt Haley's body go rigid a moment before she placed her hand in the crook of his arm and they walked toward the receiving line where Emerald and several others stood waiting to greet them. But glancing again at her, Luke decided he'd imagined it. She looked as serenely beautiful as she had the day she'd walked down the aisle of the little chapel in Pigeon Forge to trustingly place her hand in his and become his...wife.

His heart stalled. Why had that particular word come to mind? It was one that, over the course of the past several weeks, he'd been extremely careful to avoid.

"Lucien, darling, I'm so happy you decided to attend," Emerald greeted him, placing her bejeweled hand on his cheek and bringing him back to the present. Turning to Haley, she smiled. "And what a lovely young woman you're with this evening."

"This is my executive assistant, Haley Rollins," he introduced automatically. "Haley, I'd like you to meet Emerald Larson."

"How do you do, Ms. Rollins?" Emerald replied, lightly kissing Haley's cheek.

"L-lovely. It's a pleasure to meet you, Mrs. Larson." Was his mind playing tricks on him or had he heard a slight quaver in Haley's voice?

"I hope you don't mind, but I'm going to steal my grandson away from you for a few moments," Emerald declared, smiling. "There are a few people I would like for him to get acquainted with."

Luke could have cheerfully choked the old girl for dropping that little bomb. He'd avoided telling Haley that Emerald was the grandmother he'd mentioned. For one thing, theirs was a business arrangement and he hadn't felt it pertinent to their situation. And for another, he hadn't gotten used to the idea himself. Now, short of creating a scene, there was nothing he could do but allow Emerald to lead him away from Haley and over to the three men standing across the ballroom.

"Of course, I don't mind," Haley murmured, but her look clearly stated otherwise.

"I'll be right back," he whispered in her ear. "I promise that I'll explain all of this later."

She leaned away from him a fraction of an inch. The movement was ever so slight, but he'd noticed it just the same as if she'd fully recoiled from him. "Don't worry about me, I'll be fine. Take all the time you like," she professed, turning to walk in the opposite direction.

Unless he missed his guess, he was in hot water and other than omitting the fact that Emerald Larson was his grandmother, he couldn't figure out why.

"Your assistant is quite beautiful, Lucien," Emerald commented as they walked across the ballroom. "I take it there's more between the two of you?"

"That's really none of your concern, Emerald," he retorted, not at all surprised that she felt entitled to know about every aspect of his life. After all, she was the all-knowing, all-seeing Emerald Larson.

"Of course it is," she sweetly disagreed, smiling. "I'm your grandmother and I naturally want to see that you're happy." She placed her hand on his arm. "And if there's anything I can do to help, please don't hesitate to let me know."

"I seriously doubt that I'll need your assistance," he disclaimed, wondering what the hell she thought she could do that he couldn't.

"Just keep that in mind if you ever do," she reminded as they continued to cross the ballroom.

Her comments had him wondering how much she knew about his arrangement with Haley, but he didn't have time to dwell on it as they approached the three men.

"Lucien, I'd like for you to meet your brothers, Caleb Walker, Nicholas Daniels and Hunter O'Banyon," Emerald said. "Now, while you boys get to know each other, I'll return to my guests."

"She's a piece of work, isn't she?" Hunter asked, shaking his head as they watched Emerald walk back toward the ballroom entrance.

"Is she ever," Luke agreed, liking the man instantly.

"We're glad to get to know you and the rest of the Garnier side of the family," Caleb spoke up.

"Likewise," Luke answered, shaking hands with all three of his half brothers. "For the record, everyone but Emerald calls me Luke."

"Yeah, she insists on calling me 'Nicholas' most of the time," Nick disclosed, his expression reflecting his displeasure.

"When you have her kind of money, you can do anything you damned well please," Hunter summarized, laughing.

"I hear you own one of the biggest construction companies in the South and thanks to Emerald you've recently ventured into log homes," Nick described, sounding thoughtful. "Have you ever considered building in the western states? I promised my wife a new house for our anniversary and who better to build it than one of my brothers."

Luke smiled. "I haven't ventured past the Mississippi, but that doesn't mean I'm not open to the idea. If you're going to be in town for a few days, maybe we can get together."

"Save a spot at that table for me," Hunter added. "I run an air med-evac service in southwest Texas and I'd like to build an office and sleeping quarters for the on-duty crew separate from the hanger where we service the helicopters."

"And me," Caleb interjected. "You never know, I might just decide to have you build something for me out in New Mexico."

Luke had tried to tell himself that he didn't care if he ever met his half brothers. But truth to tell, he was glad for the opportunity. It wasn't their fault they had been thrown into the same set of circumstances that he, Jake and Arielle found themselves.

"How does Monday evening sound?" he asked. All three men agreed, and naming a time and place, Luke added, "I'll see if Jake will be able to rearrange his schedule and hang around another day or two and join us."

"Sounds good," Hunter confirmed, glancing toward a group of women. "Uh-oh, I think Callie's trying to get my attention again."

"Yeah, Alyssa's giving me one of those looks, too," Caleb noted, smiling toward a pretty auburn-haired woman across the ballroom.

"Then I'll see you Monday evening," Luke said.

When he turned to find Haley, Luke spotted her by the buffet table. Damned if that jerk Chet Parker wasn't standing right beside her. What the hell was *he* doing at a reception for Emerald? And did the guy have some kind of radar honed in on Haley wherever they went?

"Looks to me like the entertainment for this little bash is about to make time with your new wife," Jake taunted, coming up to stand beside Luke.

Glancing at his brother, he felt as if he was looking in a mirror. But instead of wearing a devil-may-care grin like Jake, Luke was certain his expression bordered on premeditated murder.

"He's the entertainment for the evening?"

"That's what I hear." Rocking back on his heels, Jake nodded and took a sip of the drink he held. "You do know he's most likely looking for wife number four?"

"I've heard the rumor," Luke responded, his gaze never wavering from the pair at the buffet table.

"I represented his second wife in their divorce and let me tell you, she came away with a bundle," Jake supplied, sounding quite pleased with himself.

"Good for you," Luke commented absently. He felt his blood pressure skyrocket when he watched Parker put his hand on Haley's bare shoulder. "I'll be back in a few, Jake. Right now, I have something I need to take care of."

His brother chuckled. "Let me know if you need back up with that, bro."

When he walked up and slipped his arm around Haley's waist, Luke made it a point to meet Parker's questioning gaze head on. "Haley, have you seen my sister?"

"I spoke to her a few minutes ago," she answered, her tone as cool as he'd ever heard it.

"Why don't you go find her for me?" he proposed, his gaze never wavering from Parker's. "I'd like to talk with her before we leave."

Haley glared at him for several seconds, before giving him a short nod. "Of course, Mr. Garnier. Whatever you say, Mr. Garnier."

She was less than happy when she brushed past him, but he'd straighten out things with her later. At the moment, he had to put the fear of God into one country Casanova.

"Listen up, Parker. I'm only going to tell you this once," Luke threatened, his jaw clenched so tight it felt welded shut. "Stay the hell away from Haley."

"Why should I?" Parker demanded, his tone self-assured. "You seem to keep forgetting that you bring her to these things or else she wouldn't be wandering about alone." He smiled. "A little gal like Haley makes a man think about settling down and raising a couple of kids."

"I know, that's why I married her."

"She's your wife?" Parker shook his head. "She's not wearing a ring. If you're married, why isn't she wearing your brand?"

Making a mental note to remedy that problem as soon as possible, Luke glared at the man. "That's my business, not yours. She's mine and you keep your damned hands off her."

"And if I don't?" Parker prompted, his cocky grin sending Luke's blood pressure into stroke range.

"You'll be picking up several of those capped teeth

of yours from the floor," Luke warned, halfway hoping the man would give him a reason to show that he meant business.

"Is that a threat?" Parker asked, raising an eyebrow.

Luke shook his head. "No, it's a fact."

Luke walked away before he carried out his promise and punched Parker square in the face. Taking several deep breaths to bring his anger under control, he searched the crowd for Haley. He wasn't sure who he was irritated with the most—Parker for zooming in on the fact that Haley wasn't wearing a wedding band or himself for forgetting to buy her one.

Either way, it didn't change the fact that she belonged to him, and Luke Garnier wasn't the type of man who shared what was rightfully his.

By the time Haley found Arielle in the powder room, her anger at Luke had been replaced with an undeniable sadness. There was no way he'd ever see their marriage as anything more than another one of his business deals. She'd been deluding herself when she'd thought that he might.

Not only had he introduced her to Emerald Larson as his executive assistant, he obviously hadn't shared the fact that the woman was his newfound grandmother. And if that wasn't proof enough that he viewed her only as his employee, just look at the way he'd ordered her to look for his sister.

"Haley, are you all right?" Arielle asked, clearly concerned. "You don't look like you feel very well. Should I go get Luke?"

Lowering onto one of the plush sofas in the lounge

area, Haley shook her head. "I'm fine, really. And no, I'd rather not see Luke at the moment."

"Uh-oh." Arielle walked over to sit down beside her. "What has that boneheaded brother of mine done now?"

"More like what he hasn't done," Haley informed, feeling absolutely miserable.

She wanted a baby more than anything, but what had she gotten herself into? How could marrying a man she loved with all of her heart for the purpose of having the baby she wanted so badly, make her feel so hopeless?

"You love him, don't you?" Arielle inquired, reaching to place her hand on Haley's. "That's why you agreed to his hair-brained plan to have a baby, isn't it?"

"You know about our arrangement?" she ventured, somewhat surprised.

"I know all about it," Arielle assured Haley, her smile encouraging. "When Luke told Jake about the two of you getting married and the plan to have a baby, Jake couldn't dial my number fast enough." She grinned. "I think it was just too much for poor Jake to keep to himself. But it did give me a bit of a reprieve."

"I'm sure it was quite a shock to both of you," Haley attested, nodding. "But enough about me and Luke. What about you? Your brothers—"

Obviously not wanting to discuss her brothers' concerns, Arielle interrupted, "I've known for some time that you absolutely adore Luke."

"But how? I've always been careful not to show how I felt about him."

The young woman smiled. "When I was here at Christmas, I saw the way your eyes would light up when he walked into the office. And let's face it, women are a lot more intuitive than men. You could hang a sign around your neck, advertising how much you care about him and I think Luke would probably miss it."

"Men are rather clueless, aren't they?" Haley agreed, her mood lightening ever so slightly.

Arielle nodded. "And Luke is one of the worst. When it comes to business, he's unsurpassed. But he's avoided having a real relationship so long that he doesn't recognize what is as plain as the nose on his face to the rest of us. I'm just glad he finally realized how perfect you are for him."

"You do know that our marriage is just to get me to have his heir? It's only temporary," Haley elaborated, wondering if Luke's sister really did know everything.

"That's what I was told, but I don't think that's going to be the case." Arielle gave Haley a knowing look. "I saw the way Luke reacted when he found Chet Parker talking to you. If looks could kill, they would be hauling poor old Chet to the morgue right now."

"But I've never been interested in anyone but Luke," Haley argued, shaking her head.

Arielle laughed. "I know that and you know that, but my overly obtuse brother can't see it."

They were silent for a few moments, before Haley brought up her brothers' concern. "I'm sure you know Luke and Jake are very worried about you."

The young woman sighed as she stared down at her hands. "As much as I love my brothers and appreciate everything they've done for me, there are some things they just can't fix."

Haley put her arm around Arielle shoulders. "Is there anything I can do?"

Shaking her head, Arielle raised tear-filled eyes to meet Haley's questioning gaze. "I really don't think there's anything anyone can do. I'm almost three months pregnant."

"Have you told the baby's father?" Haley asked, her heart going out to her sister-in-law.

"I've tried, but I can't find him." Arielle bit her trembling lower lip. "Please, you have to promise me you won't tell Luke or Jake. I'm just not ready to listen to a lecture right now."

"You have my word." She wasn't about to betray her sister-in-law's confidence. "But you will have to tell your brothers eventually."

"I know, but I have some things that I need to work out before I let them know." Sniffing, Arielle straightened her shoulders. "Besides, Luke and Jake would just start demanding to know who the father is so they could have one of those famous brotherly talks with him."

"You're right. And that would probably just make matters worse." Haley knew for certain they'd track the man down no matter what it took.

"My brothers don't seem to realize that I'm not ten years old anymore and these are my decisions to make, not theirs."

"If you need to talk to anyone, you know I'm as close as the nearest phone," Haley attested. She truly liked Arielle and hoped they would remain friends even after she and Luke parted ways.

"Thank you, Haley," Arielle reflected, hugging her. "I hope Luke wakes up soon and realizes how much he loves you. I really would like to keep you for my sister."

Haley tightly closed her eyes to keep a fresh wave

of tears in check as she hugged Arielle, too. She greatly appreciated her sister-in-law's good wishes, but she really held no hope for that ever happening.

Nine

On Monday evening, Luke guided Haley to the private room he'd reserved at the restaurant for the dinner meeting with his brothers, and holding the chair for her, smiled at his brothers and their wives. "Sorry we're late, but there was an accident on I-24 and we had to make a detour."

"Don't worry about it," Caleb spoke up. "We all just got here ourselves."

"Why don't you introduce your lovely date?" Jake teased, his knowing grin enough to set Luke's teeth on edge. "I've known Haley for several years, but I don't think you had the chance to introduce her to anyone at Emerald's reception."

"This is my executive assistant, Haley Rollins," Luke announced, seating himself beside her. "Haley, these are my brothers, Caleb, Nick and Hunter and their wives Alyssa, Cheyenne and Callie."

With the introductions complete, he noticed that Haley had grown extremely quiet. "Are you feeling all right?" he whispered, leaning close to her ear.

"I'm fine," she murmured, then immediately turned away to engage the other women at the table in conversation.

Deciding that getting to the bottom of what was wrong with her would have to wait until after they returned home, Luke spent an enjoyable evening getting better acquainted with his brothers. They hadn't known each other for more than a couple of days, but he knew they were building a lifelong bond and looked forward to staying in touch with them. He was also pleased to see that over the course of the evening, Haley's mood had improved. She seemed to have opened up and was enjoying the company of his sisters-in-law, as well.

"So, when are we all getting together again?" Hunter asked as the men's conversation about their various building projects began to wind down.

"If you'd like to come out to Wyoming this summer for a week or two, Cheyenne and I would love to have the company," Nick offered. "We'll give the old house a family send-off, then next summer we'll have a get-together and christen the new log home Luke's company is going to build for us."

"Absolutely," Cheyenne agreed enthusiastically. "And we'd love for you to come for a visit too, Haley."

"We all went up there last summer and had a great time," Alyssa Walker added, laughing. "I even learned to ride a horse."

"I'm sure you'd enjoy yourself, Haley," Callie O'Banyon proclaimed, smiling. "Please say you'll try."

Luke watched Haley give the women a weak smile. "That would be very nice, but I'm not sure what I'll be doing this summer. If it's all right, I'll have to let you know later."

No one besides himself and Jake seemed to think Haley's vague answer was anything out of the ordinary. But when they rose to leave, Jake made it a point to pull Luke aside.

"What's going on, bro? Why wouldn't Haley be right there with you?"

Luke shook his head. "I have a pretty good idea and you can bet your life I'm going to find out for certain."

As soon as they were comfortably seated in the back of his limo, Luke pushed the button to raise the privacy window between them and the driver. "You seemed to have a good time this evening."

She nodded. "I really like your brothers and their wives. They're all very nice."

Silence reigned for several more minutes before he asked what he thought might be the likely cause for her moodiness. "Are you still worried that we might not have been successful yet? Because if you are, don't be. I'm sure if you aren't pregnant this month, you will be shortly."

Instead of answering, she simply shrugged.

Trying to get her to open up to him was like trying to pull teeth and he was damned tired of it. "What's wrong? And don't tell me 'nothing' because you haven't been yourself for the past few days."

"I don't know what you mean." She wouldn't look him in the eye.

He shook his head. "Don't play dumb, sweetheart. We both know you're a lot more intelligent than that."

When she finally raised her gaze to meet his, the sadness in the turquoise depths caused his gut to twist into a tight knot. "If you don't mind, I'd rather not…go into it right now," she said.

He'd bet every last penny he had that she was a heart-beat away from the flood gates opening. "Okay, we'll wait until we get home," he concurred, putting his arm around her shoulders and drawing her close to his side. "But I want answers, Haley. And neither of us are going to get any sleep until I get them."

The rest of the ride home was spent in complete silence and when the driver finally opened the limou-sine's rear door and Luke helped her from the backseat, Haley's nerves were stretched to the breaking point. For the past several days, she'd been struggling with herself and having dinner with his brothers and their wives this evening had helped her reach a decision. What she had to say wasn't going to be easy and Luke certainly wasn't going to like hearing it, but she had no choice in the matter. Her survival depended on it.

While Luke locked the front door and set the security alarm, she slowly climbed the circular stairs to the second floor and steeled herself for the argument she knew was sure to ensue. She just hoped with all of her heart she could voice what had to be said before she dis-solved into a torrent of tears or worse yet, allow him to convince her to change her mind.

When she entered the master suite, Luke wasn't far

behind and after he'd closed the French doors, she turned to look at the man she loved more than life itself.

"What's going on, Haley?" he asked before she had a chance to speak. "And don't try to deflect the question again, because we both know that something's bothering you."

Tossing her purse onto the bed, she took a deep fortifying breath. "I never thought I would go back on a promise to you, Luke. And God knows that having to say this to you now is killing me. But I just can't do this anymore. I thought I could, but I can't."

His eyes narrowed as he tugged his tie loose and released the button at the collar of his shirt. "And just what exactly is it that you think you can't do, Haley?"

"*Th-this.*" She struggled to keep her voice even, but she knew she was failing miserably. "I can't continue this charade any longer."

"I think this would be a good time for me to remind you that we have a couple of written contracts," he countered, his tone so calm and collected she wanted to scream.

"You mean the prenuptial papers you had me sign?"

He nodded. "Those protect my assets and custody issues if we have a child."

"Don't worry about that," she disclosed, feeling more desolate and alone than she'd ever felt in her life. "I don't want anything from you. I just want out."

"We also have a marriage certificate. I was under the impression that made things very real. And let's not forget our verbal agreement for you to have my heir," he reminded. "In most courts, that's just as legal and binding as a written document, sweetheart."

Why did it not surprise her that he'd bring up the

threat of litigation if she tried to get out of it? But then, that's all their marriage had been to him, all it would ever be—a business deal to get what he wanted.

"Why are you doing this to me, Luke?"

"I'm not doing anything. You're the one who brought all of this up." He shrugged out of his suit coat and tossed it on a chair along with his tie. "You agreed to have my heir if I met your requirements." He started walking toward her. "I followed through with my end of the bargain and we got married. Now I fully expect you to follow through with yours and have my baby."

She held up her hand to stop his advance at the same time that she backed a few steps away. If he touched her, she knew for certain her resolve would crumble.

"Please don't, Luke. We both know this isn't a marriage. It's a..." She searched for a word to describe the biggest mistake she'd ever made. "...a farce, a sham, an outright degradation to the sanctity of marriage."

Folding his arms across his chest, he gave her a look she'd seen many times before. He was going into serious negotiation mode again. But this wasn't up for compromise.

"What do you think our marriage should be, Haley?" he asked calmly.

"Not this," she retorted, becoming more upset with each passing second. She walked over to the sitting area by the balcony doors to put more distance between them. "Whether it's a temporary situation or not, I'm your wife. But there hasn't been one single time that you've introduced me as anything more than your employee. Not to your clients. Not to your family. When you introduced me to your brothers and their wives this evening, you told them I was your executive assistant."

"And your point is?"

"We're supposed to be married. We live together. Sleep together. That makes me your—"

"So you're saying that you want me to start referring to you as my wife?" he interrupted.

How could he be so intelligent and still be so stubbornly insensitive?

"No. I want you to want to *think* of me as your wife."

"What makes you so sure I don't?"

Haley felt her stomach twist into a tight knot. He wasn't the type of man who conceded even the slightest point of an issue.

"Don't patronize me, Luke. If you thought of me as your wife, you'd introduce me to people that way. Instead of telling everyone my name is Haley Rollins, you'd tell them I'm Haley Garnier." She shook her head. "You couldn't possibly think of me as your wife. I don't even wear the basic symbol of marriage."

"A wedding ring?" he asked, his intense stare seeming to bore all the way to her soul.

"Y-yes," she said as a wave of dizziness washed over her.

"You told me the day we got married that it didn't matter that I hadn't bought you a ring," he argued, taking a step toward her.

As she fought the swirling sensation making her head pound, perspiration broke out on her forehead and she had a hard time focusing on what he'd said. "I tried to tell myself…that I didn't care…but God help me… I do."

"Why, Haley?" He took another step forward. "Why do you care so much? Why do you want me to tell people you're my wife? And why do you want to take my last name?"

The thundering roar in her ears made his voice sound as if it came from a very long distance. "B-because…I—"

"Haley!"

She heard him shout her name, but she couldn't speak and her limbs suddenly felt leaden. Swaying, she tried to focus on Luke rushing toward her, his arms outstretched.

But as the relentless spinning in her head pulled her further into the deep vortex, suddenly and without warning an excruciating pain shot through her temple and a split second later, everything went dark.

As he raced his Escalade through the dark streets of Nashville, Luke's heart pounded against his ribs with the force of a sledgehammer and his gaze never wavered from the back of the ambulance with its siren screaming and lights flashing just ahead of him. When he'd watched Haley turn ghostly pale and crumpled like a marionette with severed strings, he'd tried his damnedest to get to her, tried to keep her from going down. But she'd backed too far away from him and he hadn't had a chance of catching her before she fell and struck her head on the corner of the coffee table in the sitting area.

He took a deep shuddering breath. He would never, as long as he lived, forget the nightmarish sight of her limp, unconscious body on his bedroom floor, blood trickling down her pale cheek from the cut at her temple. And she hadn't yet regained consciousness.

When the ambulance finally turned into the emergency entrance of the hospital, Luke brought the SUV to a sliding halt not far behind and threw open the driver's door. He briefly noticed that he'd parked in a restricted zone, but he didn't give it a second thought as he ran toward the gurney being unloaded from the red and white vehicle. Let the police tow his car. He didn't care. All that mattered was getting to Haley and making sure that she received the best medical care that was humanly possible.

"Has she woken up?" he asked when the paramedics lifted the stretcher from the back of the ambulance and then rolled it through the automatic double doors into the hospital's emergency room.

"Not yet," one of the two men responded as they rushed past the nurse's station and wheeled the stretcher into a treatment room. The man's voice sounded grimmer than Luke cared to hear and fear twisted his gut into a tight knot.

"Sir, if you'll please come with me, I need to get some information from you," a woman instructed from somewhere behind him.

Turning to the nurse walking toward him, he shook his head. "Can't it wait until later? I don't want to leave her."

"I'm afraid not, sir." The woman gave him a sympathetic smile. "I know how worried you must be, but I need to get the patient's medical background from you. Now, if you'll please follow me, we can get this taken care in just a few minutes."

Luke looked at Haley through the window of the treatment room where a bevy of medical personnel had surrounded the narrow bed. There was a flurry of activity as tubes were unrolled, IVs were hung on metal poles and an oxygen mask was placed over her nose and mouth.

He shook his head again resolutely. "She needs me and I'm not leaving her."

"But sir, I have to get—"

Luke turned to glare at the woman. "Let's get this straight. You can ask me whatever you need to know right here and I'll do my best to give you the answers you need. But I'm not leaving her side. Understand?"

Realizing that she wasn't going to win, the nurse disappeared for a moment, then returned with several papers on a clipboard. Luke answered what little he knew about Haley's medical history, but when the woman wanted to know who to list as the next of kin, he had no problem giving her his name.

"And what is your relationship to the patient?" the woman asked.

Luke kept his gaze trained on the activity taking place in the treatment room. "I'm her husband."

Nodding, the nurse added it to the chart and started through the treatment room door to give the medical team the information. "The doctor will be out to talk with you as soon as he knows something, Mr. Garnier."

Luke continued to watch through the window as he thought about what he'd said to the nurse. In any other set of circumstances, he might have been surprised at how quickly the pronouncement had rolled off his tongue. But telling the nurse that he was Haley's husband had come as naturally as taking his next breath.

And that's when it hit him. He'd tried not to think

about it, denied it was happening and fought hard not to do it, but he'd fallen in love with her.

But before his realization could sink in, his heart stalled at the sight of a man in hospital scrubs walking out of the treatment room and heading straight for him.

"Mr. Garnier?"

"Is my wife going to be all right?" he demanded, tightness in his throat.

"I wish I could say she is, but at this point, we just aren't sure. We're going to have to do some tests before I can give you a prognosis." He reached out to shake Luke's hand. "My name is Dr. Milford and I'm the resident neurologist on call this evening. I'll be in charge of your wife's care and I'll do everything I can for her. But before we take her to Imaging, I need to know, is she pregnant or is there the possibility that she might be pregnant?"

"I'm not sure," Luke advised, feeling as if he was an unwilling participant in a horrific nightmare. "We've been trying to get pregnant, but I don't know if we've been successful."

The doctor nodded. "In that case, we won't risk doing a CT scan of the head because of radiation and the possible harm it could do to the fetus."

"I want you to do whatever you have to do to bring Haley out of this. Even if there is a baby and it comes down to a choice of tests to find out what's wrong, you do what's best for my wife," Luke directed without hesitation.

"We'll do an MRI and that will be safe for both of them, in case she is pregnant," Milford concluded, his voice filled with understanding.

As Luke watched, two nurses maneuvered Haley's bed through the door and out into the hall. "Where will you take her after the test?" he asked, wanting to be as close to her as possible.

"I'm having them ready a bed on the third floor. That's where we take care of our head trauma patients," Dr. Milford answered as he turned to follow the gurney. "She'll be taken there straight from Imaging and I'll meet you in the waiting room with the test results."

Getting directions from the nurse's station, Luke prayed like never before on the elevator ride to the third floor. When he found the waiting area closest to the room Haley would be taken to, he lowered himself into one of the chairs and ran a shaky hand over his face in an effort to keep his choking emotions in check. God, he couldn't lose her now, not when there was so much he needed to say to her, so much that he needed to make right between them.

What had made him so damned relentless with his questions? Why had it been so important that he force her to tell him what he'd known for weeks?

Haley was in love with him and had been for years. Hell, after getting to know her intimately this past month, he knew for a certainty that she would have never married him if she hadn't loved him.

And the ultimate irony of all of it was that he'd probably loved her just as long. He'd just been too blind to see it.

But even after he'd figured it out, he'd been an arrogant jerk about it. He'd known the hell he was putting her through, but he'd wanted her to be the one to admit her feelings, had been determined to get her to say the words first.

He reached into his pants pocket and withdrew the small black velvet box. Flipping it open, he stared at the white gold wedding band, with an array of sparkling white diamonds, that was nestled inside. He'd bought the ring just that morning and intended to surprise Haley with it right after they returned home from dinner with his brothers.

Why hadn't he bought it for her earlier? Why had he waited until Chet Parker goaded him into even thinking of it?

Luke snapped the box shut and stuffed it back into his pants pocket. He knew exactly why he'd finally purchased the ring. He'd wanted to send a message to dirtbags like Parker to keep their hands off of Haley.

He took a deep steadying breath. But now the ring meant so much more. Now the wedding band symbolized his love for Haley and his steadfast determination to make their arrangement—their marriage—permanent.

He just prayed to God that he had the chance to give it to her.

Ten

An hour after seeing the medical staff roll Haley's bed out of the treatment room for her MRI, Luke sat in the waiting room wondering what the hell was going on. The test seemed to be taking forever and the longer it took, the more worried he became.

"Mr. Garnier, if you'll follow me, we'll step into the consultation room to discuss your wife's test results and her prognosis," Dr. Milford said, motioning for Luke to follow him.

Lost in his own misery, Luke hadn't even noticed the man's approach. Jumping to his feet, he followed the man into the room and when the doctor closed the door behind them, sank into one of the chairs lining the consultation room wall.

"Is Haley going to be all right?" Luke asked without waiting for the doctor to speak.

"The MRI showed that your wife has a concussion, which we knew," Dr. Milford reported, sitting in a chair across from Luke. "And I'm relieved by the fact that we found no signs of bleeding in the brain and only a slight swelling."

"Has she regained consciousness?" Luke inquired, praying that she had.

Dr. Milford nodded. "She came to as we were taking her for the MRI."

"Thank God." Weak with relief, Luke drew some much needed air into his lungs. "How is she feeling now?"

"She's complaining of a headache, but that's common with a concussion and nothing to be overly alarmed about." He glanced at the chart in his hand. "We did have to close the wound at her temple with a couple of sutures and I want to keep her overnight for observation, but I see no reason she can't go home tomorrow—as long as she takes it easy for a few days, gets plenty of rest and has someone with her to watch for signs of complications."

"When can I see her?" Luke requested, rising to his feet. He needed to see for himself that Haley was really going to be all right.

"There's something else, Mr. Garnier," Dr. Milford added, his expression unreadable.

Unsure of what the doctor was going to say, Luke sank back down in the chair. "Is it something serious?"

Dr. Milford shook his head. "It's routine when someone is brought to the hospital to do a complete blood workup on the patient. Your wife's blood tests show that she is indeed pregnant, which could very well account for the fainting that caused her fall."

"Is that unusual?" Luke interjected, trying to

remember what he'd read on the Internet about the first few weeks of a woman's pregnancy.

"It's not uncommon for some women in their first trimester to have bouts of light-headedness," the doctor reassured, finally smiling.

Luke should have been ecstatic at the news that he and Haley had been successful, but at the moment, he was too relieved to give it a lot of thought. Just knowing that she was going to recover was all he could ask for.

"Anything else?" he asked.

Dr. Milford shook his head as he rose to leave. "Everything else checks out fine. She's in excellent health and I don't anticipate any further problems."

Thanking him, Luke shook the doctor's hand, then hurried down the hall toward Haley's room. There was so much he needed to say to her, so many things he wanted to explain. But it would have to wait until after he took her home. Besides the fact that she needed her rest, he needed time to make a few plans that he hoped would convince her of his sincerity when he told her how much he loved her and asked that she give him—and their marriage—a second chance.

As Haley waited for Luke to open the front door, then stepped back for her to enter the foyer of his mansion, hopelessness filled her all the way to her soul. He hadn't said more than a handful of words to her since arriving at the hospital to bring her home and the unfamiliar tension between them was about to kill her.

One of the nurses had told her that Luke spent the entire night in the chair beside her bed and commented about how devoted he was and how much he loved her.

But he hadn't been there when she'd wakened that morning and he'd only arrived at the hospital a few minutes before the final release papers were signed. And if that wasn't enough evidence that the problems between them were insurmountable, the fact that he hadn't once mentioned her pregnancy was.

"Do you feel like being up and about or do you need to lie down for a while?" he asked solicitously.

"No, I'd rather stay up for a while, if you don't mind."

"Whatever you feel like doing is fine." He led the way into the den, then standing there looking at her as if he was unsure of what to say next, he inquired, "How's your headache?"

"It's almost gone."

"That's good." Falling silent, he looked like he'd prefer to be anywhere else but in her presence.

"Luke, we have to stop this," she began, unable to bear another second of the strained tension between them.

Their overly polite conversation was driving her nuts. They were two strangers exchanging pleasantries, not a man and woman who had lived and loved together for the past month. And who now needed to discuss the fact that their marriage was at an end.

"I couldn't agree more. It's time we got everything out in the open and things settled between us." He pointed toward the chairs in front of the fireplace. "You're supposed to be taking it easy."

Lowering into one of the plush armchairs, she waited for him to sit down. When he remained standing, she gazed up at the man she still loved with all of her heart. She'd told herself that loving him the way she did would be enough for her, that it didn't matter if he couldn't care as deeply for her as she did him. But she had only been fooling herself. She wanted—needed—his love in return.

Unfortunately, Luke wasn't willing to open himself up to that type of relationship. And she'd come to the realization that she couldn't settle for less.

She took a deep breath. "We both know that there were a lot of things left unsaid last night."

He nodded as he leaned his shoulder against the fireplace and crossed his arms over his wide chest. "Where do you think we should start?"

"I should probably begin by telling you that I'm sorry, Luke. None of this is your fault. I accept full responsibility for making such a mess of things." She stared at her hands clenched into a tight knot in her lap. "You were right last night when you said you'd held up your end of the bargain. You've done everything I asked."

"So have you," he indicated, his voice strangely emotionless. "You're going to have my baby."

Thinking of the life she carried, Haley smiled and placed her hand over her flat stomach. "And I couldn't be happier about that. I've dreamed of the day when I would have a child of my own." Of having your child, she added silently.

"But?"

"I can't honor our agreement to stay married until after the baby is born," she disclosed, wondering how her heart could keep on beating even as it was breaking in two.

"But if I remember correctly, that was your main requirement for having my heir," he remarked, walking over to stand directly in front of her.

"And I'm sorry I got us both into this fiasco," she confessed, tears filling her eyes. "But if I don't get out of this now, I don't think I'd be able to survive our breaking up later on."

His expression turned thoughtful. "Is that the only reason you want me to give you a divorce?"

"Luke, please don't make this any more difficult than it has to be," she urged as she wiped an errant tear from her cheek.

He didn't want to hear the real reason she couldn't continue being his wife, wouldn't want to know that she was hopelessly in love with him and had been from the moment they met.

"Okay, you've had your say. Now, I intend to have mine," he declared, his voice as determined as she'd ever heard it. "You want a divorce because you're in love with me, admit it."

She wasn't surprised that he'd figured out how she felt about him. He'd had more than ample opportunity to come to that realization over the course of the past month. But did he have to humiliate her by pointing out that he didn't want her feeling the way she did about him?

"Yes, I love you," she admitted, finding it difficult to get her voice above a whisper. "I've loved you for years."

"Then before I give you my answer, there's something I think you need to know, Haley." Turning, he walked back to the fireplace and seemed to take an inordinate amount of interest in something on the mantel.

"I could have found someone else with similar characteristics, whom I could have convinced to have my heir," he explained, his back still to her. "But do you have any idea why it was so important to me that you be the mother of my baby?"

"No."

There was something in his tone that caused her heart to beat double time and a small bubble of hope to form within her soul. But she refused to allow it to grow. She wouldn't be able to bear the devastation if it turned out she was wrong.

He picked up whatever had claimed his attention on the mantel, then turning, walked over to kneel down in front of her. "The reason I didn't want any other woman having my baby, the reason I went along with your marriage stipulation and the reason I won't give you a divorce without a damned good fight is because I love you, too, Haley Garnier. More than life itself. It took me a long enough time to realize it, but I do and you might as well come to terms with the fact because I'm not letting you go that easily."

The hope she'd tried so hard to keep tamped down, blossomed and grew to fill her with a joy she'd never imagined possible. "Oh, Luke, I love you so much I ache with it," she revealed, reaching for him.

When he wrapped her in his arms to pull her close, she felt his body shudder and she knew he was experiencing the same emotion she was. "God, sweetheart, it like to have killed me when I thought there was a possibility that I might lose you."

"I'm so sorry I put you through that," she stated, kissing his cheek. "I thought the reason I started feeling ill was because I was so emotional. I had no idea about the baby."

He shook his head. "No, you have nothing to be sorry about. You were upset with me and rightly so. I've been a complete bastard not to consider your feelings in all of this."

"But you had no way of knowing how I felt," she said, loving him more with each passing second.

"Yes, I did." He cupped her cheeks with both hands and the love shining in his vivid blue eyes stole her breath and caused her heart to soar. "Maybe not consciously, but deep down I think I've always known. You wouldn't have even considered my proposition if you hadn't loved me."

Luke took her hand in his and the feel of his warmth and the strength of his love flowed through every part of her. "There's something I need to ask you, sweetheart."

"And what would that be, dear husband?" She loved finally having the freedom to call him that and to openly tell him how much she loved him.

His expression turned serious and so tender, it brought a fresh wave of tears to her eyes. "Will you marry me, Haley Rollins Garnier?"

"But, darling, we're already married."

"Marry me again," he stressed, showing her the object he'd removed from the mantel. He flipped open the top of the little black velvet box and removed a gorgeous diamond-encrusted, white gold wedding band. Then, holding it close to the third finger on her left hand, he asked "Will you do me the honor of becoming my wife again?"

"Yes, Luke. Nothing would make me happier." Her

heart filled to overflowing with love when he slid the ring onto her finger. As she gazed down at the sparkling diamonds, she couldn't believe that it was a perfect fit. "How did you know the size?"

He gave her a smile that caused her pulse to race. "I have my ways."

Kissing him until they both gasped for breath, she couldn't stop smiling. "Yes, Luke Garnier, I'll continue to be your wife for the rest of my life."

To her dismay, he shook his head. "Sweetheart, that's not what I asked you. I want to know if you'll marry me again."

She couldn't believe what she was hearing. "You mean you actually want us to go through another ceremony?"

He nodded as he pulled two folded pieces of paper from his pants pocket. Handing her one of them, he smiled. "This is the name and phone number of the wedding coordinator at the Opryland Hotel. As soon as you're feeling well enough, I want you to set up an appointment to meet with her. I've already instructed her to make this the wedding of your dreams."

Haley couldn't believe he was willing to do that for her. "But why, Luke?"

"You deserve so much better than our first wedding, sweetheart. I want everyone we know to be at this ceremony and see how special you are to me and how honored I am that you're my wife." He brushed a strand of hair from her cheek and his tender touch sent tingling sensations down her body. "And this time around, there aren't going to be any business meetings or labor disputes to keep me from being with you every second of our wedding day and night."

"I love you," she whispered, tears streaming down both cheeks.

"And I love you," he proclaimed, placing the other piece of paper in her hand. "This is the address and phone number of Millie Sanford."

"My…mother?" she reiterated, staring at the small note. "But how did you find her? I don't even remember telling you her name."

"Let's just say I know a woman with a hell of an investigative team and leave it at that," he said, giving her a smile that melted her heart. "You may or may not want to use that information, but I wanted you to have it in case you decide to get in touch with her."

Unable to stop the tears from rolling down her cheeks, she wrapped her arms around his shoulders and hugged him close as she sobbed against his shoulder. "I love you so much, Luke Garnier," she rasped when she finally managed to bring her emotions back under control. "Thank you."

He placed his hand on her stomach and when he met her gaze, the love she detected in his eyes sent delightful shivers up her spine. "By the way, I think you might want to consider reducing your hours at the office now that you're pregnant."

"Why?"

"Because if you're working all day, I can't pamper you the way you deserve," he informed, kissing her forehead.

Laying her head on his shoulder, she sighed. "I've never been pampered before in my entire life."

"I know and as your husband, I intend to remedy that problem." His tone left no doubt that that was exactly what he would do.

Placing her hand over his still resting on her stomach, she grinned. "I was thinking that I might even quit."

"Or you could work from home. That is if you think you'll get anything done with me and the baby under-foot all day?"

"What do you mean?"

"I'm going to start working from home in order to be with you through your pregnancy and help out with the baby once he's born," he announced, smiling.

Happier than she'd ever been in her life, Haley laughed. "Ever since you asked me to have a baby, you've referred to it as 'he' or your 'son.' What if we have a little girl?"

"You've mentioned that before and I've given it some thought," he said, his smile filled with love. "A little girl as sweet and wonderful as her mother would be just fine with me. We can have two or three boys a few years down the line."

She gave him a mock frown. "Two or three?"

Resting his forehead against her, he winked. "Sweet-heart, I love you so much I'll be more than willing to give you all the babies you want. Girls, boys, twins, whatever your heart desires."

"Really?" Nothing would thrill her more than having a whole houseful of Garnier children to mother.

"I love you, Haley Garnier. More than you'll ever know."

"And I love you, Luke. With all of my heart and soul."

Epilogue

After receiving good-natured advice from Caleb, Nick and Hunter, Luke smiled at Jake. "Looks like the next brother to take the plunge will be you."

Jake snorted. "If I were you, I wouldn't hold my breath. You'd end up turning blue and passing out before I take a trip down the aisle."

"Never say 'never,'" Hunter said, laughing. "It'll come back to bite you in the butt every time."

"Gentlemen, it's time to take your places," the wedding coordinator reported, motioning for them to follow the minister.

Walking to the front of the ballroom, Luke couldn't wait to see Haley. Arielle and his half brothers' wives had rented a suite at the hotel and insisted on Haley spending the night before the wedding with them. And even though he and his brothers had a great time hanging out at his house, Luke had missed being with her, holding her all through the night and waking up with her in his arms that morning.

When the double doors opened at the back of the room and the bridesmaids came down the aisle to take their places on the opposite side of the minister, his breath stalled and Luke couldn't believe how stunning Haley looked as she stepped onto the satin runner. She'd been beautiful the day they'd exchanged vows in the little chapel in the mountains, but today she was absolutely radiant.

Luke stepped forward to extend his arm and when she smiled up at him with more love than he deserved, he silently vowed to spend the rest of his life making sure she never doubted how much he loved her in return. "Are you ready to renew your vows to be my wife?"

"As ready as I am to hear your vows to be my husband," she noted, her sweet voice sending a shaft of heat straight through him.

"I love you, today, tomorrow and for the rest of our lives, sweetheart."

"And I will always love you," she promised, making him feel like the luckiest man alive.

"Isn't this just wonderful, Luther?" Emerald asked, leaning over to her personal assistant when the bride and groom turned to face the minister. "Four of my grandchildren married in a little over three years."

Luther gave her his usual stiff nod. "I'd say you've outdone yourself, Mrs. Larson."

Yes, everything had come together just as she'd

planned. With information supplied by her good friend and curator at the museum, Max Parmelli, her arrangement to hire Chet Parker for the entertainment at her reception she'd thrown for herself last month had worked out brilliantly. The young singer's interest in the lovely Haley had been just the impetus Luke needed to help him realize his feelings for her and ultimately led to Emerald watching them renew their vows.

She smiled as she gazed at the wedding party standing at the front of the Opryland Hotel's main ballroom. Luke made such a handsome groom and she'd never seen him look happier. Jake, the best man, was the mirror image of the groom and she still marveled at how much they resembled their father, Owen. She dabbed a tear that slipped from her eye with an Irish linen handkerchief. If only Owen could have realized what a precious gift his children were.

Her gaze drifted to her three other grandsons, Caleb, Nick and Hunter, and her heart swelled with emotion. It thrilled her to know that Luke and Jake had become close to their newfound brothers. And she was doubly happy that Luke had asked them to be groomsmen in his and Haley's wedding.

She sighed contentedly. Now that everything had worked out for Luke, she could turn her attention to making sure the same happened for her remaining unmarried grandchildren.

She focused her attention on Jake. He was going to be the most challenging one yet. Of all of her grandchildren, she worried that he might be the one who turned out to be just like his father. And although she'd yet to determine the best course of action to test his mettle, she had already started collecting information and she had no doubt that something would come to mind for him very soon.

Turning her attention to her only granddaughter Arielle, Emerald smiled fondly. With a baby on the way and her mother Francesca gone, the child needed Emerald now more than ever. But she had already set the wheels in motion to remedy the situation and she had every confidence that it would be brought to a satisfying conclusion, the same as her other efforts for all of her grandchildren.

"Aren't they a beautiful couple?" she queried Luther when Luke and Haley turned to walk back up the aisle as the string quartet played Pachelbel's Canon.

"A handsome couple indeed," Luther agreed, nodding.

Emerald smiled beatifically. "That's another one down."

Luther came as close to smiling as he was capable of doing. "And two more to go, madam."

* * * * *

ONE NIGHT,
TWO BABIES

BY
KATHIE DeNOSKY

This series is dedicated to Charlie, the love of my life.

A special thank you to Donna Swan, Carolyn Jordan and Lisa Swan for the Saturday Night Girls' Club. You're the best.

One

"Mrs. Montrose, I know what Derek did was wrong, but you have to give him another chance."

When Arielle Garnier looked up from her computer screen at the sound of the male voice, her heart came to a screeching halt. The man who just stopped inside her office doorway was the last person she ever expected to see again. And if the look on his handsome face was any indication, he was just as surprised to be coming face-to-face with her, as well.

His vivid green eyes pinned her to the chair. He stared at her for several uncomfortable seconds before he finally spoke again. "I need to talk to the preschool's administrator, Mrs. Montrose, about an incident involving Derek Forsythe. Could you please tell me where I could find her?"

"Helen Montrose is no longer in charge here. She sold the school and retired a couple of weeks ago." Arielle tried desperately to keep her voice even in spite of her jangled nerves. "I'm the new owner and administrator of Premier Academy for Preschoolers."

She took a deep breath and reminded herself to remain outwardly calm, even if his reappearance in her life did shake her all the way to the core. This was her territory and he was the one intruding. Besides, she'd rather walk barefoot across hot coals than allow him to think he still had any effect on her.

When he continued to stare at her, she forced herself to ask, "Was there something you needed?"

He finally shook his head. "I don't have time to play games, Arielle. I need to speak with Helen Montrose as soon as possible."

The shock of seeing him again quickly gave way to anger that he didn't believe she was the new owner. "I told you, Mrs. Montrose retired. And if you have business here at the school, you will have to deal with me."

He didn't look at all pleased with the situation, but that was just too bad. She certainly wasn't excited to be seated before the man who, three and a half months earlier, had spent a week loving her like she was the most desirable woman alive, then disappeared without so much as a backward glance. He hadn't even had the decency to call or leave her a note.

"All right," he eventually said. She could tell he wasn't happy, but instead of pressing the issue any further, he took a deep breath. "I suppose this would be a good time to reintroduce myself. My real name is Zach Forsythe."

Arielle's heart felt as if it had fallen to her feet. Among his other transgressions, he'd lied to her about his name? He was really Zachary Forsythe, owner of the Forsythe resort and hotel empire? And if he was here to discuss Derek Forsythe, did that mean he was the little boy's father? Was he *married?*

Bile rose in her throat and she desperately tried to think if she'd heard or read anything about him recently. But all she could remember for certain was that Zach Forsythe was reputed to prefer a quiet lifestyle out of the spotlight and guarded his privacy as if it were the gold in Fort Knox. Unfortunately, she didn't know anything at all about his marital status.

But the very thought that she might have spent a week in the arms of a married man sent a cold chill slithering down her spine. "Correct me if I'm wrong, but a few months ago I distinctly knew you by the name of Tom Zacharias."

He ran an impatient hand through his thick dark brown hair. "About that—"

"Save it," she interrupted, holding up her hand. "I don't particularly care to hear whatever explanation you're about to fabricate. I believe you wanted to talk about Derek Forsythe?" When he nodded, she went on. "And I assume you wish to discuss his pending suspension for biting another little boy?"

His mouth thinned into a grim line before he gave her a short nod. "Yes. You have to give him one more chance."

"I haven't been here long enough to be familiar with his past behavioral patterns, but your son's teacher said he's—"

"Nephew." Frowning, he then flashed her the same smile that he'd used to seduce her almost four months earlier. "Derek is my sister's little boy," he corrected. "I'm not now, nor have I ever been, married, Arielle."

She was relieved to hear that she hadn't done the unthinkable. But his devastating smile and the intimate tone he used to say her name made it hard to think.

"You don't have to be married to have a child," she countered, doing her best to regain a bit of her equilibrium.

"I suppose it's a personal choice," he observed, shrugging. "But I, for one, won't have a child outside of marriage."

"Whether you do or not isn't the issue here, Mr. Forsythe."

"Call me Zach."

"I don't think…"

Before she could go on, he took a step closer.

"And marriage may not be the issue, but I can't have you thinking—"

"What I think is irrelevant." Desperate to change the subject, she tried to concentrate on the matter at hand. "Derek's teacher said this is the third time he's bitten another child in the past week." She glanced at the teacher's recommendation for suspension on top of a stack of papers on her desk. "And the school has a strict three-strikes policy when it comes to this kind of behavior."

"I understand that. But he's only four and a half years old. Can't you make an exception this one time?" he asked, turning up the wattage on his cajoling smile. "If you haven't been told about my sister's accident by some of the other teachers, I won't bore you with the details, but Derek's experienced quite an upset in his life in the past few months and I'm sure that's the reason he's been acting out. Things are getting back to normal now and I'm sure he'll settle down. Believe me, he really is a good kid."

Zach or Tom or whatever he was calling himself these days was putting her in a very awkward position. On one hand, rules were rules and had been put into place to discourage students' undesirable behavior. If she made an exception for one child, she'd have to make it for all of the children. But on the other hand, if she didn't give the little boy another chance, it might appear that she was punishing him for the actions of his nefarious uncle.

"Would it help sway you if I promise to have a long talk with Derek and make him understand that it's unacceptable to bite other children?" he asked. Apparently sensing her indecision, he walked to her desk and, propping his fists on the edge, leaned forward until their faces were only inches apart. "Come on, darlin'. Everyone deserves a second chance."

After the way he'd lied to her about his name, then disappeared without a word of explanation, she would debate that issue. But his close proximity and hearing him call her "darlin'" with his rich Texas drawl caused her to shiver.

"A-all right," she finally replied, forcing herself not to lean away from him, even though it made her extremely nervous being so near.

She was willing to say just about anything to get him to turn off the charm and get out of her office so that she could draw a decent breath. Besides, the longer he stayed the greater the possibility he'd find out why she'd spent several weeks desperately trying to reach him. And at the moment, that was something she just wasn't ready to address, nor was her office the place to do it.

"If you'll explain to Derek that it's wrong to behave that way toward other children, I'll let him off with a warning this time," she decided firmly. "But if it happens again, he will have to serve the suspension."

"Fair enough." He straightened to his full height, then, stuffing his hands in the pockets of his suit pants, rocked back on his heels. "Now that we have that settled, I'll let you get back to whatever it was you were doing." Walking toward the door, he stopped and turned to give her another one of his charming smiles. "By the way, it was a very pleasant surprise running into you again, Arielle."

And jackasses have sprouted wings and learned to fly, she thought, barely resisting the urge to convey her sarcasm aloud. But before she could comment on his obvious lie, he exited her office as quickly as he'd barged in.

Sinking back into the plush leather of her desk chair, Arielle tried to think. What on earth was she going to do now?

She'd given up all attempts to find him months ago when every one of her efforts met with a dead end. Of course, now she knew why. The man she'd been looking for didn't even exist. It had been Zachary Forsythe, hotel and resort magnate, who had held her, made love to her and…lied to her. And here he was living in the city she'd recently moved to, with a nephew in her preschool.

"How did my life get so out of control?"

Burying her head in her shaking hands, she did her best to organize her scattered thoughts. She had no idea what to do, *if* she should do anything. Clearly he'd never expected to see her again, and wasn't overjoyed that he had. And she certainly wasn't thrilled with the situation, either.

Her stomach did a fluttery lurch and, placing a calming hand over it, she tightly closed her eyes as she fought to keep her emotions in check. First and foremost, she'd made a huge mistake falling for his charismatic charm. And second, she'd wasted countless hours trying to find a man who'd just proved he wasn't worth finding.

But she'd foolishly held out hope that he'd have a plausible explanation for leaving her to wake up alone all those months ago. Deep down she'd known she was deluding herself, but it was easier than acknowledging how gullible and utterly foolish she'd been. Now there was no denying that he was every bit the jerk she'd feared him to be.

She swallowed hard and, opening her eyes, reached for a tissue to dab at the moisture threatening to spill down her cheeks. Her move to Dallas was supposed to be a good thing—a symbolic gesture of leaving the past behind and making a fresh start. But he'd just ruined that. There was no way she could forget about him and move on with her life if he showed up at the school from time to time.

Sniffling, she reached for another tissue. She hated being so darned weepy all of the time, but then, that was his fault, too.

Her stomach clenched again and she automatically opened her desk drawer, reaching for the bag of crackers she kept for just such occasions. Yes, Zachary Forsythe was to blame for her hormones making her emotional, as well as her other current problems. And the most pressing problem of all was figuring out how and when to tell the biggest jerk in the entire state of Texas that even though he wasn't married as he said he would be, in about five and a half months, he was indeed going to have a child of his own.

Zach entered his executive office at the Forsythe Hotel and Resort Group corporate headquarters still thinking about his unexpected run-in with Arielle Garnier. He'd thought about her a lot since their time together in Aspen, but he'd never expected to see her again. And certainly not at the same preschool where his nephew was enrolled. But thanks to the little boy's latest antics, Zach had been put in the awkward position of pleading Derek's case to the woman he'd, for lack of a better word, *dumped* a few months ago.

Walking over to his desk, Zach sank into the high-backed chair. Swiveling around, he gazed blindly at the framed aerial photograph of his luxury resort in Aspen. He distinctly recalled Arielle telling him that she was a teacher at some nursery school in San Francisco. So why had she relocated to Texas? And where had she come up with the money to buy the most prestigious preschool in the Dallas area?

He supposed that her older twin brothers might have had something to do with that. If he remembered correctly, she'd told him that one was a highly successful divorce attorney in Los Angeles and the other owned the largest construction and development company in the south. They certainly could have afforded to front her the money to buy the school. In fact, they'd been the ones who'd given her the week's ski trip, complete with deluxe accommodations at the Aspen Forsythe Resort and Spa for her twenty-sixth birthday.

Focusing his attention on the photograph of the luxury mountain resort, Zach couldn't help but grin when he thought about the first time he'd met Arielle. It had been her engaging smile and flawless beauty that had first attracted him. Her silky, dark auburn hair had complimented her porcelain skin to perfection and she had the prettiest hazel eyes he'd ever seen. But as the evening wore on, it had been her sense of humor and obvious intelligence that had him thoroughly captivated. By the following morning, they had become lovers.

As he sat there thinking about what had been the most exciting, memorable week of his life, his office door opened. His sister slowly walked across the room to lower herself into the chair in front of his desk.

"Did you speak with Mrs. Montrose about Derek?" she asked, propping her cane against the edge of his desk. "She's always been extremely fair and since the accident, she's been very understanding about his uncharacteristic behavior."

Zach shook his head. "Helen Montrose is no longer in charge at Premier Academy, Lana."

"She's not?" There was a hint of panic in his sister's voice. "Who's taken over for her? Is he going to have to serve the suspension? Did you explain to whomever's in charge now that Derek's normally a very well-behaved little boy?"

"Arielle Garnier is the new owner and administrator," he answered, searching his younger sister's pretty face. To the outward eye Lana looked the picture of health. But she still had days when the fatigue of recovering from her horrific accident was overwhelming. "I don't want you to worry about it. I've taken care of everything and promised to have a talk with Derek about what's acceptable and what isn't. He won't have to serve the suspension, unless he bites the other children."

"That's a relief," Lana replied, finally smiling as she sat back in the chair. "He's settled down quite a bit now that I've had the casts taken off and we've moved back into the condo. And as our lives get back to normal, I'm sure his behavior will continue to improve."

With Lana having two badly broken legs, internal injuries and a couple cracked ribs, Zach had insisted that his sister and nephew move into his place during her recovery. And it was a damned good thing that he had. After her release from the hospital, Lana couldn't take care of herself, let alone see to the needs of an extremely active four-and-a-half-year-old boy.

"How did your physical therapy session go?"

Zach inquired, noticing Lana wince as she shifted to a more comfortable position. "You seem to be having a little trouble."

"I'm ahead of where the therapist expected at this stage, but it's not the exercises I'm doing that's causing my soreness today." She pointed to the floor-to-ceiling glass behind him. "It's this dumb weather. Since the accident I'm better at predicting a rainstorm than a barometer."

He glanced over his shoulder at the bright sunlight and brilliant blue sky just beyond the window. "It looks fine out there to me."

"I don't care," she objected, shaking her head. "My knees are telling me it's going to rain buckets sometime today, so grab an umbrella when you go out."

"I'll keep that in mind." When he watched her shift again, he offered, "If you'd like to go home and get some rest, I can have Mike pick up Derek from school in the limo."

Lana nodded as she levered herself out of the chair, waving Zach back down in his seat, and reached for her cane. "That might not be a bad idea. I promised him I'd bake some chocolate chip cookies for his afternoon snack. And a nap before I get started would be nice."

"Just don't overdo things."

She laughed as she made her way to the door. "No danger in that."

"By the way, I'm heading up to the ranch this

weekend. Would you and Derek like to go along?" he asked, thinking they might like to get out of town for a while. Located just north of the city, the ranch where he and Lana had grown up had become a peaceful weekend getaway.

Turning, she shook her head. "Thanks, but now that I'm doing better, I think Derek needs some uninterrupted mommy time. Besides, you know how it floods up there when it rains. I don't want to be stranded for the next few days while we wait for the water to recede. But please, give Mattie my love and tell her that Derek and I will be up to visit in the next couple of weeks."

"I'll drive myself and leave Mike here to take you wherever you need to go. If you change your mind, have him drive the two of you up to the ranch."

"I will, but don't count on us," she suggested, smiling.

After his sister left, Zach returned to work. But soon his thoughts were straying to Arielle Garnier and how absolutely amazing she'd appeared that morning. There had been a glow about her that he found completely fascinating.

He frowned. As unbelievable as it seemed, she was even prettier now than she had been when they'd first met.

But he wondered what brought her to Dallas. When they first met, she'd told him that she'd been born and raised in San Francisco and how much she loved it there. Had something happened to change her feelings? And why hadn't she moved to Los Angeles or Nashville to be closer to one of her brothers?

By the time he left the office for the day, Zach was filled with far more questions than he had answers. Something just didn't add up. And even though where Arielle lived or what she did was none of his concern, he decided to stop by the school on his way out of town. He had every intention of finding out why a woman who had been perfectly content with her life a few months ago would make such a drastic change.

"Thank God it's Friday," Arielle muttered as she pulled her raincoat close and splashed through the ankle-deep water covering the school's parking lot on her way to her red Mustang. "The whole day has been one big royal pain in the neck."

The gentle spring rain that had started shortly before lunch had quickly turned into a torrential downpour and had continued throughout the afternoon, causing the pre-K field trip to the petting zoo to be canceled. Then, if thirty extremely disappointed four-year-olds hadn't been enough to contend with, one of the little girls in the three-year-olds' class stuffed a bean up her nose during craft time and had to be taken to the urgent care facility around the corner to have it removed.

Opening the car door, she quickly closed her umbrella, threw it into the backseat and slid in behind the steering wheel. She couldn't wait to get home to her new apartment, slip into a baggy pair of sweats and forget the entire day ever happened. Since becoming pregnant, she'd started taking a nap when the children took theirs. Having missed hers this afternoon, she was not only tired, she was cranky, as well.

But her well-laid-out plan to spend a quiet weekend at her new home came to a swift end when she backed the low-slung car from her reserved space, drove halfway across the parking lot and listened to the motor sputter twice, then die. When all of her attempts to get the car going again failed, she closed her eyes and barely resisted the urge to scream. She should have known when Zach Forsythe showed up first thing this morning that it was going to be one of those days.

She sighed heavily and, reaching for her cell phone, quickly dialed the number for roadside assistance to send a tow truck. But her already low spirits took a nosedive when, after holding for ten minutes, a representative came on the line to inform her that due to the high number of calls from motorists with stalled-out cars, it would be several hours before one of their drivers could come to her aid.

As she ended the call, she glanced at the water covering the parking lot, then at the school's front entrance. She couldn't just sit in the car until they arrived and trudging back into the school through inches of water wasn't appealing, either.

But her mood lightened considerably when the reflection of car lights in her rearview mirror drew her attention. A Lincoln Navigator pulled to a stop beside her. She briefly wondered if she should err on the side of caution and refuse any offer of help from a stranger. But she instantly dismissed the thought. They were in an exclusive, very affluent area of the city, it was still daylight and how many criminals drove luxury SUVs?

But when the driver got out, opened the passenger door of her car and Zach Forsythe got in, Arielle's gratitude died in her throat. "What do you think you're doing?" she demanded.

His knowing grin caused her heart to flutter like a trapped butterfly. "It would appear that I'm going to be rescuing you."

She shook her head. "No, I don't need help." Especially from you, she added silently.

"Then why are you sitting here in your car in the middle of a flooded parking lot?"

"Maybe I just want to."

"Start the car, Arielle."

"No." Why couldn't he just go away and leave her alone?

His grin widened. "Is it because you don't want to or that you can't start the car?"

She glared at him before she finally conceded, "I can't."

He nodded. "That's what I thought. It's stalled out, isn't it?"

"Yes."

"Well, that tells me you *are* in need of my help."

"Thanks for the offer, but I'm sure you'll understand why I have to decline," she said stubbornly. If he was her only alternative, she'd just as soon fend for herself.

"Don't be ridiculous, Arielle."

"I'm not. I've already called my auto service."

"Really?" He didn't look at all convinced. "And just when is it supposed to arrive?"

"I'm sure it will be here any minute," she lied, staring at the street. Maybe if she wished long and hard enough, a tow truck would miraculously appear and Zach would disappear.

"Nice try, darlin'. But I'm not buying it." He leaned close as if he was about to share a secret. "Remember, I'm from Dallas. I know how it is around here in the spring and how long the auto club will take to get to you at this time of day. I also know that calling a cab would take just as long."

"I don't mind waiting," she repeated.

Why did he have to be so darned good-looking?

"In case you haven't noticed, it's pouring and doesn't look like it's going to let up anytime soon. You'll be lucky if anyone can get here until this time tomorrow."

"Surely it won't take that long."

"Trust me, it could be even longer. And there's no way in hell I'm going to leave you sitting here in your car all night."

"I'll just go back inside the school until they get here," she decided, thinking quickly. Sleeping on the narrow couch in her office held very little appeal, but it would be a lot better than accepting aid from a lying snake like Zach Forsythe.

After a long staring match, he finally insisted, "Let me make this clear for you, darlin'. Either you get in my SUV and let me take you home or I'm going to stay right here with you for as long as it takes to get your car towed."

"You can't do that."

He folded his arms across his broad chest and settled back in the bucket seat. "Watch me."

His overly confident smile and arrogant manner grated on her nerves. "I'm sure you have more interesting things to do with your time than sit here with me all evening, so I suggest you go do them."

"Actually, I don't."

"Then why don't you go hunt for something to do and leave me alone?"

A tiny ache began to settle in her stomach and she wished he'd leave so she could go inside and find something to eat in the cafeteria before she got sick. Her morning sickness had mostly disappeared a few weeks ago, but she still became queasy if she let her stomach get empty.

Besides, the longer she was around Zach, the greater the chance he would discover that she was pregnant. And although she would tell him that he was going to be a father, she wasn't prepared to do so at this moment. She was still coming to terms with the shock of running into him again.

Shrugging, he shook his head. "I'm not leaving until I'm certain you're okay."

"Why not? If you'll recall, you didn't seem to have that problem almost four months ago," she retorted before she could stop herself.

His smile fading, he uncrossed his arms and reached out to lightly trace his index finger along her jaw. "The circumstances are entirely different than they were then. Now, if you don't get out of this car and into mine voluntarily, I swear I'll pick you up and put you there myself."

A shivering thrill raced up her spine at his touch. "Is that a threat, Mr. Forsythe?"

"No, darlin'. That's a promise."

Two

Zach steered his SUV out of the school parking lot and onto the street. After giving him her address, Arielle plastered herself to the passenger-side door and clutched the front of her oversize raincoat like a security blanket. He'd also noticed she'd become quite pale.

His earlier irritation with her stubbornness quickly turned to concern. The woman he'd known in Aspen had been vibrant, outgoing and exuded good health. But Arielle's demeanor and the disturbing pallor of her complexion gave him every reason to believe that she was coming down with something.

"Are you all right?" he asked, glancing over at her again.

"I'm fine."

Stopping at the red light on the corner, he turned to face her. "I don't think so. You make a ghost look colorful."

She shook her head. "I'll be a lot better if you'll just take me home. Once I have something to eat, I'll be okay."

When the light changed, he gave serious consideration to taking her to her apartment, bidding her farewell, then leaving town as he'd planned. But his conscience nagged at him and he just couldn't do it.

Arielle was new to town, had no family in the area that he knew of and he'd bet his last dime that her only acquaintances were the people she worked with. How could he possibly leave her to fend for herself when she was obviously ill?

Making a snap decision, he headed straight for the interstate. She might not like it, but she needed someone with her until her illness passed. And the way he saw it, he was about the only choice she had.

"What are you doing?" she asked, raising her head from where it had rested against the passenger window. "Why did you pass up my street?"

"It's obvious you're sick and I don't think you need to be left alone."

"I told you, I'm fine," she insisted. "Now turn this truck around and take me home."

"No." He changed lanes to avoid a huge amount

of water covering the road ahead. "I'm taking you to my weekend place north of the city."

"I'm not going anywhere with…you." Her voice sounded a bit shaky and her pale complexion had taken on a sickly, greenish hue. "All I need is something to…eat and I'll be…good as new."

"I'll let my housekeeper, Mattie, be the judge of that." He'd feel a lot better having her oversee Arielle's care. Mattie had been like a grandmother to him and Lana and nursed them through every one of their childhood illnesses with a jar of VapoRub in one hand and a bowl of homemade chicken soup in the other. "Her home remedies are as effective as any prescription medication."

"I'm sure they are. But my apartment is a lot closer and…I told you, I'll be fine as soon as I—" She stopped suddenly. "Pull over. I think…I'm going to be…sick."

Zach had the SUV stopped before she could finish the thought. Throwing open the driver's door, he rushed around the front of the truck to help her out. Putting his arm around her shoulders, he supported her while she was sick, and if he wasn't sure before that he'd made the right decision, he was now. The last thing she needed was to be left alone to contend with a very bad case of the flu.

"I think I'll be…all right now," she finally said, raising her head.

After helping her back into the truck, Zach got in

behind the steering wheel and turned on the heater. "Let's get you out of your raincoat," he proposed, reaching over to help her. The garment was completely soaked. "I'm sure you're cold and uncomfortable in that thing."

"I'd rather keep it on," she objected, shaking her head as she clutched the folds of the coat. "It's water-resistant and the inside is still warm and dry."

Had that been a flash of panic he'd seen in her expressive hazel eyes? Why the hell would she be afraid to take off her wet coat?

"I'm not absolutely certain that's a good idea, darlin'."

"I am." As she leaned her head back against the headrest, he watched her close her eyes as if it was too much of an effort to keep them open. "Now, will you please stop telling me what to do and listen to me? I want to go home to my apartment."

"I'm sorry, Arielle, but I just can't do that. Try to rest. We'll be at my ranch before you know it."

"This could easily be considered a kidnapping," she relayed, sounding extremely tired.

"Not if the alleged kidnapper is only trying to do what's best for the alleged kidnappee," he elaborated, shifting the SUV into gear and merging back into the busy rush-hour traffic.

"Best in…whose opinion?" she argued, delicately hiding a yawn behind her hand.

"The only one that counts right now—mine." He

smiled at the long-suffering expression on her pretty face. "Now, try to take a little nap. I'll wake you once we get to the ranch."

When she felt herself being gathered into strong, capable arms, Arielle's eyes snapped open. "Wh-what on earth do you think you're doing, Zach?"

Lifting her to him, he gave her a grin that curled her toes inside her soggy shoes. "You're not feeling well, so I'm helping you—"

"Just because I'm not one hundred percent doesn't mean I can't get out of the truck on my own," she interrupted, desperate to put some distance between them. What if he felt the bulge of her stomach?

"You need to conserve your energy to fight whatever bug you have," he explained, setting her on her feet. When he shut the SUV's door, he placed his arm around her shoulders, tucked her to his side and guided her from the garage across the covered breezeway into the house. "Besides, I'm not running the risk of you passing out and possibly adding a concussion to your other ailments."

His secure hold caused her heart to thump even harder. "H-how many times do I have to tell you? All I need is something to eat and I'll be fine."

He stopped ushering her along when they entered the kitchen. "Mattie?"

"Stop your hollerin', Zachary. I'm old, but I ain't deaf." A gray-haired woman in her late sixties walked out of a pantry and stopped short at the sight of Zach holding her. "Did I forget about you bringin' company for the weekend?"

He shook his head. "No, but Arielle's sick and can't be left alone. Probably coming down with a bad cold or maybe even the flu and requires your expert care."

Arielle tried to push away from him. "I don't have the—"

"Hush, darlin'," he said close to her ear, causing a shiver to course through her. "Mattie Carnahan, this is Arielle Garnier. She's in need of some dry clothes. See if you can find something of Lana's for her to put on while I take her to the guest room."

He led her down a hall and opened the door to a beautifully decorated room. When he reached to help her out of her coat, Arielle shook her head and took a step back. "I don't need your help."

"You need to take that coat off," he insisted, moving toward her. "It's soaked."

She took a few steps backward. "The only thing I want from you is to be left alone. But if you feel you have to do something, find me something to eat and then take me back to my apartment. What part of that don't you understand? And exactly how can I make it any clearer for you?"

As they stood glaring at each other, Mattie walked into the room to place a set of gray sweats and a heavy pair of socks on the bed. "Honey, he can be as stubborn as a jackass when he gets something in his head." She motioned for Zach to leave. "You go get your things out of the car and I'll have supper on the table by the time you get unpacked."

Zach didn't appear to be all that happy with his housekeeper taking over the situation. "I can do that later. I need to make sure Arielle is—"

"Go," Arielle and the older woman both said at the same time.

Muttering a curse, he finally turned and walked from the room.

Mattie started to follow him. "If there's anything else you need, just let me know."

"Thank you," Arielle said, meaning it. At least the housekeeper had given her a bit of a reprieve from Zach's overpowering masculinity. "And for the record, I don't have the flu."

Mattie nodded as she stepped back into the room and closed the door. "Zachary means well, but he doesn't have any idea you're pregnant, does he?"

A cold sense of dread spread throughout Arielle's body. "I… Uh, no, he doesn't."

"How far along are you, child?" Mattie asked, her voice so kind and understanding it chased away some of Arielle's apprehension.

There was no use denying what the housekeeper had guessed, although Arielle didn't have any idea how the woman could have possibly figured it out.

"I'm only three and a half months pregnant, but I'm already starting to get a nice little bulge."

Mattie nodded. "I thought you must be showing some since you were so determined to keep your coat on and kept holding it together. That's why I brought some of Zachary's sweatshirts and pants, instead of his sister's. You'll have to roll up the legs and push up the sleeves, but I thought you might need the extra room."

"But how did you know?" Arielle was thoroughly amazed by the woman's intuitiveness.

"Some women have a look about them when they're pregnant and if ever a woman had that glow, you do," Mattie revealed, shrugging. "And if that wasn't enough, Zachary telling me that you got sick on the drive up here and your insistence that all you needed was something to eat was. I always had to keep something on my stomach when I was carrying both of my boys." She smiled. "Now, get changed and come to the kitchen. I'll make sure you get something to eat before you get sick again. Then I'm going home so that you and Zachary can talk things over in private."

When Mattie closed the door behind her, Arielle at last took off her soggy raincoat and sank down on the bed. There hadn't been the slightest bit of condemnation in the older woman's voice, but she had to have strong suspicions that Zach was the baby's father. Why else would she leave them alone?

As Arielle started taking off her damp clothes to put on the dry fleece, she sighed heavily. It appeared that the time had come to tell Zach about the baby and discuss how they would handle the issues of custody and visitation.

She wasn't looking forward to it, but it would almost be a relief to finally have her pregnancy out in the open. Other than her new sister-in-law, Haley, and her newfound grandmother, no one—not even her brothers, Jake and Luke—had a clue that she was going to have a baby.

And although she loved her brothers with all of her heart, just the thought of telling them about her pregnancy made her want to take off for parts unknown. She was no longer the ten-year-old girl they'd raised after their mother's death, but they still insisted on meddling in her life. Although she'd learned to stand up to them, if they knew, they would tell her what they thought was best for her and the baby. No doubt they'd even convince her to move closer to one of them.

But thankfully they wouldn't have the opportunity to once again play the overly protective older brothers. Now that she'd found Zach, she fully intended to handle things on her own terms. By the time she told Jake and Luke about her pregnancy, she and Zach would have hopefully made all of the important decisions.

She finished pulling the thick, warm socks on her feet then stood to go into the kitchen. In theory, her plan sounded logical and should work out. But something told her that if telling Zach he was going to be a father went like the rest of her day, she'd better brace herself for life to become more complicated instead of simpler.

When Zach walked into the kitchen, Arielle was already seated at the table with a plate in front of her piled high with mashed potatoes, vegetables and a country-fried steak smothered in milk gravy. "Shouldn't you be eating something a little lighter than that?" He frowned when he watched her take a big bite of the steak. "Chicken soup would be a much better choice for someone with the flu."

He watched her close her eyes for a moment, obviously savoring the taste of the beef. For someone with an upset stomach, she certainly had a hearty enough appetite.

"We'll talk about the reason I got sick after we eat," she replied, reaching for a slice of homemade bread. "But maybe now you'll believe me when I say I don't have the flu."

"Leave her be and have a seat, Zachary." Mattie had always called him by his given name, and although he preferred the shortened version, he'd long ago stopped trying to get her to change. "That little gal is going to be just fine."

"If Arielle doesn't have the flu, what's wrong with her?" he demanded, getting the distinct impression that the two women knew something he didn't.

Ignoring his question, Mattie set a plate of food at his usual place at the big, round oak table. "I'm gonna cross the yard to my house before the ground gets so mushy I end up sinkin' to my knees in mud. And if you need me for anything, it had better involve somebody bleedin' or somethin' bein' on fire before you call me to come back over here."

"Is it still raining hard?" Arielle asked a moment before he watched a forkful of mashed potatoes disappear into her mouth.

He couldn't get over the change in her. The more she ate, the less sickly she appeared.

"It's supposed to keep rainin' like this all weekend," Mattie informed, nodding. "And if it does, y'all will be on your own tomorrow and Sunday because I'm too old to be gettin' out in weather like this."

"Don't worry about me," Arielle responded, taking a big drink of milk. "I won't be here. I'm going to have Zach take me back to the city after dinner. But it was very nice meeting you, Mattie." When neither he nor Mattie commented, she frowned. "Is there something I should know?"

"Do you want to tell her or should I?" Mattie offered, turning her full attention on him.

"I will," he conceded, seating himself at the table.

When his gaze clashed with hers, he watched Arielle slowly put her fork on the edge of her plate, her expression guarded. "Tell me what?"

"We probably won't be going back to Dallas before the middle of next week at the earliest."

She didn't look as if she believed him. "You're joking, right?"

"I'll let you kids work this out," Mattie remarked, quickly removing her jacket from a peg by the door. "I'm goin' home before all hell breaks loose."

He heard the back door close as he and Arielle sat, staring at each other over the table. "When it rains like this, the Elm Fork of the Trinity River backs up into the tributaries and the creek between here and the main road floods out," he described. "You were asleep when we drove over the bridge, but we barely made it across. By now I'm sure it and the road are under several feet of water."

"In other words, you're telling me we're trapped?" She made it sound more like an accusation than a question.

"You could look at it as being on a minivacation," he suggested, turning his attention to his own plate.

"But I have things at school to take care of and an important appointment to keep."

He nodded. "I've got things I need to do, too. But that doesn't change the fact that I can't drive you back to Dallas until the water recedes."

Arielle's ravenous appetite suddenly disappeared. "Isn't there another road that's not flooded?"

"Not really." He shifted in his seat. "The way the creek winds around, it makes this part of the ranch a peninsula. Then, when rains are heavy, like now, the dry wash cutting through the middle of the property floods and this section becomes an island."

"That's kind of poor planning, don't you think?" she asked, raising one perfectly shaped eyebrow.

Laughing, he shrugged. "I suppose it seems that way now, but when my great-great-grandfather settled here over a hundred years ago, it wasn't. Back then, a natural water source was essential to a ranch's survival. Besides, we're two miles from the creek and there's a couple hundred acres between here and the dry wash. Not exactly a threat of being flooded out here on higher ground."

"But you knew this would happen and you still insisted on bringing me here?" If the heightened color on her face was any indication, Arielle was more than a little upset with him. "Why, Zach? Why did you do that when you knew full well how much I wanted to go home?"

"You were ill and needed someone to watch over you," he noted, stating what he saw to be obvious. "And since you don't have family close by, I was the only available choice."

She shook her head. "You're unbelievable. If I had been sick and did need someone to care for me, it would have made more sense to take me to my apartment. It was closer to the school and at least in the city, there are doctors and hospitals close by. And none of this was necessary because I'm not ill."

Truthfully, he wasn't entirely certain why he'd brought her to the ranch. Maybe it had been a way to make things up to her for leaving her in Aspen without so much as a simple goodbye. But whatever the reason, when he'd seen she was in need, he just hadn't been able to walk away.

"If you weren't sick, then why did you look like you were at death's door?" he observed, his own irritation beginning to rise. "And why did we have to stop on the way here for you to throw up?"

He watched her take a deep breath, then, as if coming to a decision, meet his questioning gaze head-on. "Do you know why I get sick if I don't eat? Or when I do eat, why I put food away like a starving lumberjack?"

The back of his neck began to tingle the longer they stared at each other. He had a feeling he was about to learn something that he wasn't prepared to hear and might not like.

"No."

"Because that's what happens to some women when they become pregnant," she said defiantly.

Silence reigned while he tried to process what she'd said. "You're pregnant?"

"Yes."

"Just how far along are you?" he prompted, his heart beginning to thump inside his chest like an out-of-control jackhammer.

Her gaze never wavered from his when she answered. "Three and a half months."

He immediately glanced at the front of the sweat-shirt she wore, but it was big on her and a little too early to notice any telltale thickening of her stomach. Unable to sit still, Zach rose to his feet and began to pace the length of the kitchen. It didn't take a math degree to figure out that the baby she was carrying was most likely his.

"And before you ask, yes, I'm pregnant with your baby," she stated, confirming his suspicions.

His stomach twisted into a painful knot as he recalled another time a woman was carrying his child. "We used protection."

"Yes, but one of the condoms broke," she reminded him.

He'd figured the chances of making her pregnant from that one time had to be fairly remote. Apparently he'd been wrong.

Nodding, he rubbed the tension building at the back of his neck. "I remember. But why didn't you tell me sooner?" Her desire to be left alone to deal with the flooded-out car and her refusal to take off her bulky raincoat suddenly made perfect sense. She'd been trying to hide the pregnancy from him. With his jaw clenched so tight it felt welded shut, he asked, "Didn't you think I had the right to know?"

He watched her expression turn from defiant to righteously indignant. "Oh, no you don't, buster."

She stood to face him. "I'm not letting you get away with playing the victim here. You *lied* to me about who you were. And up until this morning, when you barged into my office and told me your *real* name, I thought I was having Tom Zacharias's baby." She started to walk away, then, turning back, added, "And just for the record, I searched desperately to find a man who didn't even exist because I thought he needed to know that he was going to be a father." She swiped away the tears suddenly spilling from her eyes. "When all of my efforts proved useless…you can't even begin to imagine…how much of a fool I felt or…the emotional pain I went through. So don't… even go there."

Zach stood in the middle of the kitchen long after he watched Arielle rush down the hall toward the guest room. Stunned, he had a hard time believing how rapidly his life had changed in the past twelve hours. When he'd gone to the school this morning, he'd had nothing more on his mind than sweet-talking Helen Montrose into going easy on his mischievous nephew, then heading to the office to go over the contracts and blueprints for his newest resort. But along with his discovery that the old gal was no longer in charge at Premier Academy, the only woman he'd been tempted to have a relationship with since his ill-fated engagement had reappeared in his life and was pregnant with his baby.

Just the thought that he was going to be a father

caused a myriad of feelings to course through him. Had it not been for his ex-fiancée, he might have felt pride and excitement about the baby Arielle carried. But thanks to Gretchen Hayden and her duplicity, he was filled with a deep sense of apprehension that he just couldn't shake.

Five years ago, he'd thought he had it all—a thriving business, a devoted bride-to-be and a baby on the way. But all that had changed when Gretchen decided that motherhood would be detrimental to her figure and seriously limit her options should something better than being the wife of a hotel entrepreneur come along.

He took a deep breath in an effort to chase away the ugly memory of the day he'd discovered the woman he'd thought he loved had deliberately ended the life of their unborn child. All of his focus now needed to be on Arielle and protecting the baby they'd created together. And this time the outcome was going to be different than it had been five years ago. *This time,* he wasn't going to take it on faith that Arielle truly wanted his baby. He was going to make certain his child was protected.

Most of his anger dissipated as he thought about her trying to tell him about the baby and how hurt she'd been when she couldn't. But not all of it.

He understood her inability to find him after they parted in Aspen. In order to be completely anonymous, he always registered under an assumed name when he checked into one of his hotels. It was the only way to get an accurate idea of the quality of guest services and the efficiency and courtesy of the resort management. Besides, it was standard practice that guest information was kept in the strictest of confidence. If Arielle had inquired about him, and he had every reason to believe that she had, the management at the resort wouldn't have given her anything. And even if they had broken protocol and given her the name and address he'd registered under, the information would have proven completely worthless.

But that didn't explain why she hadn't told him about the pregnancy when they were in her office this morning. And she'd had ample opportunity to tell him this afternoon when he'd discovered her sitting in her car in the school's parking lot. And why hadn't she told him the real reason that she had become sick on the drive to the ranch?

His appetite deserting him, Zach removed their plates from the table, scraped the food into the garbage disposal and put the dishes in the dishwasher. He'd give her time to calm down, then he wanted answers. And he wasn't going to bed without them.

With her emotions once again under control, Arielle wiped away the last traces of her tears and sat up on the side of the bed to look around the guest room. It was decorated in shades of peach and antique white and at any other time, she would have loved staying in such a beautiful room. But at the moment, it felt like a prison cell, albeit a very pretty one.

She was stranded on a remote ranch with the man who had lied to her about his identity, abandoned her without a word, broken her heart and made her pregnant. And if all that wasn't enough, he was blaming her for not telling him about the pregnancy.

"Unreal," she said aloud.

But even more incredible was that her life was paralleling her mother's. Francesca Garnier had fallen in love with a man who had impregnated her with a set of twin boys and simply walked away. Then, ten years later, the man had shown up long enough to rekindle their romance, which led to the birth of Arielle, and once again disappeared. And when Arielle and her brothers first met their paternal grandmother a few months ago, they'd learned their father had used an assumed name.

Instead of Neil Owens, the starving artist their mother knew, their father was the infamous playboy Owen Larson, the only offspring of Emerald Larson, one of the richest, most successful businesswomen in the modern corporate world. During the ten years away from their mother, Owen Larson had fathered three other children—all boys and all with different women.

It was so bizarre, she even had a hard time believing it. But when Emerald Larson had contacted them Arielle had gained three more brothers. And Emerald had embraced the Garnier siblings as part of her family, giving each a multimillion-dollar trust fund and one of the many companies within the Emerald, Inc. empire. Arielle became the new owner of Premier Academy and moved to Dallas.

But that was immaterial. What was extremely disconcerting was, as her mother had done with her father, Arielle had fallen for a man she'd thought to be as honest and forthright as she'd been with him. But just like her father had done to her mother, Zach had deliberately lied to her to keep her from finding him.

She shook her head to chase away her disturbing thoughts and concentrated on forgetting what she couldn't change and focusing on her present dilemma. In spite of the stress and tension she had experienced or because she hadn't finished her dinner, her hunger had returned full force.

Unfortunately, if she went to find something for herself in the kitchen, she'd likely run into Zach. Though they had several things to discuss and decisions to make, she wasn't ready for that just yet. She'd already had an extremely upsetting day.

But the decision was taken out of her hands when her stomach rumbled. If she waited much longer she'd become sick again and since they were flooded in, she didn't have much choice.

Sighing, she rose from the bed, opened the door and walked right into Zach's broad chest. "Oh, I…um, didn't know you were there. Excuse me."

He placed his hands on her shoulders in a steadying gesture and she noticed his gaze immediately settled on her stomach. "Are you all right?"

Even though his touch through the thick fleece sweatshirt and the low timbre of his voice sent shivers straight up her spine, she forced herself to remain motionless. "I need something else to eat," she said, nodding.

"Yeah, that probably wouldn't be a bad idea." He released her, running a hand through his thick hair. She could tell by the action that he wasn't comfortable with the situation, either. "Neither of us finished dinner."

They stared at each other as if thinking of something to say when her stomach rumbled again. "I'd better find something in the fridge or I'm going to be sorry."

"Oh, yeah, sure," he agreed, standing back for her to precede him down the hall.

When they entered the kitchen, Zach walked to the refrigerator and opened the door. "Do you want a sandwich or would you prefer something else?"

"A sandwich and a glass of milk would be nice," she answered, trying not to think about how handsome he was.

He'd changed into a pair of worn jeans and a black T-shirt that emphasized every well-defined muscle of his upper body. Dear Lord, he was without a doubt the best-looking man she'd ever seen. She'd thought so in Aspen and she thought so now. But thinking along those lines was what had landed her in his bed and ultimately led to her current predicament. She'd do well to remember that and concentrate on their upcoming conversation about the baby and what role, if any, he intended to take as the baby's father.

"If you'll tell me which cabinet the glasses are in, I'll pour the milk," she offered, forcing herself to look away from the play of his biceps as he lifted a gallon jug from inside the refrigerator door.

"I'll take care of that." He motioned toward the pantry. "Why don't you get a loaf of bread and see if you can find a bag of chips."

As he poured two glasses of milk, she retrieved the bread and a bag of pretzels and by the time everything was on the table, her nerves were stretched to the breaking point. They were both being overly congenial and polite, but there was an underlying current of tension that was so strong, it could have been cut with a knife.

"We have to stop this, Zach," she declared, seating herself at the table.

To his credit, he didn't feign ignorance and act unaware of what she was referring to. "I don't want to upset you any more than I already have," he began, setting a couple of plates on the table. "But I'd bet my next resort project that our discussions are going to be tense at best."

"I'm sure they will be," she concurred, reaching for a package of sliced turkey. If she'd thought their talk was going to be unpleasant, the strained atmosphere now was far worse and she'd just as soon get it over with. "But putting it off isn't going to make it any easier." She nibbled on a pretzel. "Where would you like to start?"

He held up his hand. "We'll go into my study after we finish eating. I don't think it would be a good idea for you to have another meal interrupted, do you?"

"Probably not," she agreed, taking a bite of her sandwich.

They both fell silent as they ate and by the time they'd cleared the table, Arielle found herself actually looking forward to the confrontation she knew would follow. It would be a relief to get it over with so they could move forward. Zach was a highly successful businessman, much like her brothers, and she had no doubt he'd start by making demands and telling her what he expected her to do. But thanks to dealing with her brothers, years ago she'd learned to stand up for herself and she knew exactly how much she was willing to give and what she intended to get in return. And the sooner Zach came to that realization, the better.

Several minutes later, he showed her into his study. Arielle glanced around, then seated herself in one of the plush chairs in front of the stone fireplace. She wasn't about to sit in the chair in front of his desk. He would have no doubt sat behind the desk, giving him a huge psychological advantage, much like a boss talking to his employee. And she wasn't allowing him any kind of edge.

"How has the pregnancy gone so far?" Zach asked, walking over to stand by the fireplace. Once again his gaze came to rest on her belly. "Have you experienced any problems other than having to eat frequently?"

"Not really." She shrugged. "Aside from a couple of weeks of intense morning sickness, everything has gone quite well."

"As long as you eat frequently?"

"Correct."

When she'd first discovered she was pregnant, she'd hoped that once she found him, the man who had made love to her with such tender care would be, if not happy, at least interested in their child. It appeared that Zach was very interested. But she couldn't ignore how he'd lied to her. Trusting him now would be foolish.

"When do you learn the sex of the baby?" he inquired, finally raising his eyes to meet hers.

"I'm not sure. On Monday, my obstetrician planned an ultrasound to make sure everything is going well, but I don't know if the sex can be determined this early. But now I'll have to reschedule the appointment," she decided, it being pointless to remind him why.

To her surprise, he shook his head. "You won't have to reschedule. I'll call my pilot to bring the helicopter up from Dallas."

"But I thought you said we were stranded here until the water went down."

He again shook his head. "I told you I couldn't drive you back to the city, but I never said we were completely stranded. Besides, that was before I knew about the baby and the ultrasound." He gave her a determined smile. "Don't worry, I'll make sure that we keep this appointment and every other one until you give birth."

"*We?*"

"You didn't think I wouldn't be involved once I knew I had a baby on the way, did you?" There was an underlying edge of challenge in his tone and they were quickly approaching the more stressful phase of their discussion.

"To be perfectly honest, I didn't know if you would care one way or the other." She met his accusing gaze head-on. "If you'll remember, the man I thought I knew doesn't even exist."

The intense light in his dark green eyes stole her breath. "Darlin', the only difference between me and the man who made love to you in Aspen is the name."

"Really?" she dared, ignoring the swirl of heat the memory created and concentrating on the hurt and disillusionment of discovering she'd been abandoned. "So when you're not using an alias, you habitually use women, leaving them behind, without waking them to say goodbye?"

"No, and that's not what happened," he retorted, shaking his head. "That morning, I had to get back to Dallas—"

"To tell the truth, it doesn't really matter, Zach."

She could see that he was angry she'd cut him off, but that was his problem, not hers. She had her pride and didn't particularly care to hear that he'd left because he'd grown tired of her or that things between them had moved way too fast and he'd wanted to avoid an uncomfortable scene.

"The only thing we need to talk over now is where we go from here," she stated determinedly. "I'm perfectly capable of taking care of the baby's needs, so I don't want, nor do I need, monetary help from you. What I want to know is how involved you want to be in the baby's life. And will you want visitation rights every other weekend, once a month or not at all?"

His eyes narrowed as he took a step toward her. "Oh, I intend to be completely involved in every aspect of my child's life, Arielle. And as far as shared custody, visitation rights and child support are concerned, there is no need to work out any agreement."

"What do you mean?" Surely he didn't expect her to hand over full custody of her baby. If he did, he was in for the biggest, nastiest fight of his life. "I love this baby and I'm not giving it up to you or anyone else."

Closing the distance between them, he stood over her much like her older brothers used to when she'd been called on the carpet for doing something they had disapproved of. "I'm not telling you I want full custody, darlin'. But spending time with my baby and supporting him won't be an issue because once we get back to Dallas, you and I are getting married."

Three

Zach watched Arielle open and close her mouth several times before she finally said, "You can't possibly be serious."

If ever a woman had the deer-in-the-headlights look about her, it was Arielle. Good. Now that he had her attention, maybe she'd start listening to him.

"Rest assured, I'm very serious." He folded his arms across his chest as he gazed down at the woman he had every intention of making his wife. "I don't joke about something as important as taking a trip down the aisle, darlin'. If *you'll* remember, I told you this morning that I wouldn't have a child out of wedlock. And I meant every word of it."

Anger sparkled in the depths of her hazel eyes. "And as I told *you* this morning, you don't have to be married to have a baby."

"That might work for some people, but not for me. I'm of the opinion that when a man makes a woman pregnant, he stands by her and does the right thing. We will be married as soon as possible."

"Oh, no, we won't." She rose to her feet, then poked the middle of his chest with her index finger. "Let me tell you something, Mr. High-and-Mighty. You're going to have to get used to the idea of being a single father because I would never marry you even if you got down on your knees and begged me."

Zach wasn't used to having anyone openly defy him—not in the business world, not in his personal life. And if anyone did have the courage to cross him, they found themselves embroiled in a battle of wits they were most assuredly going to lose. But for reasons he couldn't quite put his finger on, he found Arielle's defiance mildly amusing, if not downright cute.

Maybe it was because of their considerable height difference. At six feet four inches, he towered over her. But that didn't seem to intimidate her one damned bit. Or it could have been the fact that he'd never had a pregnant woman get in his face and poke him in the chest to make her point the way Arielle had just done. Either way, he barely resisted the urge to smile. Their marriage was going to be anything but dull.

"Never say 'never,' darlin'."

"I'm telling you right now, it's not going to happen," she declared, shaking her head. "Being married isn't a requirement to have a baby. Other arrangements can be made for you to play an equal role in the baby's life, so you might as well start thinking along those lines and stop insisting on a marriage that is never going to happen."

Without giving it a second thought, he reached out and took her into his arms. "First and foremost, calm down. Getting upset is not good for you or the baby." Pulling her against him, he finally smiled. "And second, it *is* going to happen. So I would suggest that you get used to the idea pretty quick and start thinking about what you're going to wear and whether or not you want your brothers to give you away during the ceremony. I'm willing to wait until next weekend if you want them in attendance, but no longer than that."

Before she could protest further, Zach lowered his head to silence her with a kiss. As he covered her mouth with his, the memories of what they'd shared in Aspen came rushing back full force. From the moment he'd seen her that morning, he'd wondered if her perfect lips were still as soft and if her response to him would be as passionate and unbridled as his memories.

At first she remained motionless in his arms. But as he reacquainted himself with her sweetness, Zach felt some of her tension drain away and he seized the opportunity to deepen the kiss. To his immense satisfaction she finally parted her lips on a soft sigh and allowed him entry to her tender inner recesses. At the same time she wrapped her arms around his waist.

The signs of her acceptance encouraged him to explore her with a thoroughness that immediately had his body reminding him that several long months had passed since he'd held her, kissed her, made love to her. Stroking her tongue with his, his lower body tightened and his heart took off at a gallop. His faulty memory forgot how intoxicating her kisses were and how perfect she felt in his arms.

Unable to resist, he moved his hands to her sides and slowly slid them beneath the bottom of her sweat-shirt, up along her ribs to the swell of her breasts. He realized she wasn't wearing a bra and without a moment's hesitation, he cupped the weight of her with his palms. The soft mounds were larger, most likely due to her pregnancy, and when he lightly brushed the pebbled tips with his thumbs, her tiny moan of plea-sure indicated they were highly sensitive, as well.

But as he continued to reacquaint himself with her body, Zach pressed himself closer and the slight bulge of her stomach reminded him of their current situation and the raw feelings still churning inside him. Arielle said she loved and wanted his baby, but he'd heard that from another woman just before she deliberately caused herself to miscarry.

Suddenly needing to put distance between them, he broke the kiss and, removing his hands from her breasts, pulled the sweatshirt down and took a step back. Gratified by the dazed expression on her face, he could tell that Arielle had been as shaken by the kiss as he had. But if past experience had taught him anything, he would not allow his judgment to be clouded by the haze of desire. Besides, they had more than enough to deal with at the moment without adding another complication to the mix.

"Why did you do that?" she asked, sounding delightfully breathless.

Her cheeks had turned a rosy pink and he wasn't certain whether the heightened color was due to rising passion or embarrassment at her eager response. It was probably a combination of both, he decided as they stood staring at each other.

"Kissing you was the only way I knew to stop you from arguing with me."

She swiped at her mouth with the back of her hand as if trying to wipe away his kiss. "Well, don't do it again."

"You used to like it when I kissed you," he reminisced, stuffing his hands into the front pockets of his jeans to keep from reaching for her again.

"That was before I discovered how deceptive you are." If looks could kill, hers was sure to finish him off in about two seconds flat.

"What time is your appointment for the ultrasound?"

"Monday afternoon at three." She gave him a confused look. "Why?"

"I'll arrange for my pilot to pick us up before noon on Monday," he said, quickly calculating how long the helicopter flight would take to get back to the city. "I have clothes here, but that should give us more than enough time to go by your place so that you can get ready and still make the appointment."

She shook her head. "I'm sure you have another resort to build or some corporate thing that needs your full attention. You don't have to go with me. I'll be fine without you."

Yes, he did have to accompany her. But he wasn't about to tell her that he felt an obligation to protect his unborn child, even though she'd given him no good reason for concern.

"Clearing my calendar for the day won't be a big deal." He shrugged. "I'd already counted on spending a few extra days here because of the flooding. Besides, that's the beauty of being the sole owner. You can do what you want, when you want and nobody says a word unless they don't care about being fired."

"Let me put it this way, Zach." He watched as she clenched both fists at her sides and he could tell her frustration level was close to the boiling point. "I don't *want* you to go to the doctor with me."

"Why? You said you spent several weeks trying to find me. Now you're telling me you don't want me around?"

"I searched for you because I thought you might want to know that you'd fathered a child," she said tightly. "Not because I wanted you to go with me to doctor appointments or 'do the right thing.'"

"That's too bad, darlin'." He rocked back on his heels. "I'm going to the doctor with you and there isn't a damned thing you can do to stop me." Smiling, he added, "And I will be doing the *right thing* and making you my wife."

"I don't understand why you're being so stubborn about this, Zach," she grumbled.

"I could say the same thing about you."

Closing her eyes for a second as if trying to keep from belting him one, when she opened them, they sparkled with anger. "I give you my word that I'll tell you everything the doctor says and even make an extra copy of the picture from the ultrasound for you."

"I'm sure you would." He'd like to believe Arielle would be completely honest with him, but he couldn't be one hundred percent certain. After all, he'd trusted his former fiancée and that had ended in absolute tragedy. "But I'm a hands-on kind of guy, darlin'. I never rely on secondhand information and I want to hear for myself what the man has—"

"Woman," she corrected him. "My obstetrician is a woman."

"Okay. I want to hear what the *woman* has to say." He smiled as he reached forward and placed his hand on her pregnant stomach. "I'm the daddy. I'm entitled to know what's going on, as well as finding out whether we're having a boy or girl at the same time you do."

She shook her head and removed his hand from her stomach. "I didn't say you weren't. But did it ever occur to you that it might make me uncomfortable to have you in the room during an examination?"

Her revelation was unexpected. Before he could stop himself, he reached out to run his index finger along her creamy cheek. "Why, Arielle? It's not like I haven't been intimately acquainted with your body before."

"That was several months ago and a lot of things have changed since then," she said, looking away.

"Like what?" he asked, fighting the urge to take her back into his arms. "We're still the same two people who spent an entire week together."

As he watched, the color on her cheeks deepened. "I didn't mean *that*."

"Then what?"

"After waking up alone to find that I meant absolutely nothing to you, I don't particularly care to be around you," she declared flatly. "Nor do I care to hear the reason you left."

He regretted the emotional pain he'd caused her. But that couldn't be changed now. "I'm sorry you feel that way, darlin'. But it's something that's going to have to change, and damned quick." He caught her chin between his thumb and forefinger and, tipping it up, forced her to look him straight in the eye. "Once we get married, we'll be together all of the time. We're going to live together, go to all your prenatal appointments together and…we'll be sharing a bed."

He heard a hitch in her breathing a moment before she backed away from his touch. "I don't think so." As she turned to leave, she added, "It's not going to happen and you might as well get used to that fact just as quick."

Watching Arielle storm from the room, Zach straightened his stance. Oh, it was going to happen, all right. They would be married as soon as he could get a marriage license. When he wanted something, he went after it with a single-minded determination that never failed to net him the desired results. And that was something else *she* was going to have to get used to.

From everything she'd said and the way she acted, she was happy and looked forward to having his child. But he would not take it on faith that was the case here. That's why he fully intended to make her Mrs. Zach Forsythe and ensure his right to monitor everything that took place for the rest of the pregnancy.

Abandoning the book she'd been reading, Arielle shifted to a more comfortable position on the window seat and watched the pouring rain. She had successfully avoided Zach at breakfast by getting up around dawn and bringing a couple of muffins and a glass of milk back to the guest room. But she wasn't naive enough to think she could do the same thing for lunch.

In fact, she was surprised that Zach hadn't looked for her when she remained in her room all morning.

Sighing heavily, she lovingly placed her hand on her stomach. She could understand Zach's desire to be with his child, but it didn't have to be a package deal. Surely they could work out something that was acceptable for both of them without entering into a marriage for all of the wrong reasons.

When she finally did get married, she wanted it all—a home, a family and a husband who loved her. Not the loveless marriage she would be getting if she went along with Zach's plan.

Lost in thought, she jumped at the sudden rap on the door. Before she had the chance to answer, Zach walked in.

"Are you all right, Arielle?"

"I'm fine." At least she had been before he entered the room.

Good Lord, if she'd thought he had looked good last night, it couldn't hold a candle to the way he looked now. Zach wasn't just attractive, he was drop-dead gorgeous.

The pair of jeans he wore today were faded and rode lower on his lean hips than the ones from the night before. And he hadn't bothered buttoning his light blue chambray shirt, giving her a very enticing view of his chest and ripped abdominal muscles. Memories of him holding her to that chest as they made love, feeling every perfectly defined muscle pressed against her, caused her heart to skip several beats and her breathing to become shallow.

"Arielle, are you sure you're okay?" he repeated, frowning.

"Oh…um, sure." When she started to get up, he shook his head. "Stay right where you are. I know how hard it was for my sister to find a comfortable position, even in the early stages of her pregnancy."

"Some of the teachers at school said that being comfortable will become a very big issue the further along I get," she agreed, nodding.

Walking over to the window seat, he lifted her outstretched legs and sat down, lowering them to his lap. "Lana had a lot of trouble with her feet and legs getting tired," he said, gently massaging her foot. "Does that feel good?"

She could lie and tell him it didn't, but what was the point? He could tell from her serene expression that it did.

"Actually, it feels like heaven," she admitted, closing her eyes as he skillfully rubbed her arch.

"Have you had problems with muscle cramps?" he asked as his hands continued to work their magic.

"Not many." Enjoying his relaxing touch, she'd never realized that a foot rub could chase away tension throughout the rest of her body. "My legs cramped up a few times while I was sleeping, but that's about it."

He shoved one leg of her sweatpants up and began

to gently move his hands over her calf. "How did your brothers take the news about the baby?" he continued conversationally.

His touch caused a sense of euphoria to sweep over her and it took a moment to realize what he'd asked. Opening her eyes, she shook her head. "I haven't told them yet."

"Why not?" He moved to massage her other leg. "I was under the impression that you had a good relationship with them."

"We are very close." His hands moving over her leg made it hard to think and she paused to collect her thoughts. "But I'm almost sure they won't be happy with the decisions I've made lately."

Zach stopped his tender ministrations and a protective sparkle appeared in his dark green eyes. "They wouldn't talk you into terminating the pregnancy, would they?"

"Oh, no. Not that." She knew for certain her brothers would never do something like that. "They'll both be absolute fools over their niece or nephew."

"Then what's the problem?" he prodded, his hands once again moving over her legs with care.

"Instead of moving to Dallas, they'd want me to live with one of them." She sighed. "And as much as I adore both of them, I'd rather eat a big ugly bug than do that."

Zach threw back his head and laughed. "I see you still express yourself in a way that leaves no doubt what you mean."

The sound of his rich laughter sent a tingling sensation skipping over every nerve in her body. His sense of humor was one of many things about him that she'd found irresistible.

Shrugging one shoulder, she smiled. "Well, it's the truth. Luke would want me with him and his new wife, Haley, in Nashville. And Jake would insist that I move into his condo in Los Angeles."

"In other words, you'd have to choose between them?" Zach summarized.

"Not exactly. Either would be fine with me living with the other." She tried to concentrate on what she was about to say, but the feel of his hands smoothing over the sensitized skin at the back of her knee made that very hard to do. "For one thing, Luke and Haley have only been married a couple of months and they need their alone time. Plus they have a baby on the way and I don't think Luke could survive living with two women experiencing mood swings and emotional meltdowns at the same time."

"Oh God, no." Zach gave an exaggerated shudder. "One hormonal woman is enough to contend with, but two would send a man running like hell." He shook his head. "My sister moved in with me for a short time when she was pregnant. Her apartment was being painted. I never knew if what I said would make her angry enough to bite my head off or cause sobbing like her heart was broken." He lowered his head. "It was like living with Dr. Jekyll and Ms. Hyde."

"Your sister is single?" If his sister could be a single mother, why was Zach so insistent that they had to be married?

He nodded. "Lana wanted a child, but after several failed relationships, she decided a visit to the sperm bank was the answer for her." He stopped massaging her legs, but continued to hold them on his lap. "And before you ask, I failed to talk her out of it. But I supported her decision and help out with Derek whenever she needs me."

"Jake and Luke will be the same way with me."

"They won't have to be," he said, giving her a meaningful look. "I'll be with you every step of the way." Before she could comment, he went on, "But what about your brother in L.A.? Why wouldn't you want to live closer to him?"

"Don't get me wrong, Jake is a wonderful guy and I love him with all my heart. But living with him would drive me over the edge." Just the thought was almost laughable. "Besides, I prefer a much quieter lifestyle and I couldn't have kept up with which one of his women was the flavor of the moment."

"Moment?" He sounded surprised.

"Jake's fascination with a woman has never lasted longer than a couple of weeks," she explained.

"That could present a problem."

She nodded. "Plus the fact that they still think of me as a child."

"Hey, give them a break, darlin'." He grinned. "I

pretty much think along the same line when it comes to my sister."

She sighed. "Your sister has my heartfelt sympathy."

"So why did you decide to move to Texas?"

Gazing into his questioning green eyes, she wondered how much she should tell him. She'd been cautious about revealing her relationship with Emerald Larson to anyone. Who would believe she'd gone from a struggling preschool teacher, barely making ends meet, to an heiress with a bottomless bank account and a thriving business? She had never openly discussed her financial affairs with anyone but her brothers.

"I was presented with an opportunity to run my own preschool and I took it," she responded, settling on an honest but sketchy answer to his question. "And Premier Academy just happened to be in Dallas."

Zach stared at her wanting to ask more about her acquisition, but thankfully her stomach chose to rumble, reminding both of them that it was lunchtime.

"Uh-oh, we'd better get you something to eat before you get sick again," he stated, lifting her legs from his lap and rising to his feet. He held his hand out to help her up from the window seat. "What would you like me to make? Pasta or hamburgers?"

"You're going to cook?"

"I can handle things," he said, nodding his head. "Mattie's stocked the kitchen for my visit."

"Why don't we have something easy for lunch,"

she suggested when her stomach made its presence known again. "A sandwich would work."

"Need something pretty quick, huh?"

"I'm hungry enough to gnaw the legs off the table," she detailed as she walked into the kitchen and went straight to the refrigerator for a package of roast beef and some cheese.

"My cook in Dallas is going to love having you around," he said, laughing as he handed her a loaf of bread from the pantry. "Nothing makes her happier than feeding people."

Arielle stopped piling the sliced meat on two pieces of bread. "I won't be around for her to feed."

"Sure you will." She watched him remove the milk from the fridge, then reach into the cabinet for a couple of glasses. "Once we're married, you'll be living there, remember?"

She shook her head. "It's never going to happen, *remember?*"

His low masculine chuckle caused her heart to skip several beats. "Like I told you last night, never say 'never,' darlin'."

Four

On Monday afternoon, Zach sat beside Arielle in the obstetrician's waiting room, thumbing through a magazine. He wasn't the least bit interested in reading about or looking at pictures of maternity clothes. But since Arielle had been giving him the silent treatment ever since their helicopter flight to Dallas, it gave him something to do while they waited for her to be called to see the doctor.

Over the weekend, they seemed to have reached a truce of sorts and instead of arguing about their upcoming marriage, they had—as if by unspoken agreement—stopped talking about it completely. He still had every intention of making her his wife as soon as possible. Nothing she could say or do was going to change that.

"Arielle Garnier?"

Zach glanced up to see a nurse standing at the door leading back to the examination rooms. "Looks like it's our turn, darlin'," he said, rising to his feet, then offering his hand to help Arielle out of her chair.

Frowning, she placed her hand in his, stood and turned to face him. "It's my turn, not *ours,* and I'd rather you stay here while I'm with the doctor."

"You've made that very clear, darlin'. And I've made it just as clear that I'm going with you." He placed his hand to the small of her back and started guiding her across the waiting room.

Her body language and stormy expression indicated that he would hear all about this once they left the doctor's office. But if she thought that was enough to intimidate him, she was sadly mistaken. Nothing was going to keep him from seeing the first images of his child.

The nurse motioned for them to enter a small room at the back of the office. There she recorded Arielle's weight, then took her temperature and blood pressure. "The doctor will be in shortly," she estimated, smiling as she walked to the door. "If you'd like, you can have 'Dad' help you onto the examination table. Then go ahead and pull your top up to just below your breasts and your pants down to just below your tummy."

As the woman closed the door behind her, an odd feeling spread throughout Zach's chest. Although he'd thought of little else since learning that Arielle was carrying his child, something about the nurse calling him "Dad" made it a reality.

"For the last time, I would prefer to see the doctor without an audience," Arielle protested, her tone reflecting her outrage.

Turning to face her, he cupped her soft cheeks with his hands. "It's all right, darlin'. I know you're probably self-conscious about your stomach," he said, making certain his tone was sympathetic, even if he didn't quite understand why she was uncomfortable about it. "But that's to be expected. You're pregnant. And there's nothing I'm going to see now that I haven't already." Kissing the tip of her nose, he smiled. "Now, let's get you on that table, ready to find out what we're having—a bouncing baby boy or a sweet baby girl."

She gave him one last belligerent glare, before allowing him to help her up onto the examination table.

"Didn't the nurse tell you to expose your stomach for this?" he asked, reaching for the bottom of her maternity top.

To his surprise, she slapped the back of his hand. "I'll wait until the doctor comes in."

"Okay," he uttered, quickly releasing the hem of the garment. Zach knew better than to press the issue if he wanted to keep his head resting comfortably between his shoulders.

"My nurse told me you brought the baby's father with you for the ultrasound, Arielle," a woman wearing a white lab coat announced when she walked into the room. Closing the door behind her, she smiled and stuck out her hand. "Good afternoon, I'm Dr. Jensen."

He shook her hand. "Zach Forsythe."

"Nice to meet you, Zach." She walked to the other side of the examining table and, looking down at Arielle's rounded stomach, shook her head. "My goodness, I think you've blossomed even more since last week at your regular appointment." Gathering an instrument that looked a lot like a microphone, she reached for a tube of clear gel. "If either of you have any questions during the procedure, please don't hesitate to speak up. I like for the dad to be just as involved as the mom throughout the pregnancy and delivery."

There was something about Dr. Jensen that instilled confidence and he could understand why Arielle had chosen the woman to deliver their baby. "At the moment, I can't think of anything. But I'm betting that changes, real quick," he said, smiling.

Dr. Jensen nodded and, turning her attention to Arielle, asked, "How have you been feeling? Anything we need to address before we get started?"

Zach watched Arielle shake her head as she lifted her maternity top, then hooked her thumbs in the elastic waistband of her slacks and lowered them below her slightly rounded stomach. "I still have to make sure I eat something when my stomach gets empty, but otherwise, I've felt pretty good."

"That's not all that unusual," the doctor assured her, squeezing a generous amount of the gel onto Arielle's stomach. She held the instrument poised over the clear blob. "Are you both ready to see your little one for the first time?"

"Y-yes," Arielle answered, her voice reflecting an anticipation as strong as his own.

"Will we be able to find out whether to decorate the nursery in pink or blue?" Zach asked.

The doctor smiled. "Probably not this time, but it won't be too much longer."

Nodding, Zach reached out and took Arielle's hand in his. When she gripped his hand tightly, he knew she appreciated his support.

"Ready whenever you are," he said, his gaze never wavering from Arielle.

When the doctor began moving the scope around Arielle's stomach, a fuzzy, twitching image immediately popped up on the monitor. Zach wondered what the hell he was supposed to be looking at. But the more Dr. Jensen moved the wand around, he noticed what might possibly be an arm or a leg.

The woman pointed to the screen. "See, there's your baby's head and back." She moved the instrument to the other side of Arielle's stomach. "Let's see if we can detect the sex from this angle." Her sudden frown caused Zach's heart to grind to a halt. "What's this?" she asked, adding to his anxiety. "It certainly explains why you're a bit larger than normal."

"I-Is something wrong?" Arielle murmured, sounding as if she might burst into tears.

Zach lightly squeezed her hand in an effort to lend her every ounce of strength he possessed. "I'm sure everything is fine, darlin'."

"Oh, there's nothing wrong," Dr. Jensen confirmed, turning to them with a wide grin. "I'm just wondering how you will keep up with two toddlers when they start walking."

"Two?" Arielle echoed, her eyes round with shock.

"Twins?" Zach croaked at the same time.

Dr. Jensen laughed as she pushed the print button on the side of the monitor. "The way the first baby was lying, I couldn't see the second one until I changed sides. But yes, you're definitely having twins."

At that moment, Zach couldn't have forced words past the lump clogging his throat if his life depended on it. He was not only going to have a child, he was going to have two. Unbelievable.

His chest felt as if it had swelled to twice its normal size. Words couldn't express what he was feeling, and, leaning down, he covered Arielle's parted lips with his for a brief but intense kiss.

"Do twins run in either of your families?" the doctor inquired as she wiped the excess gel from Arielle's stomach with a handful of tissues. She didn't comment that both of them were breathing as if they'd run a marathon by the time he lifted his head and Zach figured the woman was used to displays of emotion after learning the results of an ultrasound.

Clearly in a state of shock, Arielle stared at him as if urging him to answer Dr. Jensen's question. "Arielle has twin brothers," he responded, finally getting his vocal cords to work. "But to my knowledge there aren't any twins in my family."

The doctor tilted her head. "Well, there are now." She picked up Arielle's chart and made a notation. "I see neither of you anticipated a multiple birth."

"I...uh, suppose I knew it was a possibility, but..." Looking utterly stunned, Arielle's voice trailed off as she rearranged her clothes and sat up on the side of the exam table.

"Are both of the babies okay?" Zach thought to ask as his brain began to function again.

"Actually, everything looks very good." Dr. Jensen smiled. "Both fetuses appear to be a good size and I'd estimate the right weight for this stage of their development."

Helping Arielle down from the table, he asked the doctor, "Is there anything special that we should or shouldn't be doing?"

Dr. Jensen shook her head. "As long as you feel like it, Arielle, there's no reason you can't enjoy your normal activities, including sexual relations."

He caught Arielle's warning glare and wisely

refrained from commenting on the doctor's stamp of approval for their making love. But he didn't even try to stop his wide grin.

Dr. Jensen started for the door. "I'll see you in three weeks for your regular appointment and of course, if you have any problems or questions before then, don't hesitate to give me a call."

Zach and Arielle walked together down the hall to the elevator. They remained silent on the ride to the lobby and he figured she was coming to terms with the idea of having twins.

"How long will it take you to pack an overnight bag?" he asked as he helped her into the back of his limousine.

"Why would I need to pack?" she questioned, when he slid into the seat beside her.

"Because I'm moving you into my place." It was more important now than ever that Arielle took good care of herself.

"No, you're not." She shook her head. "I'm going to go home, change into a circus tent and call my brothers to tell them the news about the baby… babies." She suddenly emitted a nervous giggle. "Oh my God, I'm having twins."

"Yes, you are, darlin'." Giving instructions to his driver to take them to her apartment, he put his arm around her shoulders. He could tell she was still overwhelmed by the news and now wasn't a good time to press her on the issue of moving in with him.

"We'll spend the night at your apartment and move you into my home tomorrow morning."

"No, we won't. You're going to drop me off at my place and then go home to yours while I call my brothers. End of discussion." She sounded quite adamant, but he noticed that she wasn't scooting away from him, was allowing him to hold her close to his side.

"Sorry, darlin', but I told you that I would be with you every step of the way." He kissed the top of her head. "And that means from here on out, we'll be doing whatever needs to be done together. Everything from doctor appointments to breaking the news to your brothers that we're going to have twins."

By the time they arrived at her apartment, the fact that she was going to be the mother of twins had sunk in and she was regaining some perspective. "I think it might be better if I'm the one to break the news to my brothers." Removing her cardigan sweater, she walked over to hang it in the entryway closet, hoping Zach would take the hint that she needed a little time alone. "While I make the call from my bedroom, please make yourself comfortable. I'll only be a few minutes." She'd given up on him going home.

"I'd rather you stay right here and make the call on the speakerphone." He shrugged out of his suit coat, loosened his tie and released the button at the neck of his white oxford cloth shirt, then walked over to place his hands on her shoulders. "I promise I'll keep quiet as long as they don't give you too much flak." He used his index finger to raise her chin until their gazes met. "But I reserve the right to break my silence at any time if I think they're upsetting you."

Where was all this concern almost four months ago when she discovered he was gone and cried for days feeling like such a fool? Or a few weeks later when she realized she was pregnant with no way of contacting her baby's father?

The heat from his hands permeated her shirt and sent an excited little shiver up her spine. Trying to ignore the way his touch made her feel, she advised, "I'm a big girl, Zach. I can take care of myself."

"You don't have to, Arielle. Not anymore." Her breath caught when he took her in his arms, but it was the look on his handsome face that sent her heart racing. "From here on out, that's my job. And believe me, I have every intention of taking it very seriously. I give you my word that I'll do everything in my power to protect you and our babies. And if I have to, I'll have no problem taking on both of your brothers to keep that promise."

She could have asked him who was going to protect her from him, but he chose that moment to lower his head and cover her mouth with a kiss so poignant it brought tears to her eyes. At first, it seemed just a kiss to seal his vow to take care of her and their babies, but as his lips moved over hers, it quickly evolved into so much more.

As Zach tasted and teased, she tried her best to suppress her reaction to him. She started to push against his chest, but just like the first night at his ranch, her will to resist evaporated like morning mist on a hot summer day and she melted against him.

She briefly wondered how she could succumb to his charm after all that had happened. But as he parted her lips with his tongue and began a tender exploration, she quickly forgot the past and lost herself to the mastery of his caress.

Heat coursed through her at the speed of light as he coaxed and demanded that she respond, drawing her into his sensual web. A tingling sensation spread throughout her entire body as he slowly moved his hands down her back to the tail of her oversize shirt.

He slipped his hands beneath the gauzy lavender fabric, then up along her ribs to cup her breasts. She knew she should call a halt to things right away and regain her senses. Nothing had changed between them. She still wouldn't complicate matters by agreeing to get married, or moving into his home. But when Zach rubbed her overly sensitive nipples through the satin and lace of her bra, all rational thought deserted her and she leaned into his embrace.

"I think before this goes any further, we'd better make that call to your brothers," Zach said, nibbling tiny kisses along her jaw to the hollow just beneath her ear. "Otherwise, there's no telling when we'll get around to it."

He continued to tease her with his thumbs. When she realized what he'd said, her cheeks heated and she started to back away from his electrifying touch. But to her dismay, he slipped his hands from her breasts and around to her back to hold her to him.

"We'll pick up where we left off after we make the call," he whispered, sending a wave of goose bumps sliding over her body.

She shook her head. "That wouldn't…be a…good idea."

"Sure it would, darlin'." He nuzzled his cheek against her hair then took a step back. "Now, why don't we make this a conference call and tell them at the same time?"

Still feeling a bit lightheaded from Zach's drugging kiss, Arielle nodded and, dialing Jake's number first, put him on hold while she called Luke. When she had both of her brothers on the line, she switched the phone to speaker, sank down onto the couch beside Zach and took a deep breath.

"I have some news to share and I decided to tell you both at the same time."

"Will this explain why you cry every time I've talked to you for the past few months?" Jake asked, sounding uncharacteristically serious.

"And the reason you've avoided talking to me?" Luke added, his tone stern.

"I'm sorry, Luke," she apologized, feeling guilty. She'd known how concerned her brothers were, but she wasn't sure how to tell them that she was in the same predicament as their mother all those years ago. "You know how much I love both of you. I just had some things that I needed to work out."

"You know we'd have done everything in our power to help," Jake reminded her.

From the corner of her eye, she noticed Zach nodding his approval, feeling the same way about his own sister. "I know you would have, but this was something I had to work through on my own."

"So you've done that and you are ready to tell us what's been going on?" The more serious of the two men, Luke never wasted time getting to the heart of the matter.

"Yeah, don't keep us in suspense," Jake urged.

Taking another deep breath, she asked, "How do you feel about being uncles to twins in about six months?"

The silence that followed proved that this was not what her brothers had expected.

"I know this comes as a—"

The first to recover, Jake interrupted her. "You're pregnant…"

"With twins," Luke finished, sounding more formidable than she'd heard in a long time.

"Who's the father?" Jake demanded.

"And how do we contact him?" Luke asked, sounding just as determined as his twin.

"Yeah, we'd like to have a little talk with the bastard," Jake spat, going into "big brother" mode.

Before she could answer, Zach took her hand in his and gave it a gentle squeeze of support. "I'm right here with your sister. The name's Zach Forsythe. Arielle and I are getting married as soon as I get the arrangements made."

"No, we're not," she contradicted, glaring at Zach. She tried to pull her hand from his, but Zach held it firmly in his much larger one. "I told you that marriage isn't required to have a child."

"And as I have told *you*, it is for me," he vowed stubbornly.

"Sounds to me like things aren't completely settled after all," Luke spoke up.

"Don't do anything until I get there, Arielle," Jake advised quickly. "And for God's sake, don't sign any legal documents until I look at them." The sudden sound of pages being shuffled came across the line and she knew her brother was checking his schedule. "I have a couple of discoveries to get through and a court date scheduled for Friday, but I'll be there first thing Saturday morning."

"Good idea," Luke agreed. "Haley and I will be there, too. And it might not be a bad idea for you to draw up a prenuptial agreement and bring it with you, Jake."

"I was thinking the same thing, bro," Jake acknowledged.

"None of this is necessary," Arielle insisted, wondering how something as simple as a phone call to tell her brothers she was pregnant had gotten so out of hand. "I'm not getting married and even if I was, I'm perfectly capable of making my own decisions."

"I think it's great you are coming to Dallas," Zach interjected as if she hadn't said a word. "I'd like to meet my future brothers-in-law. After all, we'll be family soon." He gave her an *I told you so* grin as he added, "And since I have more than enough room, I'd like to invite everyone to stay at my place." He gave her brothers his cell-phone number. "Let me know your arrival times and I'll have my driver pick you up at the airport."

"Sounds like an excellent plan," Luke affirmed as if everything was settled. "And in the meantime, give him a chance, Arielle. Seems he wants to do the right thing."

"We'll see you on Saturday, little sister," Jake added before he and Luke both hung up, ending the call.

"That went pretty well," Zach announced, sitting back and looking so darned satisfied with himself she wanted to bop him. "I think your brothers and I are going to get along just fine."

She stood up to glare down at him. "At the moment, I'd like to take all three of you and clunk your heads together."

He looked taken aback. "Why? What did we do?"

"You're all just alike. There wasn't one of you who paid the least bit of attention to what *I* want." She shook her head. "I told them I had everything under control. I even told them that I had no intention of marrying you. But did they listen? No. They'll be here on Saturday in full 'big brother' mode, ready to tell me what they think is best and expect me to go along with it." She wiped at the tears of frustration threatening to spill down her cheeks. "And you, you're too stubborn to give up on your harebrained notion that we *have* to get married."

"You're getting way too upset about this, Arielle," he noted, rising to his feet.

When he reached for her, she shook her head and, backing away, pointed toward the hall. "I'm going into my bedroom to lie down and try to forget that phone call ever happened. When I get up, I expect you to be gone. Please lock the door when you leave."

Without waiting for him to respond, she spun around and marched into her bedroom, slamming the door as hard as she could. She should have known better than to call while Zach was with her, she thought as she kicked off her shoes and stretched out on her bed. He and her brothers were so much alike it was uncanny. All three were highly successful self-made men with take-charge personalities and it really shouldn't have surprised her that they'd controlled the entire conversation.

Jake and Luke, she could understand. It had been an overwhelming responsibility for two twenty-year-old young men to finish raising their ten-year-old sister. And after all those years of making every decision for her, it had to be hard for them to admit that she'd grown up and could take control of her own life.

But Zach was an entirely different story. His insistence that they get married was just plain ludicrous. He didn't love her and the way he'd left her behind in Aspen, it was a safe bet that he'd grown tired of her, just the way her father had grown tired of her mother all those years ago.

She turned on her side and hugged one of her pillows. Three and a half months ago, she'd wanted Zach to ask her to be his bride. And if circumstances were different now, nothing could stop her from committing herself to him for the rest of her life. But it was his desire to be a full-time father that was fueling his demand, not the fact that he cared about her. And that wasn't enough.

A fresh wave of tears coursed down her cheeks. Closing her eyes, she vowed to remain true to her heart. For the first time in her life, she understood why her mother had fallen into Owen Larson's web of deceit the second time. But she was going to be wiser, stronger, than her mother had been.

Unfortunately, Zach was a powerful force and one she was finding almost impossible to resist. Each time he touched her, held her, kissed her, she lost every ounce of sense she possessed. And it was becoming increasingly more difficult not to fall hopelessly in love with him all over again.

* * *

Turning on the television but lowering the volume, Zach propped his feet on the coffee table and settled back to wait for Arielle to wake up from her nap. The phone call with her brothers had gone well for him, but she'd become upset with all of them and he intended to put a stop to it right away.

It had occurred to him after Arielle stormed into her bedroom that he should adjust his tactics with her. In Aspen, things between them had progressed way too fast and had actually been based on deception. Then, before he could tell her who he really was, he'd returned to Dallas because of Lana's accident and in the weeks that followed, had no time to follow up and explain. And when he finally did have the time, it had already been so long that he'd figured it was too late to set things straight with her. But he'd been wrong. They had a set of twins on the way and that changed everything.

He thought about the obstacles he'd have to overcome to get Arielle to agree to marry him. He'd hurt her deeply with his unexplained disappearance and the use of his alias had destroyed any trust she'd had in him. That was definitely something they would straighten out. Pressing her to get married before he explained why he'd left that morning in Aspen would be a study in futility. But he did have a fairly good idea how to get her in a more receptive mood to hear him out and he had every intention of putting his theory into action immediately.

Taking his cell from the clip on his belt, he dialed his home number and when his housekeeper answered, had her put him through to the kitchen. Telling his cook what he wanted, he instructed her to have his driver bring the special dinner over to Arielle's apartment as soon as it was ready.

Given her recent appetite, a scrumptious meal was definitely going to make points with her and hopefully put her in the mood to listen to his explanation. Satisfied with his plan, he waited for Arielle to wake, certain they'd soon be a step or two closer to a weekend wedding.

Five

She awoke to the tantalizing aroma of food. Getting out of bed, Arielle walked into her bathroom and washed the evidence of tears from her face. Zach obviously hadn't paid a bit of attention to her request for him to leave, but given his bullheaded tenacity, she really hadn't expected him to. And although she was frustrated beyond words by his dogged determination that they marry, she wasn't about to send him away until she'd sampled some of whatever smelled absolutely wonderful.

When she walked into the dining area, Zach had just lit the wicks on a couple of long white tapers in beautiful silver candlesticks. "Hey there, sleepyhead.

I was just about to wake you," he revealed, giving her a smile that warmed her all over. "How was your nap? Did you sleep well?"

"As far as naps go, it was okay," she said.

She was supposed to be angry with him, but that emotion was decreasing with each passing second. He looked so darned handsome in the glow of the candlelight and the way he'd rolled up the sleeves of his dress shirt was just plain sexy.

She swallowed hard. Her pregnancy hormones had to be completely out of whack if just the sight of his tanned forearms was enough to send her temperature soaring.

Deciding to concentrate on something besides the sexiest man she'd ever known, she pointed to the two elegant place settings filled with delicious-looking food. "What is all this?"

He pulled out one of the chairs for her. "I thought you might need something to eat when you woke up."

"I appreciate your thoughtfulness, but something to eat is soup or a sandwich," she pointed out, sitting in the chair he held. "This is a feast."

He shrugged as he lowered himself into the chair at the head of the table. "A light meal is good once in a while, but it doesn't provide enough of the vitamins and minerals you and the babies need to stay healthy."

"When did you become a nutritionist?" she quipped, picking up her napkin to place it on her lap.

"Actually, I was relying more on common sense

than knowledge," he confessed, grinning. "But it sounded pretty impressive, don't you think?"

"Yes, but you'd better be careful." She couldn't help but laugh at his smug expression. "Don't break your arm patting yourself on the back for being so clever."

The easy camaraderie continued throughout the most sinfully delicious meal she'd had in a long time. By the time they finished dessert, Arielle felt positively stuffed. "The chocolate mousse was scrumptious and, hands down, the best I've ever tasted."

Zach nodded. "I'm convinced that Maria Lopez is, without question, the best cook in the whole state of Texas."

"After that meal, she certainly has my vote," Arielle agreed, rising to her feet.

When she started to take their plates, he caught her hand in his and pulled her down to sit on his lap. "I'll take care of clearing the dishes in a few minutes."

"But—"

"Arielle, we need to talk about Aspen."

"Zach, I—"

"I've tried to tell you before and you haven't wanted to hear it, but this time, I'm not taking no for an answer," he interrupted, determined to have his say. "I'm going to tell you exactly what happened—from using another name to the reason I left that morning."

Whether she liked what he had to say or not, the time had come to hear him out. If she didn't, they'd never work out an amicable agreement to share the raising of their children.

"All right," she concurred cautiously. "I'm listening."

She felt his chest rise and fall against her side as he took a deep breath. "First of all, it's a habit of mine to use another name when I check into one of my resorts to observe how my employees interact with our guests."

"And no one has figured out who you are?" she ventured, unable to believe he'd maintained his anonymity. "Surely there are people at your hotels who have met and recognize you."

He nodded. "Of course there are. But besides arranging my visits while the resort manager is on vacation or away for a training seminar, my hotels are large enough that I can avoid being recognized by posing as—"

"Tom Zacharias, skiing enthusiast," she interjected, beginning to understand.

"That's right, darlin'. When I check in as someone else, I'm treated like any other guest." He shrugged. "And you'd be amazed at how much more I learn about guest services, maintenance and customer satisfaction than if I had made an announced visit."

"I would assume everyone would be on their best behavior if they knew who you were."

"And I wouldn't know a damned thing about the areas that need improvement."

What he said made sense, but that didn't explain why he couldn't have told her who he was. "But what about me, Zach? Why couldn't you have been honest with me about your real identity? Or do you also make a habit of having a fling with one of your female guests every time you visit one of your resorts?"

"No, Arielle, I don't." He leaned back until their gazes met. "Until you, I had never even asked another guest out to dinner."

She could tell by the light in his dark green eyes that he was telling the truth. "What made me different?"

"Besides being the sexiest, most beautiful woman on the mountain, you were funny, intelligent and when you found yourself on the expert run instead of the beginner slope, you were so damned determined to get yourself out of a bad situation, I couldn't resist." His easy smile warmed her. "When I came across you making your way down that section of the Silver Queen run, you were scared to death, but you weren't about to throw up your hands and wait for someone to find you. You had the courage to get yourself down the mountain. I admired that, darlin'."

"All right, but that doesn't explain why you didn't tell me who you really were sometime later during the week," she countered, refusing to let him off that easily.

"You're right, Arielle. I should have told you my real name." He touched her cheek with his index finger. "But you took me by surprise, darlin'. I wasn't expecting you or how fast things developed between us." His expression turned serious. "And the reason I left that morning without waking you or leaving a note was because of an emergency about my sister. If I had been thinking clearly, I swear I'd have never left without at least telling you goodbye."

"What happened?" She hadn't considered that he'd been called away because of an emergency.

"Lana was almost killed in a head-on car crash. All I could think about was getting back to Dallas to see her."

"Oh my God, Zach. Is she all right?" He'd mentioned his sister several times, but Arielle couldn't remember him speaking about her in the present tense.

"She's doing well now, but for several days after the accident, the doctors weren't sure she would pull through." He took a deep breath. "It's been a long, hard recovery for her and she's just recently started walking again."

Without a moment's hesitation, she wrapped her arms around him. She couldn't even imagine how frightening the ordeal had to have been for him. If something like that had happened to one of her brothers and she thought there was a possibility she might lose one of them, she doubted that she would have had the presence of mind to do any differently.

"And for the record, I thought about contacting you after I knew Lana was out of danger. But so much time had passed, I decided it was best just to leave things the way they were because you probably wouldn't want to hear from me, anyway," he explained, his strong arms tightening around her. "I know that's a poor excuse, darlin'. No matter how long it had been, I owed it to you to pick up the phone and let you know what happened."

"The accident was the upheaval in your nephew's life that you referred to Friday morning, wasn't it?" she concluded with sudden insight.

Zach nodded. "Derek really is a good kid. He's just had a hard time understanding what was going on and why Lana couldn't give him the attention he's used to getting from her."

"And it resulted in behavior problems," she guessed, having seen children react like that when something upsetting happened in their young lives.

Zach squeezed her slightly. "But now that he and Lana have moved back into her condo and things have settled down, he'll do a lot better."

"I'm sure he will." She smiled. "Children always do better in a familiar environment. It gives them a sense of much-needed security."

"And are you feeling a little more secure about me now?" he asked, nuzzling the side of her neck.

She fully understood why he'd left, and, to a point, why he hadn't contacted her. As time passed, it was always easier to let things be. But even if he had called her, it would only have been to explain his disappearance, not because he wanted to rekindle the relationship they'd shared in Aspen.

"Give it some thought, darlin'," he whispered. "Why don't you go into the living room and put your feet up."

Heat streaked straight through her and she had to remind herself to breathe when he brushed her lips with his. "You arranged for the meal. The least I can do is clear the table."

He shook his head. "I told you, I fully intend to take care of you and our babies and that includes making sure you don't overdo things."

"I don't think there's any danger of doing more than I should," she declared, feeling more breathless with each passing second. "I'd have to actually *do* something before I could overdo it."

"Hey, you're going to be the mother of twins in a few months. Take it easy while you can." His lips skimmed the side of her neck, sending shivers throughout her body. "Besides, I like pampering you."

A honeyed warmth began to flow through her veins and she had to remind herself that although he'd explained what happened, she wasn't entirely certain she could trust him not to disappear all over again. Their current circumstances were a direct result of her falling for Zach's line of sensuous persuasion once before and doing so again could very well be disastrous for her. But heaven help her, it certainly was tempting.

"I think I'll take you up on that offer," she decided suddenly, getting to her feet.

"I'll join you in a few minutes." He walked into

the kitchen and when he returned, he held a small cardboard box. As she watched, he started placing their plates, silverware and glasses inside.

"Aren't you going to put them in the dishwasher?" she chided, frowning.

He shook his head as he grabbed his cell phone and dialed a number. "Not when I have a driver waiting outside to take these back to my place."

"Oh, good Lord," she began, rolling her eyes as she walked over to the sitting area of the room. "Don't tell me you're going to make the poor man drive all the way to your house, then come back to get you later."

"Nope." He paused long enough to tell the chauffeur to come to the door for the box, then, ending the call, he smiled. "Remember, I told you we'd spend the night here, then go to my place tomorrow before we go in to work."

Why wasn't she surprised that he hadn't given up on that?

"After that wonderful meal, I really don't feel like arguing with you, Zach," she conceded, lowering herself onto the couch.

"Then don't." When the doorbell rang, he handed the box of dishes to his driver, closed and locked the door, then walked over to where she sat on the couch. "Let's just watch a movie and relax. It's been a big day and I think we could both use a little downtime, don't you?"

"That's about the first thing you've said today that

I agree with." She started to settle against the cushions, but he took her hand and pulled her back to her feet. "Now what?"

Before she could stop him, he sat in the corner of the couch, stretched out one long leg against the back cushions, then pulled her down to sit between his thighs. "Lean back against my chest and relax, darlin'," he ordered, kissing the back of her neck.

The sensations he evoked in her rendered her utterly speechless and without a thought to the danger he posed to her heart, she did as he instructed. The feel of his warm, solid chest against her back caused her heart to beat double-time, but when he wrapped her in his arms and splayed his hands on her stomach, her heart felt as if it might jump right out of her chest.

"What are you trying to do to me, Zach?" She didn't for a single minute believe that relaxation was all he had on his mind.

His hands glided over her stomach in a soothing manner. "I'm doing what I told you I was going to do—take care of you and make sure you take the time to unwind."

She shook her head. "You know what I mean."

He kissed her shoulder and the column of her neck. "Hopefully, I'm reminding you of how good we were together and how good we can be again."

"Zach, this isn't going to change my mind about—"

"Hush, darlin'." He picked up the remote control from the end table and turned on the DVD player. "We can talk about all of that later. Let's watch the movie."

As the opening credits of the romantic comedy he'd selected appeared on her television screen, Arielle tried to concentrate on watching the show and forget about the man holding her so snugly. But the feel of his strength surrounding her and the sexy scent of his woodsy aftershave assailing her senses made it hard to think of anything else.

The way he gently massaged her stomach, she could almost believe he was trying to release the tension that had built up over the day. But she'd learned the hard way not to allow his tender touch and charming words to cloud her judgment. And she wasn't naive enough to think his consideration had anything whatsoever to do with her. Everything he'd done, everything he'd said, had been for the welfare of the babies. Even his insistence that they had to get married was because she was pregnant, not because he cared deeply for her.

But her disturbing introspection was suddenly cut short at the feel of Zach's rapidly hardening body pressing insistently against her backside. The longing that followed the realization that he'd become aroused was staggering and had her struggling to sit up.

"I think it would be a good idea if I changed positions."

Holding her firmly against him, he nuzzled the side of her neck. "Are you comfortable, Arielle?"

Shivers of desire made it difficult to form a rational thought, let alone an answer. "Y-yes…I mean, no."

His deep chuckle vibrated against her back. "Do you want to know what I think?"

"Not really." She didn't need for him to point out the obvious.

"I'm fairly certain that my becoming hard is reminding you of how good it felt to have me inside you," he whispered. "And I'm betting that you're disturbed that you're as turned on as I am."

The feel of his warm breath feathering over her skin and the memory of the sultry passion they'd shared in Aspen had her catching her breath. "Not even close," she lied.

He had the audacity to laugh out loud. "Whatever you say, darlin'. Now settle back and enjoy the movie."

That was going to be easier said than done with his hard body touching every part of her back. Eventually she did become intrigued by the story line and before she knew it, the film had ended.

"The meal was beyond delicious and the show was very entertaining, but I'm exhausted," she recapped, yawning as she sat up. Turning to face him, she added, "I think it's time you called your driver to take you home."

"I gave Mike the rest of the night off," Zach reported, stretching his arms.

"Then I suggest you call a taxi."

He shook his head. "I don't use public transportation."

"There's a first time for everything, Mr. Forsythe. Now go home."

"Why would I want to do that, darlin'?" He lazily stroked her shoulders. "We're staying here tonight and going to my place tomorrow."

"You're unbelievable." She stared at him for several long seconds. Then, needing to put distance between them, got to her feet. "This apartment only has one bedroom and I'm not sharing."

He rose to stand in front of her. "I'll be fine right here on the couch."

Reaching out, he took her into his arms and before she could stop him, he lowered his head to press his lips to hers. A jolt of longing so intense it caused her head to spin surged through her veins and she had to put her arms around him to keep her suddenly rubbery knees from giving way.

Caressing her mouth with his, he quickly had her conforming to his demand to deepen the kiss. She reveled in the game of advance and retreat that followed. He seemed to be challenging her to explore him as he explored her and without hesitation, Arielle complied.

As she stroked his tongue with hers, she delighted in his deep shuddering groan and the immediate tightening of his embrace. Feminine power filled her, and if she hadn't been lost in the moment, she might have been shocked by her own boldness.

As the passion within her began to build, so did the realization that she was about to be swept up into Zach's sensual trap again. She wasn't stupid. The delicious candlelight dinner, the romantic movie and his refusal to go back to his own place meant he was trying a different tactic in his bid to get her to marry him. No matter how wonderful it felt to be in his arms again, to have him kiss her and know that he wanted her, she couldn't let down her guard. She'd barely survived his leaving her once; she'd never get through it if he left her a second time.

Breaking the kiss, she stepped back on wobbly legs. "Goodbye, Zach."

His expression gave nothing away as he paused for a moment before leading her by the hand to her bedroom door. "Good night, darlin'," he murmured, lightly brushing her lips with his. "If you need me, I'll be right out there on the couch."

As she watched him walk down the hall, she wondered what she was supposed to do now. She wouldn't be able to get a wink of sleep just knowing he was on her couch. Possibly in his boxer shorts. Possibly wearing nothing at all.

"Oh, dear Lord."

Hurrying into her bedroom, she closed the door then leaned back against it. She was in deep, deep trouble and it was going to be a very long night if just the thought of Zach being nude could send fire streaking through her veins and cause her pulse to pound so hard she could feel it in every cell of her body.

Zach stared at the ceiling of Arielle's living room long after he heard her close her bedroom door. If he wasn't so damned uncomfortable, the situation would be downright laughable. Hell, he'd single-handedly built and maintained a thriving empire of luxury resorts. He had several billion dollars in assets. He had a mansion with eight bedrooms, all with very comfortable king-size beds. And here he was, on a couch that was too short, his head resting on a throw pillow hard as a chunk of concrete and covered up with a stadium blanket that needed three more feet.

But other than his back was going to kill him in the morning and he was in one room while Arielle was in another, the evening had gone rather well. After her nap, he'd finally explained about Aspen, hadn't pushed the marriage issue and his body let her know in no uncertain terms how he still desired her as much now as he had then.

Now he had to convince her that getting married was in the best interest of their babies and by the time her brothers and sister-in-law arrived on Saturday, everything should be set for a weekend wedding. Granted it would be a small, family-only affair, since they didn't have time to make a lot of arrangements.

But later, if Arielle wanted something larger, they could plan a lavish wedding and reception.

Extremely satisfied with the way he was handling everything, he'd just drifted off to sleep when a woman's keening wail caused the hair on the back of his neck to stand straight up and had him bolting off the couch in less than a heartbeat. His heart hammered hard against his ribs as he made his way across the dark room and when he stubbed his toe on the armchair, he muttered a curse that would have had Mattie washing his mouth out with soap when he'd been younger. But ignoring the throbbing pain that followed, he rushed down the hall and flung open Arielle's bedroom door.

Relieved to see there wasn't someone in the room trying to hurt her, he then realized she was writhing under the duvet as if in extreme discomfort. Rushing to her, he turned the bedside light on, pushed the covers away and noticed she was desperately trying to rub her left calf.

"Arielle, what's wrong?"

"L-leg…cramp," she moaned, her normally melodic voice tight with pain.

Kneeling on the bed, he brushed her hands aside and immediately massaged her left calf as he loosened up the muscle. "Hang on, darlin'. It should start feeling better in just a minute or two."

In a matter of seconds, her expression told him the

pain was lessening. Now sitting beside her, he continued to gently rub her calf.

"That feels…much better," she admitted. "Thank you."

During the ordeal with the muscle cramp, her thin yellow gown had ridden up well above her knees and he noticed that although her stomach had rounded slightly from being pregnant, the rest of her body was every bit as shapely as in Aspen. Just the memory of having her long slender legs wrapped around him as they made love caused his body to harden so fast, it left him feeling light-headed and made him damned glad that he had on a pair of loose boxers.

Without a thought to the damage he might do to his well-crafted plan not to push Arielle too far, Zach stretched out beside her. Then, gathering her to him, he pulled the sheet over them.

"What do you think you're doing?" she demanded, her eyes wide.

He wasn't entirely sure why, but he did know it felt completely right. "The couch is too short. Besides, you might have another leg cramp and I'd rather not risk breaking my neck getting to you the next time."

"That's about the most contrived excuse I think I've ever heard," she protested, turning on her side to face him. At least she was still talking to him and not ordering him out of the room.

He laughed. "It was pretty weak, wasn't it?"

Nodding, she asked, "Seriously, what are you doing in my bed and why?"

"I wasn't exaggerating about the couch. It's about a foot and a half too short to be comfortable for a man of my height."

"I'm sure your own bed is long enough to accommodate you. You could go home."

"No, I couldn't." He brushed a strand of silky auburn hair from her cheek. "I told you I'd be here for you, no matter what. And I'll keep that promise or die trying." He paused, then, deciding to lay it on the line, added, "And the biggest reason I'm in bed with you is because I want to hold you while you sleep and wake up with you in my arms."

He could tell by the look on her pretty face that she had serious doubts about his motives. "Zach, I—"

"I'm not going to lie to you, darlin'. I want to make love to you. I want to be buried so deep inside you that you forget where you end and I begin." He kissed the tip of her nose. "But I give you my word, I'm not going to press you for more than you're ready to give. When the time is right, we'll know and nothing will stop me from giving you so much pleasure that we both collapse from exhaustion."

She finally nodded. "I truly appreciate your consideration. Unfortunately, I don't trust myself any more than I trust you."

"I can understand having a doubt or two about me,

but why can't you trust yourself?" he inquired, enjoying the feel of her soft body against his much harder one.

"My judgment isn't at its best when I'm around you." She closed her eyes, debating with herself about how much she wanted to say. When she opened them, she found him intently watching her face. "I let myself throw caution to the wind with you once before and although I want and love these babies more than life itself, I would have preferred we were…" She stopped for a moment, trying to find the right words. "That things between us had gone a little more conventionally."

He knew exactly what she meant. She'd wanted a relationship that progressed into a commitment before she had become pregnant. But that hadn't happened and there was no way to go back and change things. The way he saw it, they should move forward and make the best of the situation.

"Let's just take it one day at a time and see where it takes us." He slid his hand over her side, then around to her back to pull her closer. "But I'd like for you to promise me that you'll at least give me—give us—a chance. Can you do that, Arielle?"

He could see the uncertainty in the depths of her hazel eyes before she finally spoke. "I'll think about it."

Immense relief washed over him at her concession. If she was willing to give the matter some thought, he was wearing her down and that's all the opening he needed to achieve his ultimate goal.

Giving her a little more encouragement, he covered her mouth with his, and at the first touch, he felt a spark light his lower belly. But when she put her arms around his neck and eagerly accepted his kiss, the spark quickly turned into flames.

As he deepened the kiss, he reached down to lift the hem of her gown. Sliding his hand underneath, he caressed her leg from knee to thigh. Fire immediately streaked through his veins at the feel of her satiny skin beneath his palm and her eager response to his tongue teasing hers.

He slid his hand up her side to the swell of her breast, then took the weight of her in his hand. When he teased the tip with the pad of his thumb, his blood pressure went through the roof at the sound of her soft whimper. But it was the feel of her warm touch when she placed her hand on his bare chest, doing a little exploring of her own, that caused his body to tighten almost painfully.

He wanted her with a fierceness that defied every good intention about waiting until she was ready. And when she moved her hand to his abdomen to trace her finger down toward his navel, he was pretty sure she wanted him just as much. But he had to know for certain.

"Darlin', we've reached a line here and once crossed, there won't be any turning back," he implored, kissing his way to the hollow of her throat. "At least not without a cold shower and a lot of suffering on my part." Raising his head, he caught her gaze with his. "So if this isn't what you want, too, you'd better tell me right now and show me where you keep your bath towels."

Just when he thought she was going to tell him to take that cold shower and go back to the couch, she took a deep breath. "There are a lot things about us that I'm unsure of. But the one thing that hasn't changed is how much I want you."

"Are you…sure, Arielle?" he persisted, finding it hard to draw in his next breath.

"No. But where you're concerned, being certain doesn't seem to matter." The look in her eyes robbed him of air and caused the flames in his belly to burn out of control. "Please make love to me, Zach."

Six

As Zach brought his mouth down to cover hers, Arielle wondered if she'd lost the last traces of her sanity. Not once since their unexpected reunion had he apologized for what had taken place in Aspen. He'd explained using an alias and leaving without telling her goodbye, but hadn't said he was sorry. That didn't change the fact that with one kiss, one touch of his hand on her body, she was completely lost. It had been that way almost four months ago and it was that way now.

Wrapping her arms around him, she briefly considered how she would survive if she found him gone the following morning—or any other morning for that matter. But as he kissed and teased her with such infinite care, she quickly abandoned her disturbing thoughts and gave in to her feelings.

Heat shimmered behind her closed eyes and a tingling excitement skipped over every nerve in her body as he caressed his way to her panties, then eased them down and with her help, took them off. But when he moved to lift her gown out of the way, her heart skipped several beats and she suddenly wished for darkness.

"Zach, would you...please do something for me?" she asked, easing her lips from his.

"What's that...darlin'?" He sounded as if he had as much trouble breathing as she did.

"Would you please turn off the light?"

Leaning back, he propped himself up on one elbow. "If you're worried about what I think of your figure now that you're pregnant, don't." He shoved the sheet to the end of the bed. Then, grasping her nightgown, slid his hands up her sides and along the undersides of her arms, raising them over her head as he went. He lifted her slightly as he whisked her gown away in one smooth motion. His eyes never leaving hers, he eased her back down on the bed. "You've always been beautiful, Arielle."

It wasn't until his survey drifted ever so slowly along the length of her body that she truly believed he meant what he'd said. It almost felt as if he had physically caressed her.

"I was wrong," he amended, gently placing his hand on her tummy. He leaned down to press a kiss just above her navel. When he raised his head to look at her, the light shining in his dark green gaze stole her breath and erased every one of her reservations. "You're more gorgeous today than you were in Aspen and I have no doubt you'll be even more beautiful tomorrow."

Keeping his eyes locked to hers, he got out of bed. Hooking his thumbs in the waistband of his boxer shorts, he slowly lowered them down his long muscular legs. His sculpted physique was every bit as breathtaking as she remembered. As Zach revealed himself to her, her eyes widened when she noticed the strength of his thick arousal rising proudly from the patch of dark hair at his groin.

But it was the heated look he gave her when he got back into bed that rendered her utterly speechless. "I've wanted you from the moment I saw you again," he confessed, gathering her to him.

The feel of hard masculine flesh pressed against her softer feminine skin, the scent of his woodsy cologne and the sound of his harsh breathing sent sparks skipping along every nerve in her body. But when he caressed her back, then traced his hands the length of her spine to cup her bottom and pull her forward, his groan mingled with her moan and she instinctively knew that he was experiencing the same intense pleasure she was.

Heat thrummed through her veins as he covered her mouth with his. When he deepened the kiss, she threaded her fingers through his thick hair and boldly met his tongue with her own. She wanted him to know the degree of passion he instilled in her, the urgent hunger that only he could create and quench.

She felt his body pulse with need and her own body responded with a tightening deep in the most feminine part of her. It had been a long time since she'd been held by him this way and she felt as if she'd finally come home. Never had she felt such intimacy, such safety as she felt in Zack's arms.

He broke their kiss to nibble his way down the base of her throat, past her collarbone, to the slope of her breast. She held him to her as he took the hardened peak into his mouth, and the intensity of sensations coursing through her at the feel of his lips on her body sent a need racing through her entire being so strong it threatened to consume her.

"Please," she whimpered. "It's been…so long."

"Easy, darlin'," he warned as he trailed his hand down her side to her hip, then lower still. "I want you, too. But I want to make sure this is as good for you as I know it's going to be for me."

He parted her then and at the first stroke of his fingers, waves of exquisite delight flowed through her. His intimate touch was driving her absolutely crazy and caused an ache she knew only he could ease.

"I…need…you, Zach," she whispered, surprised

that she formed a coherent thought, let alone words. "Now."

"We're going…to do this…a little differently this time," he said, sounding winded as he sat up.

He lifted her to straddle his lap and held her gaze as he slowly, carefully, lowered her onto him. Arielle felt complete for the first time in months. As her body consumed his, she placed her hands on his wide shoulders and, closing her eyes, melted around him, reveling in the feelings of becoming one with the man who had stolen her heart all those months ago.

"You feel so…damned good," he groaned through gritted teeth.

When he was completely buried within her, he crushed her lips to his. In spite of the problems they had yet to address, she knew for certain she was in danger of falling in love with him.

"We're going to take…this slow," he described when he finally broke the kiss. "And I want you to tell me if you have the slightest bit of discomfort."

She could have told him that being with him again was the most comfort she'd had in the past few months, but the words died in her throat when he placed his hands on her hips and began to guide her in a slow rocking motion against him. Closing her eyes, heat filling every cell of her being, she knew as surely as she knew her own name that she'd never feel even a fraction of the emotions she felt for Zach for any other man.

As they moved together, his lips skimmed over the sensitive skin of her throat, accelerating the delicious tightening in her feminine core. Her mind closed to anything but the urgent need to find completion. She desperately tried to prolong the swirling sensations building inside her, but the hunger he created became a force she couldn't resist and she gave herself up to the power of his lovemaking. Clinging to him, she moaned his name as the hot tide of passion washed over her and she found release. She heard Zach groan, then felt his much larger body go completely still a moment before he found his own shuddering reprieve.

As the intensity subsided and they drifted back to reality, he asked, "Are you all right?"

Arielle sighed contentedly. "That was amazing."

"I couldn't agree more." He eased her down beside him, then collapsed back against the pillow. "But are you all right?"

"I'm wonderful."

"I know the doctor said it would be okay for us to make love, but—"

"Don't worry," she stressed, yawning. She knew he was overly concerned because of the pregnancy. "I'm just fine."

He chuckled as he pulled the sheet over their rapidly cooling bodies. Turning on his side, he then wrapped his arms around her and drew her close. "You do seem a lot more relaxed than when I first walked in here."

"Barged."

"What?"

She yawned again. "You didn't walk in here, you barged your way in."

"Whatever. I don't think you'll have any more problems with muscle cramps tonight." Zach kissed her soft cheek. "Can I ask you to do something else, darlin'?"

"What?"

"Would you take the rest of the week off?"

She looked questioningly at him. "Why would I want to do that?"

"I'd like for us to spend some quality time together, instead of a few hours here and there before or after you go to the school and I head to my office."

In Aspen they'd had an uninterrupted week of getting to know each other and that was exactly what they needed now. He needed to gain her trust.

"I just took over the school," she protested.

"That's true, but you're also the administrator now," he reminded. "You can take off any time you please."

"Can *you* take time away from your business?" she asked pointedly.

He smiled. "Of course. I'm the boss, remember?"

When she nibbled her lower lip, he could tell she was contemplating his request. "If I did take the time off, you'd have to promise me something."

"What's that, darlin'?"

"I'd need your assurance that you wouldn't bring

up the subject of marriage one time during the next four days." She raised her eyebrows. "Do you think you could manage that?"

He'd promise just about anything to get her to agree. Grinning, he nodded. "I'm pretty sure I can, provided you know I haven't given up on that particular issue."

"It never occurred to me that you would, Mr. Forsythe," she commented, hiding another huge yawn behind her hand.

"Good. Now that we have that settled, you need to get some sleep, darlin'."

When he realized that Arielle had already nodded off, Zach smiled as he reached to turn off the bedside lamp. Getting enough sleep was not going to be a problem for Arielle and one less thing he needed to worry about. Unless he missed his guess, Arielle could drift off to sleep anywhere, at any time.

As he lay there contemplating other ways to ensure she was taking good care of herself, he compared the differences between her and his ex-fiancée. Although Gretchen had told him how much she looked forward to having a baby, it hadn't taken long for her to change her tune. Within a few days of learning she was expecting, Gretchen started acting as if she thought eating was the ultimate sin and became obsessed about gaining weight. And that was just the tip of the iceberg when it came to her irrational reaction to the pregnancy.

She had complained that it wasn't a good time to have a baby and she was too tired to get out of bed. Then one morning, she'd surprised him when she got up and began an exhaustive schedule of physical exercises that he'd later realized was a desperate attempt to end the pregnancy. And in less than two weeks of nonstop exertion, sleeping very little and eating less than a bird, she'd succeeded in causing herself to miscarry.

Zach took a deep shuddering breath. He still carried a lot of guilt over not recognizing what Gretchen had been up to and his failure to protect that baby. He should have paid more attention.

But it wasn't going to happen again. The babies Arielle carried were depending on him and Zach wasn't about to let them down.

Fortunately, Arielle seemed to view her pregnancy in an entirely different way than Gretchen. Arielle indulged her hearty appetite, took it in stride that she was going to gain weight and got plenty of rest. And not one time since they'd reunited had he heard her express anything but pure joy over the prospect of becoming a mother.

Kissing the top of her head, he closed his eyes. Although he'd never intended to marry or trust another woman to have his child, he anticipated everything working out this time around. There was every indication that Arielle was not only going to be a good, loving mother to their twins, she was the most exciting, intoxicating woman he'd ever met and having her in his bed every night was definitely going to be a huge benefit of marriage.

Oh, he knew that Arielle wanted the whole package—marriage, children and an enduring love that would see them through whatever life sent their way. But caring that much for a woman put a man at risk of losing his perspective and set him up to make a fool of himself. And that was one chance Zach just wasn't willing to take again. As long as he didn't allow love to enter into the picture, he'd not only be able to keep his children safe, he wouldn't have to worry about losing his pride or his heart.

Satisfied that everything would work out, sleep began to overtake him. Although he couldn't give Arielle the love she wanted, theirs would be a good marriage based on mutual respect and a sincere fondness for each other. As far as he was concerned, that should be enough to make them both happy.

After taking her shower and calling the preschool to arrange for her assistant administrator to take over for the rest of the week, Arielle waited until she heard Zach go into the bathroom and turn on the shower before reaching for the phone again. Deciding it was probably the only time she'd have to call her newfound grandmother without him overhearing the conversation, she sat down on the end of the couch and dialed Emerald, Inc. headquarters in Wichita.

She'd been thinking quite a bit about her unexpected run-in with Zach and the fact that it had been just a little too convenient to be a coincidence. She wasn't sure how, but she'd bet Emerald Larson had had a big hand in the reunion.

Of course, she wouldn't be surprised if it turned out Emerald *had* discovered Zach was the father of her babies. Arielle wasn't quite sure how Emerald had managed it, but when she contacted her and her brothers to tell them who their father was, Emerald had admitted to Arielle that she knew all about her pregnancy and her inability to find the baby's father.

"Good morning, Mrs. Larson's office. How may I help you?" Luther Freemont answered in his usual dry monotone. Over the past few months, she'd spoken with him several times and if Emerald's personal assistant ever put any kind of inflection in his voice, she hadn't heard it.

"Hello, Luther, this is Arielle. I'd like to speak to Emerald for a few minutes. Is she available now or should I call back at another time?"

"Of course she's in for you, Miss Garnier. Please hold while I put your call through to your grandmother's private line."

Within seconds, Emerald came on the line. "Arielle, darling, what a pleasant surprise," she greeted, sounding truly happy to hear from her only granddaughter. "To what do I owe the pleasure of your call?"

"Hello, Emerald." Considering that she'd only recently learned about the woman, Arielle wasn't comfortable calling her "grandmother." But they had formed a friendly, pleasant relationship and Emerald had made it clear that she was always available whenever Arielle needed to talk. "I hope I'm not interrupting anything."

"No, dear. In fact, I was thinking about giving you a call to see how you're doing with Premier Academy. Has the transition of ownership gone smoothly?"

"Oh, yes. It's actually been easier than I anticipated," Arielle confessed, smiling. "The entire staff has been very welcoming and helpful."

"Good." Emerald paused. "And how are *you* doing, darling? I trust everything is going well with your pregnancy?"

"That's one of the reasons I called," Arielle informed. "I had the ultrasound yesterday."

"And what is my next great-grandchild going to be—a boy or a girl?"

"It's still a little too early to tell yet, but how do you feel about having another set of twins in the family?"

There was stunned silence before Emerald spoke again. "Twins? Oh, how marvelous. Have you told Luke and Jake yet? I'm sure they're overjoyed for you."

"I called them yesterday after I returned from the doctor."

"How did they take the news, dear?"

"To say they were shocked is an understatement," Arielle revealed, laughing. Now she could find the humor in her normally verbal brothers being struck speechless. "At first they were both a bit miffed that I'd waited so long to tell them, but they let that go in favor of wanting to know who the father was and how they could find him."

"Oh, I'm sure they were ready to take the young man to task. What did you tell them, dear?"

"I didn't have to tell them anything." Arielle sighed. "I made the mistake of making the call with Zach sitting right beside me. He spoke up and admitted he's the babies' father. He told them we would be getting married this coming weekend."

"You're going to marry Zachary Forsythe, the hotel and resort tycoon?"

"No, I'm not."

"I see." Emerald paused, as if she knew she'd revealed a bit more than she should have. "However did you find him, darling?"

"You tell me," Arielle prodded, knowing for certain that her grandmother had orchestrated their reunion. She hadn't told her Zach's last name.

"Me? Why, I have no idea what you're talking about."

"Oh, I think you do, Emerald. You knew I was pregnant, and it's my guess that your team of private investigators discovered who the father was and where he lived." She sighed. "Why didn't you just tell me instead of buying the preschool his nephew attends and waiting for us to run into each other?"

To her credit, Emerald didn't deny that she'd been behind the setup. "I didn't want to meddle, darling."

"You're absolutely priceless." Arielle rolled her eyes and shook her head. "I've already heard the stories of my half brothers and their spouses being brought together by your matchmaking efforts."

"That worked out quite well." Emerald didn't sound the least bit repentant. "Caleb, Nick and Hunter are all very happy now and have since thanked me for intervening."

"Is that what you're doing?" Arielle asked. "Do you think that bringing Zach and me back together is going to result in another of your heirs finding their soul mate?"

"There is that possibility, Arielle."

Deciding it would be futile to get her grandmother to admit to any wrongdoing, she took a deep breath. "I'm not sure I'll ever be able to trust him."

"Oh, darling, I know it has to be difficult after what happened in Aspen," Emerald concluded, her voice genuinely sympathetic. "But give the man a chance. I'm sure there's a reasonable explanation for his disappearance." She paused before adding, "Your and Zachary's situation is nothing like your mother and father's."

"You knew why he left that morning, too, didn't you?" Arielle was certain Emerald had uncovered everything about Zach, including why he'd deserted her. "Why didn't you tell me?"

"I have to go now, dear," Emerald declared suddenly. "Please give me a call to let me know how everything goes with you and your young man."

Before Arielle said another word, Emerald ended the connection, leaving Arielle frustrated and wondering how much more her grandmother knew about her life. And why was everyone so sure that she should give Zach another chance?

First her brothers and now Emerald had encouraged her to give him the opportunity to prove himself. But they'd forgotten one extremely important factor. They weren't the ones in danger of getting their hearts broken all over again.

"What's wrong, Arielle?" Zach asked, walking into the room wearing nothing but a towel wrapped around his trim waist.

The sight of all that bare, masculine skin stole her breath. Zach was without a shadow of a doubt the sexiest man she'd ever had the pleasure of meeting.

"N-nothing is wrong. Why do you ask?"

"You've got a frown that tells me otherwise, darlin'."

"I was just thinking about something," she mused, hoping he'd let the matter drop.

Zach walked over to stand in front of her and an excited little thrill raced up her spine knowing that he was naked under the towel. "Was there a problem getting someone to cover for you at the school?"

She shook her head as she tried to forget how wonderful his nude body had felt against hers. "No problem at all. Marylou was quite willing to take over in my absence."

"Good." He reached down to hold her hands and pulled her to her feet. "There's something I want us to do today and it doesn't include either of us going anywhere near work."

When he wrapped his arms around her and drew her close, she braced her hands on his bare chest. "What did you have in mind, Zach?"

"You'll see," he promised.

He nipped at her lower lip a moment before he traced it with his tongue. His actions quickly had her feeling as if she might melt into a puddle. But when he dipped his tongue inside her mouth, she couldn't stop her frustrated moan from escaping when he stopped and stepped back.

Taking a deep breath, he shook his head as if trying to clear it. "Go get dressed while I call my driver and have him bring me a change of clothes. Otherwise, we'll end up making love all day and miss out on what I have planned."

While he called his chauffeur, she tried to remember why she had to be cautious. The more he held her, kissed her, touched her, the easier it would be to forget all about the past and the danger he still posed to her heart. But that was something she just couldn't afford to do. No matter how many family members told her to give him a second chance, there were no assurances that their situation wouldn't parallel her parents'.

When Zach's private jet landed at the San Antonio airport, he released his seat belt, then reached over to unfasten Arielle's. He would remind her how much they'd enjoyed each other's company in Aspen. He wanted to make her forget all about the doubts she still had about him.

He stood and held out his hand to help her to her feet. "Are you ready to have some fun?" he asked, grinning.

Giving him a cautious smile, she placed her hand in his. "I've never been to San Antonio."

She gazed up at him and he thought she looked absolutely radiant. She wore a mint-green sundress that complimented her hazel eyes and peaches-and-cream complexion, and she'd drawn her hair into a sleek ponytail, exposing her slender shoulders and delicate neck.

He swallowed hard against his suddenly dry throat. It was going to take everything he had in him not to spend the day in a perpetual state of arousal. All he wanted, all he could think about, was exploring every inch of her satiny skin and spending the day making love with her.

"I thought we'd have lunch along the River Walk and visit a few of the shops, then maybe take a carriage ride," he relayed, bringing his wayward thoughts back under control. He'd considered renting a boat and taking her for a ride down the river, but decided against it. The boat might have swayed and caused her to take a fall. And that was one risk he wasn't willing to take.

"That sounds nice."

He preceded her to the exit of the plane, then reached up to place his hands on her waist to steady her for the descent down the jet's small steps. "After that we'll have to get back to Dallas to change for dinner."

"I was hoping to see the Alamo," she mentioned as they crossed the tarmac to a waiting limo. "I've heard it's a must-see."

Zach nodded. "I wouldn't think of bringing you to San Antonio without taking you to visit the Alamo. That would be downright sacrilegious."

"Is that your Texas pride talking, Mr. Forsythe?" she hinted, her tone sounding a little more relaxed.

Grinning, he gave her a quick kiss that left him hungering for more. But he ignored the urge to ravish her right there in the backseat. The day was all about having fun and keeping things light between them.

"Once a Texan, always a Texan," he finally murmured.

They rode the distance to the River Walk in companionable silence and by the time they reached the quaint outdoor café he'd selected for lunch, a modicum of his control had been restored.

"This is wonderful," she remarked, looking around.

Her eyes were wide with wonder and he was going to enjoy seeing the historic city from her perspective. She pointed to one of the shops down the way. "If we don't go anywhere else, we have to go in there."

Holding one of the chairs for her at a table with a bright blue umbrella, he waited until she was seated, then sat down across from her. When he realized she was talking about a trip to the ice cream shop, he smiled. "What's your favorite flavor?"

"Mint chocolate chip or maybe mocha fudge or chocolate ripple or…"

"I take it you like chocolate." He'd have to remember that.

Her enthusiastic nod caused her ponytail to bob up and down. "Sometimes I like a couple of different flavored scoops in the same cone. That way I don't have to choose just one. What's your favorite?"

"Vanilla."

She gave him a look that clearly stated she thought he might be a little touched in the head. "You've got to be kidding. Of all the wonderful ice cream flavors, you settle for plain old vanilla? Where's your sense of adventure?"

"I get adventurous once in a while," he remarked, thinking of something a lot more enjoyable than ice cream. Shifting to relieve the sudden tightness in his trousers, he added, "Sometimes, I have a few of those candy things sprinkled over the top."

Completely unaware of the direction of his

thoughts, she asked, "Aren't you afraid that's being just a bit too daring?"

Forcing himself to relax, he grinned. "What can I say, darlin'? I like living on the edge."

A smiling waiter chose that moment to walk over and place menus in front of them, effectively putting an end to their discussion of ice cream flavors. After giving the man their order, Zach noticed Arielle's delighted smile at the sight of a boat slowly motoring its way down the river toward them. Reaching across the table, he covered her delicate hand with his. "On our next trip, we'll take a ride the length of the river."

She paused, then treated him to a smile so sweet he could tell she was beginning to let down her guard. "I'd really like that, Zach. Thank you for bringing me here. Everything is so colorful and full of life. It's absolutely wonderful."

After the waiter brought their food, the rest of the time was spent indulging in some of the best Tex-Mex cuisine in the entire state. Zach watched Arielle polish off the last tortilla chip covered in *queso* from the sampler platter then motioned for their check.

"Why don't we get your ice cream, then walk over to El Mercado before we take a carriage ride," he suggested, handing the waiter his credit card. He needed to get her over to the market as soon as possible.

"I'm absolutely stuffed right now," she remarked, resting her hand on her stomach. "Maybe we'd better get the ice cream after everything else."

Once the waiter returned, Zach added a generous tip to the bill, then signed the receipt, slipped his credit card back into his wallet and stood up to hold Arielle's chair. "Are there any other shops you'd like to visit after we walk over to El Mercado?"

"I can't think of any," she indicated, shaking her head. "Just the ice cream shop will make me happy."

She placed her hand in his and in no time they'd made the short walk to the open-air market where the first part of his plan was about to come together.

"I'd like to buy you something to remember today, Arielle. What about something like this?" he asked, stopping in front of a vendor with an array of silver jewelry. He picked up a finely crafted filigree band with a beautiful solitaire setting. "This ring is nice."

Smiling, she nodded. "I love it. It's gorgeous. But you don't have to—"

He placed his index finger to her perfect lips. "I want to."

"It is made of the finest silver and crystal," the vendor lied right on cue.

Zach checked the attached tag, then gave his old friend, Juan Gomez, owner and master designer of one of the finest jewelry stores in Dallas, a conspiratorial wink. "What size do you wear, Arielle?"

"Five, but—"

"It will have to be resized, but that shouldn't be a problem." Turning to Juan, he retrieved his wallet from the hip pocket of his khaki pants. "We'll take it.

And if you can have it sized by the time we return from our carriage ride, I'll pay double the asking price."

"*Si*, senor," Juan confirmed, nodding happily.

"Zach, you can't do that." Her eyes were wide with disbelief—and he didn't think he'd ever seen her look more desirable.

"I most certainly can and will," he declared, giving his old friend several hundred dollars in order to make the transaction believable. He checked his watch, then placed his hand on the small of Arielle's back to usher her along before she realized what was going on. "We'll be back in about an hour. You'll get the rest of your money when the ring is ready."

His plan had worked like a charm and Arielle didn't suspect a thing. She had no way of knowing that the band was actually white gold and that the solitaire wasn't a crystal, but a white diamond of the finest clarity. Nor did she suspect that when they returned, the "vendor" would be packed up and long gone. Juan would be well on his way back to Dallas to size her one-of-a-kind wedding ring and Zach could check off one more item on his list of things to do before their weekend wedding.

Seven

"I still can't believe that vendor took off with your money and the ring," Arielle complained, shaking her head.

When they'd returned for the ring that afternoon, there had been an empty space in the open-air market where the man and his display of jewelry had once been. And even though several hours had passed since they'd returned to Dallas, changed clothes, had a wonderful dinner at an exclusive restaurant and were now on their way to the first resort Zach had built, she was still fuming.

Considering that Zach was a billionaire, it wasn't as important to him as to someone of lesser means.

And the truth was, the several hundred dollars the man had made off with wouldn't have made a dent in her bank account now—not after Emerald's trust fund to do with as she pleased.

But old habits died hard. From the time she'd graduated college, she'd made her own way on her preschool teacher's salary and that meant sometimes living paycheck to paycheck. She'd learned to stretch a dollar as far as it would go and until a few months ago, the amount of money Zach had lost to the nefarious man would have represented a month's rent for her.

"Things like that happen," he observed, shrugging as if he wasn't bothered by the incident. "I'm more concerned that it caused you to lose your appetite for the ice cream cone I promised you."

When the driver stopped the car in front of the Forsythe Resort and Golf Course north of Dallas, she waited for Zach to exit the car, then help her out. "I was too angry to worry about eating ice cream," she responded as he closed the car door.

When they started toward the entrance, he stopped in front of the lobby's ornate double doors. Turning to face her, he placed his hands on her shoulders. "I don't want you giving any more thought to the ring, the money or the man who took off with both, darlin'. I didn't lose that much. And if it's the ring you're upset about, I'll buy you another one."

"No, it's not the ring or the amount of money," she said truthfully. "It's the principle."

He leaned down and briefly pressed his lips to hers. "Let's forget about it and go inside. I want to show you around and get your opinion on something."

When he took her hand and placed it in the crook of his arm, Arielle decided to do as he suggested and drop the matter. If he didn't care about being duped, then she probably shouldn't, either.

The doorman held open one of the doors, and Zach escorted her into the opulent lobby. Her breath caught at the beauty of the hotel. From the black marble counter of the reception desk, to the cream-colored Italian marble floor tiles and the expensive paintings decorating the walls, everything was coordinated perfectly. And, although lavish, the lobby still had a comfortable, welcoming feel to it.

"Zach, this is absolutely amazing," she gasped, taking it all in. "I can't believe this was your first resort."

He looked extremely pleased by her compliment. "I really can't take all of the credit. My sister had a big hand in the choice of colors and artwork."

"Well, you both did a wonderful job," Arielle commented, meaning it. "Does your sister help decorate all of your resorts?"

Nodding, he steered her down a wide corridor toward a set of decorative white French doors. "I come up with the theme, layout of the grounds and services we'll be offering at the resort, then Lana goes to work doing her thing with color choices and decorations." When they reached the doors, he stepped forward to open them and ushered her into a small indoor courtyard. "But this is where I need your opinion. What do you think of this room?"

As she took in the bubbling fountain in the center of the glass-enclosed area, the lush green plants and shrubs ringing the marble-tiled floor and impressive stone terrace, she didn't think she'd seen anything more beautiful. "This is breathtaking, Zach."

"Originally, it was my intention to make it a sitting area for guests of the resort." He took her elbow to steady her as they descended the terrace steps and walked over to the fountain. "But it's rare for someone to venture in here and I'm thinking about using it for other purposes."

"I think your golf course adjoining the resort property might have something to do with your guests' lack of interest." She smiled. "I would imagine many of them are bypassing this in favor of getting in a few rounds."

"You're probably right." He glanced around. "One of my employees recently suggested that it could be rented out for small parties and receptions. What do you think? Good idea or not?"

"I think it's an excellent idea," she agreed, nodding. "The white wrought-iron benches and patio tables could be arranged for whatever the occasion dictates." She turned to look back at the terrace with it's ornately carved granite railing. "I could easily see this being used for something like garden club meetings, as well as family anniversary parties and wedding receptions."

"You think so?" He frowned as if giving it serious thought. "I guess it could be used for someone wanting one of those family-and-extremely-close-friends-only affairs."

When he brushed back the sides of his black dinner jacket to stuff his hands in the front pockets of his pants as he looked around the room, he looked more than handsome. He hadn't bothered to put on a tie, instead preferring to wear his white shirt open at the collar. Some fashion magazines might call it the casually chic look, whereas she thought it was just plain sexy.

"I don't suppose it would hurt to give it a try," he acknowledged, walking over to take her into his arms. "Who knows? It just might turn out to be a hit."

"I'm sure it will become quite popular among the Dallas elite for all of their…intimate gatherings," she described, suddenly feeling quite breathless.

His wicked grin sent her blood pressure soaring as he raised her arms to encircle his neck. Wrapping his arms back around her, he pulled her against him. "I've always liked intimate, but it's not a word I've ever associated with more than two people."

"R-really?"

He nodded. "My definition of intimate is you…" His lips brushed hers. "And me…" He kissed her again. "Alone…" Using his index finger, he raised her chin until their gazes met. "Making love, Arielle."

The spark of need in the depths of his dark green eyes and the husky quality to his deep baritone sent desire through her. "Zach?"

His mouth came down on hers with urgency and she returned his kiss with just as much enthusiasm. His tongue mated with hers, demanding that she respond in kind. Meeting him stroke for stroke, the feel of his body against her caused a thrill of feminine power to skip along her nerves.

No matter how often she reminded herself that giving in to temptation again would be foolish, Arielle still wanted him with a ferocity that erased all logic.

When he suddenly lifted his head from hers and stepped back, she realized where they were and why he'd ended the kiss. They were standing in a public area of his resort and anyone could have walked in on them.

Before she gathered her wits, Zach took her hand in his and led her up the terrace to the French doors.

"W-where are we…going?" she finally asked as he hurried her across the lobby of the resort and out to the waiting limousine.

He helped her into the backseat, then gave her a smile that curled her toes inside her sensible one-inch black pumps. "Take us home, Mike," Zach directed to the driver, his gaze never wavering from hers. "To my place."

The short drive to his estate seemed longer than he could imagine and by the time the limousine drove through the gates and up the tree-lined drive, Zach felt as tense as the strings on a finely tuned violin. He'd fully expected Arielle to protest going to his house, but to his relief she hadn't uttered a word of opposition.

Of course, he hadn't given her much of a chance. Back at the resort, he'd recognized the same reflection of desire in her eyes that he was sure showed in his. He hadn't been able to get her out of there fast enough.

As soon as his chauffeur stopped the car in front of the mansion, Zach opened the door and helped her out. When they'd arrived at his resort, he'd noticed several people taking note of who got out of the limo, and that could very well prove to be a detriment. The last thing he wanted was to see a picture of them in the social column with speculation about their relationship. He had a feeling that wouldn't set well with her and could upset his well-laid plans.

Standing beside Arielle, he told his driver, "Take Ray Schaffer, my head of security, drive to the ranch first thing tomorrow morning and bring back my SUV. Then you'll need to meet Arielle's brothers and sister-in-law at the airport on Saturday. I'll be driving myself and Ms. Garnier wherever we need to go for a while."

The usually stoic driver nodded and flashed a rare smile. "Thank you, Mr. Forsythe."

Closing the car door, Zach put his arm around Arielle's waist and walked with her to his front door.

Neither said a word as he punched in the security code to turn off the alarm. By the time they entered the foyer, he wondered if she realized that she was spending the night at his place. Just the thought of having her in his bed had him harder than hell.

But when he turned to face her, his heart sank right along with his hopes of a passion-filled night. Instead of the glow of desire he'd seen on her lovely face earlier at the resort, she looked as if she was ready to drop. And as much as he would like to, he couldn't ignore their day of nonstop activity and that she'd missed her nap.

Wrapping his arms around her, he leaned to kiss her forehead. "I think it's past time we got you into bed, darlin'. You're real close to being asleep on your feet."

"I should have had your driver…take me back to my apartment," she murmured, yawning.

He shook his head, breaking his embrace to place his arm around her shoulders and walk her to the circular staircase. "That would have been a terrible idea. Your apartment is farther away and it would have taken that much longer for you to get to sleep."

"I suppose you're right," she conceded as they climbed the stairs. "I don't know why, but all of a sudden, I can hardly keep my eyes open."

When they entered the master suite, he switched on one of the lamps in the sitting area, then led her over to the bed. "You didn't get a nap this afternoon. The day just caught up with you."

She yawned again and shook her head as she stared at the bed. "I really shouldn't be here. I don't have a nightgown or even my toothbrush."

He chuckled as he reached to pull the comforter and silk top sheet back. "You don't need a nightgown to sleep, darlin'. And don't worry about the toothbrush. I have an extra one." When she looked as if she was going to protest again, he walked over to the dresser and pulled a pajama top from the drawer. "If it will make you feel better, you can wear this," he offered, handing her the silky shirt. Someone had given him the pajamas as a Christmas gift a couple years ago and he'd never worn them. He preferred to sleep without the encumbrance of clothes.

Taking the shirt from him, she entered the bathroom and returned a few minutes later dressed in her panties and his pajama top. She looked so darned sweet, it took everything he had in him not to sweep her up into his arms. But he shouldn't keep her up any longer and touching her would only send him into the bathroom for a cold shower.

After he tucked her into bed, he leaned down to give her a quick kiss. "Sleep well, Arielle."

"Aren't you…coming to bed now?" she asked, sounding increasingly drowsy.

"Nope." He stuffed his hands in his pockets to keep from reaching for her. "I'm going downstairs to the exercise room for a little workout." Turning, he started for the door. "I'll join you in a while."

As Zach walked to the stairs, he blew out a frustrated breath. It would take running several miles on the treadmill and bench-pressing many pounds before he got a wink of sleep.

But he couldn't complain. He'd accomplished another very important detail for their weekend wedding. During the tour of his resort, Arielle had unknowingly given her stamp of approval on their marriage site.

Arielle opened her eyes and looked around the unfamiliar room. It took a moment before she realized where she was. Zach had brought her to his mansion last night. Sometime during the short ride here, her body had reminded her that she'd skipped her nap and fatigue had demanded she get some sleep.

Turning her head, she gazed at the sleeping man stretched out on his stomach beside her. Zach had been so wonderful and understanding when he'd realized that she wasn't up to making love. If she hadn't already been in love with him, she would have fallen for him after last night.

Her heart skittered to a halt as realization sank in. She loved him. Had never *stopped* loving him.

Now she fully understood why her mother had been unable to resist her father the second time he'd shown up. Francesca Garnier had fallen head over heels in love with Owen Larson just as Arielle had fallen in love with Zach. And love defied logic.

"What's the matter, darlin'?" Zach asked, moving to drape his arm over her stomach.

"N-nothing," she lied. "It just took me a minute to realize where I am."

His lazy smile sent a keen longing through her. "You're exactly where you're supposed to be. Here with me."

"What time…did you come to bed?" she inquired, feeling more than a little breathless.

"Sometime after midnight," he replied, rising up to prop a forearm on either side of her. He leaned down to press his lips to hers, but instead of the quick kiss she expected, his mouth molded to hers and he gathered her to him.

Her eyes slowly drifted shut as his warm, firm lips glided over hers, setting off sparkles of light behind her closed lids. When he coaxed her to open for him, she did so on a soft sigh, and the feel of his tongue mating with hers caused the longing she'd felt the night before to come rushing back stronger and more powerful than anything she'd ever felt.

A tingling warmth began to flow through her veins when he slid his hand over her side from knee to waist, and she gripped the sheet with both hands as heat coursed through her body. As Zach caressed and teased her body with his hands and lips, desire began to build inside her. As long as she lived, she would never tire of him touching her.

When he parted her silk pajama top and his palm

skimmed over her stomach to the underside of her breast, Arielle ceased thinking and concentrated on the delicious way Zach was making her feel. She wanted him with a fierceness that stole her breath. She briefly wondered when he had unbuttoned the shirt as he cupped the weight of her, then teased her tightened nipple with the pad of his thumb. But the thought was fleeting when he broke the caress to nibble moist kisses from her collarbone down the slope of her breast to the hardened peak.

A tight coil of need formed deep inside her when he took her into his warm mouth and gently teased with his tongue. As he worried the hardened tip, his hand caressed her down to her hip, then her inner thigh. She quivered from the intense sensations.

"Does that feel good, Arielle?" he prompted. Raising his head, he looked at her as he pulled her panties down her legs, then tossed them to the floor. "I think we have some unfinished business from last night that we need to take care of, don't you?"

Unable to speak, she nodded. When he cupped the curls at her apex and his finger dipped inside to stroke the soft, moist folds, she moaned and arched into his touch.

"Zach, please—"

He entered her with his finger and the coil in her belly grew to the unfulfilled ache of need from his relentless touch. "What is it you want, darlin'?"

"Y-you. Now. Inside…me."

Without another word, his lips captured hers at the same time he abandoned the delicious torture. Using his knee to spread her legs, he moved to lever himself over her. She felt the tip of his strong arousal probe her and as he pushed himself forward, she thought she would die from the ecstasy of becoming one with the man she loved.

Placing his hands flat on either side of her, he held himself off her stomach, bringing his lower body into even closer contact with hers. Never had she felt more filled, more a part of him.

Slowly he pulled his body away from hers, then glided forward to gently thrust into her, his heated gaze never leaving hers. They moved together in a primal dance and each time they met and parted, the blazing need within her grew. All too soon, she felt her feminine muscles tighten around him as she came ever closer to completion.

Zach must have sensed her readiness because he thrust into her a bit faster, a little deeper and suddenly she felt herself spinning out of control, cast into a sweet vortex with no beginning or end. Heat and light flashed behind her tightly closed eyes as wave after wave of sheer pleasure surged through her. Grasping his forearms, she clung to him.

Just as the storm within her began to subside, she felt his body go perfectly still a moment before he threw his head back and groaned. His muscular arms shook from the effort of holding himself off her and his whole body shuddered as the force of his release gripped him.

He moved to her side and collapsed on the bed. His breathing was harsh, but as he gathered her to him, he managed to ask, "Are you all right?"

Snuggling into his strong embrace, she nodded. "I feel wonderful. Thank you."

He leaned back to look at her. "Why are you thanking me? I should be the one thanking you."

She cupped his cheek and pressed a kiss to his firm lips. "Even though I'm pregnant and starting to feel a little awkward, you make me feel sexy."

"That's because you are, darlin'." His smile caused her heart to swell with so much love, she thought it might burst. "All I have to do is look at you and I'm turned on."

Feeling more relaxed and complete than she had in a long time, she couldn't keep her eyes open. "I think…I'll rest a minute or two…before I get up."

"It's still early. Why don't you get a little more sleep?"

When she remained silent, Zach grinned as he pulled the covers over them. He'd been right. Arielle could fall asleep with no effort at all.

As he lay there holding her, he decided that he couldn't afford the luxury of going back to sleep. He had too many plans to make. He had three days left before her brothers and sister-in-law flew into town. He wanted to have Arielle completely convinced that marrying him was best for both of them and have her totally committed to taking a trip down the aisle when her family arrived.

Glancing at the bedside clock, he softly kissed her cheek, then eased his arm from beneath her and got out of bed. He needed a quick shower, a cup of strong, black coffee and a couple of phone calls to some old friends to get the ball rolling. And the very first thing on his To Do list for the day would be to call Juan Gomez to see when he could pick up Arielle's ring.

He whistled a tune as he grabbed some clothes from the walk-in closet, then headed into the master bath and turned on the water in the shower. Everything was coming together nicely and Arielle would be Mrs. Zach Forsythe by the end of the week. Just as he'd promised her she would.

Eight

Arielle found Zach in the master suite's sitting room, reading a newspaper at the small table. Dressed in jeans and a forest-green polo shirt, he looked devastatingly handsome.

"Why didn't you wake me?" she asked.

Looking up, he smiled. "I thought I'd let you sleep in." Folding the paper, he set it aside and, rising to his feet, walked around the table to hold the chair for her. "Do you have any idea how cute you look in my bathrobe?"

A delightful little shiver raced through her at the feel of his warm kisses on the back of her neck. "I—I couldn't find anything else to wear."

He chuckled as he walked back around the table to sit opposite her. "I think it's the first time it's ever been worn."

"You're joking," she said, glancing down at the black silk garment.

"Nope." He shrugged. "What's the use of wearing a robe from the bathroom to the closet? I can wrap a towel around my waist just as easy."

"What happens if you have guests?"

The look he gave her set her pulse racing. "Darlin', the only other person in my bedroom besides me is you and I was under the impression you liked my lack of inhibitions."

Before she could tell him how incorrigible he was, he picked up a wireless device and pressed a button on its side. "You can bring breakfast to us now, Maria."

"*Si,* Senor Zach. I'll bring it right up," a female voice answered.

"Zach, we could have gone downstairs for breakfast," Arielle suggested as he returned the small device to the table.

"Nope." He reached across the table to cover her hand with his. "You need to eat as soon as you get out of bed to avoid getting sick."

"But I'm not used to having people wait on me," she protested.

He nodded. "I understand, darlin'. I like doing things for myself most of the time, too. But I told you that I intend to pamper you and having breakfast brought to you as soon as you wake up is part of that." He grinned. "Besides, you need to conserve your strength."

"Why?"

"Because I have something planned that I think you'll enjoy as much as our trip to San Antonio," he disclosed, rising at the sound of a knock on the door.

When he opened the door, a kind-looking, middle-aged woman with beautiful brown eyes entered carrying a tray to the table. After Zach made the introductions, she smiled. "It's nice to meet you. If there is anything special you would like for breakfast tomorrow, please let me know."

"Thank you, Maria," Arielle replied, instantly liking her. "But I doubt that I—"

"I'll let you know if there is, Maria," Zach interrupted.

The cook nodded. "Enjoy your breakfast."

When the door closed behind the woman, Arielle frowned. "Why would she think that I'll be here tomorrow morning?"

"Probably because I told her you would be here quite a bit from now on," he confessed, lifting the silver covers from their plates. "And before you get upset, I didn't say you would definitely be. Now, eat. We have another big day ahead of us."

She would have questioned him further, but the food's delicious aroma was far too tempting and she picked up her fork to cut into the omelet. "Oh, Zach," she murmured, closing her eyes as she savored the first bite. "This is wonderful."

"I swear Maria has some kind of magic touch," he agreed, nodding.

They ate in silence and Arielle felt completely full by the time she finished her last crumb of toast. "I don't dare eat here very often," she commented, placing her silverware on the edge of her empty plate. "I'd gain so much weight I'd waddle like a duck."

"You're supposed to gain weight. You're pregnant with twins." His tight tone and the slight frown creasing his forehead surprised her.

"I'm well aware of that and I expect to gain quite a few pounds, especially since I'm eating for three." She scooted her chair back and stood up. "All I meant was that Maria's food is so good, I could easily gain more weight than what the doctor recommends." She started toward the bathroom, hoping she had explained away Zach's concern. "Now, while I get dressed, why don't you carry the tray downstairs, then take me home."

"Why?"

Turning, she searched his face. Why did he suddenly seem on edge?

"You told me that you had made plans for us. Don't you think it would be a good idea if I had something appropriate to wear?"

"Oh, right." He looked a little more at ease as he picked up the tray with their empty plates. "Go ahead and get dressed. I'll be back in a few minutes."

"All right. I'll be ready."

As he watched her walk toward the bathroom, Zach chastised himself for jumping to conclusions. But when Arielle had mentioned gaining too much weight, a flashback of his ex-fiancée and her intention to starve herself into a miscarriage came rushing back.

Descending the stairs, he shook his head at his unfounded suspicions. Arielle was completely different from Gretchen and it was past time he stopped comparing the two women. Arielle was looking forward to the birth of their twins and had expressed nothing but happiness and excitement about the babies.

He took a deep breath as he walked toward the kitchen. He'd feel a lot better about the entire situation once they were married. He'd be in a better position to keep his vow of being there for her and their babies. And if everything worked as he'd planned, he should have that assurance by the end of the day.

After stopping by her apartment where she changed into a sundress and a sensible pair of shoes, Arielle sat in the passenger seat of Zach's SUV, wondering where he was taking her this time. Truthfully, she really didn't care where they went. She was enjoying the few days he'd asked her to spend with him and looked forward to whatever he had planned.

She knew it was absolute insanity to be getting in way over her head so quickly. But where Zach was concerned, she didn't have a choice in the matter. She loved him, had never stopped loving him and understood why her mother hadn't been able to resist her father. And just like her mother, there was a chance she would end up getting hurt again.

But as Zach steered the truck into a parking lot, she abandoned all speculation when she realized he was taking her to the Dallas Arboretum. "I love gardens. How did you know?"

His deep chuckle caused her insides to quiver. "Darlin', I wish I could tell you that I had some kind of insight into that. But I didn't. I just figured most women like flowers and it was a safe bet you would, too."

"Good call," she responded, smiling.

When he got out of the SUV and came to help her from the passenger side, he grabbed a medium-size insulated backpack from the backseat that she hadn't noticed before. "What's that?"

"There's a really nice picnic spot in the Pecan Grove area of the arboretum and I had Maria prepare lunch for us." He slung the carrier over one shoulder, then, taking her hand in his, started through the main entrance.

"What a nice idea," she remarked. "I haven't been on a picnic in years. At least not one without several dozen preschoolers to keep track of."

"Score one more for Zach," he declared, grinning.

"Oh, so now you're trying to make points with me?" she teased, laughing.

He leaned down to give her a quick kiss. "Darlin',
I've been trying ever since walking into your office
last Friday morning to plead Derek's case."

She could have told him that he was succeeding,
but as they walked along the tree-lined paths,
Arielle's attention was claimed by the acres of perfectly kept lawns and immaculate beds of brightly
colored flowers. Shades of bright pink, purple and
red were everywhere and mingled with lush green
shrubbery and various nonflowering plants, the
gardens were absolutely breathtaking. Enjoying the
fresh spring air and gorgeous scenery with Zach was
wonderful and before she knew it, they were walking
toward a beautiful picnic area among a grove of
pecan trees.

"A dollar for your thoughts," Zach offered as he
placed the backpack on a shaded picnic table and
began unzipping the front flap.

"A dollar?" Seating herself on one side of the
table, she smiled. "I thought that used to be a penny."

"Inflation has set in, darlin'," he explained, laughing as he removed a navy and tan checkered cloth
from the side of the pack. "I think Maria said we have
turkey and Swiss on wheat bread, some kind of cold,
chopped vegetable medley and sparkling grape juice.
I hope that's okay."

"I'm starved and it all sounds yummy," she stated,
helping him spread out the small tablecloth. "But
these days, I'm always hungry."

"Very true," he agreed, handing her two plates, two sets of cutlery and two wineglasses. "But very understandable considering you're having twins."

"My mother mentioned one time that she ate so much when she was pregnant with Jake and Luke that she gained fifty pounds." She arranged the plates and cutlery, then waited for Zach to pour the grape juice into the goblets. "It's odd how I can remember something like that, but not the sound of her voice."

"Didn't you tell me you were ten when she was killed in a car accident?" he reminded, his voice gentle. "That was a long time ago and you were only a child, darlin'. Time has a way of making things like that fade away."

"I suppose you're right."

Staring at the empty plate in front of her, she thought about their time in Aspen and the details she'd shared about her life. But Zach hadn't revealed anything about himself when they'd first met, and beyond his name, his career and the fact that he had a sister and nephew, she knew nothing about him now.

"What about your parents?" she asked, looking up to find him watching her. "Are they still living?"

He shook his head as he placed wrapped sandwiches on the plates, then opened the container of vegetables. "My mom died when I was six. There were complications from having Lana that she just couldn't overcome."

"Oh, Zach, I'm so sorry."

"It's been almost thirty years and about the only things I remember clearly about her is that she loved baking cookies and reading stories to get me to sleep at night." He sat down at the table across from her. "After she was gone, my dad hired Mattie to take care of me and Lana while he worked the ranch. Then he passed away from a heart attack when I was in my junior year at college."

Her heart went out to him and she reached across the table to place her hand on his. "I know that had to have been devastating for you and your sister."

"Lana was only an infant when Mom died, so she doesn't have any memories of her. But we were both close to Dad and it was pretty rough for a while," he admitted, staring off into the distance. When he turned his attention back to her, he asked, "What about your dad? Is he still alive? I don't remember you mentioning anything about him."

Spooning some of the crisp vegetables onto her plate, she shook her head. "There's really nothing to tell. I never got to meet him and never will." When Zach raised a questioning eyebrow, she added, "My brothers and I recently found out that he was killed in a boating accident a couple years ago."

Zach looked surprised. "I'm sorry to hear that, Arielle."

"Don't be." She took a sip of her grape juice. "You don't miss what you've never had."

When their gazes locked, she nibbled on her lower

lip as she decided how much to tell him. Not knowing anything about her father and having never met the man, she'd glossed over his nonexistent role in her life when they'd been in Aspen.

But maybe it was time to tell Zach what she'd recently learned about the man. Maybe then he'd understand why she'd been so hurt by his actions in Aspen. And why she'd been afraid that the same thing that happened to her mother had happened to her—that although the man she loved was fond of her, he couldn't love her.

She sighed as she continued to stare at him. They had to start somewhere or they'd never build the trust between them needed to raise their twins together.

"The relationship between my mother and father was anything but conventional." She took a deep breath. "They were together twice, ten years apart and only for a few months each time. But both affairs resulted in unplanned pregnancies."

He remained silent, mulling over what she'd said. "It's a shame that things couldn't have worked out between them." He took a bite of his sandwich, then after chewing thoughtfully, asked, "Your mother never found anyone else?"

Arielle shook her head. "Whether he was worth it or not, my father was her one true love and she wouldn't settle for anything less." She poked at her vegetables with her fork. "But the story doesn't end there."

He raised his brows. "There's more?"

This was the part she had trouble believing herself. "A couple of months ago, my brothers and I were contacted by a representative for our paternal grandmother. That's when we learned our father's real identity."

As she watched, Zach slowly lowered his sandwich to his plate. "He lied about who he was?"

She could tell by his expression that the uncanny parallel to their own situation wasn't lost on him. "Our father used an assumed name and Mama never knew that the man she fell in love with wasn't who he said he was. Nor did she ever learn that during the ten years between their affairs, he fathered three more sons by three different women. None of whom he bothered to marry."

"Did he know about his offspring?"

"Every one of them," she confirmed, nodding.

The frown on his handsome face left no doubt that Zach didn't approve of what her father had done. Not in the least. "Did he offer to help these women raise his children?"

"No."

"What the hell was he thinking?" Zach shook his head disgustedly. "How can a man just walk away from his kids and never be there for them or at the very least, see that their basic needs are met?"

"I don't know." She took a bite of her vegetables. "Apparently, being an irresponsible liar who preyed on women unfortunate enough to fall in love with him was one of my father's biggest character flaws."

Rising from his seat, Zach came around the table to her side, then, straddling the bench, took her into his arms. "I give you my word that I'll always be there for you and our children."

"You're going to be a great dad," she observed.

He nodded. "Or die trying." His warm smile caused her to tingle all over. "And I know you're going to be the best mom any kid could ever have."

"I'm going to do my best," she vowed, returning his smile.

A sudden gust of wind threatened to sweep their lunch off the table and, looking up, Arielle realized it was going to start raining soon. "I'm pretty sure we're about to get wet."

"We'd better pack up the picnic and head back to the truck," he responded, getting to his feet.

"Good idea." She hurried to help him gather up everything and put it back into the insulated backpack. "I may start waddling like a duck soon, but I just don't seem to have the same fondness for getting wet."

Laughing, Zach caught her hand in his and hurried her toward the parking lot. "Besides not wanting you to get wet, we need to get back to the house, anyway."

"Why?"

"I have a couple of things I need to take care of for this evening and you need a nap."

When he helped her into the passenger seat, his grin sent shivers of anticipation through her and she knew he was up to something. She waited until he rounded the front of the SUV, then slid into the driver's seat before asking, "What do you have up your sleeve this time?"

There was enough wattage in his wide smile to light the entire city of Dallas. "You'll have to wait and see. But trust me, darlin'. You're going to love it."

"Oh, Zach, I absolutely love this," Arielle said as she closed her eyes and savored the last cold bite of mint chocolate chip ice cream.

Seated across from her in the restaurant at his Dallas resort, she could hear the smile in his voice. "I thought you might. That's why I had it flown up here from the ice cream shop on the River Walk in San Antonio."

Opening her eyes, she sputtered. "I can't believe you did that. I wouldn't have known the difference if you'd had the kitchen staff open a carton from the local grocery store."

"But *I* would. Besides, I promised I'd get that ice cream for you." The tender look in his dark green gaze stole her breath as he reached across the table and covered her hand with his. "And unless there's a damned good reason, I always keep my promises, darlin'."

"Always?" she asked, knowing he was referring to something far more important than ice cream.

Nodding, he continued to hold her hand as he rose to his feet. "Come with me, Arielle."

"Where are we going?" she asked as they walked out of the restaurant and into the hotel lobby.

"Somewhere a little more private," he explained, whispering close to her ear. When they reached the doors of the indoor courtyard, he smiled. "Close your eyes."

"You're certainly being mysterious about this."

He leaned down to brush his lips over hers. "Just another little surprise. Now, close your eyes."

When she did as he requested, he opened the French doors to the courtyard and guided her inside. Even with her eyes closed, she could tell they were standing in complete darkness. "Zach?"

She heard what might be the sound of a switch being flipped on. "You can look now, darlin'."

Opening her eyes, Arielle's breath caught at the sight of tiny white lights tastefully threaded throughout the foliage surrounding the room. Even the fountain had been adorned with special lighting that made the bubbling water appear to be a cascade of sparkling diamonds.

"Zach, it's beautiful," she declared, walking to the edge of the terrace. "How did you get this done so quickly?"

"Darlin', you can accomplish just about anything if you're willing to pay the price."

He took hold of her elbow and they descended the stone steps. He escorted her to one of the patio tables covered with a pristine linen cloth. "I thought you might like to see what this will look like for those intimate gatherings we talked about last night."

"It's perfect," she mused, sitting down in the seat he held for her. "It looks like something Cinderella might have seen when she arrived for Prince Charming's ball."

"I'm glad you like it," he noted, lowering himself into the chair next to her.

As she took in the elegance of the little courtyard, intuition told her they were there for more than her approval on the room's transformation. Turning to face him, she caught him watching her closely.

"Zach, what's going on?"

His smile sent a warm rush flowing through her veins. "Do you love me, Arielle?"

"Zach, I thought we agreed—"

"Just answer the question, darlin'."

Her heart skipped several beats and time stilled as she stared back at him. She could tell him no, but they both knew it would be a lie.

"Yes," she finally answered, surprised at how steady her voice sounded, considering her body had started to quiver uncontrollably.

His smile caused her heart to pound hard against her ribs. He removed a small black velvet box from his suit jacket. Placing it on the table, he removed the ring she'd thought the vendor in the marketplace had stolen. "Arielle Garnier, will you do me the honor of becoming my wife?" he asked, taking her left hand in his.

"You agreed not to insist on our getting married," she stalled.

He shook his head. "I'm not insisting that we get married, darlin'. I'm asking you to marry me."

Everything within her wanted to tell him yes, that she would love nothing more than to be his wife and build a wonderful life with him and their children. But although Zach had asked her if she loved him, he hadn't admitted how he felt about her.

"Do you love me?" she asked, finally getting her vocal cords to work.

His gaze held hers for what seemed like forever before he replied. "You have to know that I care deeply for you, Arielle."

Her heart felt as if it dropped to her feet. "That's not what I asked you, Zach. I want to know if you love me."

"We're good together," he responded, placing the ring on the table. He cupped her face with his hands. "We can have a good life."

"Really?" Tears filled her eyes as an ache like she'd never known filled her heart. But she blinked the moisture away. "You think so?"

"I know so, darlin'." He gave her an encouraging smile. "I like doing things for you and getting things I know you'll like."

"I-Is that what you think…I want?" she prodded, her chest tightening with so much emotional pain, she wasn't sure she could draw her next breath. "Material things?"

His expression became guarded. "I promise you'll never want for anything, Arielle."

"Y-You're wrong, Zach." She shook her head. "There's only one thing I want from you. And you can't or won't give that to me."

"What's that?" he asked. They both knew what she wanted and they both knew she wasn't going to get it from him.

"All that I've ever wanted," she professed, standing up. "Your love."

Rising to his feet, he stammered, "You have to understand that—"

"P-Please…don't," she begged, backing away from him. She couldn't bear to hear him tell her that he could never love her.

"Everything will work out, Arielle. And I give you my word that I'll never do anything that would hurt you or isn't in your and our twins' best interest."

"It's too late for that, Zach," she concluded as her heart shattered into a million pieces. "You just did."

Nine

"What's going on, Zach?" Lana asked Friday morning as she slowly walked into his den. "And don't tell me nothing because I know better."

"Hey, sis." Seated in one of the chairs in front of the fireplace, Zach motioned for her to join him. "You look like physical therapy is working wonders. You're walking a lot better than you were last week."

"Don't do that," she insisted, shaking her head as she eased down in the chair beside him. "You're not going to distract me after I skipped therapy to drive over here. I want to know why you haven't been in the office all week and why you look like you've lost your last friend." She frowned. "How long has it been since you shaved?"

"A couple of days." He reached up to scratch the growth of stubble covering his cheeks as he stared at the empty coffee cup in his hand. "I just felt like taking a few days off from everything, that's all."

Lana gave an unladylike snort. "I wasn't born yesterday, so don't feed me that line of hooey. You haven't missed a day shaving since you scraped three or four hairs off your chin when you were thirteen. And you never take time off unless you're visiting one of the resorts, which we both know are working vacations. So what's wrong?"

He'd known he wouldn't be able to avoid telling his sister the truth. Even before their father had died, he and Lana had been close. She knew him better than anyone else and was just as protective of him as he was of her. There was no way she was going to leave without answers.

"In about five and a half months, I'm going to be the father of twins," he said without preamble.

His sister's silence proved his news was not expected. "Are you serious?" she finally asked, her voice reflecting her stunned shock.

He nodded. "You know I wouldn't joke about something like that."

"Dear God, Zach, I know I was out of the loop there for a while, but how did I miss this?" Lana gave him a pointed look. "I lived here with you for several months after my release from the hospital and you weren't seeing anyone."

Explaining the events in Aspen and his recent reunion with Arielle, Zach finished by telling her what happened when he proposed. "After I took her to her apartment, I came here. End of story."

"Not by a long shot, brother." Lana slowly shook her head back and forth. "I don't blame her for telling you to hit the bricks. I would have, too. If you want her back, you have some serious groveling to do."

"I don't grovel," he retorted, suddenly irritated with his sister. They usually agreed on just about everything and it irked him no end that she wasn't taking his side.

"Well, I'd say if you want a future with this woman and your twins, you'd better start." Lana placed her hand on his arm and her voice took on a gentle quality. "I know what happened five years ago has a lot to do with the way you handled this, Zach. But Arielle isn't Gretchen. From everything you've told me, she loves you and is thrilled to be having these babies. And unlike Gretchen, she obviously adores children or she wouldn't have made pre-schoolers her career."

"I'm well aware of that."

"Then stop holding Arielle accountable for something she hasn't done and wouldn't think of doing."

He shook his head. "I'm not."

"Aren't you?" Lana gave him a meaningful look.

"I know you blame yourself for not seeing what Gretchen was doing, but that's in the past and you need to let it go. And if you'll admit it, your pride took the biggest hit back then."

"How do you figure that?" he demanded, more irritated with each passing second.

"You thought Gretchen loved you and wanted the same things you did. But that wasn't the case and you can't accept that you were wrong about her." Lana sighed. "Don't you see, Zach? It's just a matter of semantics. You say you care deeply for Arielle, but you can't bring yourself to use the word *love* because you might be wrong about her, too. And that scares you to death."

His sister's insight was hitting a little closer to home than he was comfortable with. But he wasn't about to concede. "You don't know what the hell you're talking about, Lana."

"Don't I?" Her tone and knowing expression were filled with confidence as she used her cane to stand up. Then, leaning down, she kissed his cheek. "Don't let your stubborn pride get in the way of the happiness you could have with Arielle. Admit to yourself how you feel about her and take another chance, Zach. From everything you've told me about her, Arielle is more than worth the risk."

It took several minutes after Lana closed the door behind her for Zach to think rationally. At first, his sister's observations had him so angry he could have bit nails in two. But the more he thought about what she had said, the more he wondered if she might be right.

Had he been holding Arielle accountable for the sins of another woman? Was he reluctant to take another chance on love simply because he wanted to protect his ego?

As he sat there contemplating the possibilities, he couldn't stop thinking about the way the crushed look on Arielle's beautiful face and the tears filling her eyes had made him feel. Just knowing that he'd caused her so much emotional pain created a tightness in his chest that threatened to suffocate him. And every minute of every day he was away from her, those feelings intensified.

He took a deep breath, then another. The way he saw it, he had two choices. He could play it safe, continue to deny how he felt about her and be the most miserable bastard west of the Mississippi. Or he could swallow his selfish pride, tell her how much he loved her and risk finding the happiness and completion that he knew in his heart only she could bring him.

With everything suddenly crystal clear, Zach stood, walked out of the study and climbed the stairs. He needed a shower, a shave and a pair of pants with reinforced knees. If he had to, he'd spend the rest of his life on his knees, begging Arielle's forgiveness for being such a fool and asking her to give him one more chance to make things right between them.

* * *

Arielle sat down on the couch, trying to gather the courage to call her brothers and tell them not to come to Dallas for the weekend. She wasn't looking forward to telling Jake and Luke not to visit, even though she would love to see them and could really use their emotional support. But the last thing she needed was to have two brothers in full "overly protective big brother" mode telling her what they thought she should do, while she was trying to deal with a badly broken heart.

Fortunately for her, she'd already handled the situation, broken off all contact with Zach, at least for the past few days, and was deciding to merge the preschool back into the Emerald, Inc. umbrella of companies and move to San Francisco.

When the doorbell began ringing insistently, her heart skipped several beats. She only knew one person in Dallas besides her coworkers at the preschool, who at this time of day were all at work.

As she walked the few feet to the door, she considered telling him, through the door, to please leave her alone to get on with her life. But knowing Zach, he wouldn't listen.

"Arielle, we need to talk," he declared as soon as she opened the door.

She shook her head as much to deny his request as an attempt to stem the fresh wave of tears that seeing him caused. "I think we've said all there is to say, Zach."

"No, we haven't." Before she could stop him, he placed his hands on her shoulders, backed her away from the door and into the foyer, then kicked it shut behind them. "First off, are you all right?"

No, she wasn't all right and might never be again. But she wasn't going to let him know that.

"I'm doing okay," she said cautiously.

"Good."

When he continued to stand there staring at her, she took a step away from his disturbing touch. "Why are you here, Zach? What do you want from me?"

"I told you, darlin'." He stuffed his hands in the front pockets of his jeans and rocked back on his heels. "We have some things to discuss."

"No, we don't." She pointed toward the door. "Now, please, just go."

"Not until you hear me out. Then, if you still want me to leave, I will."

Knowing how futile it was to argue with him, she motioned toward the couch. "Would you like to sit down for this?"

"That might not be a bad idea," he agreed, nodding. "This could take a while."

Arielle sighed as she walked over and lowered herself onto the couch. "Let's get this over with."

He gave her a short nod, then to her surprise, sat down on the coffee table directly in front of her. She immediately leaned back against the cushions to put a bit of distance between them. If she didn't, she wasn't entirely sure she wouldn't throw her arms around him and hang on for dear life.

"About five years ago, I was an arrogant jerk who thought he had it all," he began, propping his fore-arms on his knees and staring down at his loosely clasped hands.

"And how is that different from the way you are now?" she asked before she could stop herself.

Glancing up, he gave her a self-deprecating smile. "I guess I deserve that, don't I?"

His concession surprised her, but it wasn't in her nature to be cruel. "I'm sorry. I shouldn't have said that."

"You had every right to say it and a lot more."

Why did he have to look so darned good to her? And why couldn't he sit somewhere else? Didn't he realize how hard it was for her to love him the way she did, knowing that nothing was ever going to come of it?

"As I was saying, five years ago I thought I was on top of the world and completely invincible. I was barely thirty years old and had just made my first billion, was engaged to a woman I thought loved me and had a baby on the way."

In all of her wildest imaginings, she'd have never dreamed that what he thought he had to tell her included a fiancée and a baby.

"Why are you telling me this, Zach?" She didn't want to hear that he'd been able to love one woman, but couldn't love her.

"Because I want you to understand why I've had a hard time letting myself love again," he said, his dark green gaze unwavering when it met hers. "Why I've been such a coward."

His frank assessment of himself shocked her. But before she could comment, he rose to his feet and began pacing the room.

"We hadn't been engaged long when we found out about the pregnancy," he continued, his tone reflective. "And I thought everything was going great. I was thrilled about the baby and she assured me that she was, too."

"I take it that wasn't the case?" Arielle guessed.

Zach's harsh laughter caused her to cringe. "Not even close. As soon as she heard the word *pregnant,* she started doing everything she could think of to lose the baby."

She sensed what he was about to tell her next and instinctively placed a protective hand over her stomach.

"After a few weeks of starving herself and refusing to get the rest she needed, she was successful."

"I'm so sorry, Zach," Arielle sympathized. As excited as he'd been about their babies, he must have been devastated by the woman's intentional miscarriage.

Nodding, he reached up to run his hand through his thick dark brown hair. "I'd been busy opening the Aspen resort and wasn't paying enough attention to realize what was going on." He shook his head.

"Maybe if I had, I could have convinced her to have the baby for me to raise."

It suddenly became clear why he'd been so determined to see that she ate right and when she mentioned anything about gaining weight, he'd become irritable. It also explained why he made sure she took a nap every day. He didn't trust her when she told him how excited she was about having a child and was making sure nothing happened to jeopardize the pregnancy.

"I'm not her, Zach."

"I know, darlin'. And I'm sorry for holding you accountable. I'm the one at fault for not seeing it sooner." He shook his head. "The same as I am for not recognizing what she was doing."

"You can't blame yourself for what happened, Zach. It sounds to me that no matter how attentive you were, your fiancée would have found a way to end the pregnancy."

"You're probably right," he agreed. "But at the time, all I could see were my dreams of having a family fall apart."

With sudden insight, she realized that just like her, his lack of a conventional family while growing up was what made having one of his own so important to him. "I'm sure that was extremely hard for you."

"I survived." He gave her a hesitant look. "But not without losing a good chunk of my pride."

"I'm afraid I don't understand," she commented, wondering what his pride had to do with it.

He walked back over to sit down in front of her on the edge of the coffee table. "I've always had this thing about being right. And when I think I am, come hell or high water, I won't back down."

"Mattie mentioned that when you're convinced of something, you can be extremely stubborn," Arielle relayed, recalling how insistent he'd been about her having the flu.

"That's right, darlin'. And when I discovered I'd been wrong about my fiancée, it sent me into a tailspin." She watched his chest rise and fall as he drew in a deep breath. "It was hard for me to admit that I'd been wrong about her and her feelings for me. But it was that much harder when I realized I was wrong about the way I felt for her."

"No one likes having to accept they've made a mistake and especially about something like that, Zach." She knew firsthand how difficult it had been for her to concede that she'd been wrong about him never being able to love her.

He nodded. "But then I made an even bigger mistake when I made the conscious choice not to put myself in that position again and risk taking another hit to my pride."

"In other words, you decided not to love anyone or trust that they would love you," she recapped, realizing as never before that the situation between them had been hopeless from the beginning.

"But I was wrong." He stared down at his hands a moment before he lifted his gaze to hers. "Only I didn't realize it until you came along."

Her heart squeezed painfully and she had to force herself to breathe. She couldn't bear to hear him make a false confession of love, simply to get her to marry him.

"Please don't, Zach."

"What? Don't tell you that I fell in love with you the minute I saw you out on that ski slope?" He took her hands in his as he shook his head. "I can't do that, darlin'."

Tears filled her eyes and she forced herself to pull away from his touch. She wouldn't, couldn't, allow herself to believe him. If she did and it turned out that he was lying, she'd never survive.

"I think…you'd better…go."

When he moved to sit beside her on the couch and took her into his arms, her body began to tremble uncontrollably. "I can't do this…Zach."

"I know you don't believe me and you think I'm just telling you what you want to hear," he observed gently. "But I swear with everything that's in me that I do love you, Arielle. And I'm sorry for all the heartache I've caused both of us."

"I wish…I could believe—"

Suddenly turning her to face him, he cupped her

cheeks and forced her to look at him. "Darlin', don't you think that if I was going to lie to you about how I feel, I'd have told you what I knew you wanted to hear the other night at the resort?"

What he said was true. He could have easily told her he loved her then. But he hadn't. He'd been painfully honest about his feelings for her.

"But why…now?" she mumbled, sniffing back a fresh wave of tears. "What caused you…to change your mind?"

He smiled tenderly. "I didn't change my mind. I just came to the realization that all the pride in the world isn't worth having without your love. Without you, darlin', my life means less than nothing."

The sincerity in his eyes convinced her that he meant every word he said. "Oh, Zach, I love you so much, but—"

"I know you're afraid, Arielle." He brushed his lips over hers. "But if you'll give me a second chance, I'll spend every day for the rest of my life making sure you never doubt how much I love you."

"Third."

"What?" he asked, frowning.

"You asked for a second chance. But you've already had that. This will be your third chance." She gave him a watery smile. "And I think it's only fair to warn you that it's your last. You'd better get it right this time, Mr. Forsythe, because there won't be another."

He crushed her to him then and gave her a kiss that left both of them gasping for breath. "I love you, Arielle Garnier. Will you marry me?"

She laughed. "You don't waste time do you?"

"There's been enough time wasted already," he confirmed, smiling. "But you didn't answer my question, darlin'."

Knowing she had no other choice in the matter, she nodded. "I haven't been able to resist you from the moment we met and that hasn't changed. Yes, Zach, I'll marry you."

The tears she'd been holding back spilled down her cheeks. She watched as he reached into the front pocket of his jeans and pulled out a black velvet box. He opened it, took her left hand in his, then slipped the ring on her third finger.

"How about tomorrow?"

"What about it?" she asked, loving the feel of his ring on her finger.

He chuckled. "If you'll remember I told you that I'd like to get married on the weekend."

"But I can't possibly get everything arranged in such a short amount of time," she explained, wishing with all of her heart that she could.

"Actually, there's not much to be arranged," he countered, giving her a sheepish grin.

"What have you done?" she inquired, loving him more with each passing second.

"You mean besides getting Juan Gomez to meet

us in San Antonio to have your ring sized, decorating the courtyard and fountain, arranging for the resort to cater the reception and asking my old friend Judge Morrison to sign a waiver allowing us to get married without the required waiting period and to perform the ceremony?" He chuckled. "Other than that, I haven't done a thing, darlin'."

She marveled at how thorough he'd been. "When you showed me the courtyard, you were actually getting my approval for our wedding."

"Yes. I was in denial at the time, but I realize now that everything I did, every plan I made, was because I love you and wanted to make that day as special for you as I could."

"I love you so much, Zach. And I really appreciate everything you've done, but you weren't supposed to press the issue of marriage," she reminded, putting her arms around his neck.

"I love you, too. But technically, I didn't press you about getting married," he argued, kissing the tip of her nose. "I promised I wouldn't talk to you about it. But I never promised I wouldn't *do* something about it."

As they sat on the couch holding each other, Arielle nibbled at her lower lip. If they were going to be husband and wife, there shouldn't be any secrets between them. And she still had a big, rather bizarre secret she hadn't shared with him yet.

"Zach, do you believe in fairy tales?"

"If you mean the happily-ever-after kind, I didn't until today," he confessed, resting his cheek against her head.

She smiled. "Let me tell you about my fairy god-mother."

Epilogue

The following evening, Zach stood by the fountain in the courtyard of his first resort with Arielle's brothers—all five of them—and marveled at how much they looked alike. Except for the twins, Jake and Luke, the other three all had different mothers. But there was no doubt they were related. All five men were well over six feet tall, had muscular athletic builds and bore a strong facial resemblance. Each accepted Zach into the family, in his own way.

"You do know that our little sister is always going to be right and you're always going to be wrong, don't you?" Luke asked, grinning.

Zach grinned right back. "Yep."

"And all she'll have to do is say the word and one of us will show up to kick your sorry ass," Jake proclaimed, laughing.

Nodding, Zach's grin widened. "I wouldn't expect anything less."

Caleb Walker spoke up. "I think he's going to work out just fine for our little sister, boys."

"Looks like it," Nick Daniels agreed.

"Welcome to the family, Forsythe," Hunter O'Banyon added.

When Arielle told Zach about the discovery of her three half brothers, he hadn't realized they'd all formed a bond in such a short time. But considering the mutually unique relationship they shared with Emerald Larson, they did have quite a bit in common.

His gaze drifted over to the white-haired woman sitting at one of the tables with her personal assistant, Luther Freemont. It was no wonder Arielle thought of the old gal as a real-life fairy godmother. She'd not only made Arielle's dream come true of owning her own preschool, but Emerald had brought them together again. And that alone was enough to convince Zach that she could work magic.

Checking his watch, he glanced at the French doors. Where were Arielle, her brothers' wives and Lana? As soon as the women had first congregated at his estate, they'd whisked Arielle off to find a dress to wear for the ceremony and he hadn't seen her since.

"Getting a little antsy there, Zach?" Jake noted as the other men discussed the homes Luke's construction company was building for them. "There's still time to run like hell."

"Nope. I've waited all my life to find your sister. I'm not about to lose her now," Zach declared solemnly.

"Oh man, you've got it bad," Jake observed, shaking his head. "And I thought Luke was lost when he figured out he loved Haley."

"Your time will come." Zach laughed. "And when it does, you'll go down like a ton of bricks."

Jake snorted. "Not me. Not when there's a smorgasbord of women to choose from."

"Never say 'never,'" Zach advised as the French doors to the resort's courtyard opened.

At the first sight of Arielle, dressed in a white knee-length gown, her dark auburn hair swept up into a cascade of curls, his heart stalled. He had to be the luckiest man alive and he intended to spend every moment of his life letting her know just how much he loved her.

Walking over to the terrace steps, he offered her his hand. "I missed you today, darlin'."

"And I've missed you."

"Do you have any idea how beautiful you are and how much I want you right now?" he whispered close to her ear.

Her pretty smile damned near knocked him to his knees. "Probably as much as I want you."

"Then what do you say we get this little gathering started so that we can go upstairs to the bridal suite and get started on the intimate part?" he teased.

"Excellent idea, Mr. Forsythe," she agreed as they walked over to the fountain where the Judge waited to make them husband and wife.

"Luther, isn't she the most beautiful bride you've ever seen?" Emerald proclaimed proudly, dabbing at her eyes with her lace-edged linen handkerchief.

"Miss Garnier does make a striking bride," her personal assistant concluded in his usually stoic manner.

Emerald surveyed the gathering. Nearly everyone in the room was a member of her family—a family she'd taken great lengths and spared no expense in finding. And one that she was extremely proud of.

As her gaze settled on Jake, she frowned. He seemed to be more like his father than any of her other grandsons and was, without question, the one she worried about the most.

But unlike her irresponsible son, Jake was complex and felt more than he wanted people to believe. And unless she missed her guess, he had been more deeply hurt than any of the others by their father's abandonment.

She sighed. Only time would tell if his devil-may-care attitude was nothing more than a smoke screen to hide his true, caring nature. And once he moved to Kentucky, taking charge of the enterprise given him as part of his legacy, the clock would start ticking.

"I now pronounce you husband and wife," the judge declared, drawing Emerald's attention back to her now-married granddaughter and her handsome new husband.

"Well, Luther, we've been successful in setting things right once more," she asserted, smiling.

"Yes, madam, it's worked out just as you planned," he agreed.

"Is everything in place for Jake's move to Louisville?" she asked, rising from her seat.

Luther gave her a stiff nod. "The documents have been signed for him to take immediate possession of the Hickory Hills Horse Farm the first of next month."

"Excellent."

Emerald smiled contentedly as she and her assistant walked over to congratulate the lovely couple. She and Luther made a good team and had successfully helped five of her six grandchildren find true happiness.

Kissing the bride and groom and wishing them a long and happy life, Emerald placed her hand in

Luther's folded arm as they walked toward the buffet table on the far side of the room. "Well, Luther, that's another one down. And only one more to go."

*   *   *   *   *

THE BILLIONAIRE'S
UNEXPECTED HEIR

BY
KATHIE DeNOSKY

This series is dedicated to Charlie, the love of my life.

And a special thank you to my editor, Krista Stroever.
Here's to new beginnings.

One

"Hi, I'm Jake Garnier, the new owner of Hickory Hills."

From the corner of her eye, Heather McGwire saw the man stick out his hand in greeting, but she chose to ignore the gesture. She knew who he was and she'd just as soon have a snake crawl up beside her. Jake Garnier was the last person she wanted or needed to have to deal with this close to the big race. But now that he was the new owner of the thorough-bred farm she managed, there was no way of getting around it. She either had to get used to working for him or stick it out until after Stormy Dancer won the Southern Oaks Cup Classic, then look for employment elsewhere.

Besides, after what they'd shared, she took exception to the fact that he didn't even have the decency to remember her. The thought hurt more than she would have imagined or was comfortable with.

When she remained silent, he stared at her a moment as if trying to place her. "Heather?"

His smooth baritone caused her nerves to tingle and her heart to speed up, reminding her that a little over a year ago all it had taken was the rich sound of that voice to make her lose every ounce of sense she ever possessed. Now it only made her want to smack him for being the biggest jerk to ever draw a breath.

"Jake." She barely managed a short nod of acknowledgement.

Standing with her forearms resting on the white board rail surrounding the practice track, she concentrated on the stopwatch in her hand as Dancer passed the quarter-mile post and headed down the backstretch. The top contender for the prestigious Southern Oaks Cup Classic, the thoroughbred was on pace to break his own record.

"Come on, Dancer. You can do it." She glanced from the watch to the horse. "Just keep it up."

"I remember you mentioning that you worked at a thoroughbred farm, but I wasn't aware that it was

Hickory Hills," he said, sounding a lot happier to see her than she was to be seeing him.

"For the record, I'm the manager here." As Dancer headed for the home stretch, she added, "The name of the farm and where it was located never came up. Besides, you weren't that interested in hearing personal details, were you?" She glanced his way, and it was apparent her hostility didn't set well with him.

"Heather, I don't know what you think I've done, but—"

"It doesn't matter now," she interrupted. She didn't care to be reminded of how foolish she'd been.

He was silent for a moment. "At the risk of pissing you off further, how have you been?" he asked tightly.

Like you really want to know. If you had, you wouldn't have refused to take my phone calls.

She shrugged. "I've been all right." She didn't bothering asking how he'd been because she had a fair idea of what he'd been doing since they parted ways and didn't particularly care to hear the specifics.

"Is that our contender for the big race?" he asked, pointing toward Dancer.

Doing her best to ignore the man beside her, she urged the jockey, "Let him have his head, Miguel. Turn him loose." She glanced at the silver stopwatch again, and clicked the button on the side as the big bay sprinted past them. "Fantastic."

"I take it that was a good run?"

When Jake leaned close to see the time, his arm brushed hers and a tiny jolt of electricity shot straight through her. "It was excellent," she said, gritting her teeth and backing away. Turning to make her escape, she added, "Now, if you'll excuse me, I have work to do." She barely suppressed the urge to when he fell into step beside her.

"I'd like for you to give me a tour of the farm if you have the time."

"I'm sure you need to unpack first," she said. Thanks to the mansion's housekeeper, Clara Buchanan, Heather had received a phone call the moment he passed through the security gates at the end of the half-mile-long driveway leading up to the mansion.

She desperately tried not to notice how his outstretched arms caused his snug hunter green T-shirt to outline the muscles of his broad chest and emphasize his well-developed biceps when he stretched. "I've been cooped up in the car for the past four days on the drive from Los Angeles and it feels good to be out in the fresh air again."

"Mornings around here are pretty busy—we have our daily workouts and grooming," she hedged.

When they reached the stables, she grabbed a lead rope by one of the stalls, slid the half-door back, then eased inside to attach it to Silver Bullet's halter in an effort to escape Jake's disturbing presence.

"All right," he said, stepping back as she led the big dappled gray gelding out of the stall and down to the tack room. "This afternoon will be soon enough."

She shook her head as she tied the rope to an eye hook by the tack room door, attached another rope to the halter, then tied it to another hook on the opposite wall of the wide stable aisle. "That won't work. My schedule is pretty full today and to tell you the truth, tomorrow isn't looking all that good."

"Clear it for this afternoon." Jake's no-nonsense tone indicated that he was quickly running out of patience.

For the first time since he walked up beside her at the practice track, Heather met his irritated blue gaze full-on with a heated one of her own. "Will there be anything else, Mr. Garnier?"

Scowling, he stared at her for several long moments before he finally shook his head. "I'll be back after lunch." Turning to leave, he added, "And you might as well plan on working late this evening. After you show me around, I intend to meet with the other employees, then I want to go over the accounting records."

As she watched him walk away, a nudge against her leg had her glancing down at the big Bernese mountain dog that had sidled up beside her. "You could really use some work on your guard dog skills, Nemo. Instead of taking a nap in my office, you're supposed to keep varmints like him away."

The dog didn't act the least bit repentant when he looked up at her adoringly and wagged his thick black tail.

Returning her attention to the matter at hand, she released a frustrated breath as she picked up a brush and began grooming the gray. She had no idea how he'd managed to get his hands on Hickory Hills, but she'd told herself when she learned Jake was the new owner that she'd be able to handle seeing him again. That she could keep what happened between them all those months ago separate from their working relationship.

Unfortunately, that was going to be a whole lot easier said than done. The sound of his voice carried with it the memory of him calling her name as they made love.

Closing her eyes, Heather rested her forehead against the big thoroughbred's shoulder. Over the past year, she'd done everything she could to convince herself that Jake wasn't that good-looking, that her perception of their only night together had been clouded by loneliness and the haze of too much champagne. But she realized now that she'd been in deep denial.

Jake Garnier was well over six feet of pure male sex appeal and it was no wonder that he had an endless stream of women clamoring for his attention. With broad shoulders and narrow hips, he had the lean, muscular body of an athlete. When they'd met at the thoroughbred auction in Los Angeles, he'd been striking in a suit and tie, but today in jeans and a T-shirt, he was raw sensuality from his thick black hair to the soles of his outrageously expensive running shoes.

Sighing heavily, she went into the tack room, retrieved a saddle, then returned to place it on the horse's back. She tightened the saddle's girth, then bridling Silver, led him out of the stable toward the practice track.

As much as she'd like to forget what happened that night in L.A., she couldn't regret it. Jake was arguably the biggest player on the entire West Coast. But there was an earnestness to his charm that she'd found completely irresistible. And she was reminded of how captivating it was each and every time she gazed into her baby daughter's eyes. Eyes that were the same cobalt blue and held the same sparkle of mischief as Jake Garnier's.

Walking back up the path from the immaculately kept stables, Jake wondered what the hell had just taken place. He wasn't used to getting the cold shoulder from women and Heather's blatant snub didn't sit well.

There were only two things besides his siblings and highly successful law practice that caught and held his attention for any length of time and that was fast, flashy cars and shamelessly uninhibited women. And to his immense pleasure, the first frequently attracted plenty of the latter.

So why did one woman's obviously low opinion of him matter? He wasn't sure, but there had been a sparkle of hostility in Heather's eyes that had taken him completely by surprise.

Thinking back to the first time he'd seen her, he still couldn't believe how captivating she'd been. He'd attended a thoroughbred auction to personally see that the woman he'd represented in a bitter divorce sold the horses she and her husband had purchased as an investment. Jake had quickly lost interest in the parade of equine offerings and looking around spotted a pretty little filly of the human variety to divert his attention. And from the moment he introduced himself to her, he found Heather to be the most enchanting woman he'd ever had the pleasure of meeting.

They'd spent the rest of that day and one incredibly sensuous night together and over the course of the past year he'd come to the conclusion that he should have asked for her last name and a number where he could reach her. It was totally out of character for him and something he'd never contemplated before. Once he parted ways with a woman, he never looked back, never had the slightest regret about not contacting her again. At least he hadn't until Heather.

But surely she wasn't angry that he hadn't kept in touch over the fifteen months since. Besides the fact that he didn't know how to reach her, it was a well-known fact that he wasn't looking for a relationship of any kind and that none of his liaisons went any further than a good time.

He had no idea if that's what the problem was, but he had every intention of finding out and settling the animosity between them once and for all. If she was going to be running the horse farm that his newfound grandmother, Emerald Larson, had insisted he take over, it was essential that they get whatever had her panties in a twist straightened out so they could at least be civil.

In the meantime, he needed to unpack and put in a call to Emerald, Inc. headquarters to find out what the hell Emerald had up her sleeve this time. Given her track record of setting her grandchildren up to find their soul mate, he wasn't naive enough to think that she wasn't attempting to do the same thing with him. He wasn't sure how she'd done it, but she had to have discovered that, however brief it had been, that he and Heather had a bit of history.

But the old girl was in for a big disappointment if she thought her tactics were going to work with him. He wasn't looking to settle down with a wife, kids and the requisite canine. Nor was he inclined to trade his sleek little red Ferrari for a family-friendly minivan with car seats and clumps of dog hair.

With a plan of action to set down a few ground rules for both Emerald and his farm manager, Jake followed the path around the antebellum mansion to the circular drive in front where he'd parked his sports car. Just as he pressed the remote on his keychain to open the trunk, a teenage boy wearing stylishly ragged jeans, an oversize chartreuse T-shirt with It Is What It Is screen-printed on the front and a red baseball cap turned backward on his head came out of the house to greet him.

"Hi, Mr. Garnier," the kid said, crossing the veranda and bounding down the steps. He came to a sliding halt at the side of the car, then stood staring at it as if in awe. "Suh-weet."

"Thanks," Jake said, chuckling at the way the boy stretched the simple word into two syllables. "And you are?"

"Daily." He grinned. "My dad was a horse trainer before he died and talked my mom into naming me after the Daily Double at Churchill Downs." He reverently circled the car. "Dude, I have *got* to get me a ride like this when I get old."

Jake realized that the kid was talking to himself and meant no disrespect. But the comment reminded him that within a few short weeks he'd mark his thirty-seventh year and he supposed that in the eyes of a young teenager, he was probably considered a fossil.

Smiling, Jake reached into the trunk for the

suitcase he'd packed for his short stay at Hickory Hills. But Daily jumped forward to grab the handle.

"I'm sorry, Mr. Garnier. I didn't mean to get so carried away looking at your car." He hoisted the suitcase out of the trunk. "My grandma sent me out to get your luggage and take it upstairs for you."

"You're Mrs. Buchanan's grandson?" Jake asked, following Daily up the steps of the veranda.

The boy nodded. "Grandma's in charge of the house and Heather is in charge of everything else." Daily's youthful face suddenly split into a wide grin. "Wait until you meet Heather. For an older chick, she's way hot. Having her to look at every morning makes my chore of mucking out stalls a lot easier."

When Emerald and her stoic assistant, Luther Freemont, had met with him to turn over ownership of the farm, they'd informed him that Clara Buchanan was the live-in housekeeper. But they hadn't said a word about Heather being the farm manager. That just reinforced Jake's theory that Emerald was definitely up to something. Why else would she mention the name of the housekeeper and leave out all reference to the woman who ran the majority of the farm?

"I've met Heather." The kid couldn't be more than fourteen or fifteen years old, but it seemed he already had an appreciative eye for the ladies. "And I agree. She's very pretty."

When Daily opened the double doors and stood back, Jake entered the foyer and immediately felt as if he'd taken a step back in time. Decorated with furniture he had no doubt were period antiques, he half expected to see a woman in a wide hoop skirt descend the sweeping circular staircase. Or more likely a Kentucky colonel dressed in a white suit and holding a mint julep come strolling out of the study.

"Grandma told me to take your luggage up to the west wing," Daily said, walking toward the stairs. "If you want me to, I can show you where your room is, Mr. Garnier."

"Lead the way." When they reached the top of the staircase, Jake grinned. "I'll bet sliding down a banister like this one is as close to being on a roller coaster as you get without going to an amusement park."

"Oh, dude, talk about a rush," Daily said, his voice enthusiastic. He stopped suddenly, a concerned expression crossing his youthful face. "Uh, you probably don't want me doing that because of scratching the finish."

"It's water under the bridge now." Jake shook his head. "But I'm not as concerned with a few marks on the wood as I am about you taking a fall. That's a long way down and you could be badly injured."

"You won't tell my grandma, will you? She'll kill me if she finds out."

Jake took pity on the kid. "As long as you don't

do it again, I think we can keep it between the two of us."

Clearly relieved to hear Jake would be keeping his secret, the boy smiled. "Thanks. You're really cool, Mr. Garnier."

"I'll take that as a compliment." Every time Daily called him Mr. Garnier, he felt as old as dirt. "And while you're at it, why don't you call me Jake?"

After a delicious lunch, Jake strolled back down the path leading to the stables and couldn't help but wonder if he'd lost his touch with the opposite sex. He'd never had this much trouble with women in his entire life. If things didn't change, he just might end up developing a complex.

Emerald, for one, was purposely avoiding him and unless he missed his guess, she'd continue to do so for a while. She had to know he was on to her latest matchmaking scheme and no doubt wanted to avoid having him tell her to mind her own damned business.

But Mrs. Buchanan's sudden disappearance right after serving him lunch was a complete mystery. She'd been friendly enough when he first walked into the kitchen. But as soon as she put his plate in front of him, she'd apologized and rushed off to the housekeeper's quarters as if she thought he was contagious.

And then there was the chilly reception he'd

received from Heather that morning. Her body language and obvious contempt let him know in no uncertain terms exactly how she felt about his re-appearance in her life. But try as he might, he couldn't figure out why. He hoped for better luck with her during their meeting this afternoon, but he wasn't fool enough to count on that happening.

Entering the stable, he walked past several stalls to the opposite end of the structure where the manager's office was located. He wasn't the least bit surprised that Heather was nowhere in sight. Given her attitude toward him, he really expected no less. He wasn't, however, prepared for the very large black dog that got up from a blanket in the corner, walked over and stretched out on top of his feet.

"At least you're friendly," he said, reaching down to pet the dog's head.

Irritated that she'd obviously blown off his request to set up a meeting with the farm employees, he extricated his feet from beneath the animal and covered the short distance to where the brood mares were kept. He found Heather bent over a horse lying on its side in one of the stalls, and his mouth went completely dry. She was dressed in a pair of faded blue jeans and a pale pink T-shirt. With the denim hugging her shapely little bottom to perfection, he didn't think twice about taking in the delightful view.

As she straightened, an older man Jake assumed

to be one of the grooms brushed past him to enter the stall and hand her a pair of rubber gloves. When she pulled them on they extended up to her shoulders.

"What's going on?" he asked, venturing farther into the enclosure.

"The stork is going to make it before the vet." She knelt down behind the horse in the middle of the oversize stall. "Jake, I want you to hold her head to keep her from trying to get up, while Tony and I take care of things on this end," she instructed.

Jake wasn't used to anyone issuing him orders, but something in Heather's tone had him kneeling down to carry out the directive. As he watched, the man she'd called Tony held the horse's tail, while she helped guide the foal from the mare. She quickly lifted a membrane away from the colt's nose, then vigorously massaged the animal's small, wet body with a towel.

"Is that to make sure it starts breathing?" He found her skill and efficiency to be very impressive.

Nodding, she pulled off the gloves and stood up. "He was doing pretty good on his own, but it never hurts to have a little insurance when it comes to foals this valuable." She smiled down at the weak little creature. "We may be looking at the next Triple Crown winner."

Rising to his feet, he moved away from the mare's head as she started to get her legs under her. "Do you have to do this sort of thing very often?"

Before she could answer his question, the cell phone clipped to the waistband of her jeans rang, and she stepped out of the stall to take the call.

Jake turned to the groom. "By the way, I'm Jake Garnier, the new owner here."

Grinning, the man nodded. "I figured as much. Welcome to Hickory Hills."

"I have to go up to the main house for a few minutes," Heather interrupted, stepping back into the stall. "If you have any questions about the brood mares, training schedules or the farm's daily routine, Tony can fill you in."

Jake walked over to stand beside her. "I think I'll go with you, then you can show me around."

"There's really no need." Her long golden brown ponytail swayed back and forth as she shook her head. "I'll only be a few minutes and there's no sense in you walking all that way just to turn around and walk back."

Had that been a hint of panic he'd detected in her soft voice? Why didn't she want him going with her?

"I don't mind at all," he said, placing his hand to the small of her back to usher her along. There was no way she'd leave him behind now. "Afraid of a little exercise?"

Jake could tell she wanted to protest at his wise-crack, but clamping her lips together, she quickly stepped away from his touch and preceded him out of the stall. Neither spoke as they walked side by side up the path to the back entrance of the mansion and he couldn't help but wonder what she was trying to keep from him. And he had no doubt there was something. He hadn't been an attorney for the past twelve years without learning to recognize when someone was trying to conceal a secret.

When they entered the kitchen, Jake stopped short at the sight of Clara Buchanan with a crying baby in her arms. Never in a million years would he have thought the emergency calling Heather away from work would be a baby. But his astonishment was compounded tenfold when Heather hurried over to them and took the child from the housekeeper. The baby instantly calmed down and it was obvious that Heather was the child's mother.

"I think she might be running a little bit of a fever," Clara said, touching the baby's round little cheek.

Heather nodded. "I thought she felt warm when I got her up this morning." She tenderly pressed her lips to her daughter's forehead. "I think she might be trying to cut her first tooth."

"That's what the pediatrician said when I called her." The housekeeper smiled fondly at the tiny girl. "But I wanted to let you know and see what you thought about taking Mandy in to her office."

"It might not be a bad idea to have a doctor check her over," Jake said from behind her.

He knew even less about babies than he did about horses. But he and his twin brother, Luke, had raised their ten-year-old sister after their mother was killed in a car accident and remembered that when a child had an elevated temperature it was always better to err on the side of caution.

"Just to be on the safe side, I think I will take her to see Dr. Evans."

"I'll get the diaper bag," Clara said, disappearing down the hall toward her apartment.

As she and Jake stood in uncomfortable silence while she waited for Clara to return, Heather felt as if her nerves had been stretched to the breaking point. Was Jake aware that he was standing barely four feet away from his own daughter? Had he noticed that Mandy had his blue eyes and dark hair?

Ever since she'd learned that he was taking over Hickory Hills, she'd wondered how she was going to break the news to him about the baby. But she hadn't anticipated him meeting their daughter before she had a chance to tell him about her.

He hadn't said anything. Maybe he hadn't noticed how much Mandy looked like him. If that was the case, she'd be able to explain everything in a much less rushed fashion. She hoped.

"Needless to say, I won't be giving you that tour of the farm this afternoon or holding the meeting you wanted with your employees," she finally said as she cradled the baby close.

He nodded. "That's understandable. We can re-schedule for tomorrow morning or even the day after if she's still not feeling well."

When the housekeeper came back into the room, he reached out and took the diaper bag from her. "I'll help Heather and the baby get to the car."

"Call me when you get back to let me know what you find out from the doctor about our little angel," Clara called after them as they left the house.

"Would you mind letting Tony know that he's in charge until I get back?" Heather asked as they walked the short distance to the carriage house.

Jake shook his head as he watched her open the back door of the older-model sedan parked in front. "No problem. I'll take care of it. Is there anything else?"

"Not that I can think of."

When Heather turned to put the baby in the car seat, the little girl looked at him over her mother's shoulder for the first time and he felt as if he'd been flattened by a steam roller. He couldn't have gotten his vocal cords to work if his life depended on it and simply stood back as Heather got into the car and drove away.

As he watched the vehicle disappear around the corner of the mansion and head down the drive toward the main road, his heart pounded against his ribs and he found it extremely hard to draw air into his lungs. The baby had dark hair and big blue eyes.

Eyes the color of cobalt. The same color of cobalt that met his gaze when he looked into the mirror each morning to shave.

Two

That evening, when Heather answered the insistent knocking on her cottage door, she wasn't the least bit surprised to find Jake standing on the other side. In fact, she'd been expecting him. She'd known that once he saw Mandy it was just a matter of time before he put it all together.

"We need to talk." Instead of waiting for her to invite him in, he took hold of her elbow and propelled her back into the living room, kicking the door shut behind him. "I want answers and I'm not leaving here until I get them, Heather."

"It never crossed my mind that you would," she

said calmly. She wasn't going to allow him to upset or stress her out in any way.

"That baby belongs to me, doesn't she?" he demanded, cutting right to be heart of the matter.

"*That baby* has a name—Amanda Grace. I call her Mandy. She's almost seven months old." Heather walked across the room to pull the nursery door closed to keep their raised voices from disturbing her daughter. "And if by belong, you mean are you her biological father? The answer is yes."

"What happened? I used protection."

Was he actually questioning that he was the father of her child?

"I'm well aware of that. It obviously had a defect." She raised an eyebrow. "Surely you're aware that nothing is one hundred percent effective except abstention. And if we'd gone that route—"

"We wouldn't be having this conversation," he finished for her.

"Exactly." She looked him directly in the eye. "But let me assure you, Mandy is your daughter."

He shook his head. "I wasn't questioning that. She looks just like me."

Heather watched a muscle work along his lean jaw as Jake stared at her for what seemed like an eternity. She could tell his anger was bordering on outrage, but that was just too bad. As far she was concerned, not knowing he'd fathered a child was his own fault and she wasn't about to let him turn the blame back on her.

"Did you even think about getting in touch with me when you discovered you were pregnant?" he finally asked, his voice low and menacing.

Heather had told herself that she wasn't going to let him get to her, but his accusatory tone angered her as little else could. "I really don't think you want to go there, Jake. Believe me, you won't like hearing what I have to say."

"Go ahead. Try me." He took a step toward her. "I told you I'm here to get answers."

"Then I would suggest you drop the intimidation tactics as well as the idea of being the wounded party in all of this because you're not." When she turned to walk into the kitchen to put a little more distance between them and the nursery, she fully expected him to follow.

He didn't disappoint her. "Did you or did you not consider letting me know that you were expecting my child?"

Turning on him, she took a deep breath in an effort to calm down. She had a lot to say and she was going to savor every second of it. She'd wanted this conversation for over a year, but never thought she'd have the chance to have her say. She wasn't going to allow herself to lose momentum by becoming overly emotional. She refused to give Jake that kind of power over her.

"I not only considered letting you know, I spent my first trimester leaving messages that I needed to talk to you urgently." She met his angry gaze head on. "*You* never returned my calls, and I wasn't comfortable leaving that kind of information with your secretary."

"I—"

Holding up her hand to stop whatever lame excuse he came up with, she went on, "Then I spent the second trimester trying to convince myself that there had to be a reasonable explanation for you ignoring my requests to get back to me. It turns out I was wrong. There wasn't a good reason, other than you really are an insensitive, self-absorbed jerk who uses women, then casts them aside."

He opened his mouth to no doubt refute her assessment of his character, but she cut him off again.

"And somewhere during the course of my third trimester, I came to the conclusion that you really didn't deserve to know about our daughter and that we were both going to be a lot better off without you in our lives." She folded her arms beneath her breasts. "Any more questions?"

Heather could tell by the stunned look replacing the angry expression on his handsome face that she'd gotten through to him.

Rubbing the back of his neck as if to relieve tension, he shook his head. "I have my secretary—"

"Screen your calls so that you don't have to deal

with uncomfortable situations with the women you've bedded," she interrupted. When he remained silent, she knew that her comment had hit a little too close to home. "And you don't have to worry, Jake. Mandy and I are just fine on our own."

His eyes narrowed. "You're going to try to cut me out of her life?"

Heather shook her head. "That's not what I said. I'm telling you that you're off the hook. You're free to go back to Los Angeles and resume your life as if nothing happened. I don't want or need your help—financially or otherwise. I'm perfectly capable of taking care of and providing for my daughter. I just thought you had the right to know about her."

"She's mine, too."

Having had her say, she suddenly felt drained of energy. "I'm relieving you of that responsibility, Jake."

"I think we need to get this straight once and for all, Heather."

He stepped forward to place his hands on her shoulders. The heat from his touch seeping through her T-shirt and the determination she detected in his deep baritone sent tingles zinging straight up her spine. But when he used his thumb and forefinger to lift her chin until their gazes locked, the sensation danced across every nerve in her body.

"I accept that it was my own damned fault I

didn't know about the pregnancy. But it doesn't mean that now that I'm aware I have a child I don't intend to be a big part of her life. And that will be much easier for me to do when I move you and Mandy into the mansion with me."

"That's not going to happen, Jake. We're very happy right here in the carriage house."

"We'll see about that."

Before she could protest or step away, his mouth covered hers and the feel of his firm lips once again caressing hers with such care caused her head to spin. She tried with all of her might to remain unaffected, but her traitorous pulse took off and a delicious warmth began to flow through her veins.

Placing her hands on Jake's wide chest, instead of pushing away from him as she intended, she reveled in the feel of his strength beneath her palms and the steady beat of his heart. This was total insanity. He'd used her, then cast her aside with little or no regard for her feelings. But when he traced the seam of her mouth with his tongue, she parted her lips without so much as a second thought and allowed him to deepen the kiss.

As he wrapped his arms around her and pulled her more fully against his large frame, he teased her with a tenderness that caused every fiber in her being to quiver to life and her stomach to flutter wildly. The excitement she'd experienced in his arms fifteen long months ago began to fill her from head to toe and it scared her as little else could. Losing herself to Jake's kiss was the very reason they found themselves in their current set of circumstances.

"Please…stop," she said, leaning away from him.

Jake immediately put a bit of space between them, but continued to hold her loosely in his arms. "All things considered, I probably shouldn't have done that." He gave her the same seductive smile that had been her downfall that night in Los Angeles. "But I'll be damned if I'm sorry I did. You have the sweetest lips I've ever tasted."

She shook her head. "Forget my lips. It's not going to happen again."

He stared down at her for endless seconds and just when she thought he was going to argue the point, Nemo chose that moment to come lumbering in through the doggie door. Finding the two humans standing face-to-face, he apparently took it as an open invitation to push his way between them and plop his big, bulky body on top of their feet.

"What's his deal?" Jake asked, staring down at the dog. "Every time he sees me, he traps my feet beneath him."

Thankful for the distraction Heather stepped back then knelt down to scratch the big gentle dog behind his floppy ears. "It seems to be a trait of his breed. I think they realize that they're too big to sit on your lap, so they lay on your feet to be close to you."

Jake bent down to pet Nemo's thick, black coat. "So I guess this means he likes me, huh?"

"It looks that way." Only inches apart, they stared at each other for endless seconds before she straightened to walk back into the living room to peek inside the nursery door.

She should have named the dog Benedict Arnold. Nemo was supposed to be loyal to her, not cozy up to the enemy like they were long lost friends.

"What did the pediatrician say this afternoon?" Jake asked from behind her shoulder. "Is she cutting her first tooth or is something else wrong?"

Unaware that he'd followed her, Heather jumped as much from the unexpected sound of his voice as from his close proximity. "Uh…yes, she's teething. The doctor said she has two that should be through her lower gum by the end of the week."

"She'll start feeling better after that happens, right?"

Heather nodded as she pulled the door to and moved away from him. The concern in his voice touched her and that was something she didn't like one bit. It was much safer for her to think of him as the shallow, uncaring man who refused to take her phone calls, than a daddy worried about the welfare of his baby girl.

"I think it would be a good idea if you leave

now, Jake." She walked over to open the front door. "I have to be up by five in the morning and I really need to get some sleep."

Glancing at the gold watch on his left wrist, he nodded. "I have a lot to do tomorrow and need to be up early myself."

He walked over to her, then cupping her cheeks with both hands lightly pressed a kiss to her lips. As he raised his head, the determination she saw in his incredible blue eyes sent a shock wave all the way to her soul.

"If you and the baby need me before morning, don't hesitate to give me a call. You have my word that from this day forward, no matter what I'm doing or where I am, I'll always be available for you and our daughter."

Once the front door closed behind him, Heather squeezed her eyes shut against the tears of frustration threatening to spill down her cheeks. She'd known the former owner was looking to sell, but why did Jake Garnier have to be the new owner of Hickory Hills? What cruel quirk of fate had caused their paths to cross again? And why, after all that had happened, did she still find him to be the most handsome, irresistible man she'd ever met?

When he'd introduced himself at the annual thoroughbred auction in Los Angeles, he'd not only charmed his way past her defenses and swept her off her feet, he'd stolen her heart, as well. She'd always heard about love at first sight, but she'd never given it a lot of thought, never believed it would happen to her. Not until last year. Not until Jake.

Swallowing hard, she reminded herself of the disillusionment and emotional pain she'd suffered when he refused to return her calls and she'd realized she meant absolutely nothing to him. It had taken her a long time to move past that and no matter how drugging his kisses were or how wonderful it had felt to be in his arms, she wasn't about to put herself in that position again.

Besides, it wasn't just her emotions at stake anymore. She had Mandy's well-being to take into consideration, as well. And Heather wasn't going to stand back and watch her daughter bond with Jake, then be devastated when he moved on like the playboy he was.

As he walked down the long driveway toward the big wrought-iron entrance gates, Jake still couldn't quite wrap his mind around everything that had happened. In the span of a few hours, his life had changed in ways he could have never imagined. He had reconnected with the only woman he'd ever regretted not keeping in touch with, learned that by taking over Hickory Hills she'd become his employee and discovered that a little over six months ago she'd given birth to his baby.

Unbelievable.

But as he thought about Heather making several attempts to get in touch with him, his gut burned with anger. He deeply regretted that she'd been forced to go through the pregnancy alone. If his secretary hadn't become overly zealous about screening his calls, she wouldn't have. He'd have not only been there for Heather throughout the pregnancy and birth, he wouldn't have been cheated out of the first six months of his daughter's life.

His daughter.

Jake's heart slammed against his ribcage and he took several deep breaths. He had a tiny baby girl who looked just like him.

It blew his mind that he had a child. Fatherhood had been something he'd never expected to experience. And it wasn't because he didn't like little kids. He did. He'd just made a conscious decision years ago never to marry and have one of his own.

His own father had twice walked away after impregnating his mother, and even though Jake didn't think he was capable of doing something like that, he hadn't wanted to take the chance. What if he carried the same narcissistic gene that had caused his father to shirk his responsibilities to his children in favor of pursuing his next good time?

Jake shook his head. It was all a moot point now. He had a daughter. And even though it scared the living hell out of him to think that he might somehow let her down the way his father had his children, Jake was going to do everything he possibly could to be a good father.

Lost in his disturbing introspection, it took a moment for Jake to notice the shadowy figure climbing over the gates at the end of the drive. "Daily?"

The boy froze halfway over the gate. "Mr. Garnier, I…oh, dude, this probably doesn't look real good, does it?"

"No. It looks like I just busted you for sneaking out of the house." Stopping a few feet from where the boy was perched, Jake planted his feet and folded his arms across his chest. "You want to come down from there and tell me why you're out this late, as well as why you don't want to alert anyone up at the house that you're leaving by activating the gates?"

When Daily dropped to his feet in front of Jake, he seemed to take a great interest in the tops of his untied high-top tennis shoes. "It's kind of personal, Mr. Garnier."

Jake hid a smile. "Want to tell me what her name is?"

The boy's head snapped up so fast, Jake wouldn't have been surprised if Daily had suffered whiplash. "How did you know I was going to meet a girl?"

Jake did his best not to laugh out loud at the astonished look on the kid's face. "I know it's probably hard to believe, but I was fourteen once, Daily."

"I'll be fifteen in a couple of weeks," the boy said, straightening his skinny shoulders.

"That's still too young to be out this late. Not to mention the fact that you don't have your grand-mother's permission."

The boy's shoulders slumped. "Yes, sir."

"I think you'd better give your girlfriend a call and tell her that you won't be able to make it this evening," Jake suggested.

As he watched Daily whip out a cell phone and rapidly punch in a text message, a knot began to form in the pit of Jake's stomach. In about thirteen years some pubescent boy with more hormones than good sense could very easily try to set up a midnight meeting with his daughter.

He barely managed to suppress a groan. He'd already raised one girl through the teen years when he and his twin brother finished raising their younger sister, Arielle. And just thinking that he was going to have to do it all over again with his own daughter was enough to give him an ulcer. His only consolation was that this time he'd be sharing that responsibility with Heather, instead of his brother who had turned out to be as clueless as he'd been.

When the boy slipped his cell phone back into his jeans pocket, Jake motioned toward the tree-lined drive leading up to the mansion. "Come on, Daily. I think it's time we both called it a night."

They remained silent for some time before Daily asked, "Are you going to tell my grandma about me trying to sneak out tonight?"

Jake shook his head. "No, I'm not. But you are."

"Me?"

"Part of growing up is learning to accept responsibility for your actions," Jake said, reminding himself as much as Daily.

"I'm gonna be grounded for the rest of my life," the boy complained when they entered the mansion through the kitchen door.

"I doubt it will be that long," Jake said, chuckling. "But as long as you're going to be sticking close to home for the next week or so, there are a few things around here I'm going to need help with. Do you think you'd be interested in the job?"

"A real job? Really? Oh man, that would be awesome," Daily said, his voice suddenly filled with enthusiasm.

"You'll have to keep up with your other chores and check with your grandmother first, to make sure she has no objections." Jake gave the boy a pointed look. "Right after you tell her about what happened this evening and accept whatever punishment she deems necessary."

Daily nodded. "I will."

"Then you'd better get some sleep," Jake warned. "We have a big day ahead of us."

"Yes, sir."

As he watched the teenager hurry down the hall to his grandmother's apartment, Jake headed for the stairs. He'd made Heather a promise and he fully intended to keep it. While she oversaw Stormy Dancer's morning workout and attended to whatever else her job entailed, he and Daily were going to get her and the baby moved from the carriage house into the mansion. And once he accomplished that, he had every intention of spending the rest of his stay at Hickory Hills getting to know his daughter.

"Jake Garnier, how dare you?" Heather demanded when she found him sitting at the desk in the study. She was angry enough to bite nails in two and it was all his fault.

His unrepentant grin when he looked up made her want to throw something at him. "I assume you're referring to the moving of the baby's things and yours from the carriage house to the rooms upstairs?"

"You know good and well that's what I'm talking about. You had no right to do that."

He walked around the side of the desk to stand in front of her. "I don't know why you're so upset," he said calmly. "I told you last night that's what I intended to do."

She couldn't believe his arrogance. "And I told you it wasn't going to happen. Mandy and I are perfectly fine in the carriage house. It's all she's ever known."

"I'm sure you're happy." He took another step toward her. "But you'll be even happier here. There's a lot more room. And besides, it will be more convenient for all concerned."

"You've got to be joking." Where did he come up with that idea? "It might be more convenient for you, but it certainly isn't for me."

He was a lot closer than she was comfortable with. But there was no way she was going to back away. That would only give him the satisfaction of knowing he still had an effect on her.

"I fully intend to be a big part of my daughter's life," he said, sounding so darned reasonable it made her want to punch him.

"We live less than a hundred feet away. How is moving to the big house going to change anything?"

He gave her a smile that caused her heart to skip a beat. Just because he smiled at her it wasn't going to get him off the hook.

"I want to watch you put her to bed at night and get her up in the morning."

"You could do that at the carriage house."

"So you're telling me that you want me to move in with you and Mandy?" he asked, giving her that same charming smile.

"N-no. That wasn't what I said at all and you

know it." She should have known he'd twist her objections around to suit his purpose. After all, he was an attorney. "You knew what I meant. You could stop by around those times, then leave."

He took the last step separating them, then lightly touched her cheek. She suddenly had to remember why she was angry with him.

"If Mandy wakes up in the middle of the night, I want to be able to get up with her." He shook his head. "If I'm here and the two of you are in the carriage house, I can't do that."

"Take my word for it, being awakened from a sound sleep is highly overrated," she said before she could stop herself.

"I'm sure that taking care of her by yourself and trying to work has been very tiring at times. Wouldn't it be nice for a change to have someone sharing that responsibility?"

When he looked at her the way he was doing now, Heather was lucky to remember her own name, let alone what he'd asked. "No. I'm fine with the way things are."

"I could get up with her while you sleep," he pressed.

The heat from his touch branded her and the scent of his aftershave made her want him to hold her, kiss her and… She swallowed hard. She needed to escape his presence before her traitorous body had her agreeing to go along with what he wanted.

"I—I don't mind at all being solely responsible for Mandy," she insisted.

"But you don't have to be, honey. Not anymore." He moved his hands down to her waist, then pulled her into his arms. "I'm here now and you don't have to do everything alone."

"Please, Jake," she interrupted. "Don't." Pulling from his arms, she somehow found the strength to back away from him. "I won't try to stop you from being part of Mandy's life. But I want you to keep a couple of things in mind before you take that step. First and foremost, it's all or nothing. You're either her father for life or not at all. I don't want her becoming attached to you, then you walk away when you get tired of playing daddy. And second, count me out. I'm not part of the package."

He stared at her for several long moments before he slowly shook his head. "You have my word that I will never do anything that isn't in her best interest or yours."

"Good. Because hurt my daughter and you'll have me to deal with." She could tell from his expression that he meant what he said—now. The only problem was, whether they intended to or not, people sometimes broke their promises and others ended up getting hurt.

"Now that we have your main concern out in the open and settled, are you and the baby going to stay here in the mansion?" he asked, seating himself back behind the desk.

"Jake, I don't think—"

"I've missed out on a lot with her already, Heather." His chest rose and fell as he took a deep breath. "All I'm asking is that you give me a chance to get to know my daughter and build a relationship with her."

She knew if she and the baby did stay in the mansion with him, she would be taking a huge risk for both Mandy and herself. If she hadn't known that before he kissed her last night, she did now. No matter how much he'd hurt her or how hard she tried to resist his charm, she still found Jake to be six feet two inches of pure temptation. And that could very well prove to be disastrous for her if she didn't keep her wits about her.

But she'd told him she wouldn't stop him from trying to bond with Mandy and she couldn't, in good conscience, deny either of them the right to get acquainted. And while he was getting to know their daughter, she intended to learn more about him, his family and where he grew up. After all, she had the right to know about her daughter's father.

Heather sighed heavily. Unfortunately, now wasn't the time to put him through the third degree. Aside from the fact that she'd already put in a grueling day, she was still too angry. She wanted to be calm, rational and in complete control when she talked to him.

"We'll stay in the mansion as long as you're here at Hickory Hills. But only on one condition."

His eyes narrowed ever so slightly before he asked, "And what would that be?"

Walking to the door, she turned back. "I meant what I said about not being part of the equation, Jake. Don't count on me to be one of your…diversions when you get bored."

Three

Jake frowned as he watched Heather place their sleeping daughter into the small baby bed that he and Daily had set up earlier in the day. "Is that thing full size? It looks awfully small."

When she placed her finger to her lips, it was all he could do not to groan. He couldn't forget the kiss they'd shared the night before and wanted to once again taste her sweetness and feel the softness of her perfect mouth beneath his own. But he knew better than to push. She'd outlined her conditions and he had to admit it was probably for the best. It wouldn't be long before they had to address some very sensitive issues concerning shared custody and how they were going to raise Mandy. If they became involved, it could make doing that a lot more difficult. He just wished that the attraction between them wasn't as powerful now as it had been when they first met. That would certainly make things a lot easier.

"It's a mini crib," she whispered, drawing his attention back to his question.

He waited until she turned on the baby monitor, clipped one of the receivers to her belt and they'd both stepped out into the hall before he asked, "Why didn't you get a regular size bed for her?"

"The room I turned into the nursery at the carriage house is small and I wanted to save space," she answered as they started downstairs.

"What about when she gets a little older?" he asked, following her. He didn't like the idea of his child being in a room that was too small when she had every right to live in the mansion and enjoy the spaciousness of any one of the spare bedrooms. "How will you fit a regular size bed into that room and still have enough space for her to play?"

"When the time comes, I'll convert the room I use for a study into another bedroom." At the bottom of the steps, she turned to face him. "Why are you asking about this now? It won't be an issue for another year or two."

He smiled as the germ of an idea took root. "I

was thinking that the two of you could live here in the mansion even after I go back to L.A."

"No. That's not an option," she said, shaking her head until her ponytail swayed back and forth.

"Why not?"

She started toward the hall leading to the kitchen. "Because it's not *my* home."

Reaching out, he took hold of her arm and the feel of her soft skin beneath his palm sent heat straight to the pit of his belly. He did his best to ignore it. "This is my house now and Mandy is my daughter. She has every right to live here."

Heather gave him a look that stated in no uncertain terms that she didn't like his idea one damned bit. "But it's not mine, Jake."

He knew as surely as he knew his own name that there was a good deal of pride holding her back from accepting his offer. "I'm telling you it can be, Heather."

"I work for you and living in the carriage house is part of my contract."

"I'm offering you an amendment to that agreement." Barely resisting the urge to pull her into his arms, he hastened to add, "You don't have to make a decision about the move being permanent now. But I would like for you to give it some serious thought." Unable to stop himself, he reached up to brush a wayward strand of hair from her soft cheek. "It would make life for you and Mandy a lot more comfortable than being cooped up in a space where there's barely room for one."

Before she could come up with any more excuses why she and Mandy shouldn't live in the mansion permanently, he reluctantly dropped his hand to his side and crossed the foyer to enter the study. If he hadn't put some distance between them, there had been a very real possibility that he would have acted on his first impulse to grab her and kiss her until she agreed to his proposal. And that would have been a huge mistake.

It would take a fool not to see that just like a magnetic force, the attraction between them was too strong to fight and impossible to resist. But at this point, she didn't trust him anymore than she would a snake coiled to make a strike. And until he proved himself to her and they worked out an agreement to raise their daughter, he had no other choice but to bide his time and no doubt end up taking more than his share of cold showers.

He sighed heavily as he lowered himself into the chair behind the desk and reached for the phone. As he punched in his brother's number, he thought about the irony of it all. The only woman he hadn't been able to forget was back in his life, was the mother of his only child and thought him lower than the stuff she scraped off her boots after a trip through the stables.

"My life is just about as freaking wonderful as it can get right now," he muttered sourly.

"As a matter of fact, mine is going pretty good, as well," Luke said, laughing.

Wallowing in his own misery, Jake had missed hearing his brother answer the phone. "Good to hear, bro. How are things in Nashville?"

"We couldn't be better. Haley has passed the point where morning sickness is an issue and we're just waiting for the sonogram to see if we're having a boy or a girl." His twin sounded happier than Jake could ever remember.

"Glad to hear my favorite sister-in-law is feeling better," he said, wondering if Heather had experienced a lot of problems with morning sickness when she'd been pregnant with Mandy.

They were both silent a moment before Luke asked, "So what's wrong, Jake?"

"What makes you think there's a problem?"

He wasn't surprised by his brother's intuitiveness. As with many twins, he and Luke shared a sixth sense where the other was concerned and instinctively knew when things weren't going right. But Jake wasn't entirely certain how to deliver the news that upon his arrival at Hickory Hills he'd discovered he had a daughter and avoid having to listen to the I-told-you-so speech that was sure to follow. Luke had been warning him for years that his "love 'em and leave 'em" ways were going to catch up to him one day.

"You're talking to the only person who knows

you better than you probably know yourself." Luke paused. "So you want to tell me what's going on?"

"I have a daughter." Jake hadn't meant to deliver the news quite so bluntly, but once the words were out, he realized there wasn't any easier way to say it.

"Whoa! You want to back up and say that again?"

"You heard me," Jake said, wanting to reach through the phone and throttle his twin. "I have a six-and-a-half-month-old daughter named Mandy."

His brother was silent for so long, Jake wasn't sure they hadn't lost the connection. "And you found this out when you moved to the horse farm Emerald gave you?" Luke finally asked.

"Yeah." He took a deep breath. "Heather's the manager here at Hickory Hills. I'm betting when the old girl's investigators found us, they discovered that a woman I met at a thoroughbred auction last year had become pregnant from our one night together."

"That explains why you ended up in a place about as far removed from your life in Los Angeles as it's possible to get," Luke agreed. "Arielle and I wondered why you were given an enterprise that was totally out of your element when we were given businesses in our respective career fields."

"I don't know why Emerald didn't just tell me about Heather and Mandy instead of blindsiding me like this," Jake complained. "Didn't she think I would step up and do the right thing?"

His brother made a strangled sound. "You're getting married?"

It was Jake's turn to choke. "Hell, no. You know how I feel about marriage. It's not for me."

"Don't knock it until you've tried it," Luke advised. "I didn't think I was husband material, either, and look at me now."

"Whatever."

They were silent a moment before Luke asked, "Why didn't the baby's mother tell you about the pregnancy?"

"She tried, but my secretary didn't see fit to give me the messages." Jake made a mental note to call the woman the first thing in the morning and discuss her not bothering to give him a list of callers.

"Ah, if you'll remember, I told you—"

"Don't say it, bro."

Luke's laughter grated on Jake's nerves. "So when do we get to meet our niece and her mother?"

"That's the reason I called. How would you and Haley like to come up to Louisville for the Southern Oaks Cup Classic in a couple of weeks? The favorite to win the race came along with the farm."

"Sounds good," Luke said. "I assume you're inviting Arielle and Zach?"

"Of course, along with the rest of the clan."

A few months ago, when he and his siblings learned that the most successful woman in the corporate jungle was their paternal grandmother, they'd also been informed that they had three half brothers. After meeting them at one of Emerald's receptions and finding themselves in the unique position of being the unexpected heirs of one of the world's richest women, they'd become friends.

"And before you ask, I fully intend to invite our illustrious grandmother and her stiff-as-a-board assistant, too. She and I are going to have a little talk about her withholding information about my daughter," he added.

Luke snorted. "Good luck with that."

Making plans to talk again before the impromptu family reunion, Jake hung up, then called his other siblings to invite them to the gathering. With promises from all to attend, he walked into the foyer and ran right into Heather.

"Are you all right?" he asked, placing both hands on her waist to keep her from falling. A jolt of electric current as strong as a lightning strike shot through him and when she looked up, the awareness he detected in her aqua eyes let him know that she'd felt it, too.

"I—I'm fine."

"I'm sorry, I didn't see you," he said, filling his senses with her. The scent of her herbal shampoo and the feel of her softness beneath his hands sent heat coursing straight to the region south of his belt and his body's reaction was not only predictable, it was inevitable.

"I…was just…on my way upstairs." She sounded delightfully breathless and sent his blood pressure up a good ten points or so.

As if an invisible force held them captive they remained silent for so long, Jake finally forced himself to speak. "I…uh, was on my way to take a shower and call it an evening myself."

Still operating on West Coast time, he hadn't even entertained the idea of calling it a night. But he did need a shower. A cold one.

She nodded. "Well…I guess I'll see you in the morning."

"What time does Mandy wake up?" he asked, still holding her at the waist.

"Early."

Finally forcing himself to step back, he motioned toward the staircase. "Then it would probably be a good idea if we call it a night."

As if awakening from a trance, she blushed suddenly and ducking her head, started walking toward the steps. "Good night, Jake."

"Night."

He stood in the foyer long after Heather reached the second floor and disappeared down the hall. The sound of her voice and the realization that she would be sleeping just down the hall from him had him fully aroused in less than a heartbeat.

Taking the stairs two at a time, he made a beeline for the master bathroom. By the time he reached his bedroom, he'd already stripped off his shirt and left a trail of clothing on his way to the shower.

As he stood there punishing his body beneath the frigid spray, he couldn't help but wonder how long Heather was going to deny the chemistry that flowed between them. They could fight it, try to run from it and argue that it even existed, but it was just a matter of time before they made love again. He had no doubt about that. The only question was when.

With a record-breaking crop of goosebumps and his teeth chattering like the wind-up ones found in a novelty store, he turned off the water. He grabbed a thick towel and began to vigorously dry off. They were going to have to work out the agreement for Mandy, and Heather had to come to her senses and accept the inevitable. He didn't particularly like shivering his ass off in a shower so cold he could spit ice cubes.

"Heather, I'm sorry, but I'm not going to be able to watch Mandy for you this afternoon. I forgot that I have an appointment with the high school counselor to get Daily enrolled and set up his freshman schedule."

"I suppose I could take her with me," Heather said slowly, wondering how she was going to attend a meeting at Churchill Downs with a baby in tow.

"We can change that to another day, Grandma,"

Daily offered, sounding hopeful. "I don't care. I'm not all that into school anyway."

"Young man, you'd better get 'into it' real fast," Clara said sternly. "You're in enough hot water as it is after that stunt you pulled the other night."

"Listen to your grandmother, Daily. If you want a car like mine when you get 'old,' you're going to need a good job. And that takes education."

"Yes, sir," Daily answered, shoveling a fork full of scrambled eggs into his mouth.

Looking up, Heather's heart skipped a beat as she watched Jake stroll into the kitchen and seat himself at the head of the table. Dressed in a light blue polo shirt that emphasized the width of his broad shoulders and a pair of jeans that hugged his muscular thighs like a glove, he wasn't just his usual good-looking self. This morning, he was white-hot. Busying herself with Mandy's breakfast, she tried her best not to stare.

"What time is the meeting?" Clara asked. "Maybe we'll be back before you have to leave."

Heather shook her head. "It's a luncheon meeting and probably won't be over until late afternoon." She spooned a bit of baby cereal into Mandy's eager mouth. "I'll just take her with me and hope she has a good long nap during the speeches."

"I can watch her," Jake spoke up as he took a couple of strips of bacon from the platter in the center of the table.

"That's okay. I'm sure you have better things to do." She wasn't at all comfortable leaving her daughter with a man who she was almost positive had zero experience babysitting an infant.

Smiling, he shook his head as he took a sip of his coffee. "I don't have anything going on this afternoon. Besides, it will give Mandy and me a chance to get acquainted."

"Really, it's not a problem," she said firmly. "I'll take her with me."

An ominous silence suddenly reigned throughout the kitchen as Jake put down his coffee cup and their gazes locked. "Don't be ridiculous, Heather. She's my daughter, too. I have every right to watch her while you're busy."

"No way!" Daily said, his eyes wide. "You're Mandy's dad? I didn't know that."

"Come on, young man," Clara said, removing the boy's plate from the table. "You can finish your breakfast in our apartment before you go down to the stables to muck out the stalls."

"But, Grandma—"

"You heard me," the housekeeper said, cutting him off. "These two need to talk and they don't need you hanging on their every word. Now move."

Heather waited until Clara and a reluctant Daily left the kitchen before she turned her full attention back to Jake. "How many babies have you taken care of?"

"None."

"That's what I thought." When Mandy protested loudly, Heather spooned another bite of cereal into her mouth. "You don't have the slightest idea what to do with a baby."

His frown deepened. "I've got to start somewhere."

"My daughter isn't an experiment."

"She's *our* daughter." He placed his hand on top of hers. "I know you're worried I won't know what to do. But I promise, I'd never let anything hurt her."

She could tell from the sincerity in his voice and the look in his eyes that he meant every word he said. But he admittedly had zero experience with babies.

"I won't let her out of my sight the entire time you're away," he promised.

"Jake, I'm not at all comfortable with—"

"I'll even stay in the same room with her while she takes her nap," he interrupted.

"Have you ever changed a diaper?"

"No, but it can't be that hard to figure out. Besides, I'm a quick study," he said confidently. "You can show me how to put a new one on her before you leave."

She barely managed to hide a smile at his misguided self-assurance. He had no way of knowing that their daughter thought diaper changes were great fun and the perfect time to exercise her legs by kicking like a little karate champion.

"What about lunch?" she asked, beginning to realize she didn't have any other option. She couldn't get out of the meeting and it was no place for a baby. "Do you think you'll be able to feed her?"

"I watched you feed her breakfast and it didn't look all that difficult." He grinned. "Piece of cake."

Spooning the last bit of cereal into her daughter's mouth, Heather wiped the baby's face. "You'll call me if you have even the slightest problem?"

"Of course."

She lifted Mandy from the high chair and handed her to him. "Would you mind holding her while I wipe off the high chair and put it away?"

Jake had been too busy yesterday with the unauthorized moving of her things from the guesthouse to do more than watch her or Clara with the baby. It was time that father and daughter met officially. Besides, she needed to see how Jake was with Mandy before she agreed to him watching the baby.

He gently lifted Mandy to sit on his arm. "Hey there, Honey Bunny. I'm your daddy."

As Heather watched, the baby gazed at him intently for several seconds, then giggling, happily slapped her tiny hand against his cheek. But it was the look of awe and complete wonder that instantly came over Jake's handsome face that had her blinking back a wave of tears.

She wouldn't have believed it was possible to actually see it happen. But right before her eyes, Jake fell hopelessly in love with their daughter.

Four

When Heather returned from her meeting, she practically burst through the back door of the mansion. She'd tried several times on her drive from the Downs to call Jake on her cell phone, but he hadn't answered and with each passing second her concern increased. Searching the rooms downstairs, her heart began to pound hard against her ribs when she couldn't find either of them. Why had she let him talk her into allowing him to watch her baby?

But her anxiety turned to mind-numbing fear when she hurried up the staircase and entered the bedroom where Jake had set up the crib. The two were nowhere in sight.

In a near panic, she raced down the hall to the master suite. "If he's let something happen, I'll never forgive…"

Her voice trailed off as she came to a skidding halt just inside the suite door and a knee-weakening relief washed over her. There in the middle of the king-size bed her daughter lay curled up on top of Jake. Both were out like a couple of lights.

Leaning against the door facing, her panic began to recede and as she stood there catching her breath, she couldn't help but be touched by the moment. Heather knew for certain she'd never forget the poignant sight of her tiny baby girl sleeping so trustingly on her daddy's wide bare chest. For the second time in a matter of a few hours, she found herself blinking back tears.

Quietly, so as not to disturb either of them, she gently lifted Mandy into her arms and, walking back to the bedroom where the crib was, placed the baby in the small bed. Turning on the monitor, she clipped the receiving unit to the waistband of her khakis and turning to leave, came face-to-face with a wild-eyed Jake.

"Dear God, Heather, why didn't you wake me up to let me know you were taking Mandy?" he demanded. "When I opened my eyes and she wasn't there, I—"

Heather placed her index finger to his lips to silence him when the baby moved restlessly and let out a little whimper. "I'm sorry," she mouthed. She motioned for him to follow her out into the hall. "You looked like you might be a little tired from babysitting and I thought I'd—"

"Give me a heart attack," he finished for her.

That's when she realized that he'd been as terrified as she had when she'd been unable to find them. "I really am sorry. I didn't mean to frighten you."

Running a frustrated hand through his thick black hair, he took a deep breath. "I've never been that scared in my entire life."

As they stood there, she couldn't help but stare at his bare chest. Every muscle was well-defined and as her gaze drifted lower, she had an almost uncontrollable urge to reach out and trace her fingers over each one of the ridges on his abdomen.

"W-what happened to your shirt?" she asked instead.

"Oh, that." He frowned. "Do you know how disgusting baby food spinach looks? And dear God, it smells even worse. But when it gets on clothes, it's just plain nasty."

She laughed. "It is pretty gross, isn't it?"

"It's horrible." He made a face. "I thought I was going to lose it a couple of times when Mandy decided to take a handful and rub it in her hair."

Heather couldn't stop laughing. "Don't tell me. You set the dish too close to the high chair."

Nodding, he chuckled. "By the time lunch was

over, she had more food on her than in her. And I'm positive our daughter could hold her own in a frat house food fight."

"No doubt about it," she agreed, smiling. "Any other problems? How did the diaper changes go?"

"When I finally got her to hold still it went all right. Up until then, it was a little hazardous." He rubbed his flat stomach. "She's got a hell of a kick." His expression turned serious and he fell silent a moment before reaching up to touch her cheek. "Thank you, Heather."

The back of his knuckles stroking her skin sent a shaft of longing all the way to her toes. "W-what for?"

"For today." His voice took on a husky quality that stole her breath. "For giving me the chance to get to know my daughter."

Without a second thought, she closed her eyes and leaned into his tender touch. She might have been able to resist had it not been for the sincerity in his tone and the genuine gratefulness in his amazing blue eyes. But no matter how much she tried to fight it, he was the man who had stolen her heart all those months ago and given her a precious baby daughter.

"I want to kiss you, Heather."

His whisper made her feel warm all over. "T-that probably wouldn't be a good idea."

"Oh, I disagree, I think it's an excellent idea." His

firm lips lightly grazing the shell of her ear and his warm breath feathering over her skin caused excited little shivers to course throughout her entire body.

She was flirting with danger. This was Jake Garnier, player extraordinaire. But even as she tried to reason with herself, she swayed toward him.

Apparently, that was all the encouragement he needed because the next thing she knew he wrapped his arms around her and pulled her close. She opened her eyes just in time to watch him slowly, deliberately, lower his head and when his mouth covered hers in tender exploration, she thought she just might melt into a puddle at his feet.

As his tongue stroked her lips apart, her eyes drifted shut again and the intensity of his kiss caused her head to spin. But when he coaxed, demanded and persuaded her to respond, every cell in her body tingled to life and Heather found herself holding on to him for support.

She should stop him. It wasn't smart to kiss the man who obviously hadn't wanted anything more to do with her until he learned that she'd given birth to his daughter. But the thought evaporated when Jake crushed her to him and she felt his hard muscles against her tightening nipples and his insistent arousal pressed into her lower belly.

Her knees threatened to buckle and a swirling hunger began to flow through her when he moved his hand to cup her breast, then chafed the hardened tip through the layers of her clothing. She wanted him with a fierceness that frightened her more than she'd ever thought possible.

Jake must have sensed the change in her because he slowly eased away from the kiss, but continued to hold her close. "We've got plenty of time."

She could deny that having him kiss her, that being in his arms and having his body entangled with hers wasn't what she wanted, too. But they'd both know it was a total lie.

"No, it can't happen, Jake." It was hard to be convincing when his large hand still covered her breast. But she couldn't seem to find the strength to pull free of his arms.

"I'm not going to stand here and argue. Right now, I have to take a shower."

As she watched him retreat to the master suite, Heather couldn't help but wonder if she shouldn't take her daughter and run as fast as she could back to the safety of the carriage house. It was obvious that no matter what she said, he wasn't going to listen to her. And living in such close proximity was going to make resisting him extremely difficult.

But thankfully with the Southern Oaks Cup Classic only two weeks away and all of the activities that preceded it, they were both going to become very busy in a very short time. If she could just hold out a few more days, everything should be fine.

She was going to have to attend to Dancer seven days a week and make sure that he was ready to run the race of his life. And as the owner of the favorite to win the Cup, Jake would be away at the almost non-stop receptions and balls that were held to celebrate the annual event.

With her going to bed early in order to oversee the thoroughbred's dawn exercises and Jake sleeping in after being out late with Louisville's social elite, their paths probably wouldn't cross more than a handful of times. And the few times they did, it would most likely be in a public setting for pictures and publicity for the race.

Then, by the time the festivities came to a close, Jake would no doubt be bored with the comparatively slower pace of Hickory Hills and more than ready to head back to his exciting life in Los Angeles. She and Mandy would move back into the carriage house and once again settle into their comfortable, familiar routine.

As Jake sat in the study thumbing through a pile of invitations to teas, receptions and balls being held in honor of the big race, he frowned. How the hell was he supposed to work things out and reconnect with Heather when he was going to have to attend a string of social events?

But staring at the elaborate print on one of the invitations, a slow smile curved the corners of his mouth. The words "and guest" had him rising from his chair.

"Clara, could you watch Mandy for a few minutes while I walk down to the stables to talk to Heather?" he asked when he entered the kitchen.

"No problem." She smiled when he handed her the baby monitor. "How long has our little angel been down for her nap?"

"About a half hour." He checked his watch. "I'm not sure how long she sleeps, but I'll only be a few minutes."

"Take your time." Clara grinned as she motioned toward Daily seated at the kitchen table peeling a pile of potatoes. "We won't be going anywhere for at least the next two weeks."

"I keep telling you, Grandma. When somebody's grounded, it doesn't mean they have to do stuff like this," the boy complained. "It means they just can't go anywhere."

Jake hid a smile as he left the mansion and walking past the pool, started down the path toward the stables. Since his grandmother learned about his plan for a late night rendezvous, Daily had mucked out stalls, mopped floors, polished silver and performed any other menial task she could think to assign him.

In a few days, the kid would get a bit of a reprieve from doing household chores. Jake had already talked to Clara about having Daily help him with a few projects to improve the place. The housekeeper had readily agreed and expressed her gratitude for Jake's influence with the boy. It seemed that Daily was having a hard time adjusting to his mother re-marrying after the death of his father and she'd sent him to Hickory Hills in an effort to keep him out of trouble.

Shaking his head, Jake couldn't help but wonder what his friends in L.A. would think of that one. With his reputation for partying and entertaining a differ-ent woman every night, he was the last person most people would want influencing their teenage boy. But since his arrival at Hickory Hills, Jake had found that he was enjoying the slower, laid-back pace and had started thinking less and less about getting back to the hectic schedule he'd kept for the past several years.

Maybe it had something to do with finding out he'd fathered a child. Or it could be that it was just so vastly different from his usual lifestyle the novelty hadn't worn off yet.

He frowned. So why didn't going back to L.A. sound all that appealing?

As he entered the stable, another thought occurred to him, but he dismissed it. He refused to believe that he might finally be ready to settle down. That was just ludicrous. Of course, he wanted to return to his condo and highly successful law practice. He'd be a fool not to want that.

Greeting Tony and another groom as they attended

to one of the thoroughbreds, Jake relegated his self-analysis to the back of his mind. It was amusing to think that he owned over two dozen of the finest animals in the country and he'd never been on the back of horse in his entire life.

"What's up?" Heather asked when he walked into her office. "Is everything all right?"

Jake nodded. "Mandy is taking a nap and Clara is making Daily rue the day he even thought about sneaking out to see his girlfriend by making him peel potatoes for dinner."

Heather's smile sent a shockwave of heat straight to the pit of his belly. "Poor Daily. I doubt that he'll be eager to try that again."

Jake barely managed to suppress his frustrated groan. He seriously doubted she realized just how pretty she looked with soft curls escaping her ponytail and her creamy cheeks flushed from the early summer heat.

But it was her coral lips that fascinated the hell out of him. Since kissing her outside of Mandy's room two days ago, all he'd been able to think about was doing it again and a whole lot more. And it was the "whole lot more" that was about to drive him over the edge.

"Jake did you hear what I asked?"

"Uh…sorry." Lost in his own misery, he hadn't realized that she'd been talking to him. "What was that again?"

"I asked if you needed something," she said patiently.

Oh, yeah, he needed something all right. But she didn't want to hear what that was.

"As a matter of fact, there is something I need your help with." That was an understatement, he thought sardonically. Forcing himself to focus, he sat down in the chair in front of her desk. "I have a million receptions and a couple of balls over the next two weeks."

She nodded. "That's part of the Southern Oaks Cup celebration and as Dancer's owner, you're expected to make an appearance."

"From the number of invitations I've received, I'm beginning to realize just what a big deal this is," he said, choosing his words carefully. Over the course of the past several years, he'd gotten into the habit of attending parties without a date. Now, he couldn't believe how out of practice he had become at asking a woman out. "And I'd really like for you to go with me."

He watched her open and close her mouth several times before she found her voice. "You can't be serious."

He smiled. "I'm very serious. I wouldn't have asked you to be my date if I weren't."

"I…um, appreciate it, but I can't," she said, her eyes still wide with disbelief.

That wasn't the answer he wanted to hear. "Why not?"

"I'm going to be far too busy overseeing Dancer and preparing for the race to be able to attend." Her smile looked suspiciously relieved when she added, "I'm sorry, but you'll have to go without me."

It was perfectly clear to him why she was turning him down. The more time they spent together, the bigger the possibility she could no longer deny the pull between them. And that was the very reason he was going to insist that she go with him.

"But you would attend the various functions with me if not for your job, right?"

"Well…I…uh…since I'm not about to quit, it's not an issue," she hedged.

He knew he had her and if the look on her pretty face was any indication, she knew it, too.

Rising from the chair, he walked over and called for Tony to come to the office. When the man walked to the door, Jake smiled. "From now until the race is over, you're in charge of the stables. I want Heather free to concentrate on overseeing Dancer's training, preparations for the race and attending social functions."

The man looked as if he thought Jake might be joking. "Me?"

"Yes," Jake answered decisively. "Do you think you can handle the job?"

He watched the man's gaze cut to Heather, then back to him. "Sure. I can handle it, but—"

"Then it's settled." Jake shook Tony's hand. "If

anything comes up, you're still to consult with Heather."

When he turned to walk back and lower himself into the chair in front of Heather's desk, she looked as if she might blow a gasket. "What do you think you're doing?"

"I'm relieving you of your other duties until after the race is over." He smiled. "This way you'll be able to focus on Dancer and the race and attend the social side of this thing with me."

"You can't do that to me," she said, standing up to pace back and forth behind the desk.

"Sure I can."

She stopped to glare at him. "I have a signed contract that says otherwise. You may own this place, but I run it. I'm in charge and I call the shots."

"You're still in charge, Heather." He hadn't anticipated that she'd get this upset.

"At least running this farm will look good on my résumé," she muttered.

He narrowed his eyes. "You haven't been looking for a position elsewhere, have you?"

"Not yet," she admitted belligerently. "But you just made the decision to start the search a lot easier."

Rising to his feet, he walked around the desk and took her into his arms. "Look, you're still in charge. You're still overseeing Dancer's racing career. That hasn't changed. I'm just making it easier for you to concentrate your efforts on him."

"Get real, Jake. We both know the reason you relieved me of the majority of my responsibilities was purely self-serving. You want me to attend the social events with you. That's the only reason you did this."

He took a deep breath. "That's the way it started out. But the more I think about it, the more it makes sense for Dancer to be your top priority now."

"I can't argue that," she grudgingly agreed.

"And won't it make the next two weeks easier if you can turn your sole attention to that goal?"

She slowly nodded.

"I'm sorry I usurped your authority, but I'm used to being the one in charge." He kissed the top of her head. "From now on, I'll consult with you before I make a decision about the stables."

She leaned back to look him square in the eyes and he could tell she was only slightly less furious with him. "You'd better, because if you interfere again, I'm out of here."

If he'd doubted how seriously she took her job before, he didn't now. "Understood. Now, will you please consider attending events with me. It would be nice to have someone I know at my side."

"There isn't a shy bone in your body. You'll do just fine without me."

He smiled as he brushed an errant strand of golden brown hair from her soft cheek. "Yes, but I want you with me."

"I told you, I'm not one of your diversions while you're here," she stated flatly.

She wasn't going to give in easily. But then he wasn't, either. "Would you at least think about going with me?" he whispered close to her ear.

Staring at him for what seemed an eternity, she finally nodded. "I'll consider it, but I'm not promising anything."

Satisfied that his plan to spend more time with her had a chance, Jake lowered his mouth to hers to seal the deal with a kiss. His blood pressure skyrocketed as he slowly caressed her lips with his, and he decided he could easily become addicted to her sweetness as he savored the taste of her.

When he traced the seam of her mouth to deepen the kiss, he took advantage of her soft sigh and slipped inside to stroke her tongue with his. Teasing and coaxing, he encouraged her to explore him, as well, and when she tentatively acquainted herself with him, Jake felt as if a fire had been ignited in the pit of his belly.

But it was the feel of her breasts pressed to his chest, her nipples scoring his skin through the layers of their clothing, that caused his body to harden so fast it left him feeling lightheaded. He moved his hands down her back to the flare of her hips. Pulling her forward allowed her to feel the effect she had on him, how she made him want her. She whimpered softly and sagged against him, letting him know without words that she desired him as much as he did her.

Unfortunately, his timing was lousy. They were in her office in the stable with several people close by. And going back to the mansion was out of the question.

Reluctantly easing away from the kiss, Jake took a deep breath as he leaned back to stare down at her. He didn't think he'd ever seen a more beautiful sight. Heather's porcelain cheeks were flushed and her eyes were glazed with the haze of unfulfilled desire.

"I suppose I should let you get back to work now," he finally managed to get out through his dry throat. Before she could gather her thoughts and tear into him over kissing her again, he released her and, walking to the door, added, "Our first reception is this evening. You can fill me in on our host and hostess on the drive over to their place."

Five

Heather accepted the hand Jake offered as she got out of his Ferrari in front of the home of John and Martha Wainwright, then waited for him to hand his keys to the valet. She was still upset with him over his disregard for her authority at the farm, but the more she thought about it, the more she realized attending these social events with him could work to her advantage. If she did have to look for a position elsewhere, the contacts she made at receptions like this one could prove invaluable.

"So tell me about these people," he said as he cupped her elbow and they walked the short distance to the tall, carved oak front doors of the estate.

"John Wainwright is president of the Southern Oaks Bank and Trust and Martha is the treasurer of the local ladies' club," she said, quickly filling him in on their host and hostess. "Neither of them have the slightest interest in horses or the Classic. But they would both have a coronary before they passed up an opportunity to host a reception for it."

"In other words, they're all about showing off with a big party and getting a mention in the society column."

"Exactly."

When he handed the doorman their invitation, the man smiled broadly and swung one of the entry doors wide. "Welcome to Waincrest, Mr. Garnier." He nodded and gave her a wink. "And Miss Heather."

"Hi, Hank. How is Mae?" she asked, smiling.

The man's grin widened. "She's doing just fine, Miss Heather. Thank you for asking."

As they followed his directions past a sweeping staircase and out a set of French doors onto the terrace, she felt as if she'd stepped into a fairy tale. The place was decorated with a canopy of tiny white lights, white wrought-iron patio furniture and huge bouquets of red and white roses in marble urns. Clearly, the Wainwrights had spared no expense in transforming their lawn into a very elegant cocktail party.

"That's our host and hostess," she said, discreetly nodding toward a couple standing by the bar.

"This is why I needed you with me," Jake said,

leaning close. "You know who all these people are and what role they play in all of this hoopla."

She rolled her eyes. "Like you wouldn't have figured it out on your own."

When a waiter carrying a silver tray with glasses of champagne stopped in front of them, Jake removed two of the flutes, then handed one to her. "If I remember correctly, I think this is how we met."

She swallowed hard when his fingers lingered on hers a little longer than necessary and a feeling of déjà vu swept through her. He'd walked over to her, handed her a glass of champagne and the rest was history.

He leaned close. "Do you think the evening will end the same way it did that night?"

"With me pregnant?"

Jake's teasing smile faded. "I didn't mean *that*. But I'll be damned if I'm sorry it happened. We wouldn't have Mandy if it hadn't."

She could tell he was completely sincere, and she had to agree. "She's brought more joy into my life than I could have ever imagined."

Before either of them had a chance to say anything further, John Wainwright walked over to greet them. "You must be the owner of Stormy Dancer," the man said, turning up the wattage on his smile. Almost as an afterthought, he nodded at her. "Miss McGwire."

Wainwright wasn't interested in talking to her

and she knew why. His bank handled the accounts for Hickory Hills and he wasn't going to waste his time with a lowly farm manager when he could schmooze with the owner of one of the premier stables in the entire country.

As the man engaged Jake in a conversation about becoming a member of the local country club, Heather quietly excused herself and started to walk away.

Jake put his hand on her arm to stop her. "Where do you think you're going?"

Smiling, she pointed toward the buffet table. "I'll be over there."

She could tell he wasn't happy with the way John Wainwright had dismissed her as insignificant. But she really didn't mind being excluded from their conversation. She was far more comfortable talking to the Wainwrights' staff than she was mingling with people who thought they were better than everyone else.

"Dear, would you mind helping me?" a small, elderly woman asked politely. With a cane in one hand and a mint julep in the other, the poor woman had no way of carrying her plate of appetizers.

Smiling, Heather shook her head. "I don't mind at all. Where are you sitting?"

"As far away from these pompous asses as possible," she replied, her expression so sweet that Heather thought she might have misheard.

"Excuse me?"

"You heard right, dear. I called them pompous asses," the older woman repeated proudly. "I've finally reached the age where I speak my mind and don't give a fig what people think. Now, come. Let's find a place to sit and get acquainted."

When Heather followed the elderly lady to an empty table away from the majority of the crowd, she helped the woman get settled. "Is there anything else you need, Mrs…"

"Wainwright." The old lady shook her head disgustedly. "My son is the windbag who snubbed you in favor of kissing up to your young man." She patted the chair beside her. "Sit, dear. I need someone to talk to who doesn't act like they're something they're not." She gave a disgusted snort. "I just hate when John and Martha throw one of these receptions. They put on such airs, it's a downright disgrace."

Heather didn't know what to say. But she couldn't help but like the elderly woman and her candid observations.

"It's all right, dear." The old woman patted Heather's hand. "I have no illusions about how important most of these people *think* they are. And my son and daughter-in-law are the two biggest ducks in the puddle."

"Well, your son is the president of Southern Oaks Bank and Trust."

"Pish posh. It doesn't matter what job somebody ends up with, they should never forget where they came from." Mrs. Wainwright grinned. "I'll bet you didn't know that John grew up the son of a tobacco farmer who was land rich and dirt poor." She pointed an arthritic finger toward Jake. "But your young man seems to be different. You can tell he's got money, but he doesn't appear to act like he's better than everyone else. I'll bet he hasn't forgotten who he really is and where he came from."

Heather stared at Jake. She still knew very little about him. Busy getting ready for the race, she hadn't had the opportunity to ask where he grew up, about his childhood or his family.

Were his mother and father still alive? Did he have siblings? Could Mandy have family that Heather knew nothing about?

She didn't have a clue. But she had every intention of finding out.

As Heather continued to think about it, she had to admit that Mrs. Wainwright was correct in her assessment of him. Jake had never made her or anyone at the farm feel as if they were beneath him. Even Clara had commented that he went out of his way to make everyone feel comfortable.

Heather had watched him with the grooms and stable boys and he never failed to greet them by name or stop and talk to them for a few minutes. And he was probably the only billionaire she'd ever heard of who sat at the kitchen table to eat his meals with his housekeeper, her teenage grandson and his farm manager.

"Are you ready to thank our host and hostess for a nice evening and head home?"

Heather jumped. Lost in thought, she hadn't realized that Jake had ended his conversation with the bank president and crossed the lawn to join her and the man's mother.

Introducing him to the elderly Mrs. Wainwright, she smiled. "It was nice chatting with you."

"It was my pleasure, dear." Mrs. Wainwright placed a bony hand on Heather's arm and motioned for her to lean close. "You hang on to your young man," she said in confidence. "Mark my words, he's the real deal."

"Thank you, Mrs. Wainwright." She smiled. "I'll try to remember that."

After bidding the Wainwrights a good evening, Jake waited until he and Heather were seated in his car before he apologized. "I'm sorry, honey."

"What for?" She looked thoroughly bewildered and so damned beautiful it was all he could do to keep from stopping the car and taking into his arms.

"Wainwright had no right to ignore you the way he did." When the man dismissed Heather as if she didn't exist, a protectiveness he'd never known he possessed had consumed him and Jake had wanted to punch the bastard in his big pretentious nose.

They fell silent for some time before he felt Heather staring at him. "What?"

"Tell me more about yourself."

Glancing her way, he frowned. "What do you want to know?"

"Everything. Where did you grow up? Do you have siblings?" She laid her soft hand on his thigh and he had to concentrate to keep from steering the car into the ditch. "Does Mandy have an extended family?"

"What brought this on?" he asked, covering her hand with his to keep her from moving it. He liked when she touched him.

"Jake, we have a child together and beyond the fact that you're a successful divorce attorney in Los Angeles, I know very little else about you," she said quietly.

"There's no big mystery. My siblings and I were born and raised in San Francisco. I have an identical twin brother named Luke—"

"My God, there are two of you?" She sounded truly shocked.

Grinning he nodded. "But don't worry. He's always been the quiet, more serious one of us."

"In other words, your exact opposite." She looked thoughtful. "Is he married?"

"As a matter of fact, he just got married a few

months ago. He and his wife, Haley, are expecting their first child in about six and a half months." To his surprise, Jake found that he liked sharing details about his family with Heather. "And we have a sister, Arielle. She's ten years younger. She got married last month and is five months pregnant with twin boys."

Heather was silent so long, he thought she might have fallen asleep. "I'm so happy that Mandy is going to have aunts, uncles and cousins." She paused. "What about grandparents? Are your parents still alive?"

"No, our mother was killed in a car accident when Luke and I were twenty." He took a deep breath. No matter how long it had been, he still missed the woman who had give him and his siblings life.

"I'm so sorry. What about your father?"

He snorted. "We only met our father once. After he made our mother pregnant with me and Luke, he took off and she didn't see him again until we were almost ten. That's when he showed up, stuck around only long enough to make Mom pregnant with Arielle, then took off again." It was his turn to pause. "We recently got word that he was killed in a boating accident a couple of years ago."

"Who finished raising your sister after your mother died?" she asked, sounding genuinely concerned.

"Luke and I were in college and managed to work out a pretty good system. He would work one semester and take over most of Arielle's care while I went to school. Then I'd lay out the next semester, get a job and I'd be responsible for her while he attended classes."

"My God, Jake, that had to have been so hard for both of you." She turned her hand, palm up, to clasp his. "Did you try to get in touch with your father to see if he would send money to help out with your sister?"

Stopping the car at the entrance to Hickory Hills, he used the remote Clara had given him to open the wide iron gates. "We tried, but it proved to be impossible. We didn't even know his real name."

Her mouth dropped open. "He lied about who he was?"

Jake nodded. "We didn't find that out and who he really was until we were told he was dead."

When he drove the car through the gates, he pushed the button to swing them shut and as he they traveled the long oak-lined drive, he decided to omit his newly discovered grandmother's name. Emerald Larson was Mandy's great-grandmother but he still wasn't comfortable with the fact or with the way she manipulated her grandchildren.

"Mandy does have a great-grandmother," he said, watching Heather from the corner of his eye.

"We learned about her at the same time we found out about our father's death."

She smiled. "It's nice that you finally found each other."

"More like she found us." He shrugged. "She knew how wild and unsettled her son was and after he died, she had a team of investigators search to see if he had any children so that she could set things right with all of us."

"That's when she got in touch with you and your siblings?" Heather asked, seemingly fascinated with what he was telling her.

"Among others."

He could tell from her expression that Heather was thoroughly shocked. "You mean…he fathered more children than just you and your siblings?"

"It turns out our father took the biblical passage where it says 'Be fruitful and multiply' to heart." He smiled as he parked the car in the circular drive in front of the mansion. "He also fathered three other sons by three different women in the ten years between fathering me and Luke and Arielle."

Her eyes grew even wider. "Wow! He certainly was…um, active."

"To say the least."

Jake got out of the car and as he walked around to open the passenger door for her, he couldn't help but see the parallel between the way he'd been living his life and the way his father had. And he wasn't overly proud of it. But he was different from his father in one very important way. Jake was going to be there for Mandy where his father had failed his children in every way possible.

When Heather got out of the car to stand in front of him, he didn't hesitate to put his arms around her. "I know it seems like I've been living my life a lot like my father did, and maybe to a certain extent, I have. But let me assure you, I'll always be there for Mandy…and for you."

"Jake—"

"I mean it, Heather. I'm not the irresponsible jerk my father was."

Deciding that enough had been said about his notorious father and atypical family, he let his gaze travel from her silky hair swept up into a stylish twist, down the length of her black strapless cocktail dress, to her impossibly high, black heels. In L.A. they had a colorful phrase for those kind of shoes and he seriously doubted that she realized some women wore them to send a message that they were open to a night of unbridled passion.

Groaning, he raised his head to rest his forehead against hers. "Do you have any idea how sexy you are? How beautiful?"

Before she had the chance to speak, Jake teased and coaxed her mouth with his own until she granted him the access he sought. But he was completely unprepared and not at all disappointed when

Heather took control of the kiss and touched her tongue to his.

At first tentative, her shy stroking sent electric sparks to every nerve in his being. As she gained confidence and engaged him in a game of advance and retreat, the sparks touched off a flame in the pit of his belly that quickly had him wondering if he was about to burn to a cinder.

The reaction of his body was instantaneous. He hadn't become aroused this fast since his teens.

With his knees threatening to buckle and his head swimming from a serious lack of blood to the brain, he reluctantly broke the caress. If he didn't put an end to the kiss, and right now, he was in real danger of making love to her right there on the steps of the veranda.

"Honey…I can't believe…I'm going to say this." He stopped long enough to draw some much needed air into his lungs. "Unless you're ready to go upstairs with me—to my room, my bed—we'd better call it a night."

He watched her passion-flushed cheeks turn a deep shade of rose a moment before she shook her head. "I'm sorry…I…not yet." She suddenly clamped her mouth shut, then took a step away from him, then another. "I mean…no. That's not going to happen."

When Heather turned and fled up the steps, across the veranda and disappeared into the house, Jake reached up to unknot his tie and unbutton the collar of his shirt. Then, stuffing his hands in his pants pockets, took off at a brisk walk back down the long drive toward the entrance gates.

He couldn't believe how the evening had turned out. He wasn't in the habit of divulging personal information to the women he dated. It kept things from becoming complicated when he went his way and they went theirs.

But Heather was different. For reasons he didn't care to contemplate, he wanted her to know all about him. And he wanted to learn everything about her. What had inspired her to choose her career? Did she have siblings? Were her parents still alive?

Shaking his head, he fell into a steady pace as he started back toward the house. He had no idea what had gotten into him. Yet as he got better acquainted with his only child, he had every intention of getting close to her mother, as well.

Checking on her daughter sleeping peacefully in her crib, Heather crossed the hall and, entering the bedroom she'd been using since Jake moved her and Mandy into the mansion, closed the door. What on earth had possessed her to take control of that kiss? And why had she the same as told him that at some point she would be ready to make love with him again? Had she lost her mind?

As she removed her heels and unzipped her dress, she thought about the details he'd shared with her about his family. There was a lot more to Jake Garnier than first met the eye or that he allowed people to see.

He was a self-made man who hadn't always had an easy life. He'd been there right along with his twin brother to step in and accept the responsibility of raising their younger sister, while still managing to complete his education. That had been a monumental undertaking and she could tell that he wouldn't have considered doing it any other way. He and his siblings had struggled to stay together and they'd made it. That certainly wasn't something a self-indulgent playboy would do.

She slipped out of her dress and hanging it in the closet, took down her hair and changed into her nightgown. When she climbed into bed, she closed her eyes and hugged one of the pillows tightly against her.

The more she learned about Jake, the more she admired him. Considering she was finding it almost impossible to resist him, that was extremely dangerous. She couldn't afford to let go of her pre-conceived notion that he cared little or nothing about anyone but himself. If she did, there was a very real possibility that she and her daughter would both end up getting hurt.

Lying there hugging the pillow, she must have drifted off to sleep because the next thing she knew, her daughter's cries coming through the baby monitor awakened her. She tossed the pillow aside and, getting out of bed, reached for her robe. But the sound of Jake's voice stopped her.

"What's wrong, Mandy? Did my little honey bunny have a bad dream?" He must have taken the spare receiver to his room before he turned in for the night.

As she listened to him comfort their daughter, tears filled her eyes and spilled down her cheeks. It was clear from the tone of his voice that he loved Mandy, and Heather knew as surely as she knew her own name that he would be just as committed and protective of their daughter as any father could possibly be.

Without a second thought, she quietly opened her door and tiptoeing across the hall, watched Jake gently cradle Mandy to his bare chest. She waited until he put their sleeping daughter back in the crib, then walked out into the hall. "I appreciate your trying to let me sleep."

Running his hand through his thick hair, he shook his head. "Too bad it didn't work out."

When they both fell silent, Heather found it hard not to stare. Dressed in nothing but a pair of navy silk pajama bottoms, he looked absolutely… yummy. She suddenly felt warm all over.

"Heather, are you all right?"

"I…um, yes." She needed to make her escape while she still had the presence of mind to do it.

His slow smile said that he knew exactly what she'd been thinking. "I like the way you look, too." Reaching out, he traced one of the thin spaghetti straps of her gown with his index finger. "You make turquoise look real good, honey."

"I thought that was supposed to be…the other way around," she said, realizing that she'd forgotten all about her robe when she'd heard Jake talking to the baby. "Isn't the color supposed to compliment the person wearing it?"

"Not in your case, Heather." He trailed his finger down the strap to the gown's rounded neckline. "You make everything you wear sexy."

A shiver flowed through her when the tip of his finger lightly grazed the slope of her breast. "I'm… going back to…my room."

He took her into his arms. "I'd rather you stay with me."

"Out here in the hall?"

Staring up at him, she knew she was playing with fire. The feel of him holding her and the rich sound of his voice lowered to an intimate timbre caused an ache that she knew for certain only he could ease.

"I was thinking more like my room." His seductive smile sent her pulse into overdrive.

What she wanted was to go with him. What she needed was peace of mind. And that would be in serious jeopardy if she let her heart overrule her head.

She took a deep breath as she summoned every ounce of strength she possessed. "I want you to go to your room and…I'll go to mine."

"Are you certain that's what you really want, Heather?"

They both knew she was telling a huge lie. The last thing she wanted was to go back alone to the big empty bed across the hall. But making love with Jake would only add another wrinkle to their already complicated situation, not to mention pose a serious risk to her heart.

"Y-yes." Turning to go across the hall to her room, she wished she'd sounded more convincing. "Good night, Jake."

When he placed his hand on her shoulder to stop her, the look in his amazing blue gaze caused her heart to beat double time. "You can only run from this—from us—for so long." He leaned forward to kiss her with such tenderness she thought she might do something stupid like give in. "Sleep well, sweet Heather."

As she watched him stroll down the hall toward the master suite, she had to lean against the door frame to keep her knees from folding beneath her. How on earth was she ever going to be able to resist such blatant sexuality?

She somehow managed to walk into the bedroom and close the door. If it was just a matter of physical attraction, she was pretty sure she'd be successful.

But the more she learned about Jake and the more she saw how much he cared for their daughter, the closer she came to listening to her heart. And that was something she couldn't let happen again.

She climbed into bed and hugged the pillow close again. There was no doubt about it. If she intended to survive Jake's visit to Hickory Hills, she was going to have to keep her emotions in check. She was in danger of losing a lot more than her heart if she didn't. They still had yet to discuss how they were going to raise Mandy, and considering the high-handed way he'd relieved her of most of her duties, she might end up losing her job.

But as she lay there thinking about how it felt when he touched her, held her, she knew that keeping her wits about her was going to be all but impossible to do. She was falling for him all over again and there didn't seem to be anything she could do to stop it.

Six

"Where's Heather?" Jake asked when he walked into the kitchen and found Clara feeding the baby breakfast.

"Tony called. There was a problem down at the stables with one of the horses and he wanted her to come down to assess the situation." The house-keeper shook her head. "He knows Heather would never forgive him if he hadn't let her know about it."

Jake frowned. He'd put Tony in charge to free Heather from having to deal with this sort of thing until after the race. "Is there something wrong with Dancer?"

"No. I think she said one of the other studs has a really nasty cut on its pastern." She spooned a mouthful of cereal into Mandy's open mouth. "Heather's almost as good as a vet when it comes to taking care of horses and I'm pretty sure Tony wanted her to take a look at the injury to see how bad it is."

Clara might as well have been speaking a foreign language for all he understood about where the horse was injured. "How did she learn so much about horses?" he asked as he grabbed a mug from the cabinet, then poured himself a cup of coffee.

"Bless her heart, she learned from the best," the housekeeper said, smiling fondly. "Before he died five years ago, her dad, George, was the manager here. From the time she was old enough to walk, she followed him around like a shadow and soaked up everything he knew about horses."

Fascinated by the details he was learning about Heather, Jake leaned against the kitchen counter. "What about her mother? Is she still around?"

Clara snorted. "No, and I say good riddance. She was a wild one, always looking for a good time. She took off when Heather was six and they never heard from her again."

It sounded to him like Heather's mother and his father were a lot alike—narcissistic and completely irresponsible. "I think I'll walk down to the stable and see what's going on. Would you mind watching Mandy until Heather and I get back?"

"Not at all." Clara grinned as she wiped the baby's face. "Take all the time you need. The only thing I have to do this morning is come up with another list of chores to keep Daily busy after he finishes mucking out the stalls."

Chuckling, Jake wondered how much longer the woman was going to make the boy suffer for his lapse of judgment. "I have another project that I'd like his help with. Do you think you could pencil that in on the schedule for tomorrow?"

Clara nodded. "Will you need him all day?"

"Probably several days. Will that be a problem?"

"Not at all." She smiled. "What have you got up your sleeve this time?"

"When we moved Heather and the baby, I noticed the carriage house could use a fresh coat of paint and some new carpet."

As Jake left the house and walked the distance to the stables, his thoughts returned to Heather and he couldn't help but wonder how she'd slept the night before. If he was taking bets, he'd wager that she hadn't gotten any more sleep than he had.

Entering the stable, he followed the sound of a loud commotion. What had been so important that Tony felt the need to call Heather?

"Hold him while I get him tranquilized."

Jake automatically turned at the sound of Heather's voice inside one of the stalls and it felt as if his heart came up into his throat. As he watched, she, Tony and another groom jumped back just in time to keep from being kicked by a very large, extremely agitated horse.

"Heather, get out of there." He tossed the coffee cup onto a pile of straw and reached to open the stall's half door.

"Don't you dare open that door," she warned. "Just stay back. We've got this under control."

It didn't appear that they had everything in hand. It looked as if someone was about to get seriously hurt. The thought that it might be Heather had his heart hammering so hard that he thought he'd surely end up with a few cracked ribs.

When Tony and the other man finally caught hold of the thoroughbred's halter, Heather moved swiftly to jab a long needle into the animal's shoulder. The horse lurched to one side, then kicked the back of the stall with a blow that Jake knew for certain would have killed someone had it connected with one of the humans inside the enclosure. But just when he thought all hell was going to break loose, Heather and the grooms managed to open the half-door and escape.

Fear ignited an anger in him that quickly flared out of control and he was itching for a confrontation. "What the hell do you think you were doing in there?" he demanded when she stood safely in front of him.

"The job you pay me to do."

He stubbornly shook his head. "I pay a veterinarian to attend injured horses. And if the size of his bills are any indication, I pay him quite well."

As he and Heather glared at each other, Jake noticed Tony and the other man hurrying toward the far end of the barn. They apparently decided that retreat was the better part of valor.

"For your information, the vet *is* on the way." Her aqua eyes sparkled with anger and he didn't think he'd ever seen her look prettier.

"Then why were you in the stall? Why didn't you wait for Dr. Pennington to get here?"

"Because Magic needed a sedative immediately," she shot back. "We couldn't run the risk of him making the injury worse."

"I don't care," he said angrily. "You could have gotten yourself killed."

"I've been around horses all my life and I know what I'm doing," she insisted. "Besides, that horse is a full brother to Dancer and almost as valuable as he is. His stud fees alone are going to make you a fortune once he's retired from racing."

Reaching out, Jake took her by the shoulders. "Don't you understand? It's not about the money, Heather. Your safety is far more important to me than any money I could make off of a damned horse."

She stared at him for several long seconds before her stormy expression began to ease a bit. "Honestly, I really wasn't in as much danger as it might have seemed, Jake."

He crushed her to him. "Even the slightest chance of you being hurt in any way is one chance too many, honey."

As his heart slowly returned to a more normal beat, he couldn't get over the fear that had coursed through him when he saw the horse come so close to kicking her. It had rivaled the feeling he'd experienced a few days ago when he'd awakened to find his napping daughter missing from where she'd fallen asleep on his chest.

Before he could analyze what that might mean, he lowered his head to cover Heather's mouth with his. He told himself that he needed to reassure himself that she was indeed all right. Yet the truth of the matter was he'd become quite good at looking for reasons to kiss her.

Soft and pliant, her lips immediately fused with his as she wrapped her arms around his neck. But when she used the tip of her tongue to invite him to deepen the kiss, her eager response to the caress sent blood surging through his veins and his body hardened so fast it made him dizzy.

As he slipped inside and teased, he slid his hands from her back to her delightful little blue jeans-clad bottom and tried to pull her even closer. But an insistent nudge against his legs had him breaking the kiss to look down at the big dog trying to work his way between them.

"Thank God Nemo came along when he did."

Heather's cheeks colored a pretty pink as she glanced down the wide aisle to see if anyone had been watching.

"I thought you were supposed to be man's best friend," Jake groused when he bent to pick up his discarded coffee cup. He scratched behind the big dog's ears. "How would you like it if I interrupted you and one of your female friends?"

"Since he's been neutered, I doubt he'd care," she said dryly.

"Nemo, buddy, I'm so sorry to hear that," Jake said sympathetically.

She looked confused. "Why are you sorry he's been neutered?"

"It's a guy thing." Jake shook his head. "You wouldn't understand."

"The vet just arrived," Tony called from the opposite end of the stable, drawing their attention back to the matter at hand.

"Heather and I are going back up to the house," Jake said before she could answer or find an excuse to stick around. "You assist him with whatever he needs."

"No problem, boss."

"I'm not going anywhere," she stated. "My job is to stay right here and see to Stormy Magic's welfare."

"Dr. Pennington has arrived and Tony will see that he takes good care of whatever treatment the animal needs." Turning her, Jake put his arm around her shoulders and started walking them from the stable. "Besides, if you'll remember, we have a dinner meeting with a couple of the other owners and then the Southern Oaks Ball to attend this evening."

"You could go without me."

"Nope. You agreed to be my date for these things. It's too late to back out now."

She shook her head. "It was more like you pulled rank and told me I was going."

He chuckled. "Whatever. You'll need to start getting ready early."

"Why? We're not meeting the other owners until seven this evening."

"I was contacted this morning by the television network carrying the race. They want to interview us before dinner and get some footage for their *Meet the Owners* pre-race segment."

"I don't own Dancer. You do. There's no reason for me to be included in that." She shrugged from beneath his arm and stopping, glared at him. "Right after he was named the favorite to win the Classic, they showed up here to tape his daily exercises and grooming. They interviewed me then and I told them everything there is to know about Dancer." She shook her head. "This particular fifteen minutes of fame is all yours."

* * *

When Jake helped her out of the back of the limousine, Heather felt as if she'd stepped right into the middle of a three-ring circus. Cameras whirred and reporters called out questions as they walked along the carpeted runway toward the entrance of one of the oldest and most prestigious hotels in Louisville.

"This is just like a Hollywood premiere," Jake said, placing his hand to her back to guide her.

"And the very reason I would have preferred staying at home," she muttered. They'd spent an hour and a half before dinner being interviewed by the television network as well as a couple of reporters from the print media. She was more than ready to escape the spotlight.

"What was that, honey?" he asked, leaning close.

"It's not important." She wasn't surprised he hadn't been able to hear her. The noise was almost deafening.

Thankfully they left most of the chaos behind as they crossed the lobby to enter the Grand Ballroom. She waited while Jake presented the doorman with his invitation, then walking into the ornate room, looked around. The light from the massive crystal chandeliers caused the gold accents on the pristine white walls to take on a rich glow and complemented the heavy floor-to-ceiling red velvet drapes. As she continued to scan the room, she spotted a few of the same guests that had attended the Wainwrights' reception along with several well-known celebrities and foreign dignitaries.

"Is that who I think it is?" Jake asked as a sheikh and his entourage strolled past them.

She nodded. "That's Sheikh Kalid Al-Kahra. He owns Dancer's biggest competition."

"Do you think we have anything to worry about?" Jake asked.

"Not a chance." She couldn't stop her smug smile. "The sheikh's jockey has a tendency to take the horses he's riding to the lead right out of the gate and doesn't let up. By the time they reach the home stretch, the horse has nothing left for the sprint to the finish."

"I'm glad that jockey is riding the sheikh's horse and not ours," Jake said, grinning.

"The previous owner of Hickory Hills demanded the best. That's why we have Miguel Santana wearing our silks." She nodded toward a group standing off to the side of the orchestra. "See that distinguished-looking gentleman over there with all the medals and ribbons? He's the Crown Prince of Marunda. He owns the long shot."

"The Wainwright affair was small potatoes compared to the company we're keeping this evening," Jake said, accepting champagne for both of them from a passing waiter. "There are some very impressive pedigrees here this evening."

"I suppose you could say that." She accepted the

sparkling wine he handed her and took a sip. "But I'm more impressed by the horses than I am with the people owning them."

He looked thoughtful. "You really mean that, don't you?"

She nodded. "Owners like the sheikh and the prince were born into their positions in life. They didn't have to work to get where they are. But every horse starts out the same. They may have impressive bloodlines, but they still have to work and prove themselves on the track. That's something to be admired."

They fell silent for several moments before she felt him watching her.

"Is something wrong?"

"Not at all." His smile caused her pulse to speed up. "Do you realize you're the most beautiful woman here tonight?"

"I really hadn't given it much thought," she said truthfully.

She had, however, thought a lot about how handsome *he* was. Dressed in a tuxedo she knew for certain hadn't come off of a rack, he looked absolutely amazing.

When a beautiful young woman stepped up to the microphone in front of the orchestra and began to sing the song "At Last," Jake set both of their glasses on a nearby table. "Let's dance."

He took her hand and leading her out onto the dance floor, took her into his arms. The awareness suddenly arcing between them was spellbinding. Gazing into the other's eyes, neither spoke as the orchestra played and the young woman sang about finally finding love. Jake held her close, and swaying in time to the music, Heather knew that she'd remember the moment for the rest of her life.

When the song ended, the orchestra immediately played the beginning notes of another slow, dreamy love song and he pulled her more fully to him. Resting her head against his broad chest, she closed her eyes. She'd never felt more cherished, more secure than she did at that very moment in Jake's arms.

"Honey, I want you more right now than I've ever wanted anything in my entire life," he whispered close to her ear.

His warm breath caused a shiver to course through her. She could deny that she didn't want him just as much, but she was tired of lying. From the moment he arrived at the farm, she'd fought what she knew now to be the inevitable. Jake's touch, his drugging kisses and being held in his arms had worn down her defenses, and she'd lost the battle she'd waged with herself. She wanted him just as much now as she had the night they'd conceived Mandy.

Leaning back to stare up at him, the heat in his cobalt gaze stole her breath.

"How long are we expected to stay at this thing?" he asked.

Her heart sped up. "We've put in an appearance. That's all that's expected."

"Then what do you say we call it an evening and go home?" The promising look he gave her sent excitement coursing through her veins.

Before she could answer, he led her off the dance floor and out of the ballroom straight to the concierge desk. Requesting that their limousine be sent to the front entrance, Jake helped her into the backseat. He raised the window between them and the driver, then gathered her into his arms.

Touching her chin with his index finger, he smiled when their gazes met. "You do know what's going to happen when we get back to the farm?"

Her smile robbed him of breath. "Yes."

Crushing her to him, he covered her mouth with his and it suddenly felt as if the temperature in the car went up a good ten degrees. As she put her arms around his neck, she parted her lips and he didn't hesitate to deepen the kiss.

Her eager response sent blood surging through his veins and he didn't think twice about slipping his hand inside the low cut neckline of her evening gown. Caressing her breast, he touched the beaded tip with his thumb. Her moan fueled the fire building in his belly, but when she moved her hand upward from where it rested on his thigh, the rush of heat tightening his groin made him feel as if the top of his head might just come off. He would have liked nothing more than to strip her of the sexy dress and make love to her right then and there. But he hadn't made out in the backseat of car since he was in his teens and he'd forgotten just how uncomfortable it could be.

Breaking the kiss, Jake breathed in some much needed oxygen as he removed his hand, rearranged her dress, then tucked her to his side. As much as he needed her at that moment, he didn't want their lovemaking to be rushed. He wanted their first time together again to be special.

When she snuggled against him and rested her palm on his chest, he covered her hand with his. The ride to Hickory Hills seemed to take twice as long as it should have and by the time the chauffeur stopped the limo in the circular drive in front of the mansion, Jake felt as if he had enough adrenaline running through his veins to run a marathon. Without waiting for the driver, he opened the door and helped Heather out of the car.

Neither spoke as they walked the short distance to the veranda and climbed the steps. Opening the door, Jake stood back for Heather to enter and once they stood inside the foyer, he put his arms around her.

"Is Clara babysitting Mandy in her quarters for the night?"

She nodded. "She volunteered and since I wasn't

sure how long we would be out this evening, I took her up on the offer."

Kissing her until they both gasped for breath, he slipped his arm around her waist. "Let's go upstairs, honey."

When they climbed the stairs and started down the hall toward the master suite, he forced himself not to pick her up and sprint the short distance. He wanted her with a driving urgency. But he focused his entire attention on taking things slowly and refreshing her memory of how good they'd been together in Los Angeles.

Entering his bedroom, he guided her over to the side of the bed, then turning on the bedside lamp, gathered her into his arms. He kissed her forehead, her eyes and the tip of her nose.

"I'm going to kiss you all over and by the time we're finished there won't be a single inch I haven't loved."

As he nibbled his way from the hollow behind her ear down her delicate throat to her collarbone, he reached behind her to unzip her cream-colored sequined gown. When the garment lay in a glittering pool at her feet, his heart stalled at the sight of her white lacy garter belt, sheer nylons and spike heels. He didn't know a man alive who didn't have some sort of fantasy about a woman wearing one of those little scraps of lace and a pair of impossibly high heels.

"If I'd known you were wearing this, we'd have left after that first dance," he said, meaning it.

Her sultry smile sent his blood pressure off the charts as she stepped away from the gown. "When I get dressed to go out, I like feeling feminine."

He grinned. "We'll have to start going out more often."

Releasing the garters, Jake bent to slowly slide his hands down one of her thighs, taking the sheer hose past her knee and down her slender calf. He lifted her foot to remove her shoe, then pulled the nylon off and tossed it to the side. He did the same thing with her other leg and as he straightened, he leisurely ran his hands up along her thighs, enjoying the feel of her smooth skin beneath his palms.

As he raised his head to capture her mouth with his, he unfastened the garter belt and added it to the growing pile of clothing. Her soft, moist lips clung to his and he knew he'd never tasted anything quite as enticing.

He broke the kiss and holding her gaze with his, made quick work of unhooking her strapless bra. When it fell to the floor, his breath lodged in his lungs at the sight of her perfect breasts. Taking the weight of them in his palms, he watched her close her eyes and a blissful look come over her as he chafed the tips with his thumbs.

"You're so beautiful, so perfect."

"So are you," she said, bringing her hands up to

slip them beneath the shoulders of his tuxedo jacket. Sliding them down his arms, she took his coat with her and it soon joined her clothing on the floor.

His heart hammered hard against his ribs as she toyed with the studs on the front of his shirt, then slowly released them one by one. When she parted the linen to place her hands on his chest, her delicate touch caused him to harden to an almost painful state.

"I've wanted to do this since returning from my meeting at Churchill Downs the other day," she admitted as she explored him.

"Not as much as I've wanted you to, honey."

He closed his eyes and enjoyed her fingers tracing the pads of his pectoral muscles and the ridges of his belly. But when she traced the line of hair from his navel all the way down to the waist-band of his slacks, his eyes snapped open as a shaft of heat shot straight through him.

Quickly reaching to stop her, he shook his head. "I love the way your hands feel on my body, but I'd rather not start this party without you."

She raised her gaze to meet his and the need he detected in the aqua depths robbed him of breath. "It's been so long," she said breathlessly.

"I know, honey."

He kissed each one of her fingertips before he placed her hands on his shoulders, then brought his to rest at her waist. Staring down at her, he ran his index finger along the waistband of her panties and watched her eyes darken with desire.

Without a word, he slipped his fingers beneath the elastic and sliding his hands down, bent to remove the scrap of satin. When she stepped out of them and he straightened to face her, his heart stalled at the look she gave him just before she reached out to unfasten the waistband of his trousers.

Before she caused him to have a coronary, he stepped back and made quick work of removing his shirt and pants. But when he reached to remove his boxers, she stopped him.

"Do you mind?" The sound of her voice slid over him like a fine piece of silk.

"Not at all, honey," he said, grinning. "You're doing just fine."

Their gazes remained locked as she slid them from his hips and down his legs. Kicking them aside, he stepped forward and took her into his arms. The feel of her soft breasts crushed to his chest, her hardened nipples pressing into his skin, had his body feeling as if he'd go up in flames.

A shaft of need knifed through him when she skimmed her hands over his back and down his flanks, but when her slender fingers found him, Jake felt as if the intensity of pleasure would knock his knees right out from under him. As she gently measured his length and girth, he leaned down to capture one of her puckered nipples between his lips and worried it with butterfly flicks of his tongue.

Her soft moan was his reward and raising his head, he kissed her smooth cheek. "I think we'd better get into bed, honey. Otherwise, I'm not sure I'll have enough strength left to get there."

When she turned toward the bed, he reached into the night stand drawer to remove a small foil packet, then placing it under his pillow, stretched out beside her. Gathering her to him, he covered her mouth with his and let his kiss tell her how much the moment meant to him, how much he wanted her.

He'd never wanted to please a woman as much as he wanted to please Heather. "Honey, I'd like to take this slow, but I'm not entirely certain that's an option," he said hoarsely.

Heather gave him a look that sent liquid fire rushing through his veins as she wrapped her arms around his neck. "And I've wanted you just as much, Jake."

He'd been positive that she was experiencing the same desire, but having her confirm his assumption caused a fever within him that threatened to send him up in a blaze. Kissing her parted lips, he brought his hand up to cup her breast and tease the beaded tip.

When he took her nipple into his mouth, then sucked on it gently, a tiny moan escaped her lips and running her fingers through his hair, she held him to her. "That feels so…good."

Kissing his way down her smooth, flat stomach, Jake slid his hand along her side to her hip, then down her slender thigh to her knee. She shivered against him and he knew her excitement was building. He wanted to bring her to even greater heights and, trailing his fingers along the inner part of her thigh, teased the sensitive skin as he went.

"Jake, you're driving…me crazy," she softly gasped.

When he parted her and found her hot, wet and ready for him, he was the one feeling as if he might go insane. Just knowing that she needed him as much as he needed her sent blood racing through his veins and he had to use every ounce of his concentration to keep from losing the slender thread he still held on his control.

He wanted nothing more than to bury himself deep inside of her, to bring them both the completion they desired. He took a deep breath and forced himself to slow down. He was an accomplished lover and never failed to satisfy his partner. But it was more important to him than ever that he ensure Heather's pleasure above his own.

"P-please…Jake."

Apparently, she was feeling the same urgency because she suddenly moved to find his arousal, then taking him into her delicate hand stroked him intimately. A white-hot haze began to build deep within him and he had to fight with everything that was in him to keep from plunging over the edge.

"Just a moment, honey," he said, reaching for the packet beneath his pillow. Quickly rolling their protection into place, he nudged her knees apart and settling himself in the cradle of her hips, entered her with one smooth stroke.

Gritting his teeth at the mind-blowing tightness surrounding him, he leaned down to capture her lips with his as he slowly began to move within her. But the tension building between them was like a wildfire, untamed and out of control. Each movement, each kiss, fanned the flame and drove them ever closer to being consumed by the passion.

When Heather suddenly arched up to meet him and he felt the immediate tightening around him, felt her feminine muscles cling to him, he deepened his strokes. He held her close and watched in awe as the ecstasy overtook her and she let go.

With his own release close, he moved into her again. He felt Heather suddenly tighten around him one more time and cry out his name. The mind-numbing realization that he'd brought her to a second release sent him over the edge. As he surged into her one final time, shock waves so strong they reverberated throughout his entire being shook him.

Easing to her side before he collapsed on top of

her, he gathered Heather close and held her to him as they both tried to catch their breath. Shaken by the intensity of what they'd shared, Jake knew for certain that he'd never experienced anything as meaningful as their lovemaking. But even though he wasn't at all ready to try to put a name to what he was feeling, he wasn't fool enough to try to deny that it existed, either. And that should have made him nervous enough to jump out of his own skin. It was a mystery to him why it didn't.

"Are you all right?" he asked, kissing the top of her head where it rested on his shoulder.

"Mmm. That was incredible."

"I couldn't agree more." When she yawned and snuggled against him, he smiled and tightened his arms around her. "Why don't you get some sleep, honey? It's been a long day and the week has just started. We have about half a dozen more parties and receptions to attend before all of this is over."

"That many?"

"Unfortunately."

When she started to get up, he tightened his arms around her. "Where do you think you're going?"

She tilted her head up to look at him. "My room."

"I don't think so." He reached over to turn off the bedside lamp. "I want you right here."

"But—"

"I want to wake up with you tomorrow morning and make love again." He brushed her lips with his.

"I can't do that if you're in one room and I'm in another."

She nibbled on her lower lip and he could tell she was waging an internal debate with herself. "Jake, I'm not sure this is such a good idea."

He knew she was afraid of getting in over her head. Hell, he was in uncharted waters himself.

"Please spend the night with me, honey," he pressed. "Then we'll take this one day at a time and see where it goes."

She stared at him for what seemed like forever before she finally nodded. "I'll stay tonight, but that's it. And when your family arrives in a few days, Mandy and I are going to move back into the carriage house."

"Why?"

"Because by my calculations, you're going to need our bedrooms to accommodate everyone."

"This suite is huge," he said, thinking fast. "We can move Mandy's crib in the sitting room and you can sleep with me."

She stubbornly shook her head. "I told you, I'll only stay with you tonight. And we will move back to the carriage house in a few days."

He could tell she wasn't going to concede the issue. But he didn't like the idea of not having her with him, in his house, in his bed.

"All right," he finally agreed.

Apparently satisfied that he'd given up, she laid

her head on his shoulder and in no time he could tell that she'd drifted off to sleep.

As he lay there holding her and staring at the ceiling, determination filled him. Hickory Hills was her and Mandy's home and they belonged right where they were. And he was certain he could come up with some reason for them to stay in the house. All he had to do was find it.

Seven

"Heather isn't gonna like this," Daily said, looking uncertain.

Jake gave the boy an encouraging smile as they carried the sofa from the carriage house and loaded it onto a truck. "You let me worry about Heather. Just make sure you don't drop your end of this thing."

After she, Clara and the baby had left to go into Louisville for lunch and shopping, Emerald had called, prompting him to enlist Daily's help in emptying out the carriage house. Heather was probably going to throw a fit about it, but once he explained everything, she'd surely understand. The place needed to be repainted and recarpeted, and it wouldn't hurt to have some of the furniture replaced. He'd intended to make some of the renovations for her anyway, just not quite this soon.

But when Emerald finally returned his call to tell him she was accepting his invitation to attend the race, she'd asked for downstairs rooms for herself and her assistant, and in doing so handed him the perfect excuse to keep Heather and Mandy in the house with him when the family descended upon them in a few days. Due to Emerald being somewhere in her mid-seventies and her assistant, Luther, being every bit as old, she'd reminded him that climbing the staircase in the mansion might not be a good idea for them. That's when he'd come to the conclusion that the one-level carriage house was the perfect solution.

"How long before the painters get here?" Daily asked, interrupting his thoughts.

As they turned to go back inside for the last pieces of furniture, Jake checked his watch. "They should be here any time. We'd better get the rest of this stuff loaded on the truck and take it to the storage unit, so the men can get started." He was having to pay double the normal rate to get everything done in time. But in the end, it was going to be well worth it.

Daily looked almost as nervous as the night he'd tried to sneak out to see his girlfriend. "Have you

figured out how you're going to keep Heather from
finding out what's going on until everything's
finished?"

"I'm not." Jake laughed at the boy's horrified
expression.

"She's gonna kill both of us when she finds
out," Daily said, shaking his head. "It's been nice
knowing you."

"Don't worry. I'll take the heat with Heather,"
Jake assured. "You're just doing what I asked you
to do."

An hour later, he and Daily had the carriage
house emptied and the furniture unloaded into the
storage unit. The painting crew had just finished
taping the woodwork and were laying down drop
cloths when Heather, Clara and the baby drove up
in Heather's old sedan. "Jake, what's going on?" she
asked when she got out of the car.

"I'm having the place renovated," he answered,
hoping her reaction wasn't going to be as dire as
Daily had predicted.

"What do you mean by that?" she demanded, her
voice reflecting her displeasure.

"I'm having it painted and recarpeted."

She propped both fists on her shapely hips.
"What did you do with my furniture and all of my
things?"

"I stored the furniture until the work is finished
and put all of your personal effects in your room in

the mansion." He'd contemplated moving them to his room, but abandoned that idea after some careful thought. He'd reasoned that she'd be irritated enough that her plans to move back into the carriage house had to be changed, and there was no sense adding more fuel to that particular fire.

"You can't do this, Jake." Her voice shook with anger as she walked up to stand toe to toe with him. "I liked everything the way it was."

"You're on your own, dude," Daily said, taking off down the path toward the stables like the hounds of hell chased him.

"I'll go ahead and take Mandy into the house," Clara offered as she quickly moved to get the baby out of the car seat.

Jake waited until Clara crossed the patio and entered the house with Mandy, before he turned his full attention on Heather. If he was going to get himself out of the hole he'd dug with her, he figured he'd better do some fast talking.

"Before you become too upset, let me explain."

She folded her arms beneath her breasts. If looks could kill, he figured he'd be a dead man in nothing flat. "This had better be good."

"I received a call from my paternal grandmother this morning. She's going to join the rest of the family here for the race this weekend."

"And?"

"She and her assistant are both elderly." He

wasn't about to tell her that Emerald and Luther were two of the spryest septuagenarians he'd ever met and that he strongly suspected Emerald's request was another ploy to control the situation. "There isn't an elevator in the mansion and I don't think it's a good idea for them to climb the stairs to get to their rooms. At their ages, a fall could be disastrous."

He could tell by her sudden frown that she was giving his reasoning consideration. "I can understand your concerns, but you should have discussed this with me first, instead of taking it upon yourself to start changing things." She pointed to the front door of the carriage house. "That's my home and I should have something to say about what goes on with it. You had no right to get rid of my furniture."

Reaching out, he pulled her into his arms. "Honey, this whole farm is your home. And your furniture will be moved back in as soon as the work is done. I promise the only thing different will be the color of the walls and carpet."

He lowered his head and kissed her until they both gasped for air. "If you decide later to move back into the carriage house, won't it be nice to have those things already done?"

"There's still a problem of not having enough bedrooms in the house when your family arrives."

"I'll have it all worked out by the time they get here." He was just glad she wasn't still glaring daggers at him. "Now, let's go into the house so you can show me the hat you bought for the race and explain to me why all of the women wear them."

After dinner, Heather sorted through the boxes Jake had moved from the carriage house. She should have anticipated him finding a way to get her to stay in the mansion while his family visited. But she had to admit he did have a valid reason. There was no way she'd subject two elderly people to the perils of climbing all of those steps. She'd never forgive herself if one of them fell and was seriously injured.

"What are you doing in here, honey?" Jake asked from the door.

"I'm trying to organize and find a place to put everything until after your family leaves and Mandy and I can move back into the carriage house," she answered without looking up.

He walked over to sit on the bed beside her. "I meant it when I told you that I want you and Mandy to feel free to live in the mansion whether I'm here or not."

She sighed heavily. "Do we have to go over this again? It doesn't belong to me and I wouldn't feel right—"

"We'll cross that bridge when the time comes," he interrupted. "Right now, I have something I want you to see."

"This is the only free evening we've had in the past few days and I'd really like to relax." When she'd discovered they didn't have a reception to attend, she'd looked forward to a quiet, uneventful night.

Taking her hand, he pulled her to her feet. "Trust me, you're going to like this."

She allowed him to lead her down the hallway to the stairs. "Let's get this over. I have a date with the Jacuzzi a little later."

His grin caused her to feel warm all over. "Want company? I'll wash your back if you'll wash mine."

The thought of being in the bubbling water with him caused a delightful fluttering in the pit of her stomach.

"We'll talk about it later." She stopped as he led her toward the front door. "I forgot the baby monitor."

"Don't worry about Mandy," he said, opening the door. "I asked Clara to watch her." He covered her eyes with his hand. "Now, follow me."

"But she has been babysitting so much the past few days." She let him lead her out onto the veranda. "I hate to take advantage of her."

"Clara volunteered." She could hear the smile in his voice as he helped her down the steps. "I think she knows we both need some down time. Besides, she told me the other day that it's a lot easier to grandmother a baby than a teenager."

Nodding, Heather laughed. "I've seen Daily turn as red as a beet when she kisses his cheek, whereas Mandy loves it."

"Are you ready for the surprise?"

"I suppose so." She couldn't imagine why he was being so secretive.

He removed his hand. A shiny royal-blue minivan with the farm logo sat in the driveway. "What do you think?"

"Who does that belong to?" she asked cautiously.

"The farm. But it's primarily for your use."

She turned to stare at him. "Why?"

He pulled her along as he circled the car and opened the sliding side door. "I saw how cramped the backseat of your car is with Mandy's car seat and you can definitely use the room. Besides, it's not fair for you to drive your car for the farm business."

He handed her a set of keys. "Try it out."

She bit her lower lip. It was such a pretty car and would save her from having to put a lot more miles on her aging Taurus. "I'll only use it to go to meetings and to pick up things for the farm."

"Honey, I want you to feel free to use it whenever you like. I'd feel better if you and Mandy were in this than a car that could break down and strand you somewhere." He urged her to get behind the wheel, then walked around to close the side door. But before he slid it shut, Nemo jumped in and sat down on the bench seat in the back. "What the hell?"

"He likes to go for rides," she said, laughing.

Jake patted the big dog's head, then closing the door, got into the passenger seat. "I guess we'll take Nemo for a ride."

By the time they drove several miles down the road and back to the mansion, Heather had fallen in love with the new car. "This is wonderful," she said when she parked it and they coaxed Nemo out of the backseat.

"I'm glad you like it," he said, smiling warmly as he picked up a clump of dog hair from the leather seat, then tossing it to the ground, closed the door. "I'll install a car seat tomorrow and you'll be good to go."

As they walked hand in hand into the house, she started to go back upstairs, but he stopped her. "Where do you think you're going? The evening has just started."

"What do you have up your sleeve this time?" she asked, smiling.

Leading her into the den, he motioned for her to sit on the sectional couch in front of a large flat-panel television. As she sank into the plush cushions, she noticed a bowl of popcorn and a couple of soft drinks on the coffee table.

"I thought we could watch a movie together," he said, sitting beside her. He picked up a remote control, pushed a button to start the movie, then put his arms around her shoulder and pulled her close.

"We've been on the go so much lately, I figured it might be a good way to relax."

Settling back into his embrace, Heather munched on popcorn and watched the comedy he'd selected for them. She briefly wondered if Jake felt as happy and content as she did. This was her idea of the perfect evening, but she wasn't sure about him. He seemed to be enjoying the quiet evening at home. But he could very well just be marking time until he could get back to the fast-paced lifestyle he led in Los Angeles. After all, he was used to going out every night and partying until the wee hours of the morning.

"What's running through that head of yours?" he asked, startling her. He switched off the television.

"Why do you ask?"

"Because you look pensive and you're not paying attention to the movie." He used his index finger to brush a strand of hair from her cheek. "Otherwise, you would have laughed. Especially at that last part."

She stared at him for several seconds before she voiced her thoughts. "I was just wondering if you're bored yet."

He frowned. "Where did that come from?"

Shrugging one shoulder, she met his confused gaze. "You've been here a week and other than the sedate receptions and the ball last night, you haven't gone out to any of the clubs. And you've had more than enough time after you brought me home to go back out. But you didn't. I would have thought by now you'd be climbing the walls."

"Honey, I haven't missed that scene one time since I've been here." He looked thoughtful as if he couldn't quite believe it himself. "In fact, I don't find the idea of going clubbing the least bit appealing."

"Are you feeling all right?" she asked before she could stop herself.

He unbuttoned his shirt, then taking her hand in his, placed it on his bare chest. "You tell me."

Her pulse sped up. "I think you feel pretty good. Wonderful actually."

Pulling her onto his lap, he cradled her to him as he tugged her shirt from her jeans and slipped his hand under the hem. When he cupped her breast, he rested his forehead against hers. "You feel pretty awesome yourself."

A delicious warmth began to flow through her veins and she closed her eyes as she lost herself to the sensation of his hand on her sensitive skin. Was it possible that he really didn't miss his old lifestyle? Or when the first opportunity presented itself, would he revert to his old ways?

Jake covered her mouth with his and she gave up all speculation. She didn't want to think about what tomorrow would bring. At the moment, she was in his arms and that was all that mattered.

"Let's go upstairs, honey," he said, ending the

kiss. "I think your suggestion about our having a date with the Jacuzzi is an excellent idea."

Putting her arms around his shoulders, she smiled. "I thought that was *my* date."

His mischievous grin caused her heart to skip a beat. "Do you mind if I make it *ours?*"

"Not at all."

When he set her on her feet and stood, she didn't think twice about placing her hand in his and walking out of the den and up the stairs. As they entered the master bedroom, he ushered her into the sitting area and over to one of the chairs.

"Stay right here," he said a moment before he disappeared into the bathroom. A couple of minutes later, he walked back into the room and smiling, leaned down to kiss the tip of her nose. "Come with me, Heather. I have a surprise for you."

Doing as he requested, when he led her into the bathroom, she couldn't believe her eyes. The flicker of white candles in all shapes and sizes lit the otherwise dark room and the filled bathtub was already bubbling.

"When did you do this? There wasn't enough time—"

"I set the candles out and filled the tub earlier. The thermostat kept it warm for us." He took her into his arms. "I just lit the candles."

She wrapped her arms around him and laid her head against his chest. "This is perfect. Thank you."

"Let's get undressed and see if it's as relaxing as it looks," he suggested.

Taking turns removing each others clothes, Jake stepped into the Jacuzzi and eased her between his thighs. The feel of his body against hers when he pulled her back to lay against him sent electricity skipping over every cell in her being.

"This feels so good," he said as he tightened his arms around her.

"Yes, it does." She blissfully closed her eyes. "The water is just right."

His low chuckle caused goose bumps to shimmer over her. "I wasn't talking about the water." A shiver of excitement coursed through her when he kissed her shoulder at the same time his hands covered her breasts. "Tonight is all for you, honey. I'm going to love you so well that there won't be a doubt left in your mind how much I desire you."

The sound of his deep baritone promising a night of passion and the feel of his rapidly hardening body against her backside caused her to feel as if she never wanted to be anywhere else but in his arms. And that's when it hit her. She'd told herself that it wasn't happening and tried her best not to do it, but she'd fallen hopelessly in love with him.

If she'd had the chance, she might have been frightened beyond words. There was a very real possibility that she would get hurt again. But Jake didn't give her the opportunity. His hands were moving over her body with precision care and robbed her of all thought.

When he slid his palm down her abdomen to the apex of her thighs, then gently parted her to stroke the tiny nub nestled within, Heather felt as if a spark ignited in her soul. The intensity of the sensations coursing through her caused her body to hum with a need stronger than anything she had ever known.

"Jake, please."

"What do you want, Heather?"

"Y-you."

She turned her head to look over her shoulder at him. "Please make love to me."

His deep groan vibrated against her back. "Turn around, honey."

When she did as he commanded and straddled his thighs, he lifted up to meet her and entered her in one smooth motion. The feel of his hard body nestled inside of her and the hunger darkening his blue eyes stole her breath.

She watched him tightly close his eyes as he struggled for control and she knew his need was as great as hers. Without hesitation she wrapped her arms around his neck and slowly moved against him. His eyes immediately snapped open and placing his hands on her hips, he helped her set a steady pace.

Feeling more cherished than she had in her entire

life, she bit her lower lip to keep from crying out at the intensity of emotions swirling through her. She loved Jake with all of her heart and soul.

As the knowledge filled her, an undeniable tension built inside of her and she rapidly began to climb toward the peak. Jake must have sensed her readiness and deepening his thrusts, sent her over the edge. As her body clung to his, waves of pleasure flowed through her and almost immediately, she felt him tense, then give into the force of his own climax. His tremors rocked them both and she held him close as they rode out the storm together.

When they slowly drifted back to reality, Jake's heart suddenly pounded so hard against his ribs, he wasn't entirely certain it wouldn't jump out of his chest. "Dammit all to hell."

"What's wrong?" Heather asked, clearly startled by his outburst.

He set her away from him and moved to get out of the Jacuzzi. "I wanted you so much, I didn't even consider protection."

She smiled. "Oh, that."

Why was she taking it so lightly? They already had one baby they hadn't planned. And although he loved Mandy more than life itself, he didn't think having another was going to help an already complicated situation.

"Let's get out of here and dry off," he said, wondering if he'd lost his mind. As he got out of the bathtub, he handed her a plush towel, then dried himself off with another.

There was no question about it. He didn't want to make her pregnant again. Hell, he didn't know if he was a good father to one child yet, let alone two.

He shook his head in an attempt to clear it. There hadn't been one time in his life that he'd failed to use protection. Even as a teenager, he'd been conscious of the implications and responsibilities attached to an unplanned pregnancy.

"Jake, are you listening to me?" she asked, wrapping the towel around her.

He'd been so distracted, he hadn't realized she was trying to talk to him. Securing the towel at his waist, he motioned toward the door. "Let's go into the bedroom, honey. We need to talk."

"But I'm trying to tell you—"

He placed his index finger to her lips. "Not until I've had my say."

She looked thoughtful for a moment before she nodded and walking into the bedroom, sat down on the side of the bed. "I'm listening."

Unable to stand still, he paced back and forth in front of her. "There's no excuse for my forgetting to protect you." He stopped and ran his hand over the tension building at the base of his neck. "But I want you to know that if you do get pregnant because of my carelessness, I'll be there this time."

He knelt in front of her and took her hands in his. "I promise you won't have to go through everything alone like you did when you were pregnant with Mandy. This time I'll know, and I give you my word that I'll be there for you, Heather."

"Are you finished?"

He couldn't believe her lack of concern. Did she want to become pregnant again?

Nodding, he drew in a deep breath. "Yes, I think that about covers it."

"You can stop worrying. I'm not going to get pregnant." She shrugged one bare shoulder. "There was an issue of my being regular after Mandy was born, so the doctor put me on the Pill."

Instead of the relief he should have felt, disappointment settled in the pit of his belly. Had he really wanted to make her pregnant again? Had he lost what little sense he had left?

Of course not. The thought was ludicrous. But he couldn't seem to chase away the let-down feeling that accompanied her announcement.

"Why didn't you tell me?" he asked.

"The subject never came up. And besides, it really wasn't any of your business."

She was right, of course. But what he couldn't understand was why he wanted it to be.

Reaching out, she touched his cheeks with her soft hand, then leaned forward and gave him a kiss so sweet it robbed him of breath. "You wouldn't have gotten so worked up if you'd only let me explain. You really could use some work on your listening skills, Mr. Garnier."

Two hours later, after making love to Heather again, Jake held her close as she slept and thought about his uncharacteristic emotions. Not quite two weeks ago, he'd been a carefree, commitment-shy bachelor with nothing more on his mind than paying a visit to his newly acquired horse farm, sticking around for the big race and then he was supposed to be back on the road to L.A. But all that had changed with the discovery that he'd not only found the one woman he'd regretted not staying in touch with but also that she'd had his baby.

Why did he all of a sudden want all of the things he'd spent most of his adult life trying to avoid?

Tightening his arms around her, he pulled her close and tried to relax. But as sleep began to overtake him, Jake couldn't help but feel that he was walking a fine line. And once crossed there would be no going back.

"How's my little angel?" Heather asked as she picked the baby up from the crib. "Did you have a good nap?"

Mandy's happy grin as Heather changed her diaper revealed a small white place on her lower gum.

"Your tooth has broken through." Kissing her

daughter's soft cheek, Heather picked her up from the changing table and walked out of her bedroom toward the stairs. "We'll have to find your daddy and show him. He's been worried about when it was finally going to stop bothering you."

Shortly after awakening to find herself alone in Jake's bed that morning, she'd gone in search of him and found that he had moved the crib into the room she'd been using. He'd explained that with his grandmother and her assistant staying in the newly decorated carriage house there would be plenty of rooms for everyone when they descended on them later in the day.

Hearing voices when she reached the bottom of the steps, she crossed the foyer and entering the den, found several people taking their turns hugging Jake. It appeared that his family had arrived.

"Heather, I'd like you to meet the clan," Jake said when he noticed her standing just inside the door. Walking over he lifted Mandy onto his arm and put his other arm around her shoulders. "This is my daughter, Mandy, and her mother Heather."

"Please let me hold her," his sister, Arielle, said reaching for Mandy. Almost six months pregnant, she and her husband, Zach, had just learned they were expecting twin boys. "She's absolutely adorable. And she looks just like you, Jake."

As everyone greeted her and made a fuss over the baby, a bittersweet feeling filled her chest at the pride in Jake's voice. She only wished he could love her half as much as he did their baby.

When he finished making the introductions, Heather couldn't help but notice how much Jake and his half brothers were alike. All of them were quite tall, had the same athletic build and bore a strong facial resemblance. They even shared some of the same mannerisms. When his brother Hunter O'Banyon talked about the stress of being an air medevac pilot, he ran his hand over the back of his neck, which Jake had a habit of doing, too.

"Where's your twin and his wife?" she asked, noticing their absence.

"Haley had a doctor's appointment," Jake answered. "Luke said they'd meet us at Churchill Downs before the race tomorrow."

"Heather, I hear you're the one in charge of the winning horse," Nick Daniels said. "Jake told us you raised him from a colt."

Smiling, she nodded at the rancher from Wyoming. "Actually, I was responsible for choosing his bloodlines as well as helping the mare foal when the vet couldn't get here in time."

"Hang on to her, Jake," Nick advised. He put his arm around his pretty wife, Cheyenne. "Take it from me. You can't go wrong with a woman who knows her horses."

"I'll remember that," Jake said, smiling.

"Heather, do you have time to go shopping with

us?" Caleb Walker's wife, Alyssa, asked. "I've heard that it's a tradition for all of the women to wear a hat to the race."

"I got a new one a couple of days ago and I'd be more than happy to take all of you to the shop where I bought it," Heather offered. "They have a great selection, in all colors and styles."

Callie O'Banyon sighed. "A shopping trip without little ones in tow sounds like heaven."

"By the way, where are your children?" Jake asked.

Caleb chuckled as he pointed to his brothers. "We all decided to leave them with the babysitters and enjoy spending a little alone time with our wives."

"If everyone's agreeable on the shopping, we could go right after I take a nap," Arielle suggested, yawning. She handed Mandy to Alyssa, then with her husband's help, rose to her feet. "Could you tell me where our room is, Jake?"

"I'll be happy to show you where you'll be staying," Heather spoke up, earning a warm smile from Jake.

When they climbed the stairs and Heather showed the pretty young woman where she and her husband, Zach, would be sleeping during their stay at Hickory Hills, Arielle motioned for Heather to follow her into the room. "Are you up for some girl talk before I crash?"

Heather liked all of Jake's brothers and sisters-in-law, but there was something about Arielle that told Heather if given the chance they would become very good friends. "Of course."

Lowering herself to the side of the bed, Arielle smiled. "I just wanted you to know how thrilled I am that someone has finally tamed Jake. I couldn't be happier for both of you."

Heather frowned. "I think you must have gotten the wrong impression. Jake and I are just—"

"Don't tell me you're just friends," Arielle interrupted. "I've seen the way my brother looks at you and there's a lot more to the way he feels about you than friendship."

Heather wasn't quite sure what to say. She wasn't going to lie to the woman. But she wasn't certain there was anything more going on for Jake than a strong attraction and undeniable desire.

"It's...complicated," she finally said, settling on the truth. Whatever was going on between them was going to take some time to sort out. They still hadn't discussed how they were going to handle raising Mandy together with so much distance between their residences. Jake had talked about going back to Los Angeles and leaving her and Mandy the run of the farm, but that didn't mean the custody issue was settled. He could still come up with demands for equal time.

Arielle placed her hand over Heather's. "You love him, don't you?"

She didn't even think to hesitate. "Yes."

"Trust me, Jake may not realize it yet, but he's in love with you, too," Arielle said, smiling. "I've never seen him like this. He can't keep his eyes off of you."

"It's not like he has much to choose from here," Heather said dryly. "Besides the housekeeper, Clara Buchanan, who's sixty if she's a day, I'm the only other woman here at Hickory Hills."

Arielle laughed. "How many times has he been out since he's been here?"

"Other than the receptions and ball we've had to attend, he hasn't," she admitted.

"I rest my case." Arielle hid a yawn behind her hand. "I know my brother. If he didn't have some very strong feelings for you, he would have been out every night."

"I wish you were right, but—"

"I am." The young woman yawned again. "Now, why don't you go downstairs and get to know the others while I take my nap. When I get up we'll all go shopping and buy some wildly expensive hats we'll probably never wear after the race tomorrow."

Heather gave Arielle a hug, then walked out into the hall and quietly pulled the door shut behind her. She'd give almost anything for Jake's sister to be right. But she couldn't trust that Jake had changed for good. Before coming to Kentucky, he'd been perfectly content being the irresponsible bachelor with no children and no commitments. And once he was back in his element in Los Angeles, around friends who enjoyed partying all the time, he just might find that he'd missed that nonstop excitement and revert to his old ways.

Eight

"Heather, I'd like for you to meet my paternal grandmother, Emerald Larson," Jake said, wondering how she'd take the news that he was the grandson of one of the richest women in the world.

The one thing that Emerald had respected and taken great pains to protect was her grandchildren's right to privacy. She left it entirely up to them when and to whom they revealed the relationship. And as if by unspoken agreement, all six of them had been discreet and managed to keep the news fairly quiet.

As he watched, Heather's aqua eyes widened a moment before she recovered and shook Emerald's hand. "It's nice to meet you, Mrs. Larson."

"I see Jake has taken his cue from the rest of my grandchildren," Emerald said, patting Heather's cheek. "Don't worry, dear. None of the others revealed my identity until they had to, either."

"If you'll excuse me, I was just on my way to the paddock to see if Tony has everything under control," Heather said, rising from her seat.

As she started past him, Jake caught her hand in his. "Will you be back in time for the race?"

Her smile lit the darkest corners of his soul. "Absolutely. I wouldn't miss this for anything."

"Where's your assistant?" he asked Emerald as he watched Heather disappear into the crowd.

Since Emerald never went anywhere without the distinguished-looking gentleman, Jake knew he couldn't be too far away. He just hoped he didn't have to go looking for Luther in the sea of people. Churchill Downs had a record crowd and he'd probably never find the poor old guy.

"Luther is placing a small wager for me on your horse, Jake," Emerald said as she found a seat in the box section he'd reserved for the family to watch the race.

Unless she'd changed her ways, Emerald never did anything on a small scale. No telling how much she'd had Luther put down on Stormy Dancer. But it wasn't as if she couldn't afford it. She could probably buy the entire race track with all of the horses and not even scratch the surface of her bank account.

"This is such a festive atmosphere," she said, looking genuinely excited. "And I love that all of the ladies have such decorative hats." She touched the brim of her own elaborate headwear. "I think it's sad that these aren't called for on more occasions. I can remember a time when all the women wore hats for every occasion."

Jake paid little attention to what she was saying as he scanned the crowd for Emerald's assistant, Luther Freemont. When he finally spotted him, Jake breathed a sigh of relief. The man was slowly making his way through the crowd to the box section with a mint julep in each hand and a bet slip sticking out of the breast pocket of his suit.

"Mr. Garnier." Luther nodded a greeting in his usually stiff manner, then handed one of the glasses to Emerald. "Your julep, madam."

"Thank you, Luther." Emerald patted the seat beside her and the man lowered himself into it. "I'm so glad we're right here in front of the finish line. We'll be able to see Jake's horse win."

As the bugler played the call to race, his brothers and their wives began to file into the box. Jake checked his watch. Where the hell was Heather? She should have been back from checking on Dancer down at the paddock by now.

Just as the horses began their parade past the grandstand on their way to the starting gate, he saw her hurrying up the steps. "Was everything all right?" he asked, when she reached him.

"Dancer was a little more skittish than usual," she said, sitting down beside him. "Thoroughbreds are high-strung by nature—he can sense this is the race of his life."

"Which one is Stormy Dancer?" Caleb asked from behind them.

"That's Dancer," Heather spoke up, pointing to one of the bays. "Our silks are red and blue with a white stripe cutting diagonally across the jockey's chest. When they're running along the back stretch or packed up, look for the colors and you'll be able to keep track of him during the race."

"Thanks for the tip," Caleb said, picking up a set of binoculars.

"There's a lot to remember in this business," Luke said, laughing as he sat down on the other side of Jake.

"Tell me about it, bro." Glancing at his twin, he felt as if he looked into a mirror. Lowering his voice, he admitted, "I couldn't have gotten through these past couple of weeks without Heather. Every time a question was asked about Dancer or his training, she'd tell the reporters and sportscasters what they needed to know."

Luke looked thoughtful. "When's the wedding?"

"How many mint juleps have you had?" Irritated, Jake shook his head. "If I were you, I'd lay off for a while."

Luke shrugged. "Still in denial, huh?"

Before he could tell his brother to mind his own damned business, they started loading the horses into the starting gate and everyone jumped to their feet. As soon as the last horse was guided into place, the front of the chutes flew open at the same time the announcer shouted, "They're off."

The roar of the crowd made it impossible to be heard, and when the horses raced past the grandstand, Heather grabbed his hand and squeezed it until his fingers went numb. He barely noticed. He was too busy watching her. Her cheeks had colored a pretty pink and he didn't think he'd ever seen her look more breathtaking. With sudden insight, he realized that he'd underestimated how much it would mean to her if the horse she'd raised won. She'd chosen his bloodlines, overseen his development and this race was her validation—the culmination of her work.

The horses entered the backstretch and Jake noticed that the sheikh's horse was way out in front, just as Heather said he would be. Picking up the binoculars he'd brought with him, Jake searched for Dancer and found him in the middle of the pack. As they rounded the turn and headed for the home stretch, their jockey must have turned Dancer loose because he suddenly shot to the outside and made his way to the front. And as Heather predicted, the sheikh's horse started slipping back into the pack and Dancer took over the lead. By the time he sprinted across the finish line he was five or six lengths ahead of his nearest challenger and there was no doubt he'd won the race.

"We won!"

With enough adrenaline flowing through his veins to lift a freight train, Jake caught Heather up in his arms and kissed her like a soldier returning from war. He knew his level of elation had nothing to do with the their horse winning and everything to do with the relief that she hadn't been disappointed with the results of the race.

When he set her on her feet, she grabbed his hand. "We need to get down to the track. After Miguel weighs in with the saddle, they'll want you in the winner's circle."

Jake shook his head. "They want *us* in the winner's circle, honey. I may be the owner on paper, but Dancer has always been your horse and always will be."

Tears filled her eyes and she raised up on tiptoes to lightly kiss his cheek. "Thank you, Jake. That means a lot to me."

After posing for endless pictures and helping Jake get through the required interviews with the media, Heather called Clara to check on Mandy. Then, leaving orders with Tony to give Dancer an extra scoop of oats to celebrate, she joined Jake and his family for an elaborate dinner at the hotel where the Southern Oaks Ball had been held.

Once their waiter had popped the cork on a bottle of outrageously expensive champagne, Jake stood up and raised his glass. "To Heather, her excellent instincts and expertise. Today was the culmination of your hard work and the realization of a dream. May Dancer be the first on many winners under your expert management."

As everyone added their congratulations, Jake sat back down beside her. "Thank you," she whispered, blinking back tears. His recognition of her accomplishment meant more to her than he'd probably ever know.

"You deserve all of the credit and accolades for the outcome of today's race, honey." His hand found hers beneath the table and he gave it a gentle squeeze. "And I couldn't be happier for you."

When the waiter served the main course, conversation turned to catching up on what was going on in the various lives of Jake's siblings, and Heather found it heartwarming that in spite of their unconventional relationship, they'd all become good friends.

"What's up next for you, Jake?" Hunter asked. "Any more big races on the horizon?"

"I'm leaving that up to Heather," he answered. "I called a Realtor yesterday to put my condo on the market and have her find a house along the beach in Malibu for me."

As the group left the private dining room and entered the Grand Ballroom for the victory party, Heather didn't have time to dwell on what Jake might have planned as she noticed several celebrities milling around the bar. All of them had notorious reputations for partying and she couldn't help but wonder if some of them were Jake's friends.

When a singer started singing the song they'd danced to at the ball, Jake turned to her, smiling. "I think they're playing our song, Heather." Leading her out onto the dance floor, he wrapped his arms around her. "Are you happy, honey?"

She stared up at the man she loved with all of her heart. "And you?"

"Let's see. Our horse won the Classic. The family all made it for the big race. I have a sweet baby daughter with a new tooth who loves to throw baby food at me. And you're in my arms," he brushed his lips over hers. "What more could a man ask for?"

She wanted to believe that all of that would be enough for him. Unfortunately, she knew it wasn't. If he'd already started looking for a house along the beach in Malibu, where she was certain several of his acquaintances had property, he wasn't considering leaving the wilder side of life behind.

The song ended and the orchestra immediately began to play the other tune they'd danced to. Looking up into his cobalt eyes, she blinked back tears. "You arranged for those songs to be played back to back, didn't you?"

His smile made her feel warm all over in spite of the disappointment filling her. "They will always remind me of you and a very special night we spent together." He tenderly kissed her forehead. "You're so beautiful and I want you so much right now."

She loved the way his body felt against hers. "I want you, too. But—"

"I know. You don't have to say it." He shook his head. "Do you think I can charter a jet to take my family all back to their homes tonight?"

She shook her head. "I don't think that would be a good idea."

"I do."

When the music stopped and he led her off the dance floor, her earlier speculation was answered about the celebrities in attendance being his friends when a tall, dark-haired man she recognized as one of Hollywood's baddest bad boys walked toward them. "Jake Garnier, I heard you owned the horse that won today. I hoped you'd stop by this evening." The man grinned from ear to ear, showing off a mouthful of capped teeth. "Now I know this little bash is going to rock."

"What are you doing here, Cameron?" Jake asked, smiling at his friend.

"One of the actresses in my latest film is part owner in one of the nags that ran in the big race and she asked me to come along with her to watch." The conspiratorial wink he gave Jake set Heather's teeth on edge. "You know me. If a woman asks, I'm always up to the challenge." Turning his attention her way, the man's grin evolved into an outright leer. "And who do we have here?"

She felt the arm Jake had draped around her waist, stiffen. "Heather McGwire, this is the infamous Cameron Strombeck."

"Jake!" a tall willowy redhead called as she made her way across the dance floor toward them. "Congratulations. I'll bet you'll be out all night. Be sure and save a dance for me, darling."

As the celebrities continued to gravitate toward them, Heather felt increasingly more uncomfortable. It appeared that instead of having to go back home to pick up his life where it left off, Los Angeles had come to him.

"I think I'll join your family," she said, slipping from his arm before he could stop her.

She walked over to the table where the women were gathered as they waited for their husbands to return with their drinks and sank into an empty chair beside Arielle. "I hope you don't mind my joining you."

"Not at all," Callie O'Banyon said, smiling warmly.

"You and Jake looked amazing out there on the dance floor." Arielle reached over to hug her. "Congratulations, I'm so happy for you."

"Thank you. Dancer's win was definitely exciting." She knew that wasn't what the woman meant, but it was easier to change the subject than to accept good wishes for something that was never going to happen.

When the orchestra started playing again, the volume made conversation impossible and they all fell silent. Heather glanced at Jake several times and her heart broke a little more each time. He looked as if he was having the time of his life with his friends from Tinseltown. As she watched, the redhead melted against him on the dance floor. He didn't seem to mind in the least.

"I hope you don't mind but I think I'll call it a night," she said, rising to her feet.

"Heather, wait," Arielle said, placing a hand on her arm to stop her.

"I'm...um, really pretty tired. I'll see you all in the morning." She had to get out of there before she humiliated herself by dissolving into a torrent of tears. She'd done the very thing that she'd told herself she couldn't let happen. She'd started to believe that Jake might be content staying with her and Mandy. But she knew now that wasn't going to happen. He would soon be leaving Hickory Hills to return to his life in L.A. and the sooner she accepted that, the better off she'd be.

Hurrying across the hotel lobby, when she stepped out onto the sidewalk, she found Mrs.

Larson and her assistant waiting on their limousine. "What's wrong, dear?" Mrs. Larson asked, clearly concerned.

Heather forced a smile. "It's been a full day and I'm going back to Hickory Hills before I collapse."

"Would you like to ride with us?" Mrs. Larson offered. "It's past our bedtime and we'd like to get a good night's sleep before we fly back to Wichita tomorrow."

"I would appreciate it. Thank you."

She'd intended to get a cab, but she was going to have to watch her money for a while. There was no way she could continue working for Jake after what she'd just witnessed. Effective the first thing tomorrow morning she was going to resign her position as farm manager and find employment elsewhere.

"Back off, Lila," Jake demanded, setting the woman away from him. Aside from the fact that he wanted nothing to do with the woman, he didn't want Heather getting the wrong idea.

"I thought you'd be open to having a little fun for old times." Her expression turned to a pout that he was certain she'd practiced for years. He couldn't for the life of him remember why he'd ever found her attractive.

"I'm with someone else. Besides, if you'll remember, that ship sailed a long time ago. We went out a total of three times. You've got to move on."

Her lips curled into what could only be described as a snarl. "You don't know what you're missing."

"Oh, I think I do." He started to walk away, then turned back. "And don't worry. I'm sure you'll find someone to help you have a *good time* this evening. Have a nice life, Lila."

He glanced over at the table where his sister sat and breathed a sigh of relief. At least Heather hadn't been around to witness Lila's brazen move.

"Hey, Jake, would you like to go see what the clubs around here have to offer?" Cameron asked, stopping him half way across the room. "This is dull. We want a lot more action than what this horse crowd has to offer."

As he stared at the man, Jake couldn't believe he'd ever considered him a friend. A pleasure-seeker from the word go, Cameron Strombeck was about as shallow and self-absorbed as a human could possibly be. His disdain for the fine people of the racing industry—for people like Heather—grated on Jake's nerves as little else could.

"No, I'm fine right where I'm at. But you might want to check with Lila Dixon. I happen to know she's looking for a little excitement."

"Really? That could be interesting. I'll catch you when you get back to L.A., then," Cameron said, turning to find Lila. "Give me a call."

"Don't hold your breath on that happening," Jake muttered. Continuing on to the table where Arielle sat, he noticed that she looked ready to tear him in two. "What's wrong?"

"Sit."

"Where's Heather?"

"I said sit!" He didn't think he'd ever seen his sister look as determined as she did at that very moment.

"Where's Heather?" he repeated, desperately searching the ballroom for her. He saw his brothers and their wives on the dance floor and his brother-in-law, Zach, over by the bar. But Heather was no-where in sight.

"She left." Arielle shook her head. "And I don't blame her. How could you do that to her, Jake? What were you thinking?"

"What the hell are you talking about? I didn't do anything."

When he started to get up, Arielle stopped him. "Stay right where you're at, big brother. I have something to ask you."

"It's going to have to wait, Arielle. I need to find Heather."

"You and Luke have made me listen to both of you all of my life, now you're going to hear what I have to say." He'd never known his sister to be this upset with him.

"Could you make it quick?" he asked impatiently. "I've got to get to Heather and find out why she left."

Arielle looked thoughtful a moment. "She's extremely important to you, isn't she, Jake?"

"Yes."

"You love her, don't you?" Arielle pressed.

"I wouldn't go that far," he said stubbornly. He knew he had deep feelings for Heather, but he wasn't comfortable with the word *love*.

"Oh, Jake." Arielle's voice softened as she reached out to put her arms around him. "You're frightened, aren't you?"

"That's ridiculous, Arielle." He hugged her back. "I can't think of one single thing I need to be scared of."

Leaning back, she smiled sadly. "How about losing Heather? Aren't you afraid of that?"

His chest tightened painfully at the thought of never holding her, loving her, again. "You don't understand, I…"

When his voice trailed off, his sister nodded. "That's exactly what's going to happen if you don't take the chance, Jake. I don't know what's holding you back, but whatever it is, you've got to let it go."

As he stared at his younger sister, he knew that she was right. He'd avoided making a commitment for fear of turning out to be as irresponsible as his father. But he was nothing like Owen Larsen and never would be.

No other woman incited the degree of passion in

him or made him want her the way Heather did. And he'd never met any other woman who made him want to be a better person. Not until Heather.

Taking a deep breath, he rose to his feet and kissed Arielle's cheek. "For a kid, you're pretty damned smart."

"What's going on?" Zach asked when he walked up to the table.

"I have to go find Heather and do some serious explaining," Jake answered, turning to leave.

"Stop by a sporting goods store first and get a set of knee pads," Zach called after him. "If Heather is anything like Arielle, you're going to need them when you're on your knees begging her to give you another chance."

After checking with Clara to see if she could watch Mandy for the rest of the evening, Heather barely managed to make it to her room upstairs and close the door before the tears she'd been holding in check spilled down her cheeks. How could she have let herself think there was a chance that Jake was different now than he'd been over a year ago? How could she have been so stupid?

Collapsing on the bed, she hugged one of the pillows. She should have known better than to think that he had changed. Jake was Jake. He couldn't be someone he wasn't, couldn't be the man she wanted him to be. Seeing him with his friends tonight and hearing his plans to buy a house in Malibu had been all the proof she needed to see that she and their daughter weren't enough for him.

She wasn't certain how long she lay there sobbing against the pillow, but when she finally managed to stop crying, she gathered the scraps of her broken heart and got up. There were things she needed to do before she faced Jake tomorrow morning.

Going into the bathroom, she washed her face, then took off the evening gown she'd changed into for dinner and put on a pair of jeans and a T-shirt. She needed to pack her and her daughter's things and take them down to her old car, then draft her resignation.

As she opened the dresser drawers and started pulling out clothes, the sound of a car coming to a screeching halt in front of the mansion caused her to jump. Almost immediately she heard the front door bang back against the woodwork.

Hurrying to the top of the stairs to see what was going on, she stopped short at the sight of Jake, standing in the open doorway staring up at her.

"Heather, honey, we have to talk."

Nine

"I don't *have* to do anything," Heather stated flatly.

She watched him release a frustrated breath. "Would you please come down here? I need to tell you something."

"Where are your friends?" she asked as she slowly descended the steps.

"Damned if I know and damned if I care." He closed the front door, then walked over to stand at the bottom of the staircase.

"I would have thought you'd be out celebrating with them," she said, drawing on every bit of strength and pride she could muster.

"That's one of the things we need to discuss."

When she descended the last step, he started to take her by the hand, but she sidestepped him. He stared at her for a moment before he motioned toward the study. "Please follow me."

"I don't really want to discuss anything right now, Jake." Did he think hearing that he was leaving her and Mandy would make everything all right?

She walked over to the fireplace and traced her finger along the frame of a snapshot that he'd had Clara or Daily take of himself holding their daughter. Just like the photograph, she was never going to be a part of the picture. The thought caused an ache so deep inside, she had to look away to keep from crying out.

When Jake put his hands on her shoulders to turn her to face him, she backed away from his touch. "Please don't."

"Heather, honey, you have to listen to me."

"You don't have to make excuses or explain," she said, surprised that her voice remained steady. "You're an adult. You can do as you please."

"But I'm going to tell you anyway," he interrupted. "Now, will you stop arguing with me and start listening?"

Sighing heavily, she walked over to sit in one of the chairs. "Let's get this over with. I have things to do."

He stared at her for several long seconds. "What do you have to do at this time of night?"

"I need to pack."

He folded his arms across his broad chest. "Are you going somewhere?"

"I suppose now is as good a time as any to tell you that I quit effective immediately." She had to pause before she could finish. "You'll have to find someone else to manage Hickory Hills and oversee your horses."

A dark scowl wrinkled his forehead. "You can't do that."

"Watch me." A sudden anger swept through her and she started to get up.

He quickly stepped forward to block her. "I won't let you quit and I don't want you leaving."

"You can't stop me," she said, settling back in the chair.

"Dammit, Heather, Hickory Hills is your and Mandy's home." He pulled another armchair over to sit in front of her. "You belong here."

"Not anymore, I don't." She glared at him. It was much easier to let her anger build than to give into the misery of a broken heart. "You're going back to your life in L.A. and I'm staying here. But do you honestly think I want to be here when you bring a woman with you for your next visit? Or wait for you to return so that I can be a diversion while you're here?"

He shook his head. "That's not going to happen."

She watched him close his eyes as if garnering

his patience. When he opened them, there was a determined spark in the cobalt depths.

"If you'd stuck around long enough you'd have seen me decline Cameron's invitation to go barhopping with him and a few others I know from L.A."

"Didn't you want to reconnect with your friends?" she asked.

"Those people wouldn't know how to be a friend if their lives depended on it. They're too self-centered, too shallow." He sat back in his chair. "You probably won't believe this, and I wouldn't blame you if you didn't, considering my track record. But I've been tired of the party crowd for quite some time. I just didn't realize it."

"That is pretty hard to believe," she said, tamping down a tiny bubble of hope.

Sitting forward, he reached out to take her hands in his. "Honey, I'm not going to pretend that I've been a saint since you and I were together in Los Angeles. But I can tell you that after you left, I realized that something was different about me. I suddenly felt like I wanted more out of life than being part of that scene."

"So you're telling me that I caused you to have some grand revelation about yourself?" she snorted.

He laughed. "I'm a little more thickheaded than that." His expression turned serious as he stared down at their entwined hands, then looked up to capture her gaze with his. "It's not an easy thing for me to admit, but all of my adult life I've been afraid to risk my heart, afraid to love. Deep down I was afraid I'd turn out to disappoint a woman the way my father had my mother. So I ran from it. I went out to clubs and dated more than my share of women to keep from becoming too involved."

Was he telling her he was incapable of loving?

Without warning, he reached over to lift her onto his lap. "But then I met you and all that changed."

"In what way?" It felt so wonderful to be in his arms, but she couldn't let herself believe that everything was going to work out between them. When she tried to get to her feet, to escape the temptation he posed, he tightened his arms around her.

"I couldn't forget your laughter, your smile. I couldn't forget you." He nuzzled her hair with his cheek. "I found myself lying in bed at night regretting that I hadn't learned your last name, where you were from and how I could keep in touch with you. And that's something that had never happened to me before."

"Never?" She had a hard time believing that he'd been able to forget every other woman he'd ever gone out with, but her.

"It's the truth, honey." He kissed her cheek. "I never thought I'd ever say this to a woman, but I think I've loved you ever since I spotted you standing there at that horse auction."

Tears welled up in her eyes as the hope within

her burst free and spread throughout her being. "You love me?"

"With all of my heart, Heather." He cupped her cheek with his palm. "And I'm tired of running, honey. If you can find it in your heart to forgive me for being so thick-headed, I want it all. You, marriage, brothers and sisters for Mandy. I even want the minivan filled with car seats and clumps of dog hair."

"Are you sure?" she asked cautiously.

"I've never been more certain of anything in my entire life." His smile caused her heart to skip a beat. "I love you, Heather McGwire. Will you marry me?"

"Oh, Jake, I love you, too." The tears spilled down her cheeks. "But—"

"That's all I need to hear," he said, capturing her mouth with his.

Tracing her lips with his tongue, he deepened the kiss and she knew she had to take the chance. She loved being held by him, kissed by him. And knowing that he wanted to spend a lifetime showing her how much he cared for her caused her heart to swell with more love than she'd ever thought possible.

When he finally broke the kiss, he leaned back to gaze at her and the love she saw in his eyes stole her breath. "There's something else we need to talk about," he said, smiling.

"What would that be?"

"Where we're going to live."

She worried her lower lip for a moment. She'd never imagined herself living anywhere but in the heart of Kentucky's horse-racing country. But as long as she, Mandy and Jake were together, she could live anywhere.

"I've never lived in a huge city." She took a deep breath. "But they have horses in California, too."

Giving her a smile that made her feel warm all over, he shook his head. "Don't get me wrong, I love California. It's one of the most beautiful places on earth. But I think I'd like to live right here."

"Really? Why?" She couldn't have been more surprised. "You told Hunter you were looking for a house in Malibu."

"That will be our vacation home. I want you to be able to continue making a name for yourself in the racing industry," he said. "You have a real knack for choosing bloodlines and producing champions. I want you to have the opportunity to build your reputation as the best in the business."

"I could do that in California."

He nodded. "That's true. But you've already made Hickory Hills a force to reckon with. Why not continue to build it into a racing empire?"

Loving him more with each passing second, she laid her head on his shoulder. "What about your law office? It's in Los Angeles and quite successful. Are you sure you want to give all of that up?"

"Honey, I can practice law anywhere." He shrugged. "But to tell you the truth, I'm tired of helping people end their marriages." He paused a moment. "I think I'd like to give being a gentleman farmer a try and help my wife raise her champion thoroughbreds." He laughed. "Besides, having me around all of the time is going to save you and Clara a lot of grief."

She sat up to stare at him. "I don't understand."

"Mandy can practice her food-fighting skills on me, instead of you." He smiled. "And Daily's a good kid, but he's a lot like I was at that age."

"Heaven help us," Heather said, rolling her eyes.

His low chuckle sent a shiver coursing through her. "No kidding. I think Clara is going to have her hands full when he gets a little older and could use the help."

"I know she'll appreciate it."

Content with being in each other's arms, they remained silent for some time before he spoke again. "You never did give me an answer, honey."

"About getting married?"

He nodded. "You said you love me, but you haven't officially accepted my proposal. Will you marry me, Heather McGwire?"

"Yes."

"How soon?" His grin was bright enough to light a small city. "We've already wasted a year being apart and I'd like to make you mine as soon as possible."

Before she could tell him that she wanted that, too, the sound of the front door opening and several people entering the house intruded.

"It appears that your family has made it back from the victory party."

"Good." He set her on her feet, then rose to take her by the hand. "Let's go share our news with them."

When they walked out of the study arm in arm, everyone fell silent and turned to look at them expectantly.

His eyes never leaving hers, he announced, "I've asked Heather to marry me and she said yes."

Apparently shocked by the news, silence reigned, then everyone seemed to start talking at once.

"I'm so happy for you both," Arielle said, rushing over to give both of them a hug.

Luke laughed. "I told you so, Jake."

"Have you set a date?" Hunter wanted to know.

Smiling, Heather shook her head. "We haven't gotten that far."

Jake kissed the top of her head. "It can't be soon enough for me. If I had my way, we'd be standing in front of a minister right now."

"Me, too," Heather said, gazing up at the only man she'd ever love.

"Do you mean that?" Alyssa asked, stepping forward.

When they both nodded, Heather watched the

women exchange a brief look a moment before Arielle spoke up, "We can do this, girls."

"Absolutely," Callie agreed. "Would tomorrow evening work for both of you?"

"Yes, but we can't possibly get ready in time," Heather said, disappointed. "Tomorrow is Sunday. We can't even get a marriage license until Monday."

"Don't underestimate this bunch," Haley said, laughing.

"Let's make a list." Cheyenne reached into her purse for a notepad and pen. "Nick, go get Emerald and Luther. We're going to need their help with this."

"Yes, ma'am," Nick said, his grin wide as he left the house.

When he returned with the elderly pair, Emerald breezed into the room in her satin and chiffon robe to hug Jake and Heather. "This is wonderful. I can't tell you how happy I am for you." Then, before Heather's eyes, the woman turned from a doting grandmother into a decisive, corporate giant on a mission. "Luther, find out who we know in the Louisville city government and get them to open the clerk's office first thing tomorrow morning so the kids can get their license."

Distinguished-looking even in his slippers and robe, the older gentleman gave a stiff nod. "Consider it done, madam."

Turning back to the group, Emerald continued, "Caleb, Hunter and Nick, call your nannies and babysitters and tell them my corporate jet will pick them and the children up by noon tomorrow. I want the entire family to be here for this. Luke, you and Zach are assigned to helping the girls with whatever they need to pull all of this together."

"Wow!" Heather could understand why Emerald Larson was the highly successful businesswoman she was. Seeing her in action was like watching a battlefield general direct his troops.

"Heather, dear, would you prefer the ceremony be performed here or do you have somewhere else in mind?" Emerald asked, smiling.

There was no question in Heather's mind. "Right here."

"Excellent. Indoors or outside?"

"I've always dreamed of coming down that staircase to meet my groom at the bottom of the steps," Heather answered, pointing toward the sweeping structure.

Jake gave her a tender smile. "And I'll be there waiting for you."

"Another excellent choice," Emerald approved. Turning to Heather's soon-to-be sisters-in-law, the woman grinned. "Divide up the list and get started first thing in the morning, girls. We have a wedding to get ready for tomorrow evening."

When Jake walked out of the master suite the next evening, Luke was waiting for him. "Are you ready to take the plunge?"

"I never thought I'd ever hear myself say this, but it can't be too soon," Jake admitted as they descended the stairs.

Taking his place at the bottom of the steps, he looked around. He'd never loved or appreciated his family more. They'd all worked hard to pull a wedding together on the spur of the moment and everything was picture-perfect. Heather was going to love it.

When the string quartet began to play, Jake's attention was drawn to the top of the stairs and the sight of his bride robbed him of breath. Heather was absolutely stunning. Her golden brown hair lay in soft curls around her bare shoulders and the white lace and antique satin wedding gown emphasized her enticing figure. But it was her radiant smile that he knew he'd never forget as long as he lived.

As she came down the circular staircase, he heard the baby start fussing, and walking over to Clara, took Mandy from her. Then, with his daughter in one arm, he extended his other to her beautiful mother and together they walked over to stand in front of the minister to exchange their vows and become the family he wanted with all of his heart and soul.

"Oh, Luther, I was so afraid this day might never happen," Emerald said as she dabbed her eyes with her linen handkerchief. "I was worried that Jake would turn out to be like his father and remain an irresponsible philanderer for the rest of his life."

"There was that possibility, madam," Luther agreed, nodding.

As she watched the minister pronounce Jake and Heather husband and wife, Emerald couldn't help but feel a bit sad. The investigative team she'd hired to find all of her grandchildren had concluded their search and they'd reported back that there were no more heirs to be found. Her family was finally complete.

When the group gathered in the foyer for pictures, Emerald motioned for Luther to join her. "You need to be in the picture, too, Luther. You've been instrumental in helping me find my heirs."

"It was my pleasure, madam," he said, walking over to stand at her side.

"You know, I'm going to miss helping my grand-children find their soul mates," she whispered wistfully as the photographer tried to get the children to stand still for the picture.

"You've done a fine job with that task, madam," Luther said, keeping his voice low as he patted her hand. "They've all made good matches."

"After all of the unhappiness that my son caused, I'm pleased that we were able to make everything right and give them all their rightful place in Emerald, Inc." Clasping his hand with hers, she gave it a little squeeze. "Now, I can concentrate on trying to find my own bliss."

He squeezed her hand back. "I don't think you'll have far to look, madam," he said gruffly.

Turning, she gave him a happy smile. "Neither do I, Luther. Neither do I."

Epilogue

One year later

"Do any of you have the slightest idea why we've been summoned to Wichita?" Jake looked at his brothers and brother-in-law expectantly as they sat in the family room at Emerald's Wichita mansion. When they all shook their heads, he shrugged. "Me neither."

"All she told me was our presence was mandatory," Luke said, setting the baby bottle down and shifting his six-month-old son to his shoulder to be burped.

"Yeah, I told her I had plans to go to a cattle

auction in Denver and she told me to cancel it," Nick added.

"Arielle has become pretty close to Emerald," Hunter said, looking thoughtful. "Does she know anything, Zach?"

"If she does, she didn't tell me," he said, glancing over to check on his eight-month-old twin boys sleeping peacefully in their baby carriers beside his chair.

"When are she and our wives supposed to return from their shopping trip?" Caleb asked. "All of the kids will be waking up from their naps pretty soon and it'll turn into a three-ring circus again."

Hunter grinned. "Yeah, with ten kids between us, it does get a little hairy sometimes."

"This time next year, there'll be eleven," Jake said proudly. "We just found out Heather is pregnant."

"Make that an even dozen," Nick said, laughing. "Cheyenne is pregnant again, too."

"More like a baker's dozen," Caleb added, grinning like a fool. "Alyssa is close to entering her second trimester."

As they all congratulated each other, Emerald, Luther and their wives walked into the room. "I would imagine you're all wondering why I've asked you here for the weekend," Emerald said, smiling.

"It's crossed our minds a time or two," Luke said dryly.

When Heather walked over to sit on the arm of the chair beside him, Jake put his arm around her waist and gazed up at her. He couldn't believe how happy he'd been in the past year. Marrying her was the best thing he'd ever done. He loved her more with each passing day.

"I have a couple of announcements to make that will have a direct impact on all of you," she said, seating herself in an empty armchair.

"You have our attention," Jake said, watching Luther move to stand beside Emerald. Something was definitely up. Normally as stiff as a board, Jake had never seen the old gent look so relaxed.

"I'm retiring," Emerald said without preamble.

Jake was certain he could have heard a pin drop in the suddenly silent room. The first to find his voice, he asked, "When?"

"Next month." She paused to let the information sink in, then added, "And I'm appointing all of you to the Emerald, Inc. board of directors. I'll maintain ten percent of my stock, but the other ninety percent will be divided equally between my six grandchildren."

"Are you sure you want to do this?" Arielle asked, clearly concerned. "You started out with a home business fifty years ago and built Emerald, Inc. into a corporate empire. It's been your life."

Emerald smiled serenely. "I'm getting ready to enter a new chapter in my life."

"What are you up to this time?" Hunter asked, grinning.

Jake watched her glance at Luther and for the first time since he met the older man, Luther grinned.

"Your grandmother is going to do me the honor of becoming my bride," Luther said, placing his hand on her shoulder.

"We'll be getting married right after we both retire," Emerald said, placing her hand on Luther's. "Then we intend to take an extended honeymoon and travel the world. So I'm counting on all of you to see that Emerald, Inc. remains solid and the gold standard for corporate excellence."

After everyone expressed their surprise and promised not to let their grandmother down, Jake spoke up. "I think I speak for all of us when I say we wish you every happiness. If not for you and Luther, I might never have found Heather and Mandy."

Each of his siblings agreed that if not for Emerald and her matchmaking they might not have found their spouses and true happiness.

"Is there anything we can do to help get ready for your wedding?" Haley asked.

Jake didn't think he'd ever seen a brighter smile on his grandmother's face. "As a matter of fact, there is, dear. You all did such a wonderful job with Jake and Heather's wedding that Luther and I were wondering if you'd all like to plan ours."

"I think that's our cue to retire to the media room, boys," Hunter said, rising to his feet. "The Astros are playing the Cardinals this afternoon."

"If you don't mind, I'd quite like to join you," Luther said, surprising all of them. He kissed Emerald's cheek. "If you'll excuse me, my dear. I think I'll attempt to 'bond,' as the younger generation are so fond of saying, with my future grandsons."

"There just might be hope for you yet, Luther," Jake said, standing to shake the older man's hand.

To his surprise, Luther actually winked. "I have twenty that says the Cardinals win. Anyone want to place a little wager?"

As Emerald watched her grandsons and the man who had stood by her side for over forty years leave to watch the ball game together, she smiled contentedly. In her day, children born out of wedlock had been considered illegitimate and in some cases went unclaimed by their families. But she'd never considered her grandchildren illegitimate. She'd searched high and low to find them and now her life was filled with more happiness than she'd ever thought possible.

She'd done everything in her power to help each one of them discover their own happiness, and to her immense satisfaction they had.

* * * * *

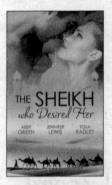

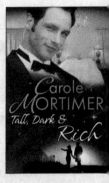

Come home this Christmas to Fiona Harper

From the author of *Kiss Me Under the Mistletoe* comes a Christmas tale of family and fun. Two sisters are ready to swap their Christmases—the busy super-mum, Juliet, getting the chance to escape it all on an exotic Christmas getaway, whilst her glamorous work-obsessed sister, Gemma, is plunged headfirst into the family Christmas she always thought she'd hate.

www.millsandboon.co.uk

She's loved and lost — will she ever learn to open her heart again?

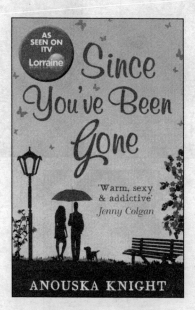

From the winner of ITV Lorraine's Racy Reads, Anouska Knight, comes a heart-warming tale of love, loss and confectionery.

'The perfect summer read — warm, sexy and addictive!'
—Jenny Colgan

For exclusive content visit:
www.millsandboon.co.uk/anouskaknight

Meet The Sullivans...

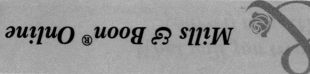
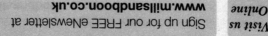

What will you treat yourself to next?

Ignite your imagination,
step into the past...
6 new stories every month

INTRIGUE...

Breathtaking romantic suspense
Up to 8 new stories every month

Medical Romance™

Captivating medical drama –
with heart
6 new stories every month

MODERN™

International affairs,
seduction & passion guaranteed
9 new stories every month

nocturne™

Deliciously wicked
paranormal romance
Up to 4 new stories every month

MODERN tempted™

Fresh, contemporary
romances to tempt all
lovers of great stories
4 new stories every month